Wisdom Lost

Book Two of Pandemonium Rising

By Michael Sliter

Corbin,
I hope you see
this as you tear into
the second book.
   -Mike

1

For Katie. You tolerate me.

Contents

Map of Ardia

ARDIA

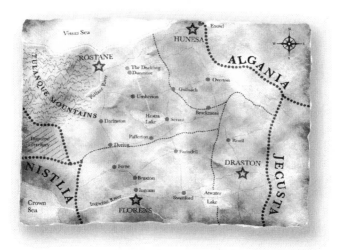

Legend

Duchy Capital	Duchy Border	Country Border
☆	....	●●●●●●●●●●●

Map of Saiwen (Southern Continent) and Imsal (Northern Continent)

Legend

Duchy Capital | Country Capital | Country Border

☆ | ❀ | - - - - - - - -

What Came Before: Solace Lost, Book 1 of Pandemonium Rising

Fenrir de Trenton, a disgraced guardsman-turned-criminal, was not particularly good at his job. His most recent task—collecting the ring finger (this being the calling-card of his employer, The House) of a retired adjudicator—went seriously awry, so that an injured Fenrir was forced to flee into the wilderness after the mishap, eventually hoping to return to Rostane, the seat of the duchy of the same name.

Merigold Hinter—serving girl from a small crossroads inn—dreamt of adventure and finding love, perhaps with her long-time crush, Saren. She has an unusual ability to draw energy from other people; it's a subtle, near unconscious power. She was always careful, lest she draw the wrong kind of attention. One evening, a man—Fenrir—arrived quite late into her inn, stinking of the road. Fenrir, despite his trials, flirted with Meri. He spoke to her of the Plateau, the great fortress towering above Rostane. An exhausted Meri became lost in his stories, and drew too much energy from him, and thus drove him to near assault her. He was stopped by her father, who battered him down from behind.

Waking up in a ditch, weak and concussed, Fenrir travelled back to Rostane, nervous about discussing his misadventures with his superiors. Indeed, Tennyson was upset at his failures, and, though Fenrir managed to talk himself out of any serious trouble, he lost his job as an enforcer for the organization and was told only that The House will have need of him elsewhere.

Meanwhile, a despondent Merigold had a chance encounter with Saren. They kissed once, in the past, but nothing more had ever happened. She pushed for a date, and Saren agreed. Excited, Merigold sought out her best friend—a more experienced lover—and learned a good deal more about lovemaking.

Fenrir, in the meantime, survived an assassination attempt, taking a wound to the shoulder. He was summoned by his father Darian, a merchant king of a trading empire. Fenrir, a constant disappointment who had run off to join the military in his youth, traded hard words with his father. He ended up with his father's fingers piercing his already-injured shoulder and was ultimately disowned, stripped of his name.

Merigold began her date with Saren, who took her for a moonlit walk. They shared a passionate kiss, and Meri decided that she wanted things to go further. However, after Saren took her to a secluded old trapper's cabin, she found herself with her ankle twisted, her body covered in sweat and bug bites, trying in vain to put Saren off. Saren, however, motivated by his disgust for her father and his anger at Meri, abused and raped her. Though she tried to protect herself, Meri finds that she was unable to draw upon Saren's energy. Her poorly-understood powers had failed her. Merigold was trapped for several weeks in the cellar of the cabin, periodically abused by Saren and two of his friends. She began to lose hope, questioning her life and religious beliefs.

Emma Dram, once Fenrir's lover and the first victim of his knife when he joined The House, was the handmaiden of Lady Escamilla. The current duke, perhaps manipulated by unknown political powers, was holding hostage nobles from across the four duchies in order to consolidate his own power. Emma observed, as always, the political happenings of the country while doing her best to serve her lady liege.

When a recovered Fenrir showed up as part of a rescue attempt, Emma was furious and tries to assault him, to be stopped only by Fenrir's quick reflexes and Lady Escamilla's anger. The three worked their way through the servant passages of the great fortress, and met Morgyn, an urchin who previously tried to rob Fenrir. The disagreeable girl was tasked with leading them through the ruins below the Plateau. Though pursued, the companions managed their way through the ruins. Near the end of their escape, several creatures—primal and feral and pale—attacked the group. Fenrir recognized these creatures as twisted, insane humans.

Saren, covered in blood and with murder on his mind, arrived at Merigold's prison. She had finally procured a weapon—a long, rusty nail—and managed to evade Saren, trapping him in the cellar that had become her home. Overwhelmed by her freedom, she headed back to her village. However, she found that the village has been destroyed, corpses cast across the scene, flora blackened and decayed. She heard a bell ringing in the chapel and meets with the survivors of the decimation.

Hafgan Iwan is a Wasmer, a humanoid race generally reviled by humans, and he also worked for The House. His efforts to assimilate with human culture have only ostracized him from both the Wasmer and humans. He met Fenrir and company, escorting them to a boat set aside for their escape. He ultimately tailed a highly suspect Morgyn. Hafgan found that she was working for a rival underground organization, Recherche Oletta, who had put the current duke in power by murdering his father. He overheard Morgyn being tasked with killing Lady Escamilla to make up for her own failures.

Merigold, after meeting with the survivors (including one of the men who abused her), traveled back to her father's inn. The young man followed her, sincerely apologizing, explaining that he had little choice. Merigold accepts his apology, but, at his touch, was overwhelmed, and she murdered him with her rusty nail.

She found the same destruction at her father's inn, bodies piled in the common room. A man arrived, drawn by the perception of great magical energy being used in the region. Cryden is a recruiter, a cautaton, a man who can sense magic. Cryden took a reluctant Merigold with him to Hunesa, one of the four duchies, on their way to Cryden's order of mages. Meri had her own plans, however, realizing through her conversations with Cryden that her father may yet live.

Lady Escamilla (and Emma's) escape from the Plateau forces the Rostanian military to mobilize early to take the four duchies of Ardia, starting with an invasion of Florens to the south. Hafgan is sent to infiltrate the military, allowing himself to become conscripted into the segregated Wasmer unit. The Wasmer, a caste-based culture, choose their warleaders based on military prowess. Hafgan, having been trained to be an elite warrior priest before leaving his own people, defeated the current warleader Siarl, becoming the equivalent of a lieutenant in the Rostanian military. He gained access to military council meetings, and observed as the Rostanian leaders lied and manipulated so that their forces believed that they are fighting a just war.

Fenrir, Emma, and their companions arrived at Brockmore, one of Lady Escamilla's holdings. She had been gathering her own forces, stripping her many holdings of soldiers and men. She held a war council, and Emma began to show some initiative despite her low standing, confronting a powerful Yetranian chaplain who was attempting to control the proceedings. Later, Morgyn sneaked into the manor in the dark of night and begged Escamilla for protection. Escamilla granted it, and Fenrir was sent to Hunesa to recruit a mercenary force to bolster the Army of Brockmore.

Merigold, holed up in an inn in Hunesa with Cryden as he sought passage overseas, realized she was pregnant, and determined to rid herself of the child once she recruited a mercenary force to help find her father. In these misguided attempts, Merigold met some bad men who attempted to steal her little money and abuse her. She stabbed one in the gut and managed to awaken her dormant powers, shredding one of her attackers into bloody bits. Fenrir, hoping to recruit the same mercenaries, walked in just afterward with the mercenary captain, and saw Merigold fall to the ground amidst the blood and gore. Fenrir returned to Brockmore, Meri and a new army in his possession.

Hafgan continued his subterfuge within the Rostanian military, but was dealing with this own problems. He had begun training other assimilated Wasmer, who were derisively called budredda (filth) by traditionalist Wasmer. This conflict built over the weeks, and the traditionalists and budredda brawled when Hafgan is gone. He arrived just as a budredda was killed. Fenrir took control, protecting his men and taking on the budredda title as a badge of honor instead of a slur.

Merigold awoke amidst the Army of Brockmore, and began to forge a paternal relationship with a surprisingly kind Fenrir. She met the same Yetranian chaplain who had argued with Emma, and found the man to be empathetic and understanding. He recounted the story of the rise of Yetra, the warring powers of Harmony and Pandemonium, and how Yetra's own struggles forged her into an instrument of Harmony. He gave a desperate Merigold hope and convinced her to keep her child and raise it in Harmony.

The Rostanian military marched to Florens, and Escamilla's forces arrived soon after. Emma found her lot in the world improved, as she spoke with the authority of Lady Escamilla. She witnessed a great battle between the Rostanians and the outnumbered, combined forces of Florens and Brockmore. Brockmore's mercenaries unleashed magical forces, and but for a twist of fate and a betrayal, they would have won the battle.

Hafgan and his expendable Wasmer were sent on a mission to guard a mysterious compound southeast of Florens, full of terrible howls and other strange happenings. The same night of the Battle of Florens, the traditionalist Wasmer staged a coup, and Hafgan's budredda were hard-pressed to fight off their brethren. During the battle, creatures burst forth from the compound, these being pale, feral beings who interrupt the coup. All the Wasmer banded together as these creatures overtake them, as they serve as a hurdle between the creatures and the Army of Brockmore. Ultimately, the well-learned Hafgan realized that these are gwagen, Feral: soulless men who have been warped by magics, harbingers of worse things to come. He determined that he must return to Wasmer territory to warn his people of this threat.

After a confrontation with Emma, Fenrir was sent to kill the duke. It was a suicide mission. Fenrir's small force managed to cause a distraction and attack the inn where the duke is staying. Two of the duke's advisors used an unknown power to immobilize Fenrir and his remaining soldiers. Fenrir managed— through a subtle power he had previously manifested—to briefly resist the magic and drive his sword through the chest of the duke. The advisors did not seem overly concerned, hinting that they might be the true power in Rostane. One caused Fenrir to lose consciousness, additionally hinting that they might have caused his original disgrace. Fenrir was presumably made a captive.

Escamilla's forces decided to withdraw, hoping that Fenrir would be successful in slaying the duke and buy them time to consolidate and rally. Emma learned that she is, in fact, Escamilla's legally-dictated heir. Morgyn, ostensibly adopted by Escamilla, slumbered in the corner of the command tent while the captains argue about next steps. The army, in the middle of the night, came under attack by the same Feral who had torn through Hafgan and his Wasmer. During the disarray, Morgyn stabbed Escamilla in her back and ran off. With her lady liege unlikely to survive, Emma found herself elevated to being one of the richest, most powerful women in the country—commanding an army that was in shambles and in desperate need of succor.

Merigold was also caught up in the battle near the baggage train. She was attacked by a terribly injured, but still strong Feral, and sought to draw energy from it. She found the creature empty. A human bereft of life force, bereft of soul. Instead, she sought power within herself, and managed to defeat the creature. But, the power that she drew on had come from her unborn child, which she lost. Soon, reunited with Cryden, Merigold considered the shambles of her life and the damage done to her and her loved ones by magic, concluding that it was her role to wipe magic from the earth.

And Merigold's father, Ragen Hinter, found himself in an unknown prison, completely bereft of light. He was confronted by a beautiful woman, a woman who had seen millennia pass and civilizations rise and fall. She was the goddess Yetra, and, calling Ragen her sweetling, she began to sap him of his lifeforce.

Prologue

"Good morning, my sweetling.

"Oh, that's right. You would have no way of knowing whether it is morning or night down here. I can assure you that it is indeed a stunningly beautiful morning. The sun is cresting the hills, glowing golden across the sky. The birds are singing lovely songs, filling the air with glee. Oh, I wish you could see and hear it.

"But, that is not to be, and I do truly apologize. The darkness, I've found, will help you recover from this ordeal. Ancient teachings—has it really been long enough for them to be considered ancient?—originally suggested the recuperating power of the sun, but I have found, over time, that those left in the sun experience great sensitivity to the light, some finding the pain unbearable. This darkness seems cruel, but it is, in fact, a kindness.

"Other kindnesses? Well, I would give you a chair, but soon you will not care about such things…. Oh, let it not be said that I am cruel. I shall send for a chair. When it becomes soiled, I will burn it. There are always more chairs, after all. Yes. There are always more.

"What is happening to you? Ah, my sweetling. You know, you have a weak heart. Have you felt a pain in your left arm, on occasion? A weakness throughout? Your body is so strong, but your heart is slowly failing you. There is nothing that you could have done. The ancient physicians would say that it is hereditary. Some things you are born with, things given to you by your parents. Sometimes, such things are gifts. Sometimes, they are curses.

"Did you feel that, just now, beneath the touch of my hand? That was your heart healing. A heart consists of four chambers, and a wall was weak. I drew upon existing tissue to strengthen it. I

15

cannot claim that as a kindness, however. No, that is simply my efforts at preservation. You see, I need your body as strong as your maenen. The two are intrinsically linked, and when I drain your maenen, your body can also suffer. It takes me such little effort to heal you, and you can provide so much more to me if you stay healthy.

"Think of this place like a farm, designed to feed multitudes. Unfortunately, this food is of a different variety. Some of us feed on maenen. Your power, your lifeforce. You, my sweetling. You have a strong maenen, contained within a powerful and rejuvenating nerring. You, if we must continue with the food metaphor, are a delicacy.

"Some harvest their crop immediately, leaving nothing left. Uprooting the plant, if you will. But, in my many, many years, I have learned that a crop will continue to yield a great deal more with patience. Although, there will be slightly less yield each time.

"Yes, you will begin to lose yourself over time. Right now, you are articulate, though tired, and can hold a complex conversation with me. You have thoughts, hopes, fears, memories. You shouted the name of your daughter and I experienced her. Merigold. Such a beautiful name. I knew a Merigold once, more years ago than you could conceive of. I wish your daughter were here, both to comfort you and also to serve as an additional delicacy, as it were. It is often the case that, if you have such a strong maenen, she likely will, as well. It depends on the mother. With you being such a handsome man, even at your age, I imagine your wife was very beautiful.

"But yes, you will begin to forget her, your Merigold. And your beautiful wife. Your old life. It will be a small mercy, I'm afraid. Eventually, you will know only the basest of emotions. Think of a predatory animal. Hunger, over time, will become your motivation. You will hunger for food and lust for coupling. You will feel as if even I am a threat to you, and your natural aggression will be multiplied at an astounding rate. Your anger. Your hatred. Those emotions that have been obscured by your humanity will be laid bare to the world.

"But, we have some time until that happens. We should cherish this time together.

"What is that? Why? Why am I doing this? That is a loaded question, my sweetling, and I've not the strength to discuss it on such a beautiful morning. Perhaps, once I've enjoyed the feel of the sun on my face, I will be able to tell you a story.

"I suppose that I have stalled enough, though I truly do enjoy your company. You are one of the few. I can feel your hatred, but I can also feel your love.

"Shall we begin?"

Chapter 1

The boys played near the great river against the express wishes of their parents, as boys often did. Threats of punishment did little to dissuade adolescent boys when there was adventure to be had. Particularly at night, when the near-full moons lit the sky, teasing the earth with their shimmering whites and blues. These were the colors of mischief. The colors of fun. The colors of magic.

Finding that the other boys had pulled ahead, Fenrir stumbled through the brush to catch up. The paths along the Fullane were so overgrown here. Not much further, and the boys would be near his and his mother's special place. He didn't want the boys to sully the little clearing—one of the few safe places that he and his mother could share. It may have been the only place where his mother smiled her real smile.

Fenrir rushed ahead to distract the boys, to lead them away from their clearing. He had seen a great turtle earlier in the day—maybe he could find it again, and focus the boys on that instead.

Suddenly, he was falling, tumbling forward, his arms flailing to catch his fall. Had he hit a root?

There was a biting laugh behind him. Sigmund Fitra pulled himself from the bushes where he'd been hiding with his leg sticking out. The skinny youth was as well-dressed as always, though they were at play. His parents never cared if he came home dirty, even if he ruined his silks. He would just get replacements. His parents gave him everything he wanted.

Through the brush, the moon glinted off Sigmund's teeth, painting them a glowing blue and giving him the visage of a demon. The stringy, angular boy was handsome and symmetrical, but Fenrir had always thought he resembled a rat. He was a couple of years older than Fenrir, but Fenrir still thought himself the stronger and the faster of the two, and could take him in a fair fight. But, Sigmund never fought fair.

"What gives, Siggy?" Fenrir asked, pushing himself to his feet and noticing the deep scrapes on his hands as he rose. He did nothing to tend to the wounds, however. Sigmund was like a predatory bird. You couldn't show injury or he would attack.

"It's not fucking Siggy, you shit!" spat the boy, his moonlit features twisting in rage, giving him the appearance of Ultner, Lord of Pandemonium. Fenrir was taken aback more by his language than anything. The boy was extremely polite and polished in public, and adults loved him.

But, rarely had they been so far from home, and certainly not at night. So far from any adults.

"It is when you trip me!" Fenrir stepped forward, fists clenched painfully, confident that Sigmund would either do nothing or back down. Astonishingly, Sigmund crossed his arms, a smile creasing his rodent face. It gave Fenrir pause for a moment. He was about to retreat himself when something hard cracked him in the back of the head. He cried out and fell on his face, the scrapes on his hands tearing open even more on the rough terrain. When he made a fist, it felt sticky with blood.

He rolled to his side, squinting up at Aiden and Ethan, Ethan holding a thick tree branch. The cause of his sudden headache, it seemed. His brothers' faces swam in his sight. He couldn't make out their features or expressions, but he imagined smug grins. They always wore smug grins.

"Fen, it looks like you fell! Do you need help up?" asked Aiden, his voice a mockery of kindness. He even held out his hand, but Fenrir knew better. He slapped it aside, despite the pain in his own palm.

Wait, was he missing a ring finger? No, that wasn't right.

Fenrir tried to stagger to his feet, but was hit by a blow he couldn't see and again knocked to the ground. He tried to roll to one side and escape, but someone leveled a kick at his aching skull, blasting stars across his vision. He was struck, again and again, until he lay moaning on his back, staring up at the twisted branches, above him like grasping fingers trying to reach the moons. Only Instar was visible, blue light giving him the impression of being underwater. The impression of being drowned.

"No, I don't—" The sound of arguing cut through waters that seemed to fill Fenrir's ears.

"That's enough. He's hurt."

"No, it isn't. We agreed—"

"But we could get in trouble."

"Enough! I'll do it."

A figure stood above him, blurry in his vision and silhouetted by the moon. The form raised its arms above its head and the wind seemed to kick up, lashing branches across Fenrir's blurry vision. It held something that appeared to be a demon's skull above its head. No, not a skull. A rock?

The rock came down, smashing into his knee. Fenrir screamed, trying to move away, but many strong hands held him in place. The rock rose once more, and again crashed into his knee with the force of a vengeful god.

Fenrir howled, eyes clenched shut to blur out the sight as if that would help with the pain.

It was agony. The shattered bones and fibers ground together like sausage being pressed in a butcher's shop.

His godsdamn, fucking knee.

***

Fenrir Coldbreaker sat up, disoriented and breathing heavily. His head throbbed, and his lower back was stiff. And his knee! Oh, did his knee ache!

He realized then that he'd been sleeping awkwardly, his leg bent back behind him. It wasn't re-shattered, thank the gods. Gingerly, he straightened out the damaged joint, grimacing as it sent waves of pain through his body. Even the best surgeons had been unable to fix him completely, either initially or afterward. No wonder he'd had that terrible dream.

But where was he? He pushed himself up from a frigid stone floor, shaking his head to clear his vision and wiping cold sweat from his forehead. Not the first morning that he'd awakened on a floor, although in Rostane, the tavern floors were typically built of splintered, wooden planks, as were the floors in his boarding house for those unfortunate nights when he couldn't find his bed. He did feel just as weak and dehydrated as he would in those situations, but didn't think he was hungover.

There was essentially no light, so Fenrir felt his way through the space. It was, indeed, a room. Mortar-stoned walls, and only a few paces wide and deep. There was a thin, barred door on one side of the room—locked, of course, as cells always were—and the place smelled like shit. On closer examination, though, the smell was actually him and whatever soiled rags he wore.

He hadn't been wearing these rags, last he remembered. No... he'd been wearing an ill-fitting set of steel armor, sprayed with the blood of Duke Penton, and he'd been surrounded by Knights of the Wolf and at least one godsdamned pasnes alnes. One of

21

those cursed magic users! He was lucky that he wasn't splattered all over the wall, like Merigold had done with those mercenaries back in Hunesa.

Despite his plight, Fenrir spared a thought for the young girl, wondering how she was. Wondering whether she was safe with the Army of Brockmore, and whether there still was an army. He'd done his part, if memory served. Hopefully, Escamilla and the rest could do theirs. He'd rather not have anything more happen to Merigold. Though she'd not told him the whole story, it was clear her recent life had been pandemonium.

The other woman in his life was also with that army. Emma Dram, his crimson-haired, sharp-tongued, cripple-handed minx of an ex-lover. Though she wasn't necessarily the one who'd gotten him into this situation, she'd delivered her orders with such certainty and finality that it felt, to Fenrir, like she'd controlled his fate. As if she had steered him into a flawed, but somehow successful, attempt on Duke Penton's life. He supposed it was what he deserved—he was the reason her hand was crippled, after all.

And, though they had been traveling together for at least a couple of months, he had never found the time, or the nerve, to apologize.

He shoved thoughts of Merigold and Escamilla and Emma from his mind. Obviously, there would be plenty of time to ponder the meaninglessness of those relationships later, given his new occupation as a prisoner. After killing the little duke—as unpopular as the man had been in Rostane, and despite the duke having started an unjust war—Fenrir would almost inevitably be executed. Likely, no one would shed a tear. Certainly not any of the ladies who'd just occupied his thoughts.

So, a cell. It wasn't a big stretch to assume he was at the Plateau. His fingertips told him that the walls were identically-cut, mortar-stoned blocks. He could feel the bumps and divots that he was so familiar with. How many hours had he stared at these blocks, focusing on any imperfection? When one is on a ten-hour guard shift, one finds stories in the walls themselves. That splotch resembled a bare-knuckled fighter, face swollen from too many fights, while that one looked like a shaggy dog. The two would walk together after the arena fights, and…

Again, Fenrir shook his head, trying to clear out the fog. Somehow, he had gotten back to the Plateau—a couple hundred miles from Florens—while remembering nothing of the trip. That distance had taken the Rostanian Army weeks to traverse, although they'd been plagued by poor organization and training on the march. Even so, he must have lost at least a couple weeks of his life, depending on how long he had been unconscious in this cell. By Ultner's soggy testicles, it must have been one of those pasnes alna, using their powers to fuck with his mind.

Some hinges screeched in the distance, and there was the sound of a metal door slamming shut. Armored, booted feet approached his cell as a light became visible down the hallway, burning his eyes like they were those of a newborn. Apparently, Fenrir would learn more about his situation without delay. He took a deep breath and attempted to focus, squinting against the light as shapes formed outside of his cell.

"He's awake," came a young voice which Fenrir didn't recognize.

"Of course; he was supposed to be conscious by now. Open the door."

This voice, Fenrir did recognize. The rising rage burned away his mental fog in an instant.

"If it isn't Fenrir the Coldbreaker, the regicide pile of shit himself." Sigmund Fitra strolled into the cell, flanked by two Knights of the Wolf, the man's rodent face twisted in a smile. As always, the skinny man was resplendent in the most expensive clothing that money could buy, and he still had the platinum Rostanian wolf emblazoned over his heart—the sign of a general in the military. Interestingly, he also had the three-masted ship of the de Trenton family on the opposite breast. It seemed like quite the conflict of interest, serving both the state and private enterprise.

"Regicide is a term reserved for king-slaying," Fenrir pointed out. "Little Penton was not a king, no matter how he styled himself. At worst, I am a murderer. But, given that we were in wartime, on opposite sides of the conflict, there is no crime. Penton was a casualty of war." He wasn't exactly trying to absolve himself, but perhaps he could anger Sigmund with knowledge. It was an excellent weapon against the ignorant.

The grin didn't leave Sigmund's face. Damn.

"Always such impertinence. However, you have reached the end. You have no friends to help you. No allies. Escamilla is dead. Her army has scattered beneath the raging storm of Rostane. Florens is ours, and Draston prepares to capitulate," Sigmund answered with smug pride.

The general must have felt personally responsible for these successes.

"Capitulate to whom?" Fenrir asked. "Penton is dead and has no heirs. Rostane must be scrambling to find a new ruler. I would expect politics to subvert the war effort. In fact, I would not doubt that Penton's successor would hail me as a hero for killing the war-hungry tyrant. Are you here to give me an award?"

"These politics are not your concern. Dukes and counts and barons are so above your current station—literally and figuratively—that you might as well not strain yourself thinking about them. Rather, you should focus on your own fate." Still with that smile. His crooked nose gave him a sinister appearance.

Obviously, Sigmund wanted Fenrir to ask about his fate. He wouldn't give the man the satisfaction. It wasn't like his circumstance would change if he knew the plan.

"How did you end up being a general, Siggy? You can barely manage to dress yourself without servants, and yet you somehow lead men? You think anyone respects someone who sucks my father's cock to get promoted? And—" A back-handed slap from one of the gauntleted knights sent Fenrir staggering backwards with an aching face.

"You will show respect to the Lord General," said the young Wolf Knight, roughly grabbing his arm.

But Sigmund's smile had finally left his face. The stinging in Fenrir's jaw was worth that.

"Again, Fenny, you must not realize your plight. I have the pleasure to inform you that the Council has deemed your presence to be a threat to national security. You are to be executed, publicly, within the month."

"Oh, so Rostane is being ruled by a council right now. Thanks for the glimpse into what's happening upstairs."

"I look forward to lowering you onto the spike myself. I expect a big turnout," Sigmund sneered, curling his lip. Fenrir remembered the boy as a youth giving him that same condescending stare. The general turned to leave.

"Sigmund, wait," Fenrir said, hanging his head, his overgrown, greasy hair tickling at his eyebrows.

"What, are you going to beg for mercy? Beg for mercy from me? Even you should be smarter than—"

Fenrir yanked out of the knight's grip and slammed his fist into Sigmund's face with all of his strength. The second knight rushed forward to restrain Fenrir as the first regained his grip, but Fenrir did not struggle. Escape hadn't been his goal.

"My Lord General, I apologize..." said the young Wolf Knight, fear plain in his quivering voice.

"You imbecile!" Sigmund sputtered from behind his hand, clutching his face. "I will see you lashed!"

"And you!" He moved his hand, revealing blood streaming from his nose and trailing into his mouth. Sigmund got within an inch of Fenrir's own face. "Let me see if we can advance your sentence. I'll see you soon."

Sigmund turned away, adding, "Soften him up. Nothing permanent; just enough to make him cry. I do not want him to be numb to the spike."

As the Wolf Knights began striking him, Fenrir smiled around the pain.

Worth it.

Chapter 2

Several thousand cavalry, resplendent in the livery of Rostane, began to trot forward, aiming for the tattered battle lines of the Army of Brockmore. The summer heat was already sweltering, and even more so due to the reflected light shining off of the twin Atwater Lakes. Ever a tourist destination, the land bridge which neatly cleaved the lakes in twain was a marvel. Its scant hundred-yard width and mile-long length was covered in tall, pink flowers that could be seen slowly blowing in the breeze, mirroring the gentle waves of the crystal-clear waters. Morning dew rose in a foggy mist, both enhancing and obscuring the beauty of the scene between the armies.

It had taken a great deal of time and patience to move her army without disturbing the flowers overmuch, but their strategy depended on these pink beauties. Lady Emma Breen, observing her armies from the relative safety of their makeshift command post, a raised platform shared by her captains, could only hope that it worked. Ferl was confident—but then, that slimy, handsome man always was. And, after all, he could count on a huge bonus if they managed a victory.

Numbering just over eight thousand, Emma's forces were ragged, though perhaps not as ragged as they appeared. Before the attack by those creatures—the same monsters who'd assaulted her and her dubious companions in the ruins under the Plateau— they'd had over eleven thousand. Now, her army more closely resembled a fraying patchwork quilt, consisting of many flags and banners with far fewer soldiers under those standards than there should have been.

First among them, though, there were Lady Escamilla's forces—Emma's forces. The Army of Brockmore, fighting under a simple apple crest. These were soldiers and guardsmen who had been stripped from Escamilla's numerous holdings all over Ardia.

Her inexperienced fighters had suffered most in the night raid made by those indefatigable creatures. They were Emma's now, thousands of men who would live or die based on her unqualified decisions.

She appraised the Florensians next, and their leader Duke Eric Malless, who sat slumped on his charger. He was young for such leadership, even younger than Emma, though he'd spent his entire life knowing that he would eventually command men. And he now commanded the best equipped force in Emma's army. The best equipped... but also the most beaten. The betrayal from within Florens, and the subsequent sacking of their city, had destroyed the hearts of these men. And those hearts only shattered further as they marched away from their loved ones, not toward them.

And then there were the two mercenary armies. Ultner's Fist—with their silver-fisted banner over a red background—was commanded by the Silver Lady, Trina Almark. This elite, if small, unit of fighting women had proven itself in both this conflict as well as many past battles, often to the chagrin of their metaphorically castrated male opponents. Ferl's Company was a less-savory group of mercenaries, and Ferl himself was not well-liked by the Silver Lady. Nonetheless, this day, he held the key to victory.

The well-organized ranks of Rostanian cavalry were only a few hundred yards away from Emma's front line. This was a poor location for a charge, though—a narrow, defensible strip of land, with terrain obscured by flowing flowers. Still, the Rostanians were confident in their training and numbers. Emma's poorly-formed and ragged line of Brockmore soldiers were too tempting of a target.

Certainly, the Rostanian commander desired the glory of such a charge, not to mention the promotion that would come with scattering the remainder of Emma's forces.

At the sight of the well-armored, well-trained Rostanian cavalry approaching, Emma—her brilliant red hair captured by a tight, headache-inducing bun—clenched her teeth, fear weakening her limbs. But, like her liege lady before her, Emma did everything she could to appear calm, collected. She wondered how much of Lady Escamilla's life had been spent hidden behind such masks. Had she ever felt fear like this?

"Arrows loose!" shouted General Anew Opine, pointing forward dramatically to signal the bugler. Emma inwardly rolled her eyes. If the bastard hadn't been so capable, his storybook mannerisms would have been laughable.

Eight hundred yellow yew warbows, wielded expertly by her trained Brockmore archers, were let loose simultaneously. As the arrows filled the sky, the Rostanian cavalry spurred forward into a canter from four hundred yards off, heading directly toward Emma and her forces. The heavy arrows fell into the middle of their ranks as they moved, raining death among the tightly-packed, mounted soldiers. Emma worked to keep from flinching as men and horses began to die at her orders.

However, unlike their own, untrained cavalry, or the conscripts their army had faced near Florens, the cavalry ahead was the elite force of Rostane. They'd been drilled and trained for such an eventuality, and so the arrows did little to dissuade the charging horses, though gaps did appear in their ranks.

"Fire at will!" shouted Opine, giving the Brockmore archers free reign. The charge came frighteningly fast, and, though men and horses continued to fall, the front ranks would collide with Emma's forces in seconds. Her soldiers, the mercenaries, and the Florensians already had their pikes dug into the ground, ready to repel the assault. But the fear was as pervasive as the stench of sweat and leather, and the soldiers were visibly jarred.

The sound of charging hooves became deafening as the Rostanians let out a powerful, incoherent war cry. Flower petals shot into the air in every direction, clouds of pink locusts amidst the rising dust. And lances were leveled, aimed for the heart of the Emma's army.

At a hundred yards, the front rank of the Rostanian cavalry disappeared. Followed by the second rank, and part of the third rank.

Horses were howling and men were screaming, impaled upon sharpened stakes and spears which had been driven into the first row of pits concealed by the flowers. Now the ground around those traps was a swirling mass of humanity and horseflesh, bones breaking in the crush, with the few men who escaped the pit so injured that they posed no threat. Rather, they posed a warning.

The Army of Brockmore had arrived four days earlier and prepared the battlefield, traveling no more than five abreast to avoid disturbing the field of flowers in the isthmus and then setting up camp, immediately digging twelve-foot-wide and ten-foot-deep pits all across the field of battle, working in ten-hour shifts. The flowers had acted as a perfect screen to conceal these deathtraps.

A trickle of cavalry managed by happenstance to pass through several small gaps in the front line of pits, but then they fell into the second row at fifty yards out. Only a couple dozen riders reached the Brockmore battle lines, and these soldiers did very little damage, taken down as they were by the long lances of Emma's infantry. Meanwhile, the main body of the cavalry was in chaos behind them, milling about and uncertain what to do. Though they were the elite, the Rostanian cavalry had never seen real battle; the skirmishes with the Wasmer, years before, had been in terrain unsuited to horse combat.

A Rostanian trumpet played the sound of retreat. This, the soldiers had drilled for. Horses moved in response, men maneuvering to gather injured and fallen men onto the backs of other horses.

"Not enough. They aren't broken, not by a long shot," murmured Captain Braston, scratching his clean-shaven face. At least his hairless face made him more recognizable, though Emma thought the beard suited the pock-marked man better.

Emma nodded in agreement. From her view, from their makeshift command tower behind their lines of defense, she could see that there was no panic. The Rostanian officers had their cavalry well-controlled and well-trained. Her nails dug into her palms. They needed to smash the cavalry, both to clear the rest of their retreat as well as send a message that the Army of Brockmore was not shattered. That they would still fight.

"They'll just regroup and go south around the lake. Or, pursue us to less defensible terrain," said Guy Empton from his chair, echoing Emma's thoughts. Since his heart episode following the reversal at the Battle for Florens, Empton had begged off command and requested an advisor's role. It had only been a couple of weeks, but he was a shadow of himself. His lanky, powerful frame—though once containing the strength to wield his great, two-handed sword—had become emaciated and gray. His face was drawn, eyes sunken into his withered face, and his thinning hair had turned gray at the temples almost overnight. And he was only thirty-eight years old, a scant ten years older than Emma.

She tried not to be vain, but she prayed to whatever gods were listening—none, in all likelihood, she knew—that she wouldn't shrivel up like that, that she wouldn't lose her crimson or curls. The stress of leading an army was immense. Not to mention holding control of a significant number of businesses and holdings scattered across the four duchies of Ardia and beyond.

Not a life Emma had chosen for herself, but one she found herself living nonetheless.

"Oh, worry not, Lady Breen." Ferl leered at Emma, a smirk twisting his handsome features. As usual, it wasn't clear if he was mocking her or just parodying the numerous others who loathed taking orders from a trumped-up handmaiden with a mangled claw of a hand. "This is exactly what we prepared for. In fact, I think it is about time to begin." He made a spinning gesture above his head with his hapler, a long-hilted, long-bladed sword popular in Hunesa, and his mercenaries reacted in an instant.

"Rethink this, boy! You are treading on the borders of Pandemonium!" intoned Ignatius Pender, chaplain of the Army of Brockmore, his chubby face red from being ignored. His proselytizing gained him no traction with Emma, of course; she loathed the hypocritical, limping cow. Ferl and Trina Almark, for all of their conflict, also held mutual disdain for the holy man and all things Yetranian. The captains, however, were split, and most other officers and rank-and-files were becoming fanatical, particularly since the attack by those white demons. "Such power should not be used—"

"Enough, Chaplain. We are set on this course of action lest we all be slaughtered," Emma snapped. Her patience for Ignatius was thinner than a needle point. She couldn't help being openly dismissive, even knowing that it would enrage the holy man. Her eyes were glued to the battlefield, however.

Across the battle line, in ten yard intervals, five men and one woman separated themselves, striding forward with their personal guard flanking them. Ferl's greenies. The five men knelt, touching their hands to the ground, while the woman, her naked feet invisible in the blowing field of flowers, simply stood there. Ashland always went barefoot; her callouses had to be as thick as leather.

Without a sound, the plant life surrounding each greenie began to turn gray, a circular pattern growing around each man like ripples in a still lake. Short grass and rough weeds, in the gaps around the flowers, began turning into charcoal. The colorless blight spread up the tall stalk of each pink flower, sucking out the green of the stalk and then the pink of the petals. Curled, colorless strings were left with pathetic, shriveled bits of confetti attached to them. Around Ashland, the flora turned completely black, ash blowing away in the breeze as she extracted every bit of power from the plants.

The Rostanian cavalry didn't react; they were focused on organizing their retreat and helping their injured, so a few soldiers walking beyond the confines of their battle line seemed a minor thing. The six greenies moved forward slowly, continuing to draw more and more color from the landscape. It was rapidly becoming a painting of a twisted, idyllic scene, one where the stylistic artist lacked any primary colors and instead used blacks, whites, and grays for effect.

Slowly, sparks of green and brown power began to travel along the ground, raising a gentle, white smoke. The magical sparks of the six greenies converged in the middle of the isthmus fifty yards in front of the battle line, merging into a much larger, seething mass of force. Ashland rushed forward then, sapping the life around her, and the power shot across the ground toward the Rostanian cavalry.

Some of Emma's own men rushed forward in their excitement, shaking weapons and cheering, while others fell back, terror as thick in the air as the rising morning dew. For most of their lives, the Yetranians had been taught of the darkness of magic, and now here it was in front of them.

The Rostanian rearguard finally noticed that something was amiss—it was hard to ignore a mass of sparkling power hurtling across a field of flowers—and raised a commotion. Chaos reigned in a matter of moments. Men directly in the path of the power spurred their horses in any direction to get away, forcing other animals aside. A number of horses, their innate, primal senses perceiving the danger, reared and ran, some even jumping into the Atwater Lakes, sending soldiers flying in all directions.

The power reached the cavalry, and both beasts and men—having seen the power of Ferl's greenies at Florens—did everything possible to avoid it. Still, some couldn't. But when the power contacted Rostanian flesh, it… did nothing. The blast traveled under the panic-stricken soldiers, their screams splitting the air like the calls of carrion birds, but no one was hurt.

Emma bit her lip despite her efforts to conceal her emotions. However, with everyone's eyes affixed to the field, not a soul noticed. Was this not going to work? If not, her men would be doomed. Not today, but certainly when they reached the open plains south of Draston.

Just as she despaired, though, the gates of Pandemonium were torn open in the middle of the retreating forces.

Cutting off the escape of the cavalry at the head of the isthmus, a thick line of green flame burst forth, sending earth, soldiers, and horses flying into the air. Or, rather, chunks of charred flesh into the air. Even several hundred yards away from the blast, Emma could smell the burning flesh as if it were pork on a nearby cookfire. Men around her averted their faces, Captain Ezram vomiting while Ignatius held aloft his Yetranian medallion in righteous fury. Pompous bastard. If Yetra could have helped them, then she would have already. No, instead, they had to rely on this magic.

And it was oh so effective.

The flame didn't follow the path of the magical sparks sent forth by the greenies. Rather, it cut horizontally across the land bridge, waterline to waterline, effectively walling off the retreat.

After the green barrier burned for about ten seconds, the flames disappeared. No smoke, no final flare... they were just gone. In their place was a fifteen-foot-wide ditch, already filling with the waters of the Atwater Lakes. At least a thousand panicked cavalry were left on the land bridge, firmly wedged between the spiked pits—which still writhed with injured and dying men and horses—and a new, deep fissure created by magic.

"By Yetra's milky teets," coughed the former General Empton, rising weakly from his wheeled chair to get a better view.

"Hideous," murmured Captain Ezram, with one other captain—Quentin, predictably—nodding his assent, disgust twisting his heavily bearded features. Ezram was a quiet one, but a fervent Yetranian. He had previously been a captain of the guard in one of Escamilla's fisheries near Hunesa. Thousands of men and women worked at that location, capturing fish and lobster, preparing them for travel and shipping them inland. Emma recalled that Ezram had obtained funding to have a Yetranian chapel built on site, and altered work shifts to ensure that every single worker would be able to attend a Yetranian ceremony each week. In fact, it wasn't optional for any under his command.

Emma would have to keep an eye on him.

General Opine—seemingly exalting in his victory—said something to his aide, who rushed to the bugler and signaled a sounding for the general advance. The ranks moved forward in a ragged line, some rushing forward and turning the sapped flora to ash while others held back in fear, reluctant to touch any ground where the greenies had stepped. Officers shouted orders in response, and not a few lashed out with spear butts to get the men moving more quickly.

As the army approached, the Rostanians began their surrender with barely a whimper. Men dismounted, throwing aside their weapons before Emma's forces even reached the pits. Her men knew how to circumvent the pits, of course; others had brought planks, but the pits were so full of the dead and dying that there was no place to cross them via the slats of wood. Instead, men moved between them and then began collecting weapons, herding both prisoners and horses toward the former battle line.

"A great victory for our noble forces! There must be over a thousand dead and wounded, even more captured," said Opine, adopting the pose of a heroic knight. One leg up on Empton's chair, his hand flat on his brow as if to obscure the sun (which was behind them). Again, however, he was too annoyingly competent to mock.

"Indeed, thanks to my greenies!" said Ferl without modesty.

"I'd like to see your men fight without this magic. The fucking cutthroats would be slaughtered, to a sobbing man," said the Silver Lady, spitting on the ground. Ferl raised his eyebrows.

"My lady. My silver-tongued, silver-haired, silver-hearted lady… without our magic, all of us would have been pierced like a Sestrian kabob. Your big-breasted warriors could not have saved us," he said with a lighthearted sneer.

"Both of you, stop," Emma ordered them, breaking into their eye contact. "This was, indeed, a great victory. Thank you, Ferl, again, for the use of your greenies. You will receive your bonus when we reach our destination."

"And where, exactly, is our destination?" asked Ferl, sticking his hands in his pockets. "Do we not just flee our enemies, tails between our legs?"

Emma ignored him. "Opine, have your most worthy men take the mounts." Most of the remaining horses of their own cavalry had been slaughtered on the night of the attack by the pale creatures they'd faced not so long ago. That strange, confident traveler they'd encountered—Cryden Renshaw, he'd been named—had called them Feral. An apt label. "Braston, Quintin,

36

Ezram. Bind the prisoners as best you can, and ensure no over-zealous—" Emma glared at Ignatius, "—soldiers harm them."

"With respect, Lady Emma, why do we not just sentence these men to death? An enemy left behind is still an enemy," Captain Quentin noted, pursing his lips as he watched the relatively orderly disarmament.

"Would you wield the blade? Would you cut the arteries of defenseless men in front of you?" Emma asked, hands on her hips. Her mutilated hand was habitually angled so only the thumb was visible; she was always conscious of it, especially when challenging these men of war.

"Well, I—"

"Have you ever even killed before? No? It is not something to easily shrug off. It stays with a person." Emma was, unusually enough, thinking of that Merigold girl, and the haunted look in her eyes after she'd learned that she'd bloodily slaughtered three mercenaries. That poor girl was likely dead now, killed by the Feral who'd raided their supply wagons.

"And these Rostanians. They may be our enemies this day, but they are still our countrymen. Should we kill them for following the orders of their superiors? Besides, if we did murder our prisoners, the rest of the cavalry would pursue us to the ends of the earth, and there would be no hope to mend our country. Vengeance is the strongest of motivators."

Quentin lowered his eyes, revealing a balding head that she'd never noticed. "Apologies, my lady. I bow to your wisdom."

"She knows a lot for a serving woman," murmured one of Ezram's aides. Emma couldn't tell which one, but she couldn't react anyway. Not the first comment she'd had to ignore, even if this one had elicited a smile on Ignatius' fat, ruddy face.

Her gaze solid on the men around her, she continued without acknowledging either the remark or the smile. "And, anyhow, leaving these men behind will force the Rostanians to choose to abandon them and continue pursuit—albeit with half as many horses—or rejoin the army in Florens. After seeing the greenies in action, I would not expect to see dust rising behind us any time soon."

"But, for the hundredth time, where are we going?" Ferl asked. "Frankly, I need to ensure that my men are getting paid, lest they begin to… misbehave. And, I'd say, after today, they deserve every yet they're given."

Emma gazed east, a considering look on her face. As if she were making the decision right then and there. They would pass within miles of Draston in a few days. Would the Drastoners provide succor to the Army of Brockmore? Could they combine their forces with the Drastoners, and would they be a match for the Rostanians? Almost certainly not. All messengers had been rejected. Not surprising, as Rostane still had possession of Michel Fraunt, the flippant son and heir of Duchess Emily Fraunt, the ruler of Draston. Likely, they had already struck a deal. Emma would be lucky if that deal didn't include military interference from Draston as her forces traveled through the duchy.

No, there was only one place to go—one place where Escamilla had cultivated relationships for years, where someone might take them in. The place where she had managed to get those invaluable yellow yew bows from, and the place where she kept a great deal of money deposited that could keep the soldiers paid, fed, and happy. For the first time in Emma's life, and likely for the first time in the lives of nearly every soldier there, they would leave their home. They would leave Ardia.

Emma pointed east, toward the border.

"We go to Jecusta. We go to Farrow's Hold."

Chapter 3

In the days following the victory over the Rostanian cavalry, Emma felt only fierce anxiety; it was a great pressure crushing her like the dark hand of Ultner. Certainly, her army had won a major victory, and word of that would spread throughout Ardia. Her men celebrated, somehow procuring barrels of whiskey despite being miles from the nearest town of any consequence. They sang and danced and bragged of their military prowess, never mind that few had bloodied their spears.

However, there was little to truly celebrate. Florens had fallen days ago, and the Rostanian forces continued to swell as minor nobles and landowners met their quotas, and as conscripts from across Florens were integrated into the infantry. Danby, Escamilla's master of information—who now served in the same capacity for Emma—had discerned that only the duchy of Hunesa still truly fought Rostane and retained their independence.

So, Emma had to lead an army of several thousand, without a supply chain, through a hostile duchy into a foreign country, where they may or may not be welcomed. Not an invigorating prospect for a seasoned leader, let alone a trumped-up handmaiden.

But, she let her soldiers enjoy a couple of days of respite. There would be little enough leisure in the months to come.

"My lady, we have a problem." Braston rushed to her side as Emma moved slowly through the disorganized camp in the early morning mist. Summer, fierce only days ago, was already giving way to autumn.

"What is it this time?" Emma asked, not breaking her stride. Her life was simply a parade of endless problems. Trying to plan ahead was like digging a well in the sand with a pitchfork. And Braston, stiff-backed and dutiful to a fault, tended to be the one to convey the news of things going awry. Emma didn't hold it against him.

"Two hundred and thirty of Lieutenant Pino's men are missing, including two sergeants. I believe... I believe they are deserters." Braston's face remained carefully neutral, but Emma could see the captain was visibly shaken. Cocks, but two hundred and thirty men! And after their victory!

"That is a lot of men," observed Emma, unsure what else to say.

"What should we do about it, my lady?"

She worked to keep her hands at her sides. "I... let me think on it."

"Yes, my lady. But, every moment takes the deserters further from our reach." Was his tone patronizing, or was it just her imagination? Was he sneering, or giving an encouraging smile?

"Gather the captains and advisors. We march in two hours, but we must speak beforehand."

"Yes, my lady." Braston nodded respectfully and hurried off, kicking at a staggering, hungover soldier who was in his way. The camp had a haphazard, disorganized quality, as if a god had sneezed tents across a field. Discipline and organization had gone to pandemonium since the Feral attack.

Emma moved through camp mindlessly, pointedly ignoring the looks that the meandering soldiery gave her, as well as the conversations that abruptly halted at her approach. She knew these men didn't respect her the way they respected Escamilla. These soldiers—men from every corner of the country—had answered Escamilla's call for arms. They'd converged at Brockmore, leaving their families to march to war. So many had fought and died for Escamilla, the Apple Lady. A person and a cause they believed in. And, now, they were left with Emma,

41

some young, unknown wench who was missing half a hand. And their doubt was evident.

Frankly, she couldn't blame them. Emma wouldn't have followed herself anywhere.

Sighing, she reached her destination, an unobtrusive and weathered tent sitting a little ways away from the camp proper. She dismissed the two Apple knights with a glance. One, a hulking monster of a man nicknamed Hammer, merely grunted and strode some distance away, his greatsword scraping at his heels. The other knight, Nail, gave her a reassuring smile, nodded, and joined his hulking brother. Licking her lips, Emma entered, crouching a bit to avoid disturbing her brilliant red hair.

The rattle of a cough accelerated Emma through the dimly-lit tent. In an instant, she was at Escamilla's side, wiping flecks of blood off of her lips and chin. Escamilla reached out, grasping Emma's hand with a surprising strength. The Apple Lady smiled a slightly bloody smile, which should have been a grotesque sight on the pale and wasted older woman. But, to Emma, it was beauteous. It meant Escamilla was having her first good day in a week. She was actually conscious today.

"Camilla," Emma said softly. "You look quite well this morning. The physicians say that you've improved." They had said no such thing, of course. Escamilla was dying. It was a slow, slow process.

"You lia…" Escamilla began in a raspy voice, but her words ended in a sputtering cough that wracked her thin body, muscles spasming as pain painted her face. Morgyn's knife, the physicians said, had passed through the woman's ribs and pierced one of her lungs. The mere act of breathing caused Escamilla great pain, while the coughing exacerbated the wound and prevented her from healing. The physicians had tried to operate, to sew up the wound and reinflate the organ, but the surgery had been unsuccessful. Emma believed that it had caused more harm than help. It was easy to assign blame.

"The notepad," Emma murmured softly, handing Escamilla a bound set of paper. Escamilla, obviously frustrated, wrote for a moment, and then held up the paper. Her typically sweeping script was sloppy.

You are a liar, girl. The physicians refuse to answer my questions and give only platitudes. If I were improving, they would fall over themselves to tell me so. And, you wouldn't look at me, just so.

"Well, I am glad to see you awake, anyhow. There is so much to tell you. The battle, first of all!" Emma swallowed the lump in her throat. Act normal, and perhaps things would return to normal. "The plan was successful, more so than we could have hoped. Many cavalry were slaughtered in the pits, and a number were taken by our arrows. Ferl's greenies, though, won the day. I don't fully understand it, but Ashland created a box of raw power, it seems, which they harnessed from trees outside the battlefield. The greenies labored to fill this box for three days, and they set it off with a magical fuse of some sort. The outcome was fantastical." Emma could still see the green flames and feel the remnants of fear and exaltation.

"Regardless, we have hundreds of prisoners."

Escamilla gestured sharply, narrowing her eyes at Emma. How are you feeding them?

"They eat what we eat… Oh. No, this is not a good idea." That much was obvious from Escamilla's expression. "But we can't kill them. I won't have the blood of hundreds of men on my hands."

Other options? Escamilla, still quizzing her via notepad, though the lady already knew the right answer.

43

"We… set them free? No supplies. No… boots. And, point them toward Draston. They should be able to manage a few days, living off the land. And the Drastoners would attribute any looting to the Rostanian Army." Emma should have thought of this sooner. Why could she only consider a problem from all angles at Escamilla's insistence?

Good. But, not perfect. See if any will join us. We cannot see every Rostanian soldier as an enemy. Some may be reluctant to battle their countrymen, or to have been following the now-dead duke. Others may respect our cause.

Emma wasn't certain what their cause was, though, anymore.

"Of course, Camilla. I will do this all at once." Emma stroked Escamilla's gray hair, perspiration leaving her hand damp. Gods, Emma would visit torture upon Morgyn, once she could capture the girl. In the aftermath of the Feral attack, things had been too disorganized to send pursuit. But, like the scummy vermin she was, Morgyn could only return to one place—the gutters of Rostane. Emma vowed to find her, one day.

Her end would be long and bloody.

How is the army? Escamilla rested her head back and closed her eyes, exhausted from the simple task of writing.

"The Silver Lady is unhappy. She lost many of her Fists in the Battle of Florens, and a handful more from the Feral. I worry she might leave us, payment received or not. That slimy bastard Ferl seems to be enjoying himself. His greenies are our only advantage, and he enjoys showing them off. Though, they represent a threat of their own." Emma sat heavily in the simple camp chair next to Escamilla's cot, thinking what to say before she continued.

"The devout Yetranian soldiers—half of our army—find the greenies to be… troubling. Their book—The Book of Amorum—preaches against use of the powers of the earth. Says it sullies the

44

soul with Pandemonium. The discontent has not grown worse than muttering and drunken boasts, but I fear tension is growing. Ignatius hasn't helped things. Ostensibly, he supports the command structure, but he speaks out against this magic in his sermons. His words are heeded, as always. Hypocritical though they may be," Emma muttered, heat rising to her face.

Ignatius would be ally. Escamilla's near-translucent hand wavered, saving herself the effort of filler words.

"I know. I will be civil, I promise." Emma would certainly attempt civility, anyway, though one look at Ignatius' falsely righteous face would likely drown that attempt like a puppy trying to ford the Fullane.

And you?

How was Emma? That was a complex question. 'Bad' came to mind. 'Overcome,' too. 'Floundering' perhaps?

"I… I am not too popular with the soldiers," she answered delicately. "They… I'm not you, Escamilla. They don't know me. They don't respect me. The officers. They seem to listen to me, but they find loopholes in my orders. I… I shouldn't be here." Emma felt tears pooling at the bottoms of her eyes, threatening to escape. She averted her gaze from Escamilla's, carefully looking straight ahead.

A slap rapped across Emma's cheek, knocking loose a few tears and leaving a stinging pain. Escamilla was on her side, propped up on one elbow, glaring at Emma. Emma almost laughed—Escamilla was here, still teaching her lessons despite her slowly wasting away.

That thought renewed the tears, and Emma began to sob anew, uncontrollably this time. Escamilla was all she had in this strange new life.

Escamilla reclined, and Emma laid her head upon the woman's chest, letting loose her sadness, which was only amplified by the sound of the breath rattling about in Escamilla's failing lungs. The older woman stroked Emma's red curls, just like she used to. It was the most solace Emma had felt in months.

After several minutes, Emma sat up, wiping her damp face on her sleeve. Though her new rank afforded her the services of a laundress, the fabric of her long-sleeved dress had even now grown dingy and worn.

"I'm sorry, Camilla. I'm not suited to this. Things seem to be falling apart, and I don't know how to fix them. We've not enough food for the march to Farrow's Hold. Ultner's Fist might leave us, and Braston, just today, tells me that over two hundred soldiers have deserted. And I can't blame them. I can't. Why would they follow me?"

Escamilla held her gaze for a long minute, the older woman seemingly beyond exhausted, but struggling against the embrace of sleep. Her jaw clenched, and she rasped a few quiet words. "You see what we… fought. Those Feral. Use that. Unite the men… against that." Escamilla whispered, with great effort, "They cannot… follow you… if they do not… respect you. Make them respect you… however you must."

Escamilla began to cough, struggling mightily to fight her failing lungs. Emma tried to comfort her, but Escamilla pushed her away, arresting her ward with a cold, stoic mask.

"You must… become hard."

***

The command tent had an empty feel, though near every officer was in attendance. They sat around the great folding table upon uncomfortable folding chairs. And while it was unlikely after weeks of travel, Emma could have sworn that the iron tang of blood lingered in the mobile structure, though there was nary a stain, so thorough were the cleaning staff.

Anew Opine sat at the head of the table, opposite Emma. A few years younger than her, General Opine displayed a wisp of a mustache which was a rather laughable attempt to hide his youth. Nonetheless, he had the confidence of a great breeding stallion. Emma had originally thought the confidence was feigned, hiding his uncertainty, but she now realized that the man had no fear, least of all of his own abilities.

"If we continue due east, we will encounter half a dozen decent-sized towns that will give us an opportunity to resupply before reaching the border," he was saying, apparently disinterested with the conversation. Heroes, it seemed, were bored with the mundane concerns of an army.

Danby met the man's gaze unblinkingly. "I've said before, that is a dangerous path. Three of those towns are walled, and all have at least a token militia. Though they'd stand no chance at fighting us, a fight is exactly what we want to avoid. We can consider Draston hostile territory, according to my agents. But we still don't want to raise the populace against us." Danby was a plain young man whose only identifying characteristic was an oft-broken nose, and he sat at Emma's side. Of those in the tent, Danby seemed the least perturbed at Emma taking command. In retrospect, given that he had been Escamilla's master of information for several years, Emma realized he'd likely been privy to her place in the hierarchy.

"I agree," remarked Trina Almark, the Silver Lady and commander of Ultner's Fist, the dwindling force of warrior women. "We need to minimize all losses, as we are already hideously outnumbered. And succor is not yet guaranteed at Farrow's Hold." The Silver Lady counted both battles near Florens as grievous losses, and had herself lost her fiery spirit.

Ferl snorted. "You've often called me a coward, and yet you fear some pitchfork-wielding bumpkins. I say we sack those towns for supplies. This is war now, and we need every advantage."

"I'd show you what a coward really is, Ferl, if you'd step from behind your greenies for more than a moment." Trina glared hotly at Ferl, obviously ready to make good on her threat. Ferl just smiled as cockily as a king.

"While we'd all be amused to see the inevitable brawl between the two of you, please do so outside of the command tent," Emma commented with a laconic wave. That seemed like an Escamilla thing to say. "Now, we do need supplies, but we can send out parties to pay for them. Unfortunately, we lost so many of our wagons that we will have to resupply more frequently than I would like."

"Is Escamilla's credit still good this side of the border?" asked Captain Quentin, a thoughtful frown twisting his mouth downward. He was an earnest, honest man who often voiced his thoughts, but never with rancor. Emma had once viewed the captains as identical, grizzled military men, but she was quickly learning how different they really were.

"That is a fair question," Emma acknowledged. Would the banks bow to the pressures of war and seize Escamilla's assets? Emma had sent trusted men, Apple Knights all, to attempt withdrawals from banks in Draston and Hunesa. They hadn't yet returned. "Thankfully, we have enough yets to carry us to the border, though the men will go unpaid until we reach Farrow's Hold."

"I don't expect that will go over well. This is a dire enough situation without having men with empty pockets," Captain Ezram said. He was a washout from Hunesa's military, so he knew enough about the life of a soldier. He often sympathized more with the men than the command structure, which was an annoying habit for all those in the tent.

"It's empty pockets or empty bellies," grumbled Opine. "And men march on their bellies."

"Away from their homes and families during wartime," said Erik Malless with a sullen shake of his head. The former duke's hair was askew, having lost the manicured, greased look that he had favored early in the march. His eyes had the glossed texture of an insomniac, and a patchy beard was coming in. He took yet another swig of a Sestrian red, wiping his mouth on his increasingly grape-stained shirt.

"Necessarily. The presence of soldiers who fought for our army would only endanger them. This is the best that we can do to protect the families. Rostanians aren't monsters, no matter who leads them." Braston scrubbed at his eyes as he spoke. Many times, he had made this argument. "Can we please stick to the topic of supplies before we break camp?"

"The men's faith will sustain them though the trials ahead," intoned Ignatius Pender, raising his head from apparent prayer. "Deontis writes that 'Yetra shall watch over all of those who live in Harmony, providing protection and guidance.' Later, in his letters as a much older man, Deontis tells us, 'I have seen faith keep a man upright when he would otherwise be slain.' Faith, my brothers, will keep our soldiers and followers focused on our goals over the coming months." Many of the captains nodded, while Danby scribbled in a small book and Malless stared at his empty cup.

He would be ally. Emma quite literally bit her tongue to prevent herself from insulting the chaplain yet again.

"Chaplain Pender is right." Cocks, the words were acid in Emma's mouth. Ignatius started, frowning. Perhaps he suspected a trick. "Faith drives our men more than money, more than food. Especially now that we know what we fight." Unease spread through the command tent. No one relished speaking of the Feral.

"We must harness that faith. We must remind the men of why we must continue this struggle, outnumbered as we are. We fight for our homes and families. We fight for our country. But, most of all, we fight against men who would unleash such creatures upon us. The Feral." Emma strove to adopt Escamilla's authoritarian tone, her implacable mask. It felt fabricated, a cheap veneer on the front of a rotting house. "Men who would use dark magicks to create and control such creatures. I want each of you captains to spend time around the fires with the men, each night, stressing the why, serving as a reminder for why we fight, for why we must stay together. Remind the men of their duty and of their faith."

An infinitely long silence filled the tent following her little speech. It felt hollow to her, speaking of faith, and Emma fully expected to be denounced as a fraud. Or that these men, spies and career military, noble and religious leaders, would burst into laughter as she was forced to flee the tent. Who was she, anyway, to speak to such men?

But, defying her expectations, each of her officers nodded in turn, their faces steady and grim. Aside from Malless, who'd apparently drifted off to sleep. Ignatius sat solemnly in his chair, grasping his Yetranian medallion with both hands. Likely trying to appear pious, though Emma could smell his satisfaction as if it were an overflowing chamberpot.

50

"That's all fine and good for your people. As long as we are still getting paid." Ferl grinned, though his tone had held a hint of a threat.

"You will get paid, as we agreed. As will Ultner's Fist." Trina did not look up, Emma noted. She would need to attempt to mend this woman's spirit, lest she lose the veteran fighting warriors.

Braston cleared his throat, shifting his gaze uncertainly around the table. Time to address the topic that Emma had been dreading.

"What shall we do about the deserters?" he asked. "I sent out trackers this morning, and the trail is clear across the grasslands. They head south—no major cities in that direction, but dozens of smaller towns. Men could get lost down in those plains. Start over, even." Braston's expression, for a moment, was thoughtful.

Emma closed her eyes, inhaling a deep breath that was tainted by the smell of burning porridge and horse dung. You must become hard. Escamilla's words rang in her mind again, and Emma knew there was only one thing to be done.

"Send twice their number of cavalry immediately. You are to disarm the men and reunite them with the Army of Brockmore. They will be spread across different companies."

"And what is to be the punishment?" These were the first words from Guy Empton, slurred from his half-dead face from where he sat in the corner in his wheeled chair.

"Each enlisted man shall receive three lashes and half-rations for three days." She donned her own mask, the mask of Emma Dran-Breen, ward of the Apple Lady and commander of this army. The mask of indomitability. The mask that brooked no question or dissent. The mask of steel.

"The deserting officers' sergeants shall be given one night to pray to whatever god or goddess they worship. Then, the next morning, they shall be dragged until dead."

Interlogue: The Birth of a Goddess

"Usually, sweetling, I am only greeted with fear. I appreciate you showing such a keen interest in me.

"But, please know that, though I love you, I cannot halt what has already begun. Your path will be the same regardless of our relationship. Over the years, I have developed many strong relationships with my donors. But it is a fleeting relationship, like so many in my life. When you have existed as long as I have, you will find that nothing lasts.

"How long? Millennia, I suppose. It does make me sound old, ancient. But, I think you would admit that I wear my age well. I see that, when you look at me, you think of your daughter. She does share some of the same characteristics—blonde, slender, and of the same height. But, in your mind, I see conflict. You still envision her as a little girl… your darling, innocent daughter. But, you realize she is a woman, a lovely young adult. And one of your strongest worries is that your protectiveness drove her to leave you, driving her into the arms of a man.

"Oh, my sweetling. This has been hard on you. It likely led to further weakening of your heart, but we've addressed that issue already. You need not worry. You know, every good father wants to protect his daughter from the world. And near every girl goes through a phase where they want to escape.

"They always come back, though it is a moot point for you, sweetling.

"You've undoubtedly heard the stories of my youth? As always, there is more mythos and embellishment—lies, really—than actual truth. Certainly, I did grow up in a safe town amidst a dangerous time. The location was such that it was well-protected by the natural landscape, and many brave men and women were willing to fight to protect it. The stories of my parents are varied.

In some, they were poorer than mud, likely to inspire the less-wealthy individuals across the various congregations over time. In other tales, they were well-off merchants. Once, I even heard they were a king and a queen—royalty. Wishful thinking, no doubt, from the various nobility across Loriayne.

"But, no. My parents were actually lamp makers. Lamp makers! I cannot believe that was lost from history. You can think of the symbolism! Spreading light across the land and so forth. They made neither the best lamps nor the worst lamps in Auqine. Average lamps that average people could afford. Silly. People had all of these conveniences, back then. And even now, many are being rediscovered. But, they never think about the people who provide them. How many times did you turn on a gaslamp in your inn and fail to think about the labor involved in gathering the metal for the frame? The work to mine the coal, to extract the liquid gas, and to ship those components to the workers who assembled the final product? I say this not with judgment, but with recognition that we all fall victim to such shortsightedness. Something that can be assembled with such meticulous attention to detail and care, the results of the efforts of many… and the world cares so very little for that.

"But I digress. I often do; it comes with age. Yes, my parents were lamp makers. My father assembled them, and my mother cleaned and polished them, and then packed them for shipping. I often helped with the business, but I wanted more than that. I had no delusions of grandeur—I certainly had no mind to lead men and women into battle or in faith. I simply wanted a bit of variety. It takes a great person to cope with routine. I was no such great person.

"Eventually, when I was… what was it… fifteen? Sixteen? I don't recall exactly. But, when I reached a certain level of maturity, a man came to visit our town. He was older than me by twenty years. He was well-spoken, and had the voice and bearing to sway the good people with mere syllables. I remember Amorum so vividly from that time. It is one of the few memories that has not withered.

"Before you ask, the book was not written by him, though it does bear his name.

"He was not a prophet, nor did he claim to be. However, he was a man of his time. He tried to teach the people of Aquine of the wars that ravaged the lands, of the people who fought back against power-hungry tyrants and so on. The world was, indeed, fractured back then. A thousand warring countries, a thousand small people vying for power. It was, as many say, true pandemonium for good people. People who simply wanted to live in peace.

"Amorum taught of this, and oh, did I listen. From around corners, behind benches, and from outside windows. Wherever I could hear his deep, narrative voice and glance at his handsome, weathered face. My father, however, did not want that. When he would catch me, he would deprive me of my little luxuries and confine me to my room. Which, as you know, sweetling, only makes a girl all the more desperate to seek what is forbidden.

"Amorum was eventually driven from town. What need do a peaceful people have for considering war when war is not at their doorstep? Such ignorance, but such wisdom at the same time.

"The stories leave Amorum out of this part of my life. Of course, they would. People would not like to think that a whore were worth listening to. But that's exactly what I was. I followed Amorum out of Auqine—quite a feat, given the security of that place. I followed at a distance for two days. And, when he camped, one night, I approached him, casting my robes aside. Even back then, in my adolescence, I knew that men's gazes lingered on me for longer than was proper. I knew that my platinum hair was a rarity, something that drew the eye. I had him almost immediately.

"We spent four glorious days in the wilderness. I have had countless lovers since Amorum. Great men and nameless men. Ugly men and strong men, warriors and scientists. A sea of faces, carried away in the vastness of my memory. But, Amorum... Not because he was my first love... No, it was more than that. He... cared.

"On the fifth day, there was a great pillar of smoke in the direction of Aquine. That part, the stories remember. I wanted to dash off, but Amorum—more seasoned, more worldly than me—held me back. He forcefully restrained me, his worried, lined face showing the truth. It was too late. One young girl and a gifted orator with some minor skill with weapons could do nothing in the face of what came. For two days, we waited. There was no more thought of sex. He attempted to calm me, speaking of peace, speaking of Harmony. Speaking of prevailing over Pandemonium through the powers of love.

"He was so misled, sweet Amorum.

"The town was ravaged. You must realize that the world was a much bigger place, long ago. Much more populous than now. My town, which would be a city by modern standards, had held over fifty thousand souls. So few remained after that. The dead were in piles, unrecognizable. Throats were torn out, limbs were ripped off, women had been raped and children abused. Men were hung and nailed to doorways. My family... my family was missing, which was almost worse than seeing them dead. Amorum tried to dissuade me, but I ran through the town, inconsolable, a shell, searching for the bodies of those I knew. Those I'd grown up with. Those I loved.

"Oh, my sweetling. I cannot believe that, even after all this time, these thoughts can still affect me. I can still see Aquine, the place of my birth, ravaged beyond recognition. It was a reflection of me. I felt such guilt, being left behind. And such rage. I feel that now. I do not enjoy feeling this way. This is torment.

"And, this is enough for now. I cannot take this anymore. I wish we had not spoken. Let me take my due and I shall see you some time soon.

"I am taking your chair."

Chapter 4

"So few problems, my dear lady, can be solved with violence. I know that is becoming your specialty, but, please, we will do this my way," Cryden Rensaw said, glancing backward at the platinum-haired girl trailing behind him.

The retort stuck in Merigold Hinter's throat. Cryden was correct in that her life, of late, had been awash in violence and death. Her hands were metaphorically stained with blood, but nearly all of it had come from protecting her own life. The cost of that, though, was high. Half a dozen lives ended—because of her.

One of those being her unborn child.

Meri clenched her teeth, shoving back her dark thoughts. These awful memories and insidious ruminations, like phantasms, eased into her mind almost at random, threatening to overcome her. But Merigold could be strong. She needed to be strong, lest she be cloaked in despair and accomplish nothing.

"When do we not do things your way, Cryden?" Merigold asked, with a fair bit of snark.

"When you run off to splatter mercenaries all over the wall of a tavern, and then join up with an army bound for war?" He didn't look back, keeping his eyes on the muddy road in front of him.

Meri grimaced, but managed to bite her tongue. And then she asked, "Are we almost there?"

"Patience, my dear lady, is a virtue," he said in that holier-than-thou tone. "But, I understand your desire for speed in this case. This place is… indeed… less than desirable."

They were in Enowl, the main port town in the duchy of Hunesa on the shores of the Vissas. They were looking for passage to Rafón via ship. Unfortunately, the entire duchy—the great city and its environs—was barricaded and locked down because of the civil war. Not a single ship was leaving Enowl; nearly all had been commandeered by the Hunesian military in preparation for the growing Rostanian threat. According to Cryden, Hunesa was dominant on the sea, and thought to curb the Rostanian land assault by threating Rostane via water.

As a result, Merigold found herself reluctantly following Cryden—in near blackness—into the seedy part of Enowl. Seediest, rather, as the entire town seemed to ooze squalor and disrepute. The paint on cheaply-built, weather-beaten houses was chipped and peeling, and windows were boarded up despite their buildings obviously being inhabited. Every third building was a tavern, too, and men who were as weather-beaten as the houses peered out at them as they passed. And people spoke forcefully and with what seemed like unspoken threats, and everyone—even the women—openly wore long knives. The muddy dirt paths were full of potholes, and Meri had nearly broken her ankle when she'd tumbled only minutes ago. Some men, obviously sailors, had laughed at her and made rude gestures.

Meri, though, was past being intimidated by men such as these. She had killed malignant men and monsters, and would not let herself be afraid. Cryden's presence was a reassurance, of course, but Meri expected she still would have shot the laughing, mocking men the same dangerous glare. She had already begun to visualize their maenen in case she needed to protect herself. Even sensing the maenen, though, was a struggle for her, giving her a piercing headache. And she hadn't tried drawing power since the day she'd lost her child.

Cryden had known she'd been questing, as he called it, for the maenen of these men. He had laid a restraining hand on her shoulder and they'd continued on.

She had moved past flinching at his touch, though it hadn't been an easy thing. However much Cryden could be irritatingly arrogant, and accidentally insensitive, he didn't mean her harm.

"It looks like we are here, Merigold. Behold the splendor of one of the most storied establishments in Enowl." Cryden spread his arms grandiosely. "Where the good and great meet, and where decisions are made that impact thousands."

Merigold actually smirked at this. Cryden had pointed to yet another dilapidated tavern in a sea of dilapidated taverns. This place was called the Lonely Mast, and the sign—with surprisingly fresh paint and stunning artistic skill—depicted a young, buxom brunette rubbing herself provocatively on the mast of a ship. The old Meri would have been appalled. Today, she barely gave it a second glance, but for the skill involved in the painting.

"Now, let me do the talking, Merigold. There is a specific language spoken by these people, and you would rather not misstep. Do not quest; do not draw. Unless things are very clearly going wrong," he added with a wry smile, his unassuming features basically unchanged.

At a time like this, Meri would have been happy to have a man like Fenrir near her, his bulky muscles acting to dissuade violence as much as anything. She wasn't exactly afraid, but she would rather avoid dangerous situations for a while. She sighed.

"Sure, Cryden. And how will I know if things are going wrong?"

"I have a feeling that will become obvious," he said with a wink. With that, he pushed open the doors and strode confidently into the maw of this tavern, Meri trailing a few steps behind him.

***

Dear fucking Yetra, did this place reek!

The inside of the Lonely Mast matched the run-down exterior. The common room was nothing like Meri's Duckling, with its organized rows of colored tables, cheery ceiling lamps, and roaring fire. No, instead, here there were small oil lamps on every third mismatched table, their light occasionally dimmed by a depressed patron leaning his hands in his head. The crowd wasn't exactly raucous at this hour, and the patrons seemed more controlled than in some of the taverns they'd passed. A couple of women, dressed in nearly nothing, lazily danced on a stage. Few were looking, and the women appeared more than aware of the lack of interest.

The acrid scent of old fish forced its way into Merigold's nose, and that was mixed with vomit and old beer. The stench was amplified by the cheap incense intended to mask the odor, but which instead exacerbated it by a factor of ten.

Though she felt an urge to cover her nose, she followed Cryden's example and acted as if nothing were amiss. The two sat down at a table, and a bar maiden was on them immediately, perhaps sensing the possibility of a decent tip. Cryden's forest green shirt was of a fine material and he wore an ornate belt patterned with silver. Meri's own clothes—a red, cotton blouse and a black skirt, split for riding—were perhaps not quite as fine, but they were the best that Cryden had been willing to purchase for her. And, of course, she wore her sapphire studs in her ears, though they didn't match her outfit. She never took them off, though.

Completing her outfit, secreted under her blouse, was her little knife, a relic from her time imprisoned underneath the cabin outside Dunmore.

"Milord, Milady! What do you need? We have local and imported brews, and some little food left for this evening, though

61

the cookfire is already extinguished. If you want, I can see what the chef can put together." The blonde girl—not more than seventeen years old, Meri guessed—had an innocent smile reflected in her eyes. Merigold was stunned. Down to a discussion of beers and the cookfire, it was like a portal into her past. A naive serving girl wanting to make a little bit of coin. Perhaps this girl's father owned this place; she seemed well-fed and unabused, surprisingly so given the quality of this place and the presence of those lazy dancers. The memories of Ragen and her old life strained against the lockboxes in her mind, and Merigold fought to keep them closed just as she fought to hold back her tears.

"My dear girl, we are neither lord nor lady, though I do appreciate the compliment," Cryden said, flashing his customary smile. He shot Meri a quick, fierce look that said 'Get a hold of yourself.' "The young woman and I will have your absolute finest wine. And, please see about the food. Maybe a small snack to settle our stomachs."

The bar maiden grinned at the "finest wine" comment, and then moved quickly to the back room. With an effort, Merigold managed to regain herself.

"Merigold, you must learn control. If you are to be a pasnes alna—which I am beginning to doubt—you cannot allow every little thing to startle you!"

Every little thing. Like recalling the death of her father and family.

"Sure, Cryden. I will try to do better," Meri promised with passable conviction. She knew he was right.

"Superb. This is a situation that we must handle with the utmost care. Losing control in any way could cost us both our escape from this civil war, along with our lives."

"I can promise it will not come to that."

"Thank you, my dear lady." Cryden leaned back, seemingly appeased, just as the blonde brought back a bottle of wine and two smooth stone decanters. Merigold did not recognize the language on the bottle.

"Where is this from?" she asked, trying to interpret the sharp letters, so unlike the Ardian.

"Rafón. Rafónese wine is some of the best available," Cryden cut in, seemingly unable to let the bar maiden answer. He always took an opportunity to show off his knowledge. "Though the climes are fairly intense, near the Filinial Sea, they grow some of the finest grapes in the world. And, they have patience in Rafón. Unlike with some of the swill made in Ardia, they allow the wine to age appropriately."

Cryden reached into his pocket and pulled out an octogonal yet, it likely being more money than the girl would see in a month. He spun it across his fingers deftly, and it disappeared in his hands before he pulled it from behind the bar maiden's ear. She squealed in delight—whether from the coin trick or the size of the coin, Meri wasn't sure. She reached for the coin and Cryden whispered something in her ear. The girl paled and shook her head. Cryden said something more fiercely, and the girl bit her lip before turning sharply and walking toward the kitchen. She left the big yet behind.

"Now what?" Meri asked.

"Now?" He poured each of them a bit of wine, swirling his around and taking a sip. "Now, we wait."

***

63

They didn't have to wait long.

Merigold had finished two cups of that fantastic Rafónese wine and was feeling a bit light-headed, particularly as her stomach was empty; that bar maiden had never come back with food. In fact, Meri didn't see her anywhere in the Lonely Mast. Merigold ran her fingers along the end of her tightly-bound braid, the alcohol exacerbating her anxiety.

Cryden didn't speak with her while they waited. They'd spoken little, truth be told, on their trip to Enowl. Once she'd recovered enough to ride, he had gotten her a pony and they'd ridden single file throughout most days, skirting around any major settlements and resting often. He had seemed distracted, lost in thought or lost in the magic. He was a cautaton, after all, a person who could sense miernes. He'd once explained to her that perceiving such miernes was a constant experience, something that he could not dampen. People with this ability often went insane before being discovered by one of the orders of pasnes alna.

Perhaps now he was lost in magic again, so quiet he was. By appearances, though, he simply enjoyed his wine and absentmindedly watching the dancers, one of which had completely given up the pantomime of dancing and just leaned against the wall, zoning out or high on kerena.

Merigold had just begun zoning out herself when a man, his face wrapped in a carmine-colored scarf, emerged behind Cryden and roughly grabbed his arm. Merigold almost jumped to her feet, but Cryden didn't react. He only lazily turned his head.

"Shall we speak in private?" he asked, unperturbed. The man grunted from behind his bright scarf, releasing Cryden's arm and gesturing him to stand, his hand resting on the hilt of a hapler at his belt. As Cryden rose, Merigold followed his example, and both were herded to a small door in the back of the bar.

The storage room was exactly what Merigold would have expected—a small, cramped room with shelves full of dried goods and cooking necessities. What she wouldn't have expected was the false floor beneath the table. The man pointed into the hole, still apparently unwilling to speak. Merigold wasn't surprised with the rudeness. What could one expect from criminals?

Without hesitation, Cryden grabbed the ledge and descended via rungs affixed to the side of the vertical tunnel. Meri, on the other hand, faltered for a moment. More than faltered, in fact. Dear fucking Yetra, this hole the ground... the darkness was terrifyingly familiar. Dripping water echoed in her brain and she felt a rising panic, building up juxtaposed urges to both flee this place and fling herself into the blackness.

Someone touched her arm and she whipped around, seeing Saren. Wait, was it Saren? Maybe Paul? She started to quest, to sense his maenen. She prepared to draw, to fight, to do whatever it took to stay out of that hole, that prison, and took a deep breath and met the eyes of her assailant.

But the man just stood there, pointing impatiently at the hole in the ground. He scratched at his scarf, likely over-warm. Merigold was in the the Lonely Mast.

She was in control. She had to be.

With a deep breath, she swung her feet over the edge and climbed down into tunnel, noticing almost immediately that it was not so dark as it had appeared in her head. In fact, it was downright cheery, so much light filtered into the chute.

"Took your time. Making kisses with our guide?" Cryden asked, sardonically raising an eyebrow.

Merigold didn't respond, but shot him a dark look. They were in, as she would have expected, a cellar. But, it was the most extravagant cellar that Meri had ever seen. Perhaps it was the most extravagant cellar in all of Ardia. All of the world, even.

The room felt as spacious as the tavern above, and on one end, spanning the entire wall, stood a latticed wine rack, containing bottles from what must have been every country in the world. On the other end, paintings covered the wall—works of art depicting famous battles, heroes of Ardia, and scapes from lands Merigold could only guess at. A great wooden table—a single piece that Meri could not imagine fitting down that hole they'd entered by— was covered in the finest foods, as well, including roasted pheasant, fruits from over the sea, and so on.

There were five people sitting around the table, too—four men and one woman, all staring at Meri, Cryden, and their silent, scarf-covered guide who'd entered behind them. The room remained completely silent as they were scrutinized. Somehow, their scrutiny was more frightening than the hapler at the belt of the man who'd guided them down the hole.

"Well, what do we have here? Few have the appropriate codes to find our lowly cellar," commented the woman sitting at the head of the table. She was not lovely; rather, Merigold would have categorized her as beefy. She had wide arms, but not the sort that carried much muscle. Her hair was cropped short in the style of many Enowlers; many worked with fish and sought to keep their various guts and slimes out of their hair. Surprisingly, the woman was not as richly dressed as Meri would have expected given the surroundings, although rich clothes would not have suited her.

"Are you the executor of Enowl, then? Resia the Blade?" asked Cryden, arms folded and his stance slightly askew.

"My reputation is confined to a relatively small circle. Perhaps you should enlighten us before Burnt Ernie there has reason to draw his blade."

Burnt Ernie? That would explain the low-fashioned scarf.

"I need a ship to take us to Rafón. Immediately," Cryden returned, his tone imperious.

The people at the table shifted uncomfortably and one of the men rose, reaching for a sword draped over his chair, suspended by a belt.

"You are evading the executor's question. And, no one makes demands of The House!" The speaker—a lithe, muscular man—drew his sword smoothly and stepped forward with confidence. Merigold stepped back, bumping into Burnt Ernie, who laid a rough hand on her shoulder.

Cryden, however, was unmoved. He slowly strolled forward to the end of the great table, making no threatening gesture. There, he reached into a pocket and the swordsman stepped forward warily, leveling his weapon at Cryden's throat. Cryden glared at the swordsman for a long moment, and the confident man seemed to waiver, his sword arm slowly sinking until his arm hung limply.

Cryden reached into his pocket and tossed a bit of metal onto the table with a clang. Meri strained forward to see what it was— was that a seven-pointed star? Crafted from white gold?

There was silence in the room.

"Where did you get that?" Resia asked, seemingly perturbed. "I know all bearers of the gold heptagram in Ardia, and you are not one of them."

"Perhaps, I do not hail from Ardia. Or, perhaps I killed one of the previous bearers." The room darkened, and Cryden seemed to tower over all in the room. A sick feeling of apprehension, of just-restrained violence, filled the cellar. The air seemed to have been sucked out of the space, and the people around the table shrank into their chairs.

"A wild one? Your tricks will not work here." Resia snapped her fingers, and the feeling lessened, though it did not vanish. The men at the table seemed to regain their composure and all began to rise, reaching for weapons. The swordsman began to raise his sword, though he moved as if underwater.

Merigold felt Burnt Ernie tense behind her, and she began to quest. She could sense the maenen of all of the people in the room save Cryden. Even Ernie, though she could not physically see him. She began to snake her hand toward where his rested on her shoulder. She had to touch him to draw his lifeforce.

And then Cryden threw back his head and laughed. "You think me a wild one? A metsikas like you? And I thought the executor of The House would be more knowledgeable about the world. And be more reluctant to show her own powers to a pasnes alna of Agricorinor." He held out one hand and a blue flame formed above it, throwing heat all around the room. Merigold shivered through her sudden sweat. How was he drawing without touching anyone? And, that power!

Resia beckoned her men to sit down, and they did so with alacrity. A pasnes alna in Ardia was enough to turn their legs to jelly, even though they had their own metsikas. Cryden cupped his other hand over the blue flame and it disappeared, the temperature in the cellar returning immediately to its base. It still felt too warm to Merigold, though. Stifling, in fact.

"Perhaps we should start over from the beginning?" asked Cryden, spreading his arms.

Resia took a deep breath, reaching under her shirt and revealing her own steel heptagram, dangling from a chain.

"Greetings, sir. What can The House do for you?" Resia's voice had dripped with sarcasm.

"Much better," Cryden said, speaking as a parent chastising a child. "Meri, shall we have a seat?"

Merigold pulled away from Burnt Ernie and sat in the proffered chair.

"And who is this one? Too young to be a pasnes alna," Resia remarked, eying Merigold with something like distaste.

"You are likely in the know regarding all things criminal in Hunesa, correct? Recall Ferl's Company, the mercenary band? She was the reason they left so quickly."

Resia did not appear impressed. "Are you telling me that this little blonde stabbed two men to death, and then splattered another all over the walls?"

"You have such little faith in my word, Resia the Blade. Merigold, perhaps you would like to show us your power? Perhaps Burnt Ernie wouldn't mind?" Cryden suggested with his typical half-smile. Merigold turned and reached toward the man, flashing her own imitation of Cryden's smile. Burnt Ernie made a throaty grunting sound and hopped back in a hurry.

The executor of The House in Enowl sighed. "Alright, enough posturing. You obviously have the better of me in this situation. So, you need a boat?"

"A ship, my dear lady," Cryden corrected her. Merigold barely restrained rolling her eyes.

"A ship." Resia's voice was flat. "You know, there are no ships leaving the harbor right now. A war is on."

"Certainly, I must believe that The House is not limited by the laws of men, nor their petty wars." Cryden poured himself some wine, the currant liquid flowing into his glass. He offered some to

Meri, but she waved it away. The Sestrian red she'd had before was gurgling in her stomach, and adding to it might have disastrous results.

"Indeed, the reach of The House is limitless. But such arrangements will take some time." Resia glanced at the swordsman who had earlier threatened Cryden. The lithe fighter was the best dressed in the room, wearing a black and silver silk coat, its material so lightweight that it must have cost a fortune. His jet-black hair was oiled back in the most modern style, and he had the easy confidence of a lord.

He shook his head firmly, meeting Resia's eyes.

"No time. We need to leave immedia—" Cryden dropped his wine glass, spilling wine on one of the men and speckling Meri with the red liquid. His eyes grew vacant and distracted, and his face fell as slack as that of a corpse.

"What is wrong with him? It's isn't a pox, is it?" asked the wine-splattered man as he twisted away from Cryden in a hurry.

"Nothing. Magic is nearby," Meri answered with dry lips, needing to fill the silence. Dear fucking Yetra, what could she do without Cryden? He must be perceiving powerful miernes nearby to have lost himself like this! She'd seen this before, on their journey. But why now?

She saw Resia glance at the man closest to her—a skinny, reptilian man. He reached into an inner pocket and pushed back his chair. Cryden was still non-responsive, even as the feeling of danger cut through the room. These people were criminals and killers, and with their main threat seemingly incapacitated, they would be quick to move.

Merigold began to quest, seeking the maenen of those occupying this lavish cellar. But, if she were to manage to kill these people—adding them to her list of victims—how would they reach Rafón?

So few problems can be solved with violence.

Swallowing her earlier impulse, Merigold waved a hand arrogantly as if nothing was amiss. "As my associate was saying, we need to leave immediately. Agricorinor awaits our return, and, as you know, they will not be denied." Merigold hoped her voice sounded confident. Her stomach was a hot stone, and her heart fluttered like a hummingbird. She also hoped that Agricorninor— the order of pasnes alna to which Cryden belonged—had some weight in this circle. Her companion had said so precious little about their final destination, and Merigold had been so distracted anyhow.

The reptilian man hesitated, looking to his leader. Resia herself seemed unsure. Merigold needed to capitalize on this uncertainty.

"Furthermore, we require a protection detail from The House, of six of your more skilled men who will escort us to the gates of Agricorinor. Trusted men, of course, who will be well-rewarded upon arrival, as will you."

Everyone in the room—save for Cryden, who remained lost to the world—had their eyes locked on Merigold. The short hairs on the back of her neck were soaked in perspiration and sticking to her collar. But, she tried not to look away from Resia. Absently, she wondered how the bulky woman had received her nickname, the Blade.

Still, no one said anything.

Merigold had never liked speaking to groups. She always preferred to listen. And, she had learned from her father Ragen that filling a silence was a poor negotiation technique. He'd traded with people from all over the four duchies, and been recognized as a shrewd dealer. He'd typically ended up better off in any trade, and would have been quite wealthy, indeed, had he not been so generous. Meri had often wished that he would instead be a little more greedy and retire, taking care of his own health instead

71

of others. She'd never fully agreed with his generosity... but she had understood his lessons.

So, Meri said nothing and only waited, resisting the urge to reach under her blouse and grip her small knife, her charm. She stared at a spot between Resia's eyebrows so she wouldn't have to look into the woman's eyes.

After what seemed like an eternity, Resia cleared her throat.

"We will need tomorrow to plan, but it will be done. Captain Jakys, it looks like your route for tomorrow night has changed. Prepare your ship and gather your crew. Quietly, of course."

Captain Jakys, the man in silver and black, gave Resia an incredulous look, his mouth hanging open as if he wanted to argue. Resia glared, and the man gulped.

"It will be as you request, Resia. Assuming this man... recovers... in time." Jakys spoke like a noble, but evidently he was a ship captain. To Meri's untrained eyes, he looked Sestrian—dark hair, tan complexion, and with a hooked nose.

"Oh, I am quite well. Thank you for your concern," Cryden said, speaking as if he hadn't just missed five very dangerous minutes. "Shall we mark our alliance with a drink?" Cryden picked up the bottle of wine and offered some to Meri. This time, she did not wave the bottle away.

He gave Merigold a small, secret smile as he filled her glass with the crimson wine.

Chapter 5

Morning came rapidly, as it often does when one lays down one's head only a couple of hours before sunrise.

Nonetheless, Merigold was brimming with energy. Having successfully survived the ordeal with the executor and her various lackeys beneath the Lonely Mast on her own, she felt prepared to do anything. She could overcome the ghosts that had been haunting her. She could survive the long trip through rough seas and foreign lands to Agricorinor. She could learn about her powers, her ability to draw maenen. And, perhaps she could find a way to fulfill her desperate promise to herself.

For the first time in a long time, she prayed an ardent prayer of thanks to Yetra, who she suspected might be giving her strength after all.

Meri dressed in an ash-gray blouse with a cobalt scarf to highlight her sapphire studs. She held her tiny knife—a long, bent nail with its cloth-wrapped handle stained brown with blood—for a moment before stuffing it under her blouse. Having the weapon touching her skin made her feel safe. Even with her powers, it brought her a sense of security she couldn't truly give voice to.

She finished packing her clothes and went to meet Cryden in the common room of the tiny Enowler inn. The place was on the better side of town, but that wasn't saying much when Enowl was a stinking, sinking marsh populated by folks who had the fortitude or poor taste to ignore their own living conditions. This nameless inn was nothing like her Duckling. There was no pride in ownership. No extra polish on the bar, but dust and grime in the corners, and the fireplace was heaped with the ash of nights past. The proprietor—a greasy, balding man with the frightening smile of a predator—was aloof and inattentive, and the food was sub-par, if Meri was being generous.

Truly, she would never find another Duckling.

"My dear lady, you seem almost cheerful this morning," Cryden greeted her, already sitting at a small table in the common space. The long evening seemed to have worn him down to the nubs. His eyes were heavy, and his usually pristine clothing was wrinkled as if he had gone back to bed after getting dressed. His face lacked his signature sardonic smile.

"You, my dear man, look the opposite," said Meri, her eyes twinkling and a smile tugging at the corners of her mouth.

Cryden sighed, exhaustion practically leaking from him. "There are strong forces at work nearby. Even had we had enough night to sleep, I would have been unable."

"What forces? What is wrong? What even happened last night?"

"The process of miernes detection is not an exact science, my dear. I have told you before, it is more of an impression, a sense." He glanced around the room. It was nearly empty, aside from a man who had been sitting at the bar, bent over a flagon since the night before. He could have been a statue for all that he'd moved.

"Surely, a man of your experience can read quite a bit into an impression," Meri responded, sitting across from him and leaning forward. Cryden was quite susceptible to flattery, she'd learned. Which was fine; she'd used to work for tips.

"And, suddenly, you again are interested in the world? Last night—or very, very early this morning, rather—has changed you." Meri raised her eyebrows, beckoning him to continue. "So, I have previously explained to you how being a cautaton allows me to sense the miernes? That different miernes leave different impressions based on the type, and how these impressions are stronger based on the power of the draw?"

Merigold nodded, meeting his eyes. She did truly need to learn.

"Well, there have been some extremely strong draws of late. Not just here. Over the entire country. I felt it, my dear lady, as I traveled to find you. And, I felt it here—well, in Hunesa—last night. Quite strong. Too strong." Cryden rubbed his eyes, and then waved to the proprietor. The man ignored him.

"Is that why you went into some sort of trance? Zoned out?"

"Zoned out? Oh, yes. That. I certainly did feel a great power last night." Cryden smiled slightly.

"And you were nonresponsive, practically a corpse. Don't you remember?"

Cryden's smile grew wider.

"What happened?" Merigold remained confused. Cryden had been paralyzed, even spilling his valued wine on his even more valued clothing.

"We can call it your first lesson. A test, if you will." He tapped the table in a quick rhythm with his fingers, then leaned back as if brimming with pride.

"What? A test?" Meri's jaw dropped. They could have been killed!

"I wanted to put you in a situation where you had to use your wits instead of your powers. You can fight. You can kill. That is well-established. However, if you seek to become a pasnes alna, particularly in my order, intelligence, wit, and cleverness are just as important. More important, in fact. Did I not tell you that very little of use can be accomplished by killing?"

"Few problems can be solved with violence," muttered Meri, echoing Cryden's words from last night and glaring at him with all the vitriol she could muster.

"What?"

"That is what you said. Few problems can be solved with violence."

Cryden smirked and then again waved to the proprietor, who began to saunter over with the urgency of a tired tortoise. He considered the conversation over, clearly but Merigold refused to let it go.

"So, you pretended to be lost in the magic—surrounded by men with weapons and a woman armed with her own magic—to teach me a lesson? Couldn't you have just… taught me in the conventional style?"

"I didn't exactly pretend. I was perceiving a great deal of power from the direction of Hunesa, and it did consume a large portion of my focus. But, I was segmenting. Something that you will learn to do if you are to be successful. The biggest part of my consciousness was scouting and learning what I could learn about whatever powers ran rampant through the night. But I was still more than aware of the surroundings of my physical body. Had there been reason to worry, I could have returned to my body in an instant and neutralized any threats. There were no worries."

"Cryden, you still could have told me," Merigold muttered, knowing not what else to say, but hoping to at least inflict the pain of guilt. It had worked well with Ragen, but Cryden was apparently immune.

The proprietor finally made it to the table, and Cryden ordered some fried potatoes and greens for breakfast. Enough for three, he said, very specifically, banging his hand on the table to punctuate each syllable. The innkeeper eyed them suspiciously, probably with good reason, and ambled back toward the kitchen. Cryden looked back at Merigold, his gaze intense and worldly.

"My dear lady, a test is not a test without stakes. Had you known it was a test, you may have held back. Knowing that you could rely on me, you likely would have panicked, or given up, or simply failed. I gave you a situation where you had to succeed. And, my dear lady, you did succeed. Quite marvelously, I might add. I was actually impressed." He smiled that sardonic smile.

This felt like a violation to Merigold, but she couldn't find any holes in Cryden's logic. And, Dear Yetra, she did feel accomplished after last night. Capable. A feeling she'd rarely had since leaving Dunmore on that night with Saren. She actually felt alive, for the first time since… well, since she'd lost so much.

"I'm uncertain whether to be upset or to thank you," Meri said cautiously. "Now, must I fear that everything from here to Agricorinor is a test?"

Cryden chuckled. "My dear, everything in life is a test. A test of your skills. A test of your knowledge. A test of your endurance. Even a test of your relationships. So, yes, I will be testing you at every turn, but so will every other damned thing in the world."

Her life had been so easy before, in Dunmore. She'd had her worries, of course. Did she have a nice dress for the Ascension festivities? Would she find a good man? Did they have enough food for the luncheon following the Yetranian weekly service? Would she ever get to see Rostane and the Plateau, or the wider world?

Trivialities, all of them.

The world had been testing her since, and Yetra knew that she had failed.

"Cryden, you mentioned that you sensed great powers at work in the night. What are they?"

"Again, you surprise me. I expected you to dwell on the test." He glanced at the kitchen, now tapping his fingers impatiently. The man was apparently hungry.

"Don't be evasive," Meri told him.

Cryden's face darkened, but it did not come with that feeling of anxiety and danger. Another lesson learned last night was that Cryden could alter the environment, or the emotions of those around him, by using his powers. She'd stored that information, planning to observe it further. Maybe she could learn how to do that, and maybe it would help her in some future test.

"What I felt—what I have been feeling," he answered at length, "—was a perception of great violence, pain, and warmth. And not just from one draw. From many. What I felt, Merigold, was the creation of Feral. All over this country. Which is why, my dear, we must get to Agricorinor as soon as possible."

Meri couldn't help but feel a shiver. She remembered the Feral who'd attacked her, broken and bleeding but still fighting to kill her, to taste her blood. These things would not be stopped by anything short of death.

Cryden glanced to the right, noticing the proprietor carrying a tray heaped with food. "But first, my dear lady, we should eat some breakfast. Journeys should never begin on an empty stomach."

***

It seemed that all things related to The House happened at night. Certainly, crime, extortion, and manipulation must occasionally happen under the light of the sun, but Meri imagined that such things were more at home in darkness, barely illuminated by the waning twin moons.

She and Cryden had spent the day shopping and preparing for the journey. Cryden was reluctant—and almost comically so—every time he had to pry open his purse and hand out a yet, but now they both had a full wardrobe appropriate for sailing and the subsequent overland travel in the winter, as well as a supply of dried meats and hard-as-rock bread. Cryden had lectured her on the importance of always carrying your own supplies rather than being reliant on others to feed you. Cryden had also reluctantly sold their horse and pony and changed his Ardian yets to Rafónese oros and a handful of Sestrian flins. Their journey would take them through both countries, though they'd only briefly be in Sestria.

Merigold would finally get to see the world. Though, now, her heart ached to return to her old, boring, and forever-lost life.

Currently, she stood behind Cryden near the docks, awaiting their escort. There were no torches or lamps lighting this area of town, and although there were guards nearby, they ignored the pair. Cryden had said they'd either been bribed or were in the employ of The House, paid to look the other way in the case of illicit goings-on, which was basically all that happened here. Anyhow, men were coming and going from the seacraft, likely to and from various taverns if their raucous behavior was any indication.

The moons shed little light, and Merigold jumped at every bit of movement. What was to keep Resia the Blade from betraying them? A little fear? A golden, seven-pointed star? She had no trust in these people. What kind of honor could a criminal have?

Cryden stood easily, arms folded and apparently lost in thought. His light cloak, trimmed with an intricate silver pattern, blew in the heavy breeze. He looked every inch a powerful pasnes alna, very much unlike a man who tended to blend into the background. She found herself staring.

And then leaping in the air as a man emerged from the shadows nearby and spoke to them at full volume.

"You the pasnes alna? Come with me." The man, dressed in all black, immediately turned and strode down the docks, his feet making hardly a sound on the wooden planking.

Merigold followed slightly behind Cryden.

She had never imagined there were so many ships in the world as were at these docks. Though the moons provided little illumination, many of the boats and ships were bright with lamps and busy with activity despite the hour. The masts made for a veritable forest—sometimes with three or more spouting from a single ship—and the docks may as well have been a labyrinth. She had no idea how the ships closest to land would navigate their way to open water. In Dunmore, they simply had rowboats, though foragers would often simply wade through the shallows, finding it quicker and easier. Mayor Marsh had had a small sailboat that he'd used for leisure during the wet season, when Dunmore Lake was actually deep enough for sailing to be worthwhile, and Merigold had been in awe of the thing, always wishing for a chance to sail on it. Larger boats than the mayor's sailboat hung from the side of these Enowler ships, held simply as back-ups!

It wasn't long until they reached their destination—a three-masted ship, relatively small compared to some of the behemoths blotting out her vision.

"A caravel," muttered Cryden, his features crinkling with distaste. "It might mean a rough ride."

Resia the Blade greeted them in front of the boarding plank, four figures flanking her. Meri again felt a flurry of fear, questing out to sense their maenen. If this were a betrayal, then she would not be taken easily.

"The pasnes alna. I trust that this ship will do?" Resia asked, her face barely visible in the dim light.

"I assume there are no other, bigger options? Those galleons, perhaps, over yonder?" Cryden asked, gesturing to a pair of gigantic ships visible against the horizon.

"I assure you, this ship will get you where you need to go. The Graceful Whale is the fastest smuggling craft we have."

"Smuggling?" Merigold echoed, before she could stop herself. But smuggling was almost certainly the least of these people's crimes, she knew. And, why should she have qualms when she had killed several men herself? Murder was certainly a worse crime than smuggling.

"Yes, smuggling. Will that be a problem, girl?" Resia's voice was harsh.

"Certainly not. I just wanted to make sure I heard correctly."

"You did. And now, your escort." Resia stepped aside, reveal three men and a woman.

"I would see those who will work with us." Cryden snapped a finger and a small light formed in his hand, causing all four to step backward hurriedly, but deftly.

Two of the men had olive-colored skin, short-cropped dark hair, and slightly slanted eyes. Sestrian men. And, she would guess that they were twins, so identical were their faces and builds. The third man stood out more prominently; he was an unusual sight, indeed. Huge, towering above the rest of them, he wore an open vest that revealed an ample, pale stomach. The only hair on his head stretched from ear to chin, and he had a great, silver ring of metal tunneling through his cheek. It created a secondary entrance into his mouth, and Merigold could see his clenched teeth. It was horrifying, and it drew the eye away from the other couple dozen piercings around his head.

The woman was built like Resia—stocky and wide—with the exception being that she had a great deal of visible muscle. More than most men, in fact. Her face was… well, if Merigold was being honest, this woman had the face of a dog she'd once seen traveling with a noblewoman. The thing had had a very smashed face, being so ugly it was nearly cute. However, the "nearly cute" part did not translate to this woman, though Meri felt immediately guilty for thinking such a thing.

"The brothers are Remy and Marius. The big man with more metal than face is Ill'nath, a Pintan islander somehow marooned on land." The man grunted and perhaps smiled, though this expression was more frightening than anything. "And, Lisan the Arrow is the muscle-bound beauty before you."

"There were to be six men," said Merigold, feeling her own daring. "That was the deal."

Resia's eyes flashed. "In case you didn't notice, we are at war. The House included. Four is a compromise, and you will deal with this. Besides, I would pit these four against any six." There was finality in her voice.

"Four is more than enough, my dear lady. I expect a quiet journey," Cryden said. "I look forward to getting to know each of you."

"We must be going," hissed a voice from the ship. Captain Jakys, the lithe noble from below the Lonely Mast, still seemed to be in an ill-temper. "Our window is closing. Get those passengers aboard."

"This will all be adequate. Thank you for your willing assistance, Executor," Cryden said wryly. He seemed much recovered from the morning, and his smile and sarcasm had recovered in turn.

"Always a pleasure. I trust these seeds will yield fruit?" Resia asked with some hesitation.

"Agricorinor will know of your assistance. Come, Meri. We must hurry so that we can sit for a week."

Merigold boarded the ship, nearly losing her balance immediately. The deck seemed to bob and weave below her feet, and she grabbed onto the railing to stay upright. One of the sailors gave an unkind, mocking laugh.

"Easy now, Meri. You will get used to this. Or, you will be violently sick for a week or two," Cryden offered, with what sounded like actual sympathy in his voice. He looked pale in the moonlight.

"Captain, where are our bunks?"

"Below. You two have the honor of the first mate's cabin, as a well-rested first mate is apparently less important than your comfort," Jakys snapped.

"I completely agree," Cryden said, obviously baiting the man. The captain met Cryden's eyes and did not back down.

"If you hadn't some magic on your side, I would toss you overboard."

"Lucky for me, then, that I have what you call magic," Cryden returned, cockiness oozing from him like the smell of fish emanating from the ocean. "Now, if we are done intimidating each other and measuring cocks—mine is bigger, by the way—what is our path?"

The captain turned to the side quite rudely.

Merigold's legs already felt weak from the motion of the sea. How could a ship moored to a dock move so much?

"We cross the Vissas Sea and take a direct route to Polanice in Rafón. Two hundred and forty leagues or so. What other path could we possibly take?" As clear as the stars in the sky, the captain was irritated that they were aboard.

"I just wanted to ensure that our thinking converged. With the correct winds, how long will this take?"

"With ideal winds, a little over a week. Realistically, though, traveling north at this time of year, it will be three or more."

Three weeks aboard this oversized wooden duck? Merigold already felt the effects of the sea on her weakened limbs, and couldn't imagine spending that kind of time here.

"Fantastic. We will be there before we know it." Cryden's voice was dry, but the captain had already turned to begin issuing orders to his men. "Come along, Meri. Let us find our bunk and see if you can find your balance."

Merigold wobbled after Cryden, already ardently missing Ardia. Or at least the feel of stable land beneath her feet.

Chapter 6

The filthy girl, footsore and stiff, finally approached the southern gates of Rostane amidst a disorganized mash of marching soldiers, meandering peasants, and purposeful traders. Morgyn scratched at her dirty chestnut hair; she'd likely gotten lice, somehow. Certainly not the worst thing that she'd experienced, but the thought almost brought her to tears—she'd have to shear her hair off again, and it was finally growing out. A couple months of relative safety and comfort, traveling with Lady Escamilla and her army, must have made her soft.

There was no room for that in her life.

Slim and standing just over five feet, Morgyn had little trouble weaving her way through the mess of people at the gate. Security seemed tighter, and the gate guards were interviewing every person desiring to enter the city. On the wall above stood a dozen guards with crank bows leaning on the crenelations. Rostane was at war. Or, rather, Rostane was winning a war, and whoever was in charge since the little duke had been skewered wanted to keep it that way.

Heavily armed and armored guards, however, were a very minor barrier to someone who had been dodging and outrunning more motivated pursuers throughout her entire life. Besides, the gate guards generally didn't give a shit.

Morgyn broke into a nimble run before she reached the head of the crowd. She stumbled over someone's shoe and heard a shout, but she managed to keep her feet and remain moving forward. The guardsman were completely unprepared for a bundle of rags dodging through their ranks, and not a single one laid a hand on her. They shouted out an alarm, but only a couple of guards started after her.

"Stop! It's just some urchin," bellowed a commanding voice as Morgyn reached the first alley, leapt a fallen pile of lumber, and splashed in the waste that was so common in the side paths of Rostane.

Just some urchin. Not the worst she'd been called. And, not true anymore. Now, she was a traitor, a killer, a spy, and an urchin. Basically, she was the worst kind of person. But that didn't matter.

Morgyn continued down the alley, ducking behind a pile of pungent trash in one smooth motion. It was a familiar move, a comfortable move. How many times had she darted into the cracks between buildings in order to hide amidst refuse? It was sad how natural it felt for her to dwell among the filth of Rostane. She'd become a fucking maggot.

She waited several moments, but saw no signs of further pursuit. Why waste the manpower chasing some piss-poor little guttersnipe? There were enough of them languishing in the dirty parts of Rostane, mostly the leavings of prostitutes, and one more throwaway wouldn't threaten national security. Truth be told, she'd counted on that.

Morgyn took a second to take a bite of an apple she'd filched earlier in the day, her last bit of food. She was starving, but ate sparingly; who knew when she would get her next meal? Hunger was a familiar feeling; she been struggling for scraps of food for her entire life and it showed in her diminutive, malnourished frame. Her mother (the woman who she figured was her mother, anyway) was a tall woman—quite a leggy whore—but those traits did not manifest in Morgyn. She was like the undersized puppy that couldn't reach the teat.

At least she could use her size to her advantage. People tended to underestimate her.

That wouldn't help her now, though. Being underrated might help her, say, smack a hulking idiot in the side of the head in the darkness, but it wouldn't protect her from the people she needed to deal with. Bad people. Terrible people.

People who made the things that Morgyn had done seem like charity work.

Morgyn twisted up from her crouch and darted down the alley, easily avoiding the refuse that had always littered her world. She was off to report to her superiors, to share how she'd stabbed an old woman in the back. As if they wouldn't already know.

She was off to find the Patriarch of Recherche Oletta.

***

In advance of meeting with an important person, some would worry about their appearance, about their cleanliness. About their odor. But Morgyn had learned that she was less likely to be struck when a potential striker worried more about catching a disease—or getting lice—from a filthy little guttersnipe. Dirt was her friend in this.

The location of the Patriarch and his ilk was ever-changing. But, for one who knew the signs, he was relatively easy to uncover. Morgyn continued down that first alley until she came to the rear of an antiques shop, a place that she'd often visited to hock her various finds. She hadn't lied to Escamilla that night in the ruins—she loved exploring and relished the opportunity to discover old artifacts and the remnants of those who'd come before her. If she hadn't needed to eat, or if she'd had a single safe place to store them, Morgyn would never have sold any of them. She loved her spearheads and her carvings. Her old writings in languages that she didn't understand. Her shiny rocks, said by the superstitious to be remnants of great magical battles from the earth's beginnings.

She wasn't a Scholar or a Savant, though, unlike most of her acquaintances, she could actually read the trader's tongue. No, her interest in old things was not academic. Rather, it was a sort of reminder that there was something bigger than all of Rostane. Bigger than all of the people who spit on her and hit her and ignored her. Something greater than this so-called modern city that allowed little girls to be dumped in the gutter, forced to live in shit, and to steal and lie and fight for a bit of old meat. That forced little girls to kill.

And, it reminded her that if something even greater than Rostane could fall, then so could this cesspool of a city.

Morgyn pulled out her ogra, a thin, black stone that she kept hidden in a buttoned pocket, or in a shoe or hanging on a thong—wherever she could keep it from prying eyes. The thing was opaque from a distance, just a shiny black rock, thin as paper but seeming to reflect all light. But, when held to the eye...

Everything was tinged in red. The wall, the sky, the crud at her feet. And, scrawled in bright white letters was a series of numbers. Morgyn repeated them silently a few times, and then tore the ogra from her eye. The thing always made her feel dizzy and wrong. And, it made her feel... furious.

The numbers were coded, as well, but Morgyn had that memorized. It was a simple code. She supposed that, when you had to have a strange rock to even see these numbers, a simple code was as good as a complex one. It gave her an address on the eastern side of town, a rougher part of town. A place where she had spent most of her life.

Of course, that would probably not be her destination. It would just be the location of the next code. Which would probably lead to another. And maybe another. She was rarely lucky enough to find the right code the first time. With a tired sigh and a suddenly grumbling stomach, she set out toward her next stop.

The numbers on the east side led her to the Oaken Barrel, which was luckily not much further. The tavern was a favorite of the Recherche Oletta, partially because the terrible food would keep out most decent folk, and partially because the apartments upstairs provided a good deal of privacy.

Morgyn sat down in a corner of the dreary tavern. Though it was still light outside, none of that light thought to enter this place. Why would it bother? Nothing worth seeing happened here. She squinted in the dim light, glancing at the occupants. Mostly sad drunks at this time of day—decent folk would still be working and the prostitutes would not yet be out of bed. Well, they would still be sleeping—that was the point. They spent most of their time in bed.

"What you want?" A serving woman limped up to her—a Wasmer woman. Few enough of those wandering around Rostane, and she recognized this one. Female Wasmer were much smaller than their male companions, but otherwise similar in appearance. They had the dual fangs, fuzzy faces, and extended fingers of the men, though women tended to be more delicately featured. Narrower chins, no lower beards, tighter cheekbones, and smaller ears. This woman was brunette, and she wore her hair in the trademark braids of the Wasmer people. She must have had dozens of the things springing from her head like vines springing from a single stem.

"Dilys, how are things?" Morgyn asked, adopting her wide-eyed, eager young girl persona. Most everyone liked her better when she acted like that, lilting her voice and speaking quickly, asking questions and talking about her little adventures.

Had she not been born to a whore, perhaps she would really have been that girl.

"Little Morgyn Aranon! I be missing your smiling face near here! It be brightening this dark place." Dilys mouth split in a smile, grotesque but at least authentic, making her a joyful gargoyle. "Where you be being, little girl?"

"Oh, here and there. I found a great, new place to play, and some new friends! Though, one was a bit of a blockhead." Fenrir. That old fuck.

"There always be one like that." Dilys was all affection. When most Rostanians saw a Wasmer, they averted their gaze or crossed to the other side of the street. Others would taunt and shout. A select few might hurl more than insults. It was quite similar to how they treated Morgyn, she knew.

Dilys was one of the few people who was truly kind to her. Not so much a friend—Morgyn had none of those—but always friendly. Always kind, though she was treated so poorly. Perhaps she sensed a kindred, ostracized spirit in Morgyn.

"Yes, there is. But I really needed to come home, you know, Dilys. There is so much to do, and I do have to work."

Dilys' face darkened at that. "You be knowing what I am thinking about that, little girl. You be too young to mix up with those people. It not be safe."

"Oh, Dilys. That is exactly why it is safe! No one would suspect that a little girl might be listening to them." As far as Dilys knew, Morgyn was simply a spy. Not an agent navigating the dangerous bounds of multiple underground organizations. Not a thief, and definitely not a killer.

"Anyhow, little girl, you be needing to take care." Dilys briefly rested her elongated fingers on Morgyn's shoulder. Maybe, this was what it would have felt like to have a mother, Morgyn thought briefly. "I be getting you some stew, no needing to pay, of course."

"No, Dilys. I just need you to send a message." Her stomach was chewing on itself, but she needed to get this over with or she might lose her nerve. It was too important for that to happen, though.

Dilys sighed, a growl coming from her bestial mouth. She gave Morgyn a firm look. "I will let them know that you are here."

The Wasmer limped away toward an opening in the back of the inn, one that led to the upper levels. A shaggy fellow sat nearby, staring blankly at his mug as if the alcohol within held all of life's answers. Dilys touched his shoulder and whispered something into his ear. The man twisted to his feet, belying his obvious drunkenness, and disappeared upstairs. A different man rose from the bar, staggering a bit, and fell into the seat by the door a few minutes later. Sentries.

It wasn't long until the original sentry returned and tapped Morgyn on the shoulder. She jumped and cringed. Time to play the cowering, broken street girl, in terrible awe of Recherche Oletta. This was less of a pantomime, given what these people had done and were willing to do.

Morgyn hunched her shoulders and reluctantly followed the man upstairs.

Down a run-down hallway, they came to an unassuming door. Certainly not a portal to Pandemonium, though Morgyn wouldn't have been surprised if Ultner were on the other side. Her escort rapped on the wood three times in quick succession and the door squeaked open a crack, a beam of light falling on Morgyn's face. Like the sun shining through a hand lens onto a bug.

Her escort patted her down, even checking her boots. He caught her eyes before he spoke. "No sudden moves. No resistance. Answer all questions when they are asked, and do not speak otherwise." The man reeked of booze, but his breath had the faint aroma of mint. Clever and careful. That was Recherche Oletta.

Morgyn took a deep breath and pushed into the room.

Just an office, as always. The set-up was always the same, though the location was transient. There was a chair behind a heavy oaken desk, which she assumed had to be disassembled and reassembled every time there was a shift in location. Morgyn studied the very unusual imperfection in the wood while averting her gaze from the man standing behind the desk, hands braced behind him in a very formal posture.

"Morgyn, my little double agent, finally returned from her failed quest," came the nasally voice of the man.

"Patriarch," Morgyn said, leveling her gaze at him. Her demeanor switched yet again, to that of a brazenly confident, street-wise thug. She had found, with the Patriarch, that he was going to beat her regardless. If she were submissive to begin with, he would hit her for longer. If she were brash, he would beat her into submission, which ultimately led to less pain. It was counterintuitive to wear this mask in front of this man, but it brought her the least pain.

The Patriarch of Recherche Oletta was a slightly stocky, but somehow agile, man of average height, and likely Alganian, although his heritage was unclear because of the almost sickly pallor of his skin. He always wore dull brown robes, outwardly to signify his obeisance to the greater good and his rejection of wealth, although his robes were crafted from the finest silk. Upon his flat nose sat a set of spectacles, like a scholar might wear in order to avoid squinting at their books. But, his spectacles were not made of glass. No, they were formed of shiny black ogra.

The Patriarch was intelligent, meticulous, and terribly erratic. He was the waterfall at the head of the Tullane River, with its white, rushing water somehow contained within this man. In contrast, Morgyn's mouth was as dry as an old whore.

"I did not fail," Morgyn said.

The Patriarch did not move. No immediate beating—that was unusual.

"You did not fail? You did not fail when you aided our enemies in leading Lady Escamilla in her escape? You did not fail when you were caught in Brockmore? Though, I must say, you must have done some fast talking to get out of being executed."

"I did not fail! I stabbed Lady Escamilla in the back, right through the ribs. If she did not die immediately, she surely did soon after." Morgyn remembered that night vividly. She had feigned sleep for hours, waiting for those pompous captains to finish their discussion. That Duke Eric Malless, especially, had made the night drag on. Morgyn had nearly drifted off every time he'd opened his mouth.

But Morgyn had known that it would be her last chance at Escamilla—she'd been alone with the lady so rarely. The army had decided to retreat, and, in the midst of the confusion, she had hoped that she would find an opportunity. Escamilla had slumbered when an attack came—those same terrible screams that Morgyn had heard in the ruins. They'd served for a much better opening than Morgyn could have imagined. She had crept up behind Escamilla while the woman had spoken with Emma, taken a deep breath, and driven a purloined dagger into her back. Then, she'd escaped Emma's clumsy attempts to catch her and run off amidst the battle.

The flight that night had been terrifying. Pale white shapes darting through the night; primal screams weakening their legs. Escamilla's soldiers being murdered all around her, some in their underclothes as they struggled to arm themselves against the unexpected attack from those fierce, indefatigable enemies. Morgyn had fled, blindly, to the north. When morning had come, she'd still been stumbling through the fields north of the battlefield. No pursuit. For all she had known, the entire Army of Brockmore had been destroyed.

It had been a long journey back to Rostane, too. Morgyn had traveled slowly, staying off the main paths and taking a circuitous route in case of pursuit and to avoid any armies or foraging troops. She'd stolen food wherever she could, but the countryside had been picked clean by the armies. She had gone hungry, more often than not, but it hadn't been the first time. She'd still continued moving forward, the rough journey both distracting her from her thoughts and giving her time to think.

She hadn't wanted to kill Escamilla. The woman had been kind to her, treating her as if she were more than a street girl, more than a tool. Under the worst circumstances, Escamilla had begun to treat Morgyn almost like a daughter. But, Escamilla hadn't been her family.

And Morgyn hadn't had a choice.

"What good would Escamilla's death be to me when her army had already arrived at Florens?" the Patriarch demanded. "When they had already killed thousands of Rostanian troops?" His posture was tight, as if he were working to control his anger. But he still did not move.

"Besides," he added, "Escamilla still lives."

What? She had felt the knife slide between the lady's ribs! The blood had stained the fine clothes that Escamilla had given her, and had dried on her hands and in her hair.

Every Morgyn's cocky persona had nothing to say to this. She felt a sudden dread.

"But, no matter. I fear that I have put too much on you, girl. More than you can handle. I can sometimes be... reactive." Morgyn could see her surprised reflection through his ogra spectacles.

What trick was this?

"I can handle whatever you send my way," she said, licking her lips.

"Can you, girl? Could you, perhaps, help me take this city, this country? Could you help squash the opposition, that bastard Tennyson and his ilk? The resistant nobles, the foolishly stubborn merchants?"

The Patriarch turned suddenly in a smooth motion that hinted at his strange agility. His back was to Morgyn as he considered the blank wall. The room was silent for a long moment, and Morgyn began to fidget. Why was he acting like this?

"Like I said, I can handle anything." Her voice rang hollowly through the small room that suddenly seemed much larger.

"Perhaps I will take you up on that offer, girl. Now, sit for a moment. Please, girl." The pleasantry had grated from his mouth, as if those words had rarely crossed his lips.

This was more chilling than the Patriarch's typical violent streak. He seemed like a great, black-eyed spider, ready to wrap her in his web and inject her with his venom.

"Aye," Morgyn said, sitting on the visitor's side of the desk and learning forward on her elbows in a bold pose. What she wanted to do was shrink into this chair, but she clung to her false confidence as if she were hanging from a rain gutter, dangling over the city streets.

"Now, tell me what you've learned." The Patriarch spun back toward her, lowering himself into his chair with the easy grace of an alley cat.

And so Morgyn spoke, telling him of her time with Escamilla, amidst her forces. She told him of Fenrir, the buffoon who'd beaten the shit out of her and hung out around the mercenaries. Fenrir was already infamous, having killed Little Duke Penton. She told him of Emma, the serving girl who'd seemed to gain power among the army as they'd marched, and that she was Escamilla's successor. She even mentioned that strange woman, Merigold Hinter, who'd purportedly blown some of Ferl's Company to bits with magical powers.

The only bit she held back was the discussion of religion with that chaplain, Ignatius Pender. The Patriarch likely didn't want to hear of the proselytizing. And besides, Morgyn kind of… well, yes, she liked the story of Yetra. It gave her a strange, unfamiliar feeling. Hope, maybe?

The Patriarch stayed silent throughout the entire story. He may have been asleep behind his ogra spectacles, for all the expression on his face.

"Anything else?" he asked, expectantly.

"No, that's it. And, my reward?" Bold, she knew. Or stupid.

"Your reward? For now, we will say 'your life' and be done with it." There was a hint of a smile on his chapped lips. The hairs rose on the back of her neck.

"Well, what should I do with my life, Patriarch, that you've so freely given? The House will be after me, and I've seen what they do to traitors."

"As if you didn't know the risks."

"Aye, but I thought it would afford some protection."

The Patriarch clenched his fists, skin turning white and highlighting the brownish scabs on his knuckles. Morgyn tried to swallow. She'd gone too far.

"Why don't you go spend some time with those slugs? You just need to stay alive for a few days, girl. Then, I will send for you."

The Patriarch stood, obviously dismissing her. She pushed back from her chair and began to rise, herself.

"Oh, girl."

Morgyn paused, partially crouching over her chair.

With unnatural speed, he reached across the table and hooked her in the mouth, sending her stumbling to the ground. Her lip tasted of sweet blood, and her head spun from where it had just struck the floor. The whimpering squeak she let out was not entirely feigned.

"Never question me. You, and those you care about, live by the grace of Oletta. I will not tolerate more failure. Now, get out of my sight."

Morgyn scrambled to the door and slid into the hallway, wiping blood on her already-filthy sleeve.

That had actually gone much better than expected.

Interlogue: Lust

"Oh, sweetling. I apologize, it has been longer than usual. I had some things that needed my personal intervention. And, I truly apologize for my rash behavior upon our last meeting. The emotions can become overwhelming at times, as I know you can understand. I can see that you have not been without pain in your life.

"It is beginning to happen, just by degrees. I can see you beginning to lose yourself. But, you still have so much of your mind, which is impressive! It is your body that is betraying you.

"Your lust, at the moment, is clearly standing in the gentle light.

"Do not feel embarrassed. In fact, I feel flattered that I can still elicit such a reaction from a man such as you. A rarity, you are. I know enough about you now to say that you are a good man. And, I have been in desperate need of a good man, of late. I am pleased that my followers got one correct, particularly after so many mishaps.

"Please, know that even a good man has his share of temptations. I know of yours, and you are forgiven. This girl…. Come to me… you recognize this girl, no? With this lovely auburn hair and a figure to rival my own? Yes, I know you lost yourself, spending several nights in passion with this girl. Sandra is her name? I see you look at Sandra now with lust in your eyes. Your primal emotions are revealed to the world. And yet, I say to you, you are forgiven. You are merely a human. An animal, really. The lust you feel now, that you try so hard to fight, is natural.

"Leave her be? Of course, sweetling! I do not harvest women. They make an… insufficient end product. Useless, really. They lack the aggressions and hungers of men, at least in any way that would be useful to me. That, and, when I harvest, I take on some of the characteristics of my donors. I have found that too many women can make me... soft. Doing the... things I must do can become more challenging if women enter my donor cycle.

"Women can serve me in other ways. This girl, here. I find her hair to be pleasing, so I enjoy having her in my sight during the day. She is well-treated, of course. You need not worry.

"Such kindness in your heart. I know this must be hard for you. I know you resent this girl. That you feel like she tempted you, stole your fidelity to your wife, though she is long passed. But, you kept your faith. The fact that you feel that way tells me again: You are a good man.

"I tell you now. Your wife has passed. Fidelity has no meaning. You did not betray her; you could not betray her. Regardless, would she not want you to be happy? Would she not want you to experience the pleasures of flesh again, since she was forced to leave you?

"I have told you that I have also struggled with lust, in my time. Amorum... Amorum took my away from myself, and I could barely control my basest instincts when he came into my life. Ultimately, lust both saved and shattered my world.

"Would you not like this girl now, sweetling? I still see your lust, unabated despite the shame of your memory. Would you not like for me to return your chair, and allow this girl to gently mount you and curtail your lust, though briefly? Would you not like to run your hands through her gorgeous, flaming hair, feeling the silken flow melt through your hands?

"I see that the answer is yes. Your hands—your entire body— shakes with anticipation. And yet, you would still resist, despite your worn humanity. You surprise me, sweetling. You are stronger than most. You are braver than most. And, remember that

I have known so many, many men when I say you are dumber than most.

"Girl, you may return to the above. On your way up, please stop and ask one of the Lanei to bring a chair back to this man. I have a feeling that he will be thankful for that comfort, come next visit."

Chapter 7

The muscular man strained against his bonds, his veins standing out on his skin like vivid blue scars. Two Wasmer struggled against the bearded man's strength, each bearing a rope looped around the man's wrist. And then the man suddenly stopped his struggle, throwing his captors off balance. He ripped one hand free and tackled the Wasmer on his left, landing three crunching, heavy blows before two other Wasmer tore him off their companion, dragging him to the ground. A third Wasmer joined the fray, wrapping his arms around the man's flailing legs and finally subduing him.

"Why do you keep trying?" Hafgan Iwan demanded, pushing through his men to see the familiar commotion. Rin Yanso, former captain of the Rostanian Army, snarled at him as usual, even as the Wasmer tightened the loops on the big man's wrists.

"I will never submit to you, Wasmer," Yanso spat, the last word coming as a fierce curse from his tongue. "You might yet drag me to Pandemonium, but I'll make you suffer every step of the way."

Hafgan appraised the man. It had taken weeks for Yanso to fully recover from the injuries inflicted by the gwagen that terrible night. The Rostanian captain and the Wasmer had simply been in the way as the soulless creatures had flowed over the walls of the compound toward the Army of Brockmore, but they'd not been spared a great many causalities. Yanso had very nearly been killed, but there was a deep strength within him, an inner drive handily matched by his very real physical prowess.

The minute that Yanso had recovered enough to be fully cognizant of his situation, he'd begun his escape attempts. First, he'd tried riding off on one of their few horses, bareback, before a mounted Wasmer had managed to knock him from the saddle with the butt end of a spear. Then, he'd overpowered one of his guards—breaking the poor Wasmer's jaw—and limped off into the night. The Wasmer had had no trouble tracking Yanso with their superior night vision, but it had been a true fight to bring him down even with him being injured.

As Yanso had grown stronger, his many injuries healing, his escape attempts had grown ever more fierce. Hafgan was continually amazed that he continued fighting, often in the face of spearpoints. The men had strict orders not to harm Yanso more than necessary, though, and the Rostanian took full advantage of it.

"Were you to leave us now, you would be dead within days. The Tulanques are inhospitable in the best of times, and with winter approaching, you would find yourself lost, hungry, and frozen," Hafgan told him, folding his arms.

Yanso stood tall and strong against Hafgan's scrutiny. "Better dead than a prisoner to you fucking cretins. You bird-sucking, shit-eating, goat-faced... fucks."

"You only be a prisoner because you make it so," said Paston, Hafgan's second-in-command. The shorter Wasmer scratched at his omnipresent facial hair, self-conscious of his Wasmer heritage even in front of a single human. The lieutenant had grown accustomed to shaving his face clean, twice per day, but he could no longer feed that habit. After hundreds of miles of marching, much of it through the harsh terrain of the Tulanque Mountains, luxuries like sharp razors, warm clothes, and adequate food were just dreams of the past.

"I be saying we just toss him off the mountainside and be done with it," growled Enric, nursing a bruised arm from the earlier scuffle. Enric somehow managed, despite their lack of supplies, to continue keeping his head and face shorn of hair. His pale, hairless head was crimson from the cold, but he seemed unaffected.

"It'd be preferable to spending another day with you fucking goats!" Yanso responded, relaxing in the arms of his captors.

"As much as I'd prefer to see you broken at the bottom of the mountain, we need you," Hafgan said, shifting his balance to his left leg. Ever since that arrow had ricocheted off his right hip, weeks ago, there'd been a nagging pain whenever he stood still. "It would be better for you, for all of us, if you just came along easily."

Yanso seemed to slump, as if finally relenting. Of course, that wasn't the case, and Hafgan was expecting the sudden activity when Yanso lunged out of the relaxed grips of his guards, grabbing a dagger from the belt of one as he passed. With a fierce precision belaying his musculature, he thrust the dagger at Hafgan's unarmored chest. Hafgan easily sidestepped, making no riposte. Yanso caught himself and followed up on his attack before being yanked back by his bonds. He slavered and snarled like a feral dog on a leash.

"Release him," Hafgan said, the chill wind tousling his overgrown hair.

"Sir?" Paston asked, licking the space where his second set of dogteeth used to be.

"Is my Ardian lacking?" No, his diction was near perfect. There was nothing like commanding men to polish a Wasmer's tongue. "I said, release him."

Reluctantly, the Wasmer released the ropes. Yanso glanced to each side, sensing a trick, but none of the Wasmer reacted. So, Yanso cut through his bonds with the stolen dagger and faced Hafgan, squinting against the bright sun which was amplified by the snowy peaks surrounding them.

"What's this game, Wasmer?"

"No game. You best me, you leave. We'll even give you supplies. You can maim me, kill me. Whatever you must do," Hafgan said, his voice growing monotone as he reached for his hedwicchen—the center, the emptiness that was so critical to this battle. His muscles reached a state of relaxed readiness, his mind emptying itself of his many worries and fears, memories and insecurities. Rather, he was fully immersed in the moment, as if the moment were the sky and he were a cloud.

There was nothing unnoticed, nothing beyond his capacity for understanding. Everything around him signaled a pattern and hinted at what was to come. To the untrained, the amount of information could be overwhelming, overpowering all five sense. A master, though, could focus, filtering the noise and extracting the most important details. Yanso began a furious set of attacks as Hafgan effortlessly compiled the details of this particular fight and opponent.

One. Yanso's lip curled slightly just before he made an attack.

Two. His right leg was weaker; his movement was slightly hampered by some old injury.

Three. He'd learned his thrust improperly. The weapon angled slightly upward, which would prevent his weapon from sliding between the ribs.

Four. Hafgan himself was struggling on dodging to the right, as pushing off his left hip still caused him pain.

Five. Paston was on the threshold of interfering, readying himself to trip Yanso with his spear.

Hafgan made a harsh negating motion with his hand, meeting Paston's eyes. He ducked under another telegraphed attack by Yanso, slapping his opponent in the ear—a horrid insult to the big man. Yanso bared his teeth at Hafgan, a wild ape attempting to intimidate another, before launching a half a dozen more strikes.

All of which Hafgan dodged, parried, or ducked. Half of which he punctuated with a slap to some part of Yanso's head.

"You fucking goat—stand and fight!" Yanso snarled. His eyes darted from side to side, looking for other methods of escape. His gaze settled on Enric for a split second longer than the rest of his surroundings. The hairless Wasmer leaned lazily against the butt of his spear, obviously confident of the outcome of this battle.

Even within his hedwicchen, Hafgan could not move fast enough.

Yanso stepped hard toward Hafgan, but it was a faint. He pivoted on his weak leg, lashing about with the dagger at the surprised Enric, who dropped his spear as he leapt backwards off-balance, taking a deep gash across his chest. Yanso scooped up the spear just as Hafgan hurtled into him, bearing him to the ground. Somehow, the huge Rostanian captain retained his grip on the weapon and managed, in the tangle of flailing limbs, to wrap the haft around Hafgan's neck.

There should have been fear surfacing within Hafgan, the panic of a fish flopping on the beach. The haft dug into his neck like a vice, cutting off his ability to breathe. Yanso was driving a powerful knee into his side now, causing a flair of agony in his healing hip like the jab of a knife. And yet, within his hedwicchen, Hafgan felt no urgency. He recognized his emotions as if he were reading them from a sheet of paper, and simply used this information. Action was necessary.

Yanso was stronger, a bull of a man. But, the hearn doethas had taught Hafgan to fight strength with intelligence based on keen observation. Though Yanso was weeks out from his major injuries, like Hafgan, he was not fully recovered. Hafgan's first elbow being driven into Yanso's previously shattered ribs merely elicited a grunt and a tightening of the haft around his neck. The second, however, forced a scream that echoed across the mountains like the call of a thousand demons.

The third blow sounded with the audible crack of a bone snapping.

The big captain cried out, dropping the spear as Hafgan spun around, smacking a booted foot across the side of Yanso's face and driving him to the ground. Through his hedwicchen, Hafgan was aware of his bruised neck and burning lungs, but that knowledge wasn't enough to deter him from pinning Yanso to the rocky ground. He dug his elongated fingers into the man's rib whenever his struggles grew too fierce.

"Stop this foolish game," Hafgan said in a hushed monotone. "You fight and you fight. You hate and you hate. And for what?"

Yanso gazed up at Hafgan through pain-filled eyes, every breath a wheeze. His shaggy hair, sweaty from exertion, hung down over his face like a mask. The thick, shaggy texture betrayed some Rafonese heritage somewhere far in his past.

"For what?" Yanso chuckled, which turned into a hacking cough that likely wracked his body in pain.

"Yes, for what? Why hate the Wasmer with such passion?" Hafgan expected that Yanso had fought in the border skirmishes, and experienced some loss at the hands of his kinfolk in years past. He was of age for that to be the truth. But what did he keep fighting for?

"You, Wasmer, searching for some reason behind my hatred of you and your kind," Yanso hissed, wary of aggravating his injury. "Perhaps expecting that your people wronged me in some way. Stole my family away, or killed a comrade in the skirmishes. Some tragic backstory to explain why I despise you. The fact is, I've suffered no loss to you fucking goats. You have neither harmed me nor those around me. I didn't fight in your skirmishes, and no one I know personally was affected."

Hafgan looked hard at Yanso, wishing his hedwicchen allowed him to peel back the man's skin and understand his thoughts. The big man smirked in return, blood splashing over his teeth from a blow that Hafgan didn't remember delivering. A dull urge to break the man's nose tickled at the edge of Hafgan's hedwicchen, but he ignored it.

"It is not anything that you have done, Wasmer. It is what you are. You are alien. You are not human. You scum are an abomination, an affront to creation. You seek to walk among us, live among us, pretend to be human. Pretend to have a goddess-given soul. But, you are empty. Soulless freaks!" Yanso's eyes were intense, filled with a burning, irrational hatred. "You, the ones they called budredda, are the worst offenders. You think that you will trick us into believing you're human. You think that we are so stupid? You seek to live among us? Be one of us." Yanso spat crimson with a bitter chuckle. "Never. We will never accept you goat-fucking freaks. You soulless, fuzz-skinned fucks."

Hafgan stared at Yanso, allowing his hedwicchen to dissipate. Some things required emotion for interpretation. Never had he seen or experienced such unadulterated hatred, such a pure and yet unfueled rage. If the big man spoke true, his detestation was based in nothing. Nothing at all! No Wasmer had ever hurt him, and yet their very existence—the fact of Hafgan's existence— drove this man to such extremes of hatred that he was willing to fight, and kill, without provocation.

Emotion always seemed stronger after the hedwicchen, in the way that the taste of an apple was so extremely tart after one fasted. Hafgan felt a rage overtake him, a muscle-shaking, teeth-grinding rage. A rage that he could scarcely control, looking at this man. This small, insignificant man so bent on hating him for his birth, not for anything he had done. Something that Hafgan had dealt with for his entire life among humans, which was somehow embodied in this uncouth Rostanian captain. This bigoted human. This... fucking scum of a subhuman bastard.

Hafgan jammed stiff fingers against the man's broken ribs, holding steady as Yanso writhed and struggled. He drew in close to Yanso's face, smelling his travel-stale breath and feeling its heat against his furred cheeks.

"You pitiable, hateful man. You speak of souls? Doesn't your Yetra say 'the soul is a measure of kindness a man spreads to others, friend or enemy?' Does she not say that 'the soul is strengthened by a man's conviction to others?' You, the hateful and vitriolic person that you are, must have a malformed, diminished soul. You are nothing more than a bitter, vicious dog, longing to be put down."

Yanso grunted and heaved for breath against the pain, his eyes glistening with agony and rancor. He had breath for only four words. "Goat... faced... shit... fucker!"

Hafgan's rage, barely held in check by his haern doethas-trained will, broke free. He slammed his forehead against Yanso's face, feeling a crunch as the man's nose broke. As Yanso's hands darted to his new injury, Hafgan intercepted a wrist and slammed it against a nearby rock, breaking the bone with a crunch. Without hesitation, he next punched the man across the face once. Twice. Three times.

And then he was borne to the ground, the weight of Paston and Alwyn preventing him from killing Rin Yanso. He struggled mightily and two other Wasmer jumped into the pile. Slowly, the fury lessened. His senses returned. His other emotions surfaced, primarily those of guilt and shame. He took several deep breaths against the pressure of his men and squeezed his eyes tightly before locking his gaze with Paston's.

"We be needing him, Lieutenant. We be needing his account of the attack. We be needing any intel—without harming him, you said."

Paston appeared stupefied at the sudden violence perpetrated by his superior. Hafgan was typically so calm, so controlled. When was the last time anger had taken him like this? Not for years, not since... not since Hackeneth. That day with Taern Llegyn...

"Sir?" Paston asked, reaching down a hand to help him up as the other Wasmer scattered.

Hafgan ignored Paston, walking over to where Yanso still lay on the cold ground, illuminated by an oddly reddish sun that had finally broken through the chill clouds. His face was a ruin of blood and bruises, and he cradled his wrist against his stomach, though his ribs must have been like a dagger in his side. What had come over him, to commit such intense violence against this man? He'd dealt with such hatred for years, and he knew the type of man that Yanso was. Why had this time been different? Shame sat in his stomach like old, sour goat's milk.

Paston stood slightly behind him, his presence like a heavy conscience. Hafgan didn't even glance back.

"Bind his ankles and bind his wounds. The captain will continue with us, and I do not expect him to cause us any more trouble."

Chapter 8

Fenrir couldn't remember a time when his body had not ached.

Always, the knee pained him. That was a foregone conclusion. The thing had been mangled, after all, by that twiggy bastard Sigmund. His shoulder, torn by knife and fingers only months before, never stopped throbbing. Martis Aieres—his trusted friend and a skilled physician—had said the pain would fade, particularly if he continued to do the strengthening exercises forced upon him during his recovery. But it was also a foregone conclusion that he was going to neglect the exercises, and would have even if he hadn't been caught up in escaping from the Plateau, recruiting a mercenary army, engaging in a civil war, and so on, not to mention the assassination of a duke.

The rest of his body was covered with new and fading bruises, small scrapes, and a couple of oozing lacerations that just wouldn't heal. How could they heal when he was beaten every couple of days at Sigmund's orders?

Fenrir had expected to be executed days ago. Weeks ago? He wasn't certain how long he had been down here; no light reached the interior of the Plateau, and he wasn't fed with any regularity. The fat he had built up during the time since his disgrace in the council chamber above had melted away. Muscles were atrophying, too, so much so that it was an effort to rise. But there was no reason to rise, really.

Maybe he deserved to be executed. He had relived that night, the night of the raid on Little Duke Penton, over and over again. He was a soldier, true. But, even a soldier shouldn't kill his friends.

Silas had been a friend to Fenrir from the earliest days of his military career. When the other recruits had beaten and abused him, an older Silas had pulled them off and dished out punishment of his own. He'd been a protector in the truest sense, his mere presence and the threat of reprisal keeping Fenrir safe. Sometimes, it had chafed Fenrir that he needed such protection; he'd often operated under the arrogant illusion that he could take care of himself. But, with his merchant background, he'd been hated among the peasant recruits, and there was only so much a single man—let alone a boy—could do against many. Silas may even have saved his life a few times.

And Fenrir had repaid that pleasure by killing him, twenty years later.

He remembered seeing Silas guarding the stairs that would lead him to Duke Penton, watching the action unfold from his weird, disembodied state. The man had recognized Fenrir in an instant and lowered his weapon. He'd not been a threat, not at that point. Nonetheless, Fenrir's weapon had torn across his throat. In his memory, his sword moved in slow motion, parting skin, tissue, and arteries as blood spurted unevenly across Fenrir's breastplate. Silas' face was not pained. No, it held recognition, surprise.

Accusation.

Fenrir tried to convince himself that he'd had no control. In the past, when he'd been in his phantom state—floating above his body like a ghost—he'd merely been an observer to his body acting in service of his goal. At least, that was how he understood the process. Martis seemed to think he was delusional, that his out-of-body experiences were either a result of drinking too much, frequent concussions, or a trick of memory. But Fenrir knew there was more to it than that.

It was fussy, in his memory, but hadn't he resisted the magic that had crippled Tilner Pick and his remaining soldiers? Had Phantom-Fenrir made that happen? Savant Iolen and Lord Faris had seemed to think there was something special about Fenrir, though neither had sullied their fancy robes by coming down to see him in prison. The last Fenrir remembered, one of them had used magic on him, causing him to pass out.

Could that be why he'd fainted, all those years ago, in the council chamber? Could Faris or Iolen have knocked him off his feet with magic?

Probably. But to what end?

Fenrir tended to suppress those thoughts as his mind ran in circles during his imprisonment. It didn't matter. What mattered was that he had killed his friend, and was himself slated to die.

When he'd killed Silas, Fenrir may not have been in control. But, he had the aching feeling that, even had he been in full command of his body, he still would have done the same thing. Silas had been an obstacle because of Fenrir's orders to kill the duke. There'd been no time for a conversation, and his men would have finished Silas anyhow, rather than leave an armed man at their backs. Silas' death had thus likely been unavoidable, so why did Fenrir feel so low about it?

Maybe because he had never really seen himself as a bad person. Sure, he drank a good deal, and did his best to manipulate women into sleeping with him. But those were victimless crimes. Some husbands may have disagreed, but, had they been decent husbands, their wives wouldn't have ended up in his bed (or him in their bed).

And, sure, he worked for the most powerful underground criminal organization in Ardia, cutting off the ring fingers of men and women who wronged The House, or those who contracted with The House. But he was just the tool in those situations. He was just the knife—and did you blame the knife when someone ended up cut? If he hadn't committed the deed, then someone else would have. He might just as well get paid for the task.

His mind briefly pictured Emma, pinned down by his knee as his knife cut through her hand, sending fingers and a chunk of flesh flying to the ground. Fenrir remembered the agony in her eyes. The gut-wrenching surprise.

He shook his head at the thought, clenching shut his eyes. Silas' torn arteries briefly floated in his vision.

Shit, maybe he was a bad person. Maybe he'd been a bad person all along.

After all, he had killed his brothers.

Well, one brother, anyway.

Jingle. Creak. Clunk.

Someone was coming. Perhaps it was his time.

***

"You look—and smell—like shit, boy," came a gravelly and terrifyingly familiar voice from outside Fenrir's cell. Though the light momentarily blinded him, there was no doubt as to the speaker.

"Father," Fenrir responded, his own voice cracking from disuse and dehydration. "Or, should I say Principal de Trenton?"

"Say as you wish," said Darian de Trenton over the sound of the cell being unlocked. Two soldiers pushed inside—one man, one woman, both of them resplendent in the vivid blue of de Trenton. Blue Adders both of them, from the elite fighting force under the control of his father. They were the best. Each soldier, even the much smaller woman, could have disarmed and dismantled Fenrir at his fighting peak. Now, beaten and emaciated, he'd stand a better chance against a horde of wolves in winter.

Fenrir's eyes adjusted, and he saw his father for the first time in months. The older man was unchanged. Younger, even, though perhaps that effect came from the smile that twisted his face. Gods, it was Fenrir's own smile flashing back at him. A charming, crooked smile that could disarm a lady at twenty feet and make a friend of an enemy at thirty.

Darian rarely smiled.

"Henson, Ingla. You are dismissed for the moment. I hadn't expected the boy to be such a… shambles." Darian waved his arm.

"Yes, my lord," said the soldier Fenrir presumed to be Ingla, the petite Sestrian women with a smart salute. The Blue Adders left quickly, their steps reverberating in unison off of the flagstones and echoing through the prison.

Father and son—if they could still truly be defined as such— regarded each other silently for a few moments. Fenrir struggled to his feet, failing to hide the effort required.

"'My lord,' is it, now?" Fenrir coughed, wiping his bearded face.

"Again, I let people call me as they wish. If it gives my people some comfort, during this tumultuous time, to treat me as a lord, who am I to stop them?" Darian's smile widened.

"Ever the martyr, my lord," Fenrir said.

"Tell me, boy, how is your shoulder?"

"Some shit got in the wound, but I managed to fight that infection." Fenrir, the master of tact.

Darian regarded Fenrir for a moment with his Pandemonium-black-blue eyes, and, as always, Fenrir felt he had to make an effort not to squirm. Here he was, imprisoned with nothing to lose except his life, and even that had a short time limit attached. And yet, Darian still held such power of him.

Interestingly, that realization gave Fenrir courage.

"Why are you here? You've already disowned me, my lord. Threatened me to stay away from you and your holdings—which I have, by the way. Are you here to revel in my pain? Watch as your unfortunate offspring is given to the Spike? Laugh while it happens while drinking a fine wine?"

Darian did laugh, then, with surprisingly good-natured mirth. Fenrir flinched back from the unfamiliar sound.

"No, boy. I am here to thank you, in fact. You have done me quite the favor."

"What could I have done for you?" Fenrir's mouth hung wide open with the shock of the thought.

"Murdering our poor little duke, of course."

"How could that have helped you?" Fenrir asked.

"Oh, Rostane has become quite a different place in recent months, boy. Interestingly, many of Rostane's fine nobles have found themselves discredited, tangled in scandals, or in deep, insurmountable debt." Darian's smugness hinted as to the origins of these various turns in circumstance.

"Let me guess. Somehow, you, my lord, have turned this to your advantage?" Fenrir suggested, leaning back against the always-damp stone wall. His legs were too weak to hold him up unaided any longer.

"Such cleverness," drawled Darian. "Listen, boy. The time of nobility is done. It is an outdated concept. Why should a person be given the right to rule simply due to the loins from which he sprang? There is so much incompetence in this country. The little duke is a prime example. His father was a fine man, a modern man. Whereas his son was an insecure and pompous buffoon. Unfortunately, boy, great men do not always breed great offspring."

"Subtle, my lord."

"Subtlety seems lost on you. Anyhow, those who run our country should be those proven to be competent, not those who have the 'correct' blood. A country, after all, is little more than a large business. And who better to run a business?" Darian crossed his arms, raising an eyebrow expectantly.

"You?"

"By the gods, absolutely not! This is not a job for any one person! No, a voting council is most appropriate. A council composed of the best the country has to offer, those who have shown, over the years, that they can proficiently manage people and yets. Certainly, I would fit that description, as would others. It is a shame that your Lady Escamilla was lost in the civil war. Though I had my share of conflicts with the woman, she would have been an excellent addition."

Sigmund had told Fenrir that Escamilla was dead, but he'd held out hope that the little shit was lying. His father, however, was so matter-of-fact that Fenrir knew the strong, cradle-robbing old woman was gone. His success in killing the little duke was meaningless. Their little army must be lost, scattered, and Florens taken despite all their efforts.

What had happened to Emma?

Fenrir fought to keep his face blank.

"Why would you care to run the country? You already have everything you could ever want." Darian was a frugal, severe man, not given to splendor or lavish living. By the gods, aside from his single vice—a love of fine, imported wine—the merchant king might as well have been a poor man.

"As if you have any idea what I want. You took no interest in the family business, remember?" Darian asked.

"You took no interest in your family," Fenrir retaliated.

A silence again filled the scant space between the men, Darian standing tall and threatening, with Fenrir leaning wearily against the wall, too resigned to feel his typical fear. Family was always a tense topic between the two men. Last time they'd discussed family, Fenrir had ended up disowned—and with Darian's fingers buried into his shoulder up to the knuckles.

Family…. Did Darian know that his brother still lived?

"No matter," Darian broke the silence. That had to be a first. "You ask why I would want to be involved in the governance of the country. Though the answer is complex, as is everything, I will simplify things for you. Open trade, boy! Rostane—all of Ardia—is one of the most closed-minded countries when it comes to trade. Import taxes are charged whenever a good enters the city. Export taxes are charged whenever a good leaves the city. Taxes are higher and higher, the further a good travels or is intended to travel. Even within the damned country, tariffs are charged from duchy to duchy."

"This is about money?" Darian must have a deeper vault than anyone in Rostane, if not Ardia!

"It's more than money, boy. It's about the world. Here we are, holed up in our little dens, our little cities. Hoarding our goods, our specialties, our wealth. These tariffs and taxes… they halt progress. They halt advancement of the world, the opening of borders. They prevent sharing of cultures, the mixing of peoples. Meanwhile, the taxes do little to benefit the peoples of our country. They fill the coffers of the nobles, who go on to squander

117

the wealth on meaningless pursuits instead of reinvesting in the country, research, and people," Darian finished scornfully.

His father. Apparently quite the philosopher, scientist, and proponent of multiculturalism. Meanwhile, he'd neglected his own family to the point that his son was rotting in prison.

Also, Fenrir had little doubt that the motives ran deeper than open trade. Darian was not quite so good of a man.

"Got it. Open trade, my lord. Well, I am pleased to see you so elevated in the world. But, if you would please excuse me, I would expect that my next appointment will be arriving soon," Fenrir said, turning away from his father to jokingly attempt to tidy his hair.

Surprisingly, Darian barked out another laugh.

"Sometimes, you are actually funny, boy. I've missed that, from time to time. No, your final appointment is here at this moment. You are coming with me. I have need of you."

"With you? You've disowned me! And I think I'd rather face the Spike," Fenrir announced, pushing away from the wall and taking a step toward Darian. The older man smirked.

"Oh, boy, you are still disowned. That has not changed. You can keep your ridiculous name. Coldbreaker? Ha." Unparalleled humor from his father.

"Then what could you possibly want from me?" Fenrir asked.

"Saving your life is not enough to secure your help for one simple task?"

"No."

"Fine, boy. I need to secure the Council's rule in this country. As I am sure that you know, there are many... clandestine elements in this city. They are a rot on the framework of society. Erosion of the foundations of our culture. They hold far too much power over many of those in charge. They must be eliminated. So, let us start small."

Darian reached out, placing his hand on Fenrir's shoulder. Fingertips—perhaps unintentionally—resting on the cloth covering Fenrir's jagged, pink scar.

"I need you to destroy The House."

The House. The most powerful underground organization in the country, and Fenrir's employer for the last couple of years. A group of very dangerous people; Fenrir had seen their work. The Spike would be a mercy compared to how they treated those who shared their secrets or betrayed them.

"No thanks, my lord."

Darian's hand gave Fenrir's shoulder a quick squeeze and the man stepped back, scratching at his chin.

"Did you know that the Kerrig Trading Company went under?" Darian asked, conversationally. "Indeed, just a few months ago, they sold their final warehouse in Draston, not too long after I saw you last. I have to say, that was a rare miscalculation on my part, thinking that it was an alliance worth forging. Peirson Kerrig is near destitute, as is his daughter Bethany."

Bethany Kerrig... the awful shrew of a woman who Darian had forced a younger Fenrir to marry. Fenrir's heart began to pound.

"I offered them a buyout, however. With much more generosity than I should have, but they did have something I wanted."

Gods, no. By Ultner, not even Darian would do such a thing.

"Astora now lives in my compound," Darian continued. "An intelligent girl, she is. A lovely girl, too. Two unusual traits, given her parentage."

Astora. Fenrir's daughter, named for his mother.

After one of Fenrir's extramarital affairs and the most intense argument of Fenrir's life, Bethany had moved to the Kerrig estate in Draston, taking a young Astora with her. Though they'd stayed married on paper for the sake of the trading company coalition, Fenrir had rarely seen Bethany afterward—to his delight. Neither, however, had he seen his daughter.

Astora... she must be sixteen or seventeen by now. Fenrir had thought about her on occasion, from time to time. Thought about writing. Even written a letter once, when he had been deep in his cups.

But, he had never sent it.

And now the girl was being used by his father. This evil, sadistic old fuck.

"I think that Astora may even become my heir," Darian continued. "I used to be convinced I needed a male heir; outdated thinking, that was. Your Lady Escamilla—a woman—rallied a nation to war after becoming more successful than near every other merchant in the country. Of course, her attempt failed, but that had little to do with her gender."

Darian called down the hallway to his Blue Adders, summoning them.

"The girl has such a bright future, boy. I certainly hope she manages to stay safe here in Rostane. It is a very different place from Draston, after all. Rostane can be... unkind."

Fenrir hung his head, beaten. From beneath lowered eyelids, he could see Darian's cock-blowing smile.

"Ingla, as we discussed, this prisoner will be coming with us. You are charged with his safety while we work on making him presentable again."

"Yes, my lord," said the small Sestrian woman, her eyes running over Fenrir appraisingly. She did not appear impressed.

Darian turned sharply on his heel, only glancing over his shoulder at his son.

"Oh, and do not think to betray me, boy. I have eyes everywhere, even within your former organization. If I sense even a hint of treachery, I will do what must be done, no matter how unpleasant."

Chapter 9

"Put these on," snapped Ingla in a sharp Sestrian accent, shoving a sack at Fenrir.

Fenrir glanced in the bag. Clean clothes, the first that he would have experienced since his brief time in Brockmore. A clean woolen shirt, dyed in the blue of de Trenton, his father's logo stitched on the breast.

"No," Fenrir replied, dropping the sack to the cold stones at his feet.

Suddenly, he found himself slammed against the wall, armored forearm pushing against his trachea. He could only gasp as her powerful, lithe arms cut off his air supply. He had no strength to speak of, let alone fight with.

"You trash," Ingla said, her eyes flashing in anger. "I will not tolerate your disobedience. When I say to do something, you do it. When I say put on the clothes, you put on the clothes. When I say eat, you eat. When I say sleep, you sleep. Do you understand, or are you too dense?"

Fenrir mumbled something.

"What was that?" Ingla asked, stepping back.

"I said 'you look prettier when you are angry.'" Fenrir coughed and cleared his throat, reaching down and grabbing the discarded clothing. He began to change out of his rags.

"Some privacy?" he asked, noticing that Ingla did nothing to avert her gaze. She said nothing. "Fine with me. Let me know if you like what you see," Fenrir said, shrugging and flashing her a smile. He might as well have smiled at a block of steel.

Ingla was younger than he, maybe in her early thirties. Her Sestrian heritage was evident from her olive skin and thick, tar-black hair, which was tied in a tight braid. Though she only came up to Fenrir's chin, she had an aura of command about her, and he felt himself the smaller one in the room. Fenrir was nearly certain that Darian had assigned him a female guard as a sign of disdain or in an effort to embarrass him. Truth be told, if he had to have someone at his side at all times, it might as well be a pretty lady, frightening though she might be.

"More quickly," Ingla snapped as Fenrir dressed, punctuating her words by slapping her hands together. Fenrir sighed.

"What is the plan, Ingla?" he asked.

"Do not speak my name. You will call me 'Sergeant,'" she barked.

"Well then, Sergeant, what is the plan?"

"Like Lord de Trenton said, we are to get you cleaned up. You are no good to us like that." Ingla gestured at Fenrir's now-clothed body. His arms were shaking as he buttoned the shirt, and the reek of piss and weeks' worth of dirt were even evident to Fenrir himself.

"And then?" Ingla glared at him, and Fenrir clenched his jaw. "And then, Sergeant?"

"And then, we tend to your health. Now, we must go."

Ingla shoved a gas lantern at him and then ushered him out of the cell. Fenrir stumbled as he took more than three consecutive steps for the first time in weeks. By the gods, his legs had grown so weak, and his head was spinning. And his symptoms were not limited to the physical.

He had resigned himself to death. He had given up. Pandemonium, he probably desired it.

But now he was to live again, if as a tool of his father.

Being used was not an unusual feeling for Fenrir. One of the reasons he'd joined the military as a teenager was because he

123

didn't want to be in control of his own life, or rather he did not want Darian to be in control of his life. For near twenty years, he'd been a simple tool of the Rostanian military, doing what he was told—standing there, guarding that. After his disgrace, he'd become a tool of The House. Again, doing what he was instructed for a little extra spending money, though many such tasks were unsavory and often dangerous. Fenrir had then became beholden to Lady Escamilla. He'd found an army for her. He'd slain a duke for her.

Simply because she'd asked him to.

And now his fate was sealed as his father's tool. Something that he had striven to avoid his entire life. But, what else was he to do? Allow himself to be killed? Not an option, regardless of his myriad sins. Betray his father and know that his only daughter, estranged though she may be, would be killed for his actions? That didn't seem particularly attractive, either.

Until he'd been forced to reflect on his shit-show of a life during his imprisonment, Fenrir had lived his life with few regrets. He'd drunk himself into oblivion, fucked married women, stolen and cheated, and chopped off fingers… but aside from a few cases, he'd never spent too much time ruminating or given over much time to regret.

But, of all of the actions and events in his life, of all of his mistakes and missteps, vices and moral weaknesses, Fenrir had regrets about his daughter. Fenrir regretted missing her life, much as an amputee might miss a phantom limb. And, like an amputee, Fenrir felt a strong urge to drink at the thought of what was missing from his life. The thought of actually seeing Astora— actually speaking to her—was enough to ignite in him a compulsion to seek the oblivion of the bottle. Now, the question was, where could he find a drink around here?

"Coldbreaker." Fenrir flinched as a hoarse voice whispered his name from the darkness. He halted his shamble and glanced into the nearest cell.

Lying in the corner was a man clothed in rags, much as Fenrir had been only minutes earlier. The older man's face was wasted and drawn from hunger, and his limbs were trembling as he attempted to rise. The once long and well-kempt mustaches of Tilner Pick were practically lost amidst his bushy, gray beard. Lady Escamilla's trusted confidant and most loyal man had fallen as far as Fenrir himself.

"Move!" Ingla commanded him, roughly grabbing Fenrir's arm and pushing him forward. Fenrir, despite his weakness, yanked his arm forward from her and spun, shoving Ingla forward and freeing his arm. She mustn't have expected any resistance, because she stumbled to her knees. Recovering almost instantly, she drew her short sword as she whirled around, leveling it at Fenrir's neck. He raised his arms, still holding the lantern.

"Apologies, Sergeant. Old reflexes and all that. Would you mind if I had a word with this man?"

Ingla was breathing heavily, her face screwed up with anger. She closed her eyes tightly for a moment, took a deep breath, and lowered her blade. Fenrir exhaled slightly. He hadn't truly expected three inches of steel in his throat—Darian obviously wanted him alive—but seeing Ingla's fury in that moment had made him fear it just a bit.

Ingla turned her back to Fenrir and walked three paces away, slamming her sword into its scabbard and folding her arms. Fenrir waited a moment, but the Blue Adder did not move a step. Permission apparently granted.

Fenrir leaned against the bars.

"Pick. So, they got you, too." He was very conscious of his fine clothing, of the symbol of his father.

"Coldbreaker, you saved my life that night." Pick's eyes were alarmingly focused, perhaps even fevered. Fenrir wanted to look away, but he was captured by the gaze.

Fenrir thought back to that night. He remembered seeing Sigmund Fitra, that twiggy little fuck, raising his sword to strike down Pick. Then, Fenrir had broken through the power that had bound him, ramming his sword through the little duke. Since then, he hadn't spared a thought for Pick. Fenrir felt a brief, unusual twinge at that.

"If I did, it seems it was only temporary," Fenrir said gruffly.

"Coldbreaker, you did save my life. And perhaps you saved Escamilla's, as well, that night, by killing the duke. That is more important. So much more important," Pick said, his voice desperate.

Pick didn't know about Escamilla's death, then. He didn't know that the Army of Brockmore had been routed.

"Um, well," said Fenrir, finally breaking away from Pick's wild eyes.

"Coldbreaker, please listen to me. You are a good man. Better than I thought. Much better, though you keep it well-hidden. It seems that you have a way out of here. If you can, if possible, please, give Escamilla my regards."

"Um…"

"I know you believe she does not love me, and perhaps you are right. Perhaps she never has." Pick grasped the bars, his knuckles white. "But it matters not, Coldbreaker. I love her. That is all that matters. Love is like that, Coldbreaker. Have you ever been in love? It is nonsensical, defying reason. Most emotions can be controlled or repressed, but not love." Pick wiped at his bloodshot eyes.

Love sounded like a terrible, painful thing. Something not worth the effort.

Tilner Pick must have been concealing the ache of his heart for years, the emotion no different than a cancer slowly eating away at him. His blind devotion had likely caused Escamilla pain while she'd still lived, too, as she would have had to break the man's heart on a daily basis. And, if something happened to either of the pair, the other would be devastated. Tilner Pick's heart would shatter like a fragile wine glass, and Escamilla—had the tables been turned—would have been remorseful for never returning his love.

No, certainly not worth it.

The only love Fenrir had ever known had been for his mother, and she was so far gone that he could not even remember the pleasant feelings. No, he only remembered the pain of loss, and the emptiness that had followed it. By Ultner, it had been decades and it still lingered.

"Coldbreaker, tell Escamilla that I love her. And... that I forgive her for never loving me."

"Tell her yourself when you are out of here," Fenrir replied, stepping back and glancing toward Ingla. Her fists were clenched, though she had not otherwise moved.

"You know there is no 'out of here' for me. Please, Coldbreaker. Tell her for me. Promise me."

"Pick..."

"Promise me."

Fenrir signed. "Okay, Pick. I will get her the message. I promise."

Tilner's legs gave out then, and he fell roughly to his knees. He rested his forehead against the bars as sobs wracked his body, as if

Fenrir's promise had busted a dike that had been containing the water of his emotions.

Fenrir reached out to the other man, but halted his hand inches from the man's shoulder. Instead, he turned and limped off toward his escort. Toward his father. Toward his daughter.

For a moment, Fenrir longed for his tar-black cell.

Chapter 10

Farrow's Hold, the great, pulsing heart of Jecusta. Emma had once heard it called the lovely mother of Ardia. The mother part was undeniable. Ardia had, until a hundred and fifty years before, been a territory of Jecusta, which was why they shared a language—or close to it—as well as a social structure and certain architectural styles.

Lovely, though? Only if someone felt that loveliness was crumbling squalor. If beauty was the memory of something that had once been great, something now infested by tens of thousands of aimless, parasitic ants.

"Tell me again of this place. What is it that I am looking at?" Emma asked, her voice as frosty as the winter's air. When had the heat of the summer faded into early winter? It felt as if they had been marching for a lifetime.

"Of course, my lady," said Harivor, Lord Unael's emissary. His Jecustan accent—more refined and pure than the bastardized Ardian—was pleasing, as was the fact that he deferred to Emma in all things. A rare quality these days. He sniffed loudly before beginning; the lanky, near-bald man seemed to have carried a chronic cold since she'd met him weeks ago.

"Farrow's Hold is one of the wonders of the world. Just look at the arches, my lady! The arches are of unparalleled beauty and craftsmanship. Even from here, you can see them stretch across the city, forming bridges over the many canals and connecting many of the great buildings that tear through the sky." Emma's gaze followed Harivor's pointing finger, witnessing a number of crumbling arches that would be unlikely to support even a single horse and cart. To the south, it seemed that one had collapsed some time ago, leaving a great heap of rubble that no one had bothered to remove.

"The sky must be lower here," mumbled Nail, pulling at his tattered apple tabard. Since the dragging of the deserters, Emma had taken a personal guard of Apple Knights, beholden only to her. Just in case. She'd heard her guard called the Rotten Apple Knights once or twice. Not everyone was in favor of her brutal decision.

But, the fact was that not a single soldier had left her army since.

Harivor pointedly ignored Nail's comment. "Not only do our arches soar into the sky, but our goods also fly across Saiwen. Of course, you know of the beer of our famous breweries…"

"Piss water," said Nail, scratching at his goatee in a faux attempt to conceal his words.

"…But the most valued commodities of Jecusta are the textiles. Never will you find more beautiful rugs and tapestries, hangings and art. Our techniques are more advanced here than anywhere in the world, allowing us to produce such beauties at much greater quantity and quality than anywhere else." Harivor eyed Emma. "Perhaps, my lady, should Rostane fall into your hands, we can forge a partnership rivaling that of Lord Tinst and your King Thontos. Perhaps, one day, we shall share our knowledge."

The emissary was full of vague promises and hints of collaborations. There were so many, though, that Emma thought that he actually believed that she could retake her duchy with her ramshackle and exhausted little army. At times, mayhap she actually believed that she could, but they were brief.

"Perhaps, indeed, my lord Harivor." Emma could be vague, as well. She pointed ahead of them. "Tell me, who are those people?"

A group of two men and three women struggled to heave a melon-laden cart up a steeply-inclined, unevenly-paved road leading toward the main city gate. A Jecustan merchantwoman howled at them, lashing out with a long, flexible rod. The men labored shirtlessly despite the cold, their pale skin covered in a criss-cross of tatoos. One was covered in trees, a great forest carved into his body. Another's skin was painted with birds, hundreds of multi-colored avians flying about his back in an overwhelming display of color. The laboring women, on the other hand, though of the same race, had no marks on their bodies. Their hair, however, was so long that it looped nearly to the ground and back again, tied around their necks. It must have been growing for their entire lives.

"Those..." Harivor sniffed, "...are the Oshwon." He said nothing further until Emma prompted him.

"Tell me more," she commanded.

"The Oshwon used to live in a great valley to the east, refusing our offers to bring them civilization and trade. Rather, they raided our farms and stole our children. We brought war to them and won," he said with finality.

"These are your slaves?" Emma asked, observing the Jecustan maiden beating the Oshwon.

"These are indentured servants. We were merciful, given the destruction they wrought upon our towns, our armies, and our people. There were some who called for extermination, the elimination of the entire people, lest they rise up again. Instead, we clothe, house, and feed them in exchange for menial labor. Their children are born free and can eventually become citizens." His voice made it clear that this was a charity, a gift to these supposedly savage people.

Emma observed the Oshwon for a moment more, her brow furrowing in obvious distaste. She hadn't known the Jecustans to be slavers; slavery was a thing of the past in Saiwen, a barbaric remnant of less modern times. Perhaps north, across the Vissas

Sea, it existed, but not on her continent. Not so far as she'd known.

Of course, Escamilla had said her own sister had been sold into slavery by her father.

"I've had enough history for now. Take us to Lord Unael," Emma said, gesturing at the small party that was to meet with the lord of this city, and likely the most influential man in the expansive country.

"We've yet a long way to travel to the hold, itself, and night will be approaching soon. Perhaps, it would be better…"

Emma cut off Harivor with an imperious gesture. A strangely comfortable motion of late. "No, we will meet now."

"As you wish, my lady. If you would all care to mount your horses, we will begin our trek." Not a sign of bitterness from the servile, cunning man.

Emma pulled up her black velvet hood against the cold wind with a shiver and looked forward toward Farrow's Hold. Whatever happened this evening, the place would at least be fucking warm. There was nothing, right now, more appealing than the thought of a hot meal and a soft bed.

***

How could the interior of a building be so much fucking colder than the outside?

The ancient hold, the namesake of the city, had aged about as well as a kerena-smoking whore, and little effort had been made to modernize the great fortress. Though it still loomed mightily over the city, whole sections of the stone-walled structure were cordoned off, no longer in use because the cost to maintain it was too high. There were specks of former glory here and there—an exquisitely carved column, a statue of some great lord of yesteryear, a magnificent, deadly sword collection hanging over the length of an endless hallway—but signs of decay were more pervasive.

Even in this audience chamber, where lavish splendor was flung about with abandon and gaudily-dressed courtiers milled about, the failing light of day illuminated old, damaged stone facades and ill-fitting glass in the malformed windows. Which was probably where the constant, chilly breeze and mild, irritated wailing sound was birthed.

"Lady Emma Breen," Lord Brox Unael greeted her with a curious, but friendly, tone. He rose from his red-padded chair and offered a lavish bow. No small feat, given his plentiful stomach. He was not strictly flab, however. Harivor had spoken—at exhausting length—of Unael's military past, and his successful campaigns against the Alganian encroachment twenty-five years before especially, not to mention the expansion into disputed territory with Carnofstra. And, his subjugation of the Oshwon peoples living within the borders of Jecusta.

"My Lord Unael. I am humbled by your generosity in allowing us sanctuary during this trying time," Emma said with her own polite curtsey, though she went no lower than exactly what was required by decorum. A lord he might be, but Unael was no monarch.

"Of course, my lady. Escamilla placed her trust in you, and hopefully with good reason." He flashed her a quick smile, revealing a set of opal-white teeth standing in stark contrast to his weathered face. Though at least two or three decades Emma's senior, his open, compassionate face and authentic mannerisms leant him a handsome appeal. "And, we have certain obligations to Florens." His eyes went to the side, away from Emma. "My boy, I am sorry to hear about your father. He was one of the few good men left in Rostane."

Eric Malless started, not having expected to be addressed. His eyes were red-rimmed and bleary, and he reeked of more than just the road.

"Thank you, my lord," he muttered, having little to say on the topic.

Unael peered at him and frowned briefly. "I am certain that you are famished from your long journey, and the comfort of a warm bed and warm food would be welcomed. Not to mention a comfortable place to sit." Unael nodded to a table in an alcove, laden with fruits and cheeses, where servants bringing out glazed meats elicited an instant reaction in Emma's mouth.

"With respect, my lord, I would like to speak briefly before taking respite," sEmma said, hearing a muffled groan from Nail just behind her. But, Escamilla had always said: Business before pleasure, lest you negotiate from a place of weakness or comfort. Stuffing one's face with warm food at the table of a tenuous ally might not be the best course of immediate action.

"So much like Escamilla," Unael murmured with a raised eyebrow, echoing her thoughts. "Very well. You are at my doorstep with an army of several thousand, including mercenaries of dubious reputation. You have no consistent source of supplies, and word has it that Escamilla's lands and assets have been seized by the Rostanians. That said, what would you have of me?"

The boldness, somehow, came easy. "We require the use of Jecustan military forces in retaking Ardia from the traitorous and malicious rule of the Rostanian Council. Fifty thousand soldiers should be sufficient in accomplishing this task, but only if we mobilize before Hunesa falls to Rostane."

Unael stared at his, lips slightly parted in amused astonishment. One of the advisors, or one of the handful of notables lurking about Unael's chair, broke into a loud, scoffing laugh that echoed throughout the frigid, drafty chamber. The sound lingered, and Emma fought her urge to cringe. Keep the mask in place. Just a little longer.

"My lady, you can't be serious. Even Escamilla, in all her confident arrogance, would never make such a request. Or did you term it a requirement?" Lord Unael asked, appraising Emma and her small entourage of officers one by one.

"I am indeed serious, my lord. Allowing Rostane complete control of Ardia would be a misstep on your part." There was a snort from one of the notables, a whip-thin man of advanced years. "I do not mean to insult you, of course. But you know not what we faced. The Rostanians sent forth abominations, human-like creatures that tore through our camp with base ferocity and savagery that no one had ever seen. Feral, they are called. Hundreds of them killed thousands of my soldiers. If Rostanians are willing to unleash such creatures on our army, do you think they will stop at the borders of Ardia?"

A low murmur began in the room, various nobles and courtiers reacting to her words. Emma clenched her crippled hand, the omnipresent pain helping her maintain her mask. It was a challenge, given the insulting scraps that reached her ears.

"…is insane. Why do these men follow her?"

"…Feral? A fairy-tale."

"…crippled half-wit…"

"…ginger bitch." This last comment echoed above the others, emanating from the whip-tall older man.

The murmur was rising, as was Emma's rage, becoming a great, boiling cauldron of yellow bile. Just as she opened her mouth, lips curling back, a vaguely familiar figure pushed through the courtiers. A man who was maybe in his forties, with eyes like a maelstrom, taking in everything.

"If I could interrupt, my lords and ladies." Emma caught a hint of a sneer in the man's voice, and her memory assembled the pieces. Iolen, senior Savant at the Enlightenment, recently made High Strategist for the Rostanian Army. Emma had once seen Iolen, smirking as always, administer a potion to keep the late Baron Erlins conscious while having his fingers chopped off, bit by bit.

Emma's hands and feet grew cold and clammy, and a solitary drop of sweat traced its way down her back.

"Lord Iolen. I would welcome your council in this regard," Unael said, his booming voice bringing order to the uneasy crowd. "Lady Breen, this is Lord Iolen, ambassador from the Rostanian Council. He arrived here only yesterday, so we've yet to hear what story he has to tell. We might as well make it public. Everything here always is." A hint of resentment in his voice. A military man, probably unsuited to or unhappy with the political maneuvering of the royal courts.

"Thank you, my lord." Iolen strode, confidently, to Lord Unael's side. A violation of protocol, but it immediately gave the Savant Strategist a clear view of everyone in the row. His hands were at his sides, palms facing the crowd. Escamilla had taught Emma that this posture was one of honesty and openness, signifying the he was most likely trustworthy.

Or an excellent liar.

"I come to you from Rostane, but not as an ambassador. Rather, I travel as a defector, a traitor, an apostate." The murmuring began again, a buzz of angry hornets. Unael took two steps away, eying his black-cloaked guards.

"I'm afraid I misled you in order to gain access to your noble ears, your noble minds. And, your noble protection."

"We trust not men who come to us under false pretenses, particularly those who are admitted liars," spat the whip-thin man, one hand secreted under his lavish amarillo coat. Unael took an audible deep breath.

"Patience, Lord Rential. Lord Iolen…. Well, it sounds like you are without title. Iolen, this promises to be an interesting narrative. But you must forgive my guards for being cautious." Two of the black cloaks drifted within a foot of Iolen.

"'Lord' has indeed been stripped from my name, but Savant is etched into my soul. I gave myself to knowledge long ago. Now, where was I?"

"Betraying your country?" offered Rential, still a falcon perched to attack.

"Ah yes, betraying my country. Though, I would rather say that my country betrayed me and all of its citizens. I served in the Enlightment—the great library at the Plateau—for many years, studying everything from military strategy to the most efficient way to drown a cat. My knowledge was well sought after by the various nobles across the four duchies, and I had a bit of a reputation—"

"For drowning cats?" mocked a voice from the crowd.

"For understanding of all things military. So, when the war surfaced, my services were sought by the late Duke Penton." The Little Duke. The bastard who Fenrir had somehow managed to kill, likely having died in the attempt. Emma wished, for some reason, that Fenrir were there now. He'd have something witty to say to disarm this cocky Savant. And, his presence would just be reassuring.

"I was made High Strategist, and the beast of war marched south to Florens. Our victory was inevitable, as we outmanned the forces gathered against us by a large margin, with that margin growing all the time. We had great engineers, Savants who had studied the mechanical sciences and created siege engines that would ensure that no walls could stop us. And, the little duke had managed leverage over most of the duchies, ensuring that they would fall one at a time. Even with Lady Breen's interference…" The Savant nodded at her. Could a nod be sarcastic? "…we should have been victorious."

"I wouldn't be so confident, Savant," she said. "You haven't seen all that we have to offer." A bluff. If Escamilla and her officers had any more tricks, they certainly weren't forthcoming about them.

"Oh, certainly," intoned Iolen, oozing condescension. "And perhaps the little duke and Lord Faris believed the same, for it was them who sent the Feral."

"You expect us to believe that such creatures exist?" This from another lord, an annoyingly handsome man with a perfectly trimmed goatee.

"You can believe what you wish. It does not change the truth. Feral are not creatures, monsters from children's tales. Now, are all of you familiar with maenen? Pasnes alna? Or, as it is termed in this part of the world—magic?"

Emma expected a gasp at this utterance. There certainly would have been in Rostane among the nobles in the Plateau. But, here there were nods and sneers.

"We are not the superstitious chawbumpkins of Rostane," Rential said. Nail, Emma's brave Rotten Apple Knight, growled from over her shoulder. He could be intimidating and had strong nationalist tendencies. Rential stepped back and cleared his throat. "We do not share the biases of the Yetranians."

"I thought Yetra was worshipped widely in Jecusta," Opine commented, his first words since arriving.

Lord Unael smiled. "This is true, but perhaps the leaders aren't the most devout. Suffice it to say, we have had some small experience with magic."

"Well, you should have some rudimentary understanding of how it works. To simplify it, some pasnes alna can draw power from humans and animals. You call them leeches, while the educated know them as pasnes maenen." Restrained anger marred the expressions of many in the crowd, at least the ones who were smart enough to recognize the insult. Iolen certainly had a way about him. "A human, or animal, having enough maenen drawn from them over time, will lose their ability to fully regenerate this power. They will become ruled by their basest instincts, anger and hunger. They will become stronger, faster, more vicious, unrestrained by the bounds of the rational mind that so often limit our abilities. They lust for violence and lust for blood. In short, they become Feral."

The name rang out like a hammer on an anvil, sounding over the heavy silence that finally permeated the chamber. Emma fought to restrain a visible shiver as goosebumps rose on her flesh.

"You say that they leeched the magic from these men. For what purpose?" Emma managed through her clenched teeth.

"Observant girl. At this juncture, I am not certain why they were harvesting magic in such a way. It needs further study—"

"Enough of this charade. Clearly, this man…" Rential sharply gestured at Iolen, "… and this woman…" He stabbed his finger toward Emma,"…are colluding together for some nefarious purpose. Perhaps they seek for us to mobilize our forces in order to leave our other borders unprotected, or to secret an army to Farrow's Hold."

139

The annoyingly handsome man was quick to take up Rential's sentiment. "Aye, House Hanthor will not stand for such a mockery. We will not allow these… foreigners to embarrass us with such obvious lies. My third cousin is pasnes alna—a leech, no less—and he would not be capable of such a feat. Pasnes alna are harmless charlatans—"

"Harmless?" Iolen's eyes flashed, and he reached toward the nearest black cloak. The man stumbled backwards, but not before Iolen grasped his hand, bringing the man to his knees in an instant. The second guard had drawn his sword, but the man and his weapon clattered to the ground at a glance from Iolen.

"Harmless? Let me show you what harm maenen can wreak!" His voice rose, and a circle of blue flame rose around him, just barely capturing the transfixed black cloak. The gathered lords and ladies sought to flee, but tumbled back from the audience chamber's entrance as a second pillar of blue flame rose to block off escape. Black cloaks stumbled forward uneasily, leveling swords and spears at the circle of flame. Two wielded crankbows, but they seemed unwilling to fire into the blaze.

Iolen pointed at each window with his free hand—the hand not gripping the pale black cloak—and needles of power launched into the glass, showering the room in shining, infinitesimal shards of dust. He reached toward the long table laden with food and, as if it were being closed like a book, the table folded in half with an earsplitting crunch. The panic rose in the room as Lord Unael tried to keep order, shouting commands as he rushed toward his seat to retrieve his own impotent sword. Rential had begun pounding on the locked door of a servants' entrance, shouting at the top of his lungs.

Emma's own retinue pushed her to the back, officers and Nail coming between her and the mad pasnes alna defector. Above her palpating heart, she felt a touch of pride at the show of loyalty.

"Using this man's life, I could wipe out every person in this room with ease. Every petty ruler and scrumming merchant could be burnt to ash at a flick of my fingers." He snapped his fingers, and half the crowed ducked. "But, that is not my goal." With a wave, the blue flames vanished, leaving no trace of ash or discoloration on the stones. Leaving the fearful notables wondering whether the fire had ever really existed. Iolen released the black cloak, and he tumbled to his hands and knees, breathing like he had just fought a battle for his life. Which, Emma reflected, he may have done.

"You did not come here for protection," observed Unael, leaning forward on his greatsword. Rential, red-faced and with his lips pursed in anger, stalked back to the center of the audience chamber. He shot such a look of hatred at Iolen that Emma was surprised he didn't throw himself at the Savant that very second.

Meanwhile, the guard that the Iolen had leeched from staggered to his feet, stumbling away from Iolen with an expression of wide-eyed terror. His companion still lay unconscious on the cold stones.

"No, I came to give a warning. The Rostanians are coming. The Feral are coming. And that is the least of Jecusta's—no, all of Saiwen's—problems."

"There must have been a less dramatic way to give that warning," Emma growled, pushing back to the front of her retinue, mask back in place. It may have just been his caustic, biting manner—or the flames that had just filled the room—but Emma could not envision trusting this arrogant, powerful man. Certainly, he might have the power to end everyone in this room, but that would be a short-term gain for his purposes. Whatever they were. No, this Savant pasnes alna, whoever he was, had some motive in mind. Emma just needed to find it.

Iolen grinned. "Oh, certainly. But, now my lords will be forced to fix those windows and get rid of this godsdamned draft. Plus, I certainly have everyone's attention now." Rential's, especially, judging from the way he glared at the Savant.

"Indeed, Savant. You have our attention. But, like I mentioned, we are not unfamiliar with your particular brand of magic, though you may have caught us off-guard in this singular situation. Know that it will not happen again," Unael said, standing tall and draping his greatsword over his broad shoulder. He shot a fierce look at an unassuming, simply-dressed Rafonese woman leaning against one of the pillars.

"Apologies, milord. There was no feeling about him. If there'd been more than just illusions and showing off, I would have intervened." She had a thick accent, and Emma had had trouble following her words. But, by the gods, those were supposed to have been illusions? Emma had felt the heat from the fire!

"A cautaton," Iolen mused with an arched eyebrow. "How very rare."

"And know we have other resources at our disposal. But, you can consider your warning heeded. You will, however, forgive that we must corroborate your reports with our own intelligence. And, even then..." Unael was thoughtfully scratching at his beard. "Regardless, you will remain our guest for the time being. For your own protection, of course."

"Of course, though I would not delay for long, my lords and ladies. Any postponement could be disastrous. As both the old and new Lady Breens have learned." Iolen nodded again in her direction. Unael glanced at her, too, a frown creasing his weathered face.

"And, Lady Breen, you have my leave to take up residence in the hold. In the next week, I will clear a portion of the Landon, the western district of the city proper, to contain your men. Now, I believe we have had enough excitement for one day, and we've much to discuss. But, one more thing." Unael's jaw clenched, his voice becoming quieter so that the gathered courtiers leaned in to hear. "How did Escamilla pass? Was it with great pain?"

"My lord, Escamilla still lives, though she has been unconscious for near two weeks." Even through her stony facade, Emma had to restrain tears. "It shouldn't be long. Our physicians do not expect her to finish out the week."

Unael bowed his head.

"We will find her the most comfortable apartments in the hold. The great lady should be allowed to pass in comfort, at least. It is all I can offer."

Chapter 11

So much had happened in Merigold's life over the past six months. She had been abducted and abused. Her friends and family had been slaughtered, and her home destroyed. Her father had been taken, likely killed. She had also murdered men, and she had lost a child.

But, on the bright side, she could not think about any of those terrible things while on this Yetra-damned ship. She was too busy vomiting.

Even weeks later, she had not adapted. Her head weighed a thousand pounds and her eyes twisted her sight as if the world was made of traveling circus dancers. She was constantly perspiring and sickly dehydrated, though she forced down her ration of water every day. But the smell of food made her nauseous. Watching the sailors made her nauseous. Thinking about how nauseous she had been made her nauseous!

Dear Yetra, what kind of demon had invented ships?

"I've been knocking and you haven't answered," Cryden said, pushing his way into her tiny sleeping room. He was pale, himself, and not precisely nimble on his feet. He sat heavily on the foot of her thin, lumpy mattress. She lacked the energy to pull away.

"Maybe because I didn't want to be bothered," Meri said, slurring her words like a drunkard. There'd been a storm last night, and she felt worse than ever.

"At some point, you need to be bothered. Remember our little chat about tests? Well, you have failed the test of seamanship."

"I don't care."

"If you seek to be pasnes alna, you must become accustomed to travel, and that travel will involve ships. Though I was once like you, I've learned to control…"

"I don't care."

"Merigold, sickness is no excuse for crassness," Cryden said, his tone as patronizing as a parent condescending to children.

Now, Meri found the energy to sit up. She glared the best glare she could muster.

"Cryden, if Ultner exists, and if he brings me to Pandemonium for my crimes… and if Pandemonium reflects, as written in The Book of Amorum, our worst fears and greatest discomforts, I would be thankful I was there instead of this Yetra… ass… fucking… ship."

Cryden chuckled quietly. "Being around sailors has worked wonders on your vocabulary. Come now, we shouldn't be more than a day or two from land, and you should come above to get your bearing. You will also need to start eating—I will not broker with the delay that shall occur if you pass out on your pony and break your own skull."

"Your compassion, as always, is overwhelming," Merigold hissed, feeling ill at the thought of food. Cryden was right, though. Maddeningly, he often was.

"Besides, you should speak with our protectors. We will be spending plenty of time with them on the road, and they may be more apt to jump in front of an arrow if they think you more than some weak-bellied youngling, brought low by a couple of waves." He grinned at that.

Meri pushed herself to her wobbling legs, baring her teeth at him. "Lead the way."

***

"So, she lives!" shouted one of the Sestrian brothers, reaching his arms above his head as if to give thanks to some listening deity.

"Of course, she lives. We would have dumped the body in the sea, had she passed," remarked the other, staring at his brother with furrowed brows.

"You are, and always will be, a dolt." The first brother took a long pull from a wooden bottle and bit off a hunk of bread to wash it down. He leaned easily against the ship's rail.

"Will you all just shut up?" This from the muscular woman, Lisan the Arrow, with a longsuffering look on her unattractive face.

"May we join you?" Cryden asked, guiding Meri by her arm. She'd fought it, at first, but had acquiesced to his help eventually, lest she further embarrass herself by tumbling to the deck in front of these rough people.

Ill'nath grunted toward a couple of low barrels that would serve as chairs. Cryden lowered Merigold to her seat, her feeling like a frail old lady, before seating himself.

It was near sunset, which surprised Meri since she'd thought it to be the middle of the night. There was beauty in the color burning across the water, painting the waves in oranges and reds, and even her sickness couldn't detract much from that. For a brief moment, she could understand why sailors could live this life. Nothing in all directions except open water and freedom, as well as unknown adventures. So much, she would have wanted this

146

life, even a year ago. But now she understood how the world really worked.

"So, Merigold, how do you feel?" Lisan asked, voice laced with genuine empathy.

"How does she look?" asked one of the Sestrians, the more rambunctious one.

"Remy, for the love of the Day Mother, I will nail your tongue to the deck if you keep waggling it."

"Don't do that to my brother or you'll answer to me," growled the other Sestrian, presumably Marius.

"By the gods, brother. You are just… thick. My apologies, lady," Remy said with a mocking bow to Lisan.

She rolled her eyes and then smiled at Meri. "Marius barely speaks Ardian, and even if he did, he's not strictly… well, he's not the brightest of men. So, how do you feel?"

"I am feeling better, thank you. I'm getting my sea legs." Ill'nath snorted at that, and Remy barked a laugh. Meri couldn't help but smile, too.

"Okay, well… I feel worse than I look, which must be like a used-up whore." Cryden raised an eyebrow, but all but Marius laughed. The sailors really had impacted her language. She would have to re-train her tongue once they finally find land.

"You do resemble Remy and Marius' mother," Lisan said. Remy chuckled while Marius reached for the blade at his waist. Remy placed a restraining hand on his brother's arm. The group drifted into an uncomfortable silence. Meri glanced at Cryden, and saw that his brow was furrowed in concentration. Was there magic to be felt even out here? The poor cautaton must never get any rest.

"So… Lisan. Why do they call you 'the Arrow'? Are you good with a bow?" Meri asked in an effort to fill the silence. Lisan smiled in response, as if knowing that Meri was uncomfortable.

"Aye, I'm good with a bow. Some would argue I'm the best with a bow. But, that's not where the name came from," Lisan said, her voice far away.

"Where did it come from, then, if not that?"

Lisan did not immediately respond, so Remy chimed in. "Arrows fly straight and true, at least when shot by a bowmaster. And, Lisan does the same. If she says she is going to do something, she does it. No wavering. No second thought. No accounting for obstacles or the number of armored men in the way. If all arrows flew as true as Lisan, we would all have shafts of wood in our throats."

She gave the Sestrian a sidelong glance. Remy smirked and shrugged. "Said better," she corrected him, "I am a woman of my word."

"And, you will take us to Agricorinor?" Meri asked. Cryden still made no move to engage in conversation, so Merigold thought that she might as well gain some semblance of commitment from these warriors.

Lisan smiled. "You have my word."

"And mine," chimed in Remy, as if it were a joke. He nudged his brother.

"And mine," Marius echoed his brother, right down to the intonation. Ill'nath merely grunted—whether in assent, denial, or hunger, Meri had no idea. The Pinton islander may not have even spoken Ardian. Or, maybe all of the metal in his face prevented speech. He had nearly all available areas dotted with metal, but all was dwarfed by the literal hole in his cheek, held open by a metal loop. She could see his gums and teeth through the hole, giving him the appearance of some nightmare monster.

Remy noticed her starting. "No worries about Ill'nath here. He's a decent fucker, if you get to know him. And, he doesn't bite." As if to illustrate, Remy tossed a bit of bread at his cheek-hole. The wind took the bread and carried it overboard. Ill'nath was unmoved.

"Dammit!" Remy tore off a bigger piece of bread and lined up his next throw.

"What?" Cryden leapt to his feet and staggered to the rail of the ship. He gripped the rail, hands white from the effort, his pale face damp with sweat. With gritted teeth, he stared west toward the setting sun, still glowing orange as it passed from view.

"Cryden, what is the matter?" Merigold demanded, pushing herself to her own wobbly feet.

He ignored her for a moment, and she placed a hand on his shoulder. He started, jumping as if he had forgotten she was there.

"What is it?" she asked. The warriors—aside from Marius—seemed fiercely uncomfortable now. Remy's hand was on his dagger as he eyed Cryden warily; so much for his word to protect them.

"Power, Merigold. Impossible power. Because there is nothing." Distraction was written across his face. Meri furrowed her own brow, wanting to understand.

"Nothing?"

"Yes… the sea…" He pointed to the west, and Merigold could make out a growing, flickering red glow in the distance. But it wasn't the sun. The sun had gone, had now completely set, and this was further to the north. It was flames in the distance. Something was burning.

"The sea?" Merigold asked quietly, prompting the cautaton to share more. He continued to gaze toward the west.

"The sea is dead."

Interlogue: Greed

"Sweetling! Oh, my dear sweetling! I understand that there has been a violation. I can see that you are still reeling from the event, that you are not wholly recovered, at least to the point that you can still recover. We will not end our session today with a harvest. No, rather I simply wish to speak with you and apologize on behalf of the offending party.

"One of my Erudites did not live up to his honorific. Why he thought he could come here and sample my delicacy, so to speak, I will never know. But, I can see from your maenen that he was not gentle, and I can see that your nerring has been damaged. You need time to heal, and I shall provide that. Your sacrifice, sweetling, is honorable, and I shall not give up on you simply because you need extra time. I can sate myself elsewhere, this one time.

"That Erudite, by the way, will never again walk these halls. One needs legs to walk.

"Constantly surrounded by treachery, I am. Since the very beginning, truth be told. I had told you of Aquine, how the town was heaped with the dead when I fled after Amorum. I did not tell you how the well-defended town had been taken. I was not to find out until long afterward, but I can fill in the gaps in the story now.

"Though Aquine was a peaceful town, it was at the crux of military technology. The military had weapons that could spray a variety of chemicals at enemy forces, ravaging skin and lungs. Researchers had created great projectile engines that could be reloaded in a matter of seconds, firing nets full of fist-sized balls that would burst into flame on contact. Other countries—as they existed then—had desired the technologies that were specific to Aquine. However, the town's leaders and great scientists decided to isolate themselves to promote peace. The philosophy was that, as long as Aquine could tear through any attackers with ease, no attackers would appear.

"That was an effective strategy for a long while. However, like any town, Aquine had the prosperous and the poor. The prosperous were happy with what they had, living life in peace with every comfort. The poor were too downtrodden to really act. I have witnessed, on many occasions, poor men so broken that they wouldn't shift even a few feet to avoid sitting in fecal matter and other various slimes of the gutter. No, neither the destitute nor the wealthy betrayed the town.

"Most often, people forget about the middle class. People who work hard for everything they have, and have tasted just a sliver of luxury. So many in the middle class will strive to avoid joining the poor, and do whatever it takes to join the elite. It was the middle class that betrayed the city.

"Men and women met in secret to develop a plan to sell the military technology to outsiders, and they managed to get word to one of the closest cities. To these people, Aquine was still safe, but this would give them the boost they needed to join the ranks of the rich. Oagon was willing to pay any price, of course, to gain these secrets, and a couple dozen Oagonan warriors—over the course of a week—were smuggled into the city as part of this plan. Though they were only to steal a few weapons for study, they instead seized the gatehouse and the western defenses, allowing an army into the city.

"Most of the betrayers were swept up along with the city, murdered and left for dead. But some were taken with the army as slaves, thought to have some value to the war effort.

"You recall that I searched Aquine for signs of those I loved, ignoring Amorum as he attempted to calm me. I never did find my parents. Not immediately, anyway.

"For it was my parents who led the effort to betray Aquine. My parents were traitors. My parents caused all of that pain and suffering and death because of their greed. Because of their inability to be satisfied with their lives. All of those years, I had railed against the thought of being stuck in a lamp shop, bending and polishing metal, packaging and delivering the finished products. I had thought my parents simple, unambitious people who were happy with that life. However, I had been wrong. They had been disgusted with their lot. They had tasted the luxuries available from riches, and wanted more. They were the embodiment of greed, and it cost so many lives.

"I know that you are a man without greed. You need not speak—I know it is an effort right now, after the violation. However, I have seen how you treated those around you. How you bought products that you had no need of in order to distribute your own wealth to struggling individuals. I know that you donated money—to the Yetranian chapel, no less!—to have a great bell commissioned. I know that you gave so much of yourself so others could live in comfort.

"That is a rare quality, to be without avarice. If my parents and others in Aquine had not embraced greed as a virtue, perhaps I would not be where I am. Perhaps you would not be where you are. But greed projected my live forward, changing my world, and the entire world—forever. I suppose there is a lesson to be learned, there. But I know not what it is, not now. Perhaps some philosopher or Taneo could read into that event, had they the true story. But, alas, they do not.

"Sweetling, I can tell that you are distracted today. I will not bore you with more of my life right now. But, I will ensure that you are safe moving forward. No one will touch you, aside from me. You are mine, sweetling, now and forever."

Chapter 12

"Absolutely not!" Captain Jakys answered, his voice as stormy as the sea had been over the last week. "I'm nearly rid of you people; Yetra knows how much this trip has cost me, both in lost profits and tarnished reputation. I am not delaying by approaching a burning fucking ship, which means there could be burning fucking pirates, all because you want to see something." He was practically in a slavering rage at the request; he'd been on edge, of late.

Merigold had been able to hear him raging at his first mate from her cabin.

"You must, Jackys. I will make up a portion of your profits if you do this thing for me," Cryden promised, and Merigold heard a hint of frustration in his voice. He must be desperate to see what was going on if he was actually willing to pay out of his own pocket.

"The Graceful Whale is mine. I mustn't do anything with her," Jackys said, turning away and beginning to walk toward the prow. Cryden grabbed his arm, and the man leapt back into a fighting stance, procuring a dagger from somewhere on his body. "You will not lay a hand on me, filthy pasnes alna!" he shouted. The crew began to stop their tasks, grabbing whatever weapons lay nearby. Belaying pins, hooks, and the odd dagger. Meri glanced around, finding that their protectors were conveniently nowhere to be found.

Cryden's face darkened. "I need not lay a finger on you, Alganian. And threatening a known pasnes alna is just… a terrible idea." The way he'd said 'terrible' sent shivers through Meri.

Jakys stepped back, but in front of his crew, he could not back down.

"Threatening a scion of the Menan family, and an ally of The House, is just as terrible of an idea." He twirled his knife. "Now, stand down; I will be rid of you in two days." Several other sailors closed in, weapons leveled against Meri and Cryden. She quested nervously, sensing the maenen within each man, but all were out of reach. What use was this power if she couldn't touch it until a man plunged a dagger into her throat? She gripped her little knife, pulling it from where it hung around her neck.

"Enough!" boomed Cryden, no longer the mild-mannered, sarcastic know-it-all, but a pasnes alna to the core. His robes whipped in the rough wind, and the light of the moons and nearby lanterns flashed off his eyes. He stretched out a hand, and Jakys' dagger disintegrated.

But 'disintegrated' was not the right word, not quite. It shattered, but into a thousand tiny, miniscule shards. Jakys looked at his hand in shock as a dust drifted away in the breeze. Then, crimson sprung from every surface of his appendage. With a cry, he cradled his hand against his gut and bent over double, wrapped around the injury as a human bandage.

"You fucker!" cried the first mate, Mikiton. He wound up to hurl his knife at Cryden, with Meri in his path. She threw her arms in front of her face, but no sharp pains arose. She looked up after another second, and saw Mikiton's wrist pierced by an arrow and pinned to the mast. To his credit, Mikiton did not scream, but instead moved slowly to rip the projectile out.

"Make a move, you'll have one in your throat," shouted Lisan the Arrow from across the roiling deck. She had another arrow notched.

"You fucking traitor!" Mikiton hissed through gritted teeth.

"Me, the traitor? Mikiton, you've got nerve, you thieving horse-fucker. You think Resia would be pleased to know that you've been borrowing from the shipping coffers to fuel your gambling habit? Or you, Jakys. How pleased would she, or Tennyson be, that you pulled a weapon on a pasnes alna, let alone one with a golden pentagram?"

Jakys said nothing in response, but the intensity behind his eyes conveyed a hate that could not be concealed. His lips peeled back, and Merigold's vision swam. She was disoriented, suddenly, fueled by the sickness, or maybe a lack of food. Her deranged mind saw Saren's face there, glaring up at her from the cellar, Pandemonium fueling his gaze. Such awful, awful hate, with the eyes of a Feral. With a cry, she launched herself at Saren, digging her knife into his side once. Twice. A third time.

Rough hands pulled her away, and she slashed at those, too. She quested and drew from one, feeling the clean maenen fill her own internal vessel and holding the power within herself as she desperately tried to shape it into something. No one would lay hands on her! She drew even more maenen, stretching so far beyond herself in the effort.

A brother, lovingly holding her as she lay on the ground, crying out in pain.

A man in a silver demon mask, spiriting her away from a burning barn, with her eyes stinging from the smoke and hot burns lacing her feet.

A vow, to protect, regardless of what happened in their lives.

Merigold dropped her knife, blood dripping from her hands and her vessel brimming with an abundance of maenen. She saw faces around her—Cryden, Lisan, Ill'Nath. People she did not want to hurt. Her body—her spirit—ached to discharge the stolen power. She was at capacity. Beyond capacity. The additional maenen stretched her beyond any semblance of comfort, as if she was ready to give birth to a dozen children. But, she held it. Dear fucking Yetra, she held it.

"Merigold... Meri..." Cryden said, his face drawn and tired as he stood over her. "I am sorry, but you are unwell."

She couldn't breathe. Her windpipes was closed as if she were being strangled by Saren. She rolled around on the deck with faces swimming in front of her, black and red spots splattering across her vision. She rolled on her side and the last thing she saw, before darkness took her, was Jakys, his shirt soaked in blood and his eyes staring dully back at her.

***

When she woke, the pain wasn't in her throat, as she might have expected. Rather, Meri's arms, bound as they were to her sides, were on fire, the rough wood behind her head telling her that she was lashed to a mast. From the smell, she realized she had gotten sick in her unconsciousness, and her freezing hands felt grimy, crusted as they were with dried blood.

She opened her eyes, squinting against the gray light of early morning. She felt a tin cup against her cracked lips and she gulped down the water, ending in a sputtering cough.

"Merigold Hinter, I have been unkind to you," Cryden said. His face was painted with exhaustion, as if he hadn't slept for a week or more.

"What... what did I do?" Merigold croaked. She didn't struggle against her bonds.

Cryden was quiet. The rest of the ship was silent, too, aside from the creaks and groans betraying the subtle movement of the sea. Meri couldn't see another living being from her place sitting in front of the mast she was lashed to, facing starboard. The hush was unnatural for this ship, where Meri could typically hear at least the curse or laughter of a sailor, even in her cabin, at all hours of the day and night.

"Jakys is dying, if not already dead. Punctured lungs. Last I saw, he was choking on his own blood, and medical care is hard to come by two days from land."

Merigold's head hung limply as she vomited up the little bit of water that she'd just drunk. She had killed another man, another one who'd no longer been a threat. He couldn't have hurt her, not with Cryden and his powers nearby and Lisan's arrow trained to his throat. But, her deranged mind had again twisted her reality, spitting her fears across her vision and forcing her to bloody her knife.

Time had done nothing to fix her, and she somehow knew that this was not the worst of what she had done in the last few hours.

She looked up at Cryden through her unruly mop of hair.

"What else? What else did I do, Cryden?"

Cryden sighed like he was offering the gasp of a dying man. "You drew, Merigold. You emptied and collapsed his nerring. You drew the entirety of his maenen, and held it within you. The entire essence of what he was. Remy is a shell. Living, breathing, but nothing behind it. He has been drained beyond his ability to create new maenen."

Remy. She'd barely gotten to know the man, but he hadn't seemed a bad sort. He'd been full of life and energy, brimming with personality and humor. Likely, he'd been a great warrior, too, and he had never wronged her. And, the love he'd had for his brother…. She had felt that love; it had equaled what she felt for Ragen. That love was… it was gone now.

"Why do you stay with me, Cryden, when I am such a monster?" she asked.

Cryden gave her a weak smile. "This world breeds monsters, Merigold, though you are not one of them. I have done you a great disservice. Your mind is unwell. I have not considered your life and the impact of what you have experienced. The trauma of losing your town, your family, and your child. I quest, Merigold, and your nerring looks healthy. I forget the impact that all of this has had on your mind. That is not my realm of expertise, my dear lady."

"You didn't answer my question," Meri said, and Cryden smirked at her half-heartedly.

"You are a bit different, Meri. The things that you can do… they are not typical. Pasnes alna shape miernes and use it to impact the environment. We do it in different ways, and you will learn more at Agricorinor. But, regardless, the theme is shaping— making manifest the power that we all hold within us. But, recall what you have done. The mercenaries. The Feral. You transfer raw maenen. You have the ability to reverse-fill the nerring of others with the drawn maenen. This is not an unheard of talent, but it is certainly rare."

Merigold recalled little of the mercenaries, but the Feral was burned into her memory. She had transferred the lifeforce of her unborn child into the near-empty nerring of her attacker, causing the monster to physically burst.

It was sickening to think of.

"That can't be all, Cryden. I can destroy things. You can destroy things, too. Just the way we do it is different. This magic… it is a curse. A blight. I… I should be put down, as should every other person who can draw and harm those around them." Merigold clenched her fists and strained against her bonds in an impotent rage at her own being.

159

Cryden watched her, a gentle frown on his face. "I'm sorry you see it that way, Merigold. Humanity kills, but we are not all weapons. Much good can be done with these powers…"

"Cryden! We are approaching!" Lisan called from over Merigold's shoulder. Cryden nodded heavily, and then knelt in front of Merigold, placing a tentative hand on her knee.

"Please rest, for now. I will release you later; I needed to assess your mental state. Lisan will watch over you and keep you safe…" Left unspoken, of course, was that she was in danger, likely from everyone on board—especially Mikiton and Marius. Marius may have seemed simple, but there was a fierce love there.

Cryden stood and strode unsteadily from sight. Thankfully, Merigold was not left alone with her thoughts for long, lest she continue down a dangerous path. Lisan crouched next to her, just out of sight, her presence oddly reassuring.

"I've killed people who didn't deserve it," Lisan said, almost as if she was talking to herself. "Baern the Holy was a good man, a chief among his people. But, the Day Mother wished him dead, for he was uniting the people counter to her wishes, and I did her will. That was in Piniton, far away from here. And, I once lost my temper and killed a man who did deserve to die. Onious was a pitiful excuse for a human being, treating his slaves as one might treat misbehaven dogs. But he was also a powerful man, one who paid for my food and gave me my orders. One day, he struck a woman with his ring-encrusted fingers, rendering her bleeding and blind in one eye simply because he was displeased with the hanging of her hair. I stabbed him thirty-four times, and he died. I stabbed three guards an additional seventeen times, and two of them died."

Merigold said nothing, not sure if she was expected to. Lisan was trying to bring her comfort; that was obvious. But Merigold's own case was different. Lisan, straight as an arrow, had followed her orders in one case and followed her heart in another. Meri killed without reason, without sense. Two more lives were lost now because she could not escape her past.

And then Cryden's voice came to her from where he looked out over the sea. "This is… this is wrong."

"Bad luck, this is," said the second mate, Yukron, who might well be the captain at this point, Meri guessed.

"You ever see anything like this before in your journey on the seas?"

"The wreckage, yes. I have seen many a ship destroyed in pirate attacks or crushed upon the reefs. There are at least three ships destroyed here, which tells me there was a battle. But I have never seen this. Coal black water? This is wrong. This place is cursed. I would recommend, my lord, that we do not linger. I know not what such water will do to our hull." Yukron's voice, though respectful, was laced with fear. Whether it was from Cryden, the black seas that Meri could not see, or both, Meri wasn't sure.

"This shouldn't be possible. Not anymore," Cryden said, his words carrying on the wind.

"My lord, you've seen it. And I worry about the men—we should be to Polanice," said Yukron, stepping into view. The Rafonese man, a fairly unassuming sort, was chewing on his lower lip. Cryden stepped in next to him and leaned heavily on the rail.

"Fine. I need samples, though, for study and to bring to Agricorinor. Have your men lower a barrel… wait—someone is out there!"

There was a sudden flurry of activity as Yukron shouted out orders, directing the helmsman to steer toward whomever they saw, and calling out a complicate set of commands for men to

161

yank and pull on various ropes. The boat lurched and stuttered across the apparently dead waters, the motion feeling unnatural to even Meri. The waves, it seemed, did not follow the pattern she was used to hating. And yet, she had no desire to look out and see exactly what the sea, which had shaken both a pasnes alna and seasoned sailors, looked like. She closed her eyes for just a few minutes, ignoring the activity and thinking about the dead.

With a start, Merigold opened her eyes at the sound of a thump and the sound of cursing. At least, it sounded like cursing from the tone of it—the language was completely unfamiliar.

Several sailors, Cryden, and Yukron were scattered around a fallen body, which gasped and sputtered for air as it flopped about the deck. He—as Merigold could see the person was a man— wore only skin-tight black breeches. He struggled to his hands and knees, vomiting a waterfall of black water. The sailors kept their distance, and Yukron eventually waved them off, shouting orders in Rafonese.

The man pulled himself to one knee, but neither Cryden nor Yukron made a move to help him. Merigold had never seen a man like this castaway before, and she had seen Jecustans, Sestrians, Nistlingers, Rafonese, and a variety of mutts traveling through the Duckling. But no one had looked like this man. His skin wasn't just pale; it was alabaster white, as if he had been untouched by the sun. It was near flawless, in fact, and even as his sharp-featured face twisted, there was no doubt that he was beautiful.

"Get up," Cryden said. Then, he repeated himself louder. "Get up!"

The man complied, grasping the rail for support. Yukron warily leveled a cutlass at him, balanced and ready to strike, but Cryden made no move.

"Tell me what happened here," Cryden said.

The man began to sputter a language Merigold had never heard, completely unlike Ardian. He spoke at a rapid pace until he broke off in a cough.

"Tell me what happened. I've little patience for your pantomime," repeated Cryden, anger in his voice.

Shaking on his feet, the pale castaway scrubbed at his face with his hands. His gaze was glassy and exhausted, and he crinkled his forehead in confusion. It was clear that he had little idea what Cryden was saying and was stunned at his turn-of-fate. He had probably resigned himself to the depths, to a watery grave. He reached an arm out to Cryden as if in supplication and then stepped back, hands raised, as Yukron's sword came an inch from his neck.

Cryden shook his head in frustration. Meri knew that his thirst for knowledge, for understanding what had happened here, was left unquenched. "Chain him below and leave a guard," he said finally. "We will try a discussion when he's somewhat recovered."

Yukron nodded and called out to some sailors. Again, the pale man tried saying something and stumbled forward, and Cryden reached to steady him on instinct. It was a ruse, though, as the man recovered, dashed forward with a wicked hook, and connected solidly with Cryden's face. The pasnes alna spun and smashed his head on a crate. Yukron brought his sword up, but not before a bare foot kicked the weapon aside, and a second spinning kick sent Yukron reeling. The pale man scooped up the fallen cutlass and glanced around hurriedly. Did he think to take the entire ship alone, and then sail it back? And, back to where, if he did? With the unnaturally fast way that he moved, could he?

Lisan cursed from Meri's shoulder, and Merigold could see her fumbling with a sealskin bag, retrieving a dry string to affix to her bow. The deck was crowded with sailors, but an arrow could end this much quicker.

Cryden was just heaving his injured and drained body to his feet, holding a wavering hand toward his attacker. The pale man spun, slashing his sword across Cryden's stomach. The pasnes alna, always so obstentatiously quiet, howled in agony before falling to the suddenly blood-slick deck. Merigold now struggled against her bonds, questing desperately for something that could free her.

As always, she felt her own nerring, her reservoir of power, within her. It was such a familiar feeling that she almost ignored the subtle differences. The ponds of her power were slightly more expansive… there was more to her right now. Not much—it was just as if the pond contained a few dozen gallons more water—but it was there. And, there were still remnants of maenen that she had drawn from Remy. The power even felt like Remy.

She focused, as Cryden had taught her, and made an effort to shape the maenen. She aimed her hand, pinned to her side, upwards, and she envisioned a beam of energy, white and hot. She forced her nerring to expel the power, as if she were squeezing a bladder to force it out. As the power exited her nerring, it was shaped by her will. Untrained, certainly, but strong. She was strong. She had survived so much. She was a killer and a survivor. She could carve her way through a couple lengths of rope.

With a sharp pain, the beam of light shot from her hand and mostly severed the fibers. They fell slack around her and she glanced down at the new burn on her arm. She ignored the pain, though—what was a burn compared to her life, of late?—and pushed herself slowly to her feet.

The pale man turned his head toward Merigold as he finished another sailor with an effortless slash across the throat. His eyes widened slightly, illuminated by a dozen lanterns and whatever waning light filled the sky.

"Maneer?" he asked, clearly. "Maneer, kyoo yaha?" He suddenly spun his sword about in a blur, deflecting an arrow shot by Lisan, who had finally found a clear shot.

"Shit. Get back," she said, yanking Meri back behind the mast. Meri caught herself before falling, trying to get a glimpse of Cryden over Lisan's shoulder. All she could see were several motionless lumps, and was even unable to tell Cryden from the other fallen sailors. Lisan shot another arrow, which the pale man also deflected with ease. He was preternaturally fast and precise, moving as if everyone else were wading through water. Lisan tossed her bow aside with a disgusted snort, placing her hand on her sword.

The castaway turned back toward Meri, stepping over a body, and Lisan drew her sword and surged forward without a sound. She met his blade with her own, swinging her short sword with a speed that belied her musculature. The castaway nodded appreciatively as he sidestepped her attack. He set Lisan off-balance with a serious of impossibly fast jabs. She worked frantically to keep the tip of his cutlass from her chest, finding no room to riposte. He caught Lisan with an unexpected and fierce kick to the shin then, and she fell backward, moving with the momentum to keep the bone from shattering.

Ill'nath appeared from the left, swinging a great club with a roar and distracting the castaway warrior from Lisan. Meri darted to Lisan's side, pulling the other woman to her feet. Lisan, ignoring the battle for a moment, gripped Meri's shoulder and trapped her with her deep brown eyes.

"This Menogan is beyond our skills," she said grimly.

"Menogan?" asked Meri.

"A people far from here. Few know of them, but I am extremely well-traveled. Later, though. We need to take him down before more are hurt." Ill'Nath stumbled over a body, barely holding his own. Only his immense strength gave the Menogan pause. That, and the size of his club. Merigold noticed that he had a deep cut, bleeding freely, from his bare chest.

"What can I do? I'm... I'm without power. I could barely burn the ropes."

Lisan gripped her hand, her eyes intense. "Take what you need from me. No more, no less."

Merigold was paralyzed at the thought. She had no control; she would draw too much maenen and hurt Lisan. Maybe even kill her, or turn her into a shell like she had Remy. And, if she did draw, could she even shape the power correctly? But she quested anyway, and could sense Lisan's nerring pulsing with healthy maenen. Her head throbbed, as it always did now when she quested.

Ill'Nath roared as the Menogan left a glistening wound in his thigh. He lost his balance and stumbled backwards, with the Menogan launching himself forward for a killing strike.

"Do it!"

Meri drew, tapping into Lisan's maenen like a mosquito sucking blood. Like a leech. She felt the maenen flow into her nerring, distinct from her own power, oil on water. As always, it offered a sensation that was a combination of exhilarating and nauseau-inducing, her skull throbbing like a heartbeat. For a moment, Merigold was overwhelmed by the feeling, Lisan's power flowing into her unabated.

Meri was tied in the hull of a boat, terrified and unable to move.

She was bound and collared, forced, with a half a dozen others, to haul a great crate off of a boat.

Time slowed to a crawl. Lisan was on her knees, her face slack, eyes empty. A tear drifted down her cheek at the speed that a mountain might crumple. The Menogan had his cutlass raised above him in a two-handed grip, Ill'Nath below him, heaving his club in an attempt to protect his body in a fashion that would clearly be insufficient.

Meri recalled the Battle of Florens, Ferl's metsikas flinging power in a dozen different ways. Spikes, beams, spinning scythes—effective methods for killing en masse. She couldn't risk missing, though, or this Menogan's sword would bite into Ill'nath's neck. She wouldn't allow another of her protectors to be hurt, not with Lisan making this sacrifice.

When Meri had been a bit younger, Ragen had asked her to dispose of a number of cracked ceramic dishes, to bury them out behind the inn. Merigold, in a particularly nasty mood that day because of an argument with Sandra about spending the night with a strange old Jecustan noble, had decided to cart them off into the woods and shatter them. She had chucked the first one out about twenty yards, shattering the plate against a tree with a satisfying crack. The second throw had accomplished the same. After ten in a row, Merigold's mood had been much lighter, and she'd realized that she had a natural skill in tossing plates. Heaving them about all day had given her an excellent feel for their heft and nature, it seemed.

Not even realizing what she did, Meri shaped Lisan's maenen into a disc that was a perfect replica of a plate from the Duckling, down to a small crack running throughout. The thing formed and hovered above her hand, glowing red and angry. She'd gleaned from Cryden that she must propel the object with her mind, so presumably size and shape should not matter. However it was projected with the mind, though, it could still be impacted by the elements.

Merigold cut off her draw from Lisan and time snapped back into focus. She launched the glowing disk forward with an intense thought and started forming a second one immediately. The first hissed toward the Menogan and his raised cutlass. Somehow, the pale warrior saw the maenen projectile hurtling toward him and twisted backwards, mid-thrust. Rather than striking Ill'nath, he lashed out at Meri's plate while leaping backwards.

His cutlass connected solidly with the plate. And, just like those she'd used to toss in the woods, it shattered.

Pieces hissed in all directions, burning into the deck and fallen bodies. But, most of the shrapnel shot right into the body of the Menogan. He dropped his cutlass and howled like a madman for the space of a long breath. He did not fall, but hugged his arms around his torso. Meri could see oozing burns all over his body and could smell the still-cooking flesh. The scream paused for the space that it would take a man to fill his lungs, and then it started again.

He suddenly stood up straight and tore at his face. A piece of her plate must have been slowly burrowing into his skull. The light of the deck lanterns shone straight through a gaping, oozing hole in his midsection. Merigold fell to her knees, heaving without anything left in her stomach to pass. The garbled scream from the Menogan was cut off abruptly, and she heard his body slump to the deck, his pain mercifully ended.

"Merigold. He would have killed all of us; you did the right thing," whispered Lisan, her voice hoarse and weak, her head hanging.

But the right thing looked an awful lot like torture. A minute ago, the man had been the picture of life, of vitality. He'd been leaping, slicing, talking…

"Maneer," said Merigold, her mind snapping to the look the Menogan had given her earlier. Raised eyebrows, mouth slightly agape. He'd recognized her, or at least thought he did. And he'd been surprised.

"What?" Lisan coughed, her face sickly.

"You said you know of these people—do you know their language? He called me 'Maneer'. What did that mean?"

Lisan, face painted with a sick exhaustion, shook her head with uncertainty. "I'm not fluent by any means, and I can't be sure what you heard."

"Tell me."

"It means... It means 'sister'."

Chapter 13

The Rostanians lived their lives in the shadow of the Tulanques, thinking about the mountains only to curse them for shorting the days by blocking the setting sun. At best, some might stop occasionally and appreciate the view of those great knives tearing through the sky and seemingly cutting the very clouds. Few ventured into the mountains, though, aside from the miners and scant remaining goatherders who still carved a living from the inhospitable granite.

They did not generally appreciate the vast beauty and terror that were the mountains, particularly as winter firmly grasped Saiwen. The Rostanians might instead complain of the mild snow that occasionally covered their streets and roofs, the ice that might cause an old woman to slip or a cart to become mired. Amidst the high paths of the mountains, though, a sudden blizzard could hit without warning, wind tearing through clothes and flesh, threatening to grab a human body and toss it to the rocks below like a sadistic child discarding an insect.

Hafgan noticed none of this, though, his body was so accustomed to the cold. He had some small worries that he'd grown soft living among the humans. That he'd gotten slow and weak. Certainly, he had developed a taste for the rich food of Rostane. The seasoned, roasted chicken; the cheese-covered potatoes. The sausage gravy that they put on everything. But, his body remained true, strong and resistant to the harsh climate.

"This fucking snow," mumbled Enric. The hairless Wasmer was less adaptive than Hafgan.

"If you'd be putting on a hat, maybe it'd bother you less," Paston mumbled, in a bad humor himself.

"If you both grew as much hair on your balls as your faces, you'd be fine," Alwyn commented. One of the new additions to his budredda, the young Wasmer had been born in Rostane, though to a traditionalist family. He spoke impeccable Ardian, even if it did sound stilted on his tongue. He was one of those who'd decided to desert instead of following Siarl in his mutiny against Hafgan.

Hafgan remembered finding the tired Alwyn wandering the woods—the man practically shaking with exhaustion, but threatening the budredda with his uncertain spear anyway. Alwyn had fully expected to be slaughtered for desertion, or for not telling Hafgan of Siarl's plan, but had not planned to die without testing his mettle. Hafgan had approached the man, waving his omnipresent budredda away and tossing his own spear aside. He'd walked forward until the point of Alwyn's spear had rested on his chest with just enough pressure to scrape his skin. He'd then looked into Alwyn's eyes and taken his measure. Another man, scared and alone, having no place in the world.

"Come," Hafgan had said, simply. And Alwyn had.

"How much further to Hackeneth, anyhow?" asked Alwyn, his deep brown eyes seeming nearly black against the snowy backdrop. He wore his hair braided in the manner of the traditionalists, but was rapidly adopting the practices of other budredda, including filing down his second set of dogteeth.

"Not much," mumbled Hafgan. "Just be ready." His return to the Carreg Da was not going to be a joyous event, neither for his men nor himself. No one rejoices when the bastard son returns bearing outlandish warnings and accusations. Particularly when that son had very publicly vowed never to return. That vow was only emphasized by its covering of Wasmer blood.

"That be a fallacy. You cannot be always ready, Lieutenant," Enric said, scratching at his chest. The wound inflicted by Yanso had been deep and required a couple dozen stitches, and it certainly still ached. Thankfully, the cold of the mountains helped forestall any infections.

"Perhaps not, but you should at least be ready when two men fight with cold steel, a mere feet from where you lounge on your spear," Hafgan pointed out, leveling his best commanding glare. The hairless Wasmer blanched, glancing away hurriedly. Enric's tendency to complain seemed to have returned with the bad weather and his injury. Hafgan needed to get him back under control before the negativity spread among an already dissatisfied group of Wasmer.

His original budredda, aside from Enric, were loyal as ever. Even more dedicated to him, even, as they had passed the trial of blood together, repelling Siarl's attack and surviving the gwagen. Some new recruits, like Alwyn, had found a comfortable place among the budredda. The majority of his three dozen soldiers, though, were simply Wasmer who weren't sure what to do, but saw a strong leader in Hafgan. His people ever bowed to strength, even those who moved and lived among humans. The Wasmer caste system was ingrained into them; warriors followed the strongest among them. Not the most intelligent or the most cunning, but the best fighter. And, in Hafgan's estimation, he had no worries in that regard.

But, leading by martial prowess was much like commanding a vicious dog. They may listen and obey commands, but if they sensed a weakness, your jugular was going to end up torn out.

Hafgan always took the role of vanguard in their march through the Tulanques. As part of his training, he had spent three months alone in the mountainous terrain, being hunted by his leaders. He had become intimately knowledgeable about the paths, hideaways, and caves, as well as locations of rival clans. Using this hard-gotten knowledge, he now steered his budredda unerringly toward the Carreg Da, toward Hackeneth, without encountering any major settlements. He knew they were watched;

they had crossed through Flam Madfall territory for much of their march. But, this clan had been largely decimated in wars with the Carreg Da, and both Rostane and Florens, as well as from constant raids on their western borders by the Yearer Inos. They were not likely to mount an attack unless clearly threatened.

A week ago, they had passed into Carreg Da territory, and still they were watched. The worst part was that, now, Hafgan knew the watcher.

This day, they had journeyed down into a valley, staying to the low ground where they were somewhat sheltered by the wind. They no longer lit fires at night; the effort needed to keep a fire burning in the snow was better spent creating makeshift shelters or burrowing into the snow and huddling together for heat. They were moving into a more populous area now, held by the many goatherding and farming villages that scraped a mean living from the odd fertile patches throughout the valley. One of the larger surface towns—Reneth—was on their path. Hafgan expected to be stopped there, by representatives from the Dyn Doethas sent ahead to escort him into the heart of Hackeneth with as little fuss and fanfare as possible.

Therefore, he was surprised when his watcher confronted him two days out from Reneth.

Listening to Enric, Paston, and Alwyn bicker, and occasionally chiming in himself, Hafgan almost missed the watcher until they were nearly upon him.

"Hafgan Iwan, as I live, breathe, and shit," called the man, swaggering out into the middle of their path from where he'd leaned against a tree. The Wasmer tongue was typically a lilting, musical sound to Hafgan's ear when compared to Ardian, but this man's voice was hoarse, cracking as he spoke. It was as if he had inhaled smoke for too long, and could only just force air past his ravaged windpipe.

"Do I know you?" Hafgan asked, sticking to Ardian. He waved back his little entourage of budredda to a safe distance, all of them responding without question—although Paston seemed the most reluctant. Hafgan had no idea how this might go, but his men being nearby would just complicate things.

"Always a funny man. A funny, stupid, funny man." The Wasmer barked a discordant laugh. His grimy brown hair, cut shorter than typical Wasmer style, stood out in all directions. His white war robes—if that's what they'd once been—were so filthy that Hafgan had originally thought they were black. But the bastard sword strapped sheathless across his back was well-cared for, and it gleamed in the light of the pale sun.

"What are you doing here?" Hafgan asked, eyes on the hilt of that sword, noting the hourglass glyph etched into the pommel. Not a typical Wasmer weapon; his people preferred to battle with the spear. But, Hafgan was familiar with this particular weapon. He'd once wielded it.

"Me? Me? This is all my land." He spread his hands grandiosely, taking in the trees, the valley, the great peaks that rose above them. "You, though… you are the trespasser. You are the encroacher. You are the invader."

That was true. Hafgan no longer belonged here in these mountains. With these people. He'd willingly—purposefully—left the Carreg Da nearly five years before, leaving no path for a friendly return. Or, truthfully, a return of any sort. There was no welcome waiting for him here. No open arms.

But Hafgan still said nothing, waiting for the watcher to continue his speech.

"So, tell me. Why do you return, a host of budredda at your heels?"

"You tell me, Yurin. Why do you continue to serve the Dyn Doethas like a stinking wet dog?" Hafgan growled through his

174

shaved teeth. Yurin, always a couple of inches taller, looked slightly down at him, completely still. And then he broke into another wheezing laugh, leaning backwards and howling his glee into the sky. The echo was unnerving, but Hafgan did not reach for his hedwicchen.

"You, Hafgan. You, you, you." Yurin started circling Hafgan. Not as if he were preparing to battle, but just sort of undulating around him, almost as if he were a drunkard staggering about without a care in the world. He almost appeared to stagger, but Hafgan knew better. This man was canny, and his style unpredictable. No warleader taught their men to fight like Yurin could fight.

"Me, me, me," said Hafgan, staring straight ahead even as Yurin moved out of his vision. It was a risk, showing such disdain for this dangerous man.

"It amazes me that you have so little to say, and that you cling to that broken language from below. You sound like a fool, and that will gain you no friends among the Carreg Da."

"I do not seek friends."

"The heart of the matter, then. What is it that you seek?" The crunching of the snow was directly behind Hafgan. And yet, Hafgan continued to stare straight ahead.

"I cannot share that with a goat-fucking dog. I need to speak with Taern, if he still manipulates from the shadows. If not, I'll settle for whomever wields the Dyn Doethas." For a long moment, there was only silence. Hafgan braced himself, worried that he had gone too far with his insults.

Something impacted his head, a glancing blow, and Hafgan flung himself forward. He twisted in midair, grabbing at his belt knife and holding it in front of himself protectively as he landed on his back.

There was no follow-up attack. Yurin stood ten yards away, grinning the grin of a madman, his dual fangs glistening and opalescent. In his hand, he held a second handful of snow, packed into a tight ball. Hafgan pulled himself to his feet, brushing the remnants of the snow from his hair.

"A snowball, Yurin? Are you a child as well as a servile dog?"

The madman's grin did not dim. "You can call me dog, if you desire. If that makes you feel superior. Hafgan, some of us were meant to serve rather than lead. If that is how I keep my place among my people, then so be it."

"It is not that you serve. It is who you serve. Spineless manipulators and murderers who seek to control their people through lies and fear." Hafgan could not keep the rancor from his voice.

"Murderers you seek to meet with." Yurin's smile finally broke. He crushed the snowball in his hand.

"That is because I still serve, despite everything. That is because I still strive to help our people, just as I did years ago. I will not see them undermined or destroyed from within. And, from what I have seen, that is exactly what is happening."

Was that why he was here on this errand? Did he still care so much about his people that he was willing to risk his life in giving this warning about the gwagen? Or was it something else? Hafgan could feel the anger bubbling up at his core like puss escaping from a festering wound. He still did not seek his hedwicchen. He needed to know what he felt, what was truly guiding his actions here.

"So, Hafgan." Yurin strode up to Hafgan, this time with no wavering. He paused an arm's length away, his eyes somewhat unfocused. "You want to help us, then. You want to… I don't know… bestow upon us the gift of knowledge? Take control of us yourself? Lead us to a gentler life?"

176

Last time he'd tried to share knowledge with the Carreg Da, it had not gone so well.

"No, Yurin, I am done with that. I simply seek to give a message, something that goes beyond the petty manipulations of the Dyn Doethas. Something that threatens the lives of the clans in the mountains as well as the lives of those below. I come with a warning."

Yurin's shifting gaze was suddenly stoic and hard, flashing both with anger and sadness. The filthy Wasmer closed his eyes tightly for a long moment then, as if in deep concentration. When he opened them, the madman's smile returned.

"Well, good luck with that then," Yurin said in halting Ardian. He started down the valley in the same direction as Hafgan's final destination, again adopting the gait of an uneven drunk. Before disappearing from sight, he called over his shoulder. "I will see you in Hackeneth in a few days. No one will stop you."

Hafgan shook his head and relaxed the tension in his shoulders.

His brother had always been a bit odd.

Chapter 14

Emma was on edge.

There was something about Farrow's Hold that scraped at her already bare nerves, whittling away at her tenuous grip on her psyche. It had been a week since their arrival, when Emma had thought that all she needed was a comfortable bed, a warm bath, and a few hot meals to regain a semblance of herself. She had had all of those things—though it had taken three baths to fully clean her hair—but she felt worse than ever.

It may have been the great hold, itself. Surrounded by forty-foot-tall stone walls, the keep was massive, a city unto itself. Her and her officers' quarters were not in the hold proper, but rather in one of the many smaller ancillary buildings, which had once housed a noble family. The Sentael estate had clearly been void of residents for some time, though, and a deep emptiness lingered, as if the chill rooms were meant for those who'd used to reside here, long gone or longer dead. The tunnels that connected the ancillary buildings with Farrow's Hold were desolate and hollow, and though black cloaks patrolled these passages and kept them well-lit, there was a forsaken, vacuous hush to them that turned Emma's stomach.

It may also have been the people of Jecusta. The place was a hornet's nest of intrigue and plotting, nobles and rich landowners stinging each other for whatever scraps of influence they could muster. In her first day, Emma had been invited to the personal residence of Borin Lasgow, a wealthy dealer of weapons and the sole manufacturer of Jecusta's famous yellow yew bows; to the residence of Roanel Sens, the ambassador from Algania and the mouthpiece of their grand chancellor; and the residence also of Evina Linstael, the most powerful woman in Jecusta. Evina's husband, the magnate of the Eastern Sweeps, was known to be an ineffectual pedophile, and she ran a quarter of the country, in truth. Nonetheless, Emma had politely turned down all meetings, unwilling to wade into an unfamiliar morass of intrigue. No wonder Lord Unael appeared so worn and weary.

Or, it may have been the fact that Emma had no one to talk to. She could be herself in front of no one and be honest in front of no one, not since Escamilla had slipped into unconsciousness weeks ago. Instead, Emma's captains and soldiers needed to see her as hard, the fearful woman that would not hesitate to drag someone to death should that need suit her. They were reserved around her, and treated her with a respect that bordered on fear. The mercenaries' captains, Ferl and Trina Almark, were less formal with her, but she didn't trust Ferl, and Trina had not yet pulled herself out of her depression. The closest Emma had to a companion was the wise-cracking Nail—one of her Rotten Apple Knights—and even he was reluctant to engage in any meaningful conversation.

In short, Emma felt alone and empty. The mask of the hard, assertive general and politician was beginning to crack, faults forming as she struggled to hold it together.

"My lady, it is late to be traversing the tunnels, even with your omnipresent knights." Emma peered into the lamp light to see Captain Braston emerging from the emptiness. Thankfully, he'd decided to let his beard grow back out again, covering up his unsightly pock marks. Her knightly escort relaxed at the familiar face.

"I could say the same to you, Braston," Emma said with the hint of a smile. Of the captains, she felt that Braston avoided her the least. In her world, that hinted at loyalty.

"I had joined some, uh, new friends for some socialization."

Judging from the nose-crinkling smell and his glassy eyes, kerena had probably been involved, as well. Perhaps Braston was not the picture of duty that he'd portrayed while on the march.

179

"Smells like quite the social event," muttered Nail, nudging the big man at his side.

"I can be social," said Hammer, Nail's notoriously stoic brother and another of Emma's personal guard. Hammer was, as his nickname implied, a huge and powerful man. There couldn't have been many taller in the entire army, and none stronger. Emma had once seen him, single-handedly, lift a fallen tree out of the road, tossing it aside like a twig rather than allowing a minor delay for their army. He was notoriously reticent, unlike his loquacious brother Nail.

Braston had the grace to seem embarrassed. "Apologies, my lady. I take it you are visiting our Lady Escamilla?"

"Yes, I'd like to sit with her for a time." Sit, and talk to her. At least Emma could pretend as if someone was listening. She could pretend that Escamilla was well, and that her sudden rise in the world was all a bad dream.

Braston nodded. "Let me join your escort, then."

"No need for that. I have these two for company."

"Please. I could use a walk, anyway." Braston wore a pleading expression. Emma nodded and let the man save a bit of face.

The passages were strangely empty this evening. Farrow's Hold, everything within the walls, was many times the size of even the Plateau. Whereas the Plateau was supported by Little Town—with servants' quarters, barracks, food storage, and so on—Farrow's Hold was fully independent. It had been built as a fortress, long before the city had existed. Typically, the place was bustling, overflowing with not only the upper echelons and administrators that ran the city and country, but also a veritable army of servants, cooks, messengers, and various other functionaries.

But, though Emma heard some discordant echoes in the distance, she and her small entourage passed no one, which only emphasized the fearful emptiness that was so pervasive of late. Their time in the tunnels was thankfully short, however, and soon they were ascending the staircases that led to the guest quarters in the main hold, the luxurious apartments where Unael was housing Escamilla during her final hours.

As if he could glimpse the ins of her mind, Braston paused for a moment, turning to her. He was looking more sober with each passing moment.

"My lady. We need to discuss the matter of… of Lady Escamilla's eventual passing. Her assets, those still available to us, will be managed by the local bankers. However, we must make decisions regarding the services." He coughed wetly into the crick of his arm. The reek of kerena wafted across the distance between them. "Unael wants to host a service, as do the Yetranians. Unfortunately, the styles are… mutually exclusive."

"Why is that?" Nail asked. None of her Rotten Apple Knights were Yetranian. She'd made sure of that.

"The noble lords, in Jecusta, are always incinerated and returned to the earth as a mark of honor," Braston explained, pausing to cough periodically. "However, the burning of a body is reserved only for the worst sinners by Yetranian law. Cremation, in this way, would mar Escamilla's legacy to so many in Ardia. So, we must either please the Jecustans or our own Yetranians."

"Sounds like a dilemma," Nail agreed, his larger brother grunting in agreement.

"Cocks," mumbled Emma, so that Nail barked a laugh at her curse. Escamilla's death, even, could not be simple. Though she'd employed Ignatius at Brockmore for years, she was anything but a devoted Yetranian. Only as devoted as necessary to forward her agenda and to pacify her Yetranian followers, in fact. Emma honestly didn't know what her lady believed in.

"We will talk about this tomorrow. Let us bring together Ignatius and Harivor; see if we can find an accord that will work for both."

"Not likely," Nail growled. He shared her fervent disdain of Ignatius, though she did her best to conceal it these days. He would be ally.

They emerged from the steep staircase into the plush-carpeted hallway that marked the western guest quarters. Typically, the gas lamps lit these passages as brightly as day, flaunting the superb, rare artwork that crowded the walls. But, half of the lamps were flickering, and the other half were off. And, there was no sign of the soldiers who should have been standing guard.

"Something's wrong!" Braston hissed, tearing a dagger out of his boot. He'd evidently left his sword behind. Thankfully, Nail drew his steel longsword while Hammer pulled his gigantic greatsword from his back. Emma probably couldn't even have lifted the thing, but Hammer could wield it with a single hand.

"Nail, you must take the lady back while Hammer and I investigate." Braston muffled a cough. "Send black cloaks and whomever else you find."

"No, I will not be left behind. Lady Escamilla could be in danger." Not that it should matter—she was an inch from death. But, somehow, it did. The thought masked the creeping fear that threatened to overwhelm her.

"My lady…" Braston pleaded.

"I will stay behind you. Now, go!"

The four crept down the hallway, Hammer and Nail leading the way, swords held ready. Braston stuck to Emma's side, dagger held in a hand that was either shaking from the kerena or from dread. Emma licked her lips and placed her hand on the hilt of her own knife. She had taken to wearing a weapon openly after dragging the men. Not that it should dissuade attackers—she hadn't a clue how to wield it effectively—but mayhap it gave her the appearance of capability.

They reached the decoratively-carved twin oaken doors to Escamilla's room. Emma gasped, and saw Nail and Hammer both stiffen, while Braston made a grunting sound. There was a… wrongness on the other side of the door. A cloying feeling that choked Emma with a cacophony of emotions. She didn't know whether to cry, sprint away screaming, or thrust her dagger between Hammer's shoulder blades. It took every bit of will power, every modicum of her spirit, to just stand in front of that door.

"You two, take down the door. We must protect the lady," whispered Braston, his breath coming in gasps.

Hammer shook his head as if to clear it, and then he split the doors wide open with a great kick from his booted foot. The doors burst open, bits of wood flung into the air as the lock was torn free. Emma peered between her warriors as they rushed into the room.

Just in time to see a great, black spear thrust into Escamilla's heart.

"No!" she cried, trying to push past her warriors while Braston held her back. She fought fiercely, elbowing Braston in the face and even reaching for her dagger before a ferocious slap stunned her long enough for him to grip her more firmly. Through her stinging cheek and a maelstrom of emotions, she became aware of the scene in front of her.

Escamilla was pinned to her bed by a spear of pure darkness, tendrils of red power laced around its stave. It was wielded by an ethereal shadow, a cloud of blackness that sucked up all light in the room. Emma felt her mind splitting just looking at this apparition, her brain unable to comprehend the utter chaos that lived inside that cloud.

Hammer was either much braver than her or taken with a rage. He sprinted toward the dark shape with a fierce war cry, covering the distance between the door and the huge, four-post bed in an instant. With a great, two-handed swing, Hammer's sword blade somehow missed the shadow, which flitted to the side. Hammer's greatsword cleaved though one of the bedposts as he stumbled to one knee. He recovered, spun, and took a burning red sword across the gut with a sizzling hiss. The smell of cooked flesh made Emma wretch, as did the sight of Hammer's intestines flopping to the ground as the sword cleaved his body like a burning poker through a chunk of ice.

The shadow leapt backwards, its fiery sword leaving streaks of light in the air. When it moved, it was in the shape of a man.

Hammer tumbled to the ground as Nail surged at the shadow with an ear-splitting howl of grief. His sword lashed out like lightening—Nail was a fantastic swordsman. The blade was deflected with glittering sparks by the red sword, which immediately riposted. Nail leapt to the side and the burning blade only scored a burning gash on his free arm. Nail next lunged forward with a precise jab, his form immaculate as he darted toward the heart of the man-figure cloaked in shadow. And, suddenly, he was tumbling to the ground, his foot severed just above the ankle.

His subsequent scream was seemingly absorbed by the shadow man.

"Run, lady!" Braston said with a thick voice, shoving her toward the staircase. Emma stumbled a couple of steps, but turned around. There was no running from this. And, Escamilla… she could not allow the great lady's body to be further defiled by whatever that creature was.

Her chaotic emotions seemed to converge into a single one: vengeance.

Braston launched his dagger into the shadow as it stood over Nail, ready to finish the fallen knight. There was a grunt as the projectile struck something solid in the heart of the shadow. With the distraction, Braston surged toward Hammer's fallen greatsword as curses spat forth from the dark mist. So, this thing could be hurt!

Braston struggled to heave the huge sword in front of his body. He was not an insubstantial man, but Hammer's weapon was as heavy as an anvil. The dark figure coalesced into a clear figure of a man, pointing one finger at Braston. A beam of blood-red light, as thin as a wooden skewer, shot from the figure's finger and pierced Braston's forehead. He dropped to the ground without a sound.

The figure, no longer cloaked in an ethereal shadow, cursed and kicked at Nail, who lay on the floor unconscious, lain flat by either blood loss or shock. The man's back was facing her. Maybe she could get to him before he turned around, ramming her shaking weapon into the monster's back. Do something before he could further harm Nail. To save even one man who'd fought so hard for Escamilla. She gripped her knife and started forward, feet making nary a sound upon the plush carpet.

The man's head jerked up, and he blinked out of existence where he'd been, only to suddenly be standing before her.

"Tsk. Tsk. Tsk. I think you should release that knife."

It fell from her good hand—whether from terror or his command, Emma didn't know. She met the eyes of the assassin, or tried to. He was wearing spectacles that were formed of an opaque, black stone. It was hard to tell around those spectacles, but he appeared to be of middle age, maybe in his early forties, with a bit of gray at his temples, though his hair was still mostly brown-blonde. There was something off about his appearance, but Emma couldn't think straight with four bodies lying strewn across the room. Her earlier courage had dissipated like a sputtering candle in the darkest evening.

"You must be the new Lady Breen, the servant girl everyone's been talking about. The red-headed, one-handed bitch, no?" He smiled a forced smile, though Emma could see the quivering rage behind it.

"Ugh, let me take these fucking things off." He turned his back to her once again, tearing off his spectacles and secreting them in a pocket of his deep black cloak.

Emma just needed to scoop up the knife and stick it in his neck…

"Better. You have no idea." He ran his hands through his hair—such a normal, human gesture from a man who'd just killed or incapacitated three fighting men and a woman in her sleep. His eyes were a deep blue and seemed to swirl like a maelstrom.

He turned back to her. "You are awfully quiet, my dear. Not at all like the bitch I was expecting."

Emma caught a glance at the spear that still pinned Escamilla to the bed. Her rage built and fed the flames of her courage. "Who are you? Why are you doing this?" she managed through clenched teeth.

"Obvious questions, but good ones. I would ask the same in your situation." He made a casual sweeping gesture toward Escamilla, as if he were shopping for fruit. "Clearly, I am not a friend. But, I need not be an enemy."

Emma steeled herself, resisting the urge to fiddle with her hands. "You didn't answer my question." He raised an eyebrow at that, which highlighted what was wrong with the man's appearance. His head, above the eyebrow and ear, was misshapen, partially collapsed. The hair masked it, but the deformity was unmistakable. Nonetheless, there was something familiar about the man, the way he moved. The way he spoke. But she'd never met a man with a smashed head before.

"You can call me 'Disorder' for now. I don't deserve a real name." His face suddenly twisted in anger, and he darted across the room to a carved wardrobe. He grunted as he toppled the great piece of furniture to the ground, kicking at it and snapping the wood. For a solid minute, he reduced the wardrobe to splintered bits of debris, grunting with the effort and punctuating blows with curses.

As abruptly as he'd started, Disorder stopped and strode back to her, stepping over Hammer's corpse and tracking blood on the lovely old carpet. It will have to be replaced, Emma thought dully, looking at the fabric. Those stains will never come out.

"Apologies. These fucking things…" he patted his pocket, "… will drive you insane if you aren't careful. One of the reasons I'd rather not do this myself."

"Then why… Why did you come here? Escamilla was going to pass in a few days at most," Emma said, stepping back from the unpredictable killer with a swallow. Maybe, if she kept him talking, someone would arrive. More Apple Knights or black cloaks, other guests of Lord Unael. Someone.

"Of course. It does seem a waste. But who am I to decide?" Disorder took a deep breath and rubbed his side, his hand coming back stained with blood. Braston's knife must have nicked him. "That bastard got me, but I'm a decent hand at healing. Well, we wanted to send a message, after that urchin failed. Escamilla going quietly in her sleep was not consistent with that message.

This should be sufficiently dramatic to get everyone's attention, don't you think?"

"Who are you people? What message?" Emma felt disconnected as she met Disorder's gaze. There was no longer that horrible surge of emotions, but rather Emma felt this was a dream. It had to be.

Disorder bared his teeth, and Emma found herself slamming into the ground, the man astride her. His forearm was across her windpipe. She struggled weakly, hitting at his face with her mutilated hand. That seemed only to fuel his rage. He pushed harder, cutting off her airflow completely.

"Don't ask so many questions! I don't want to hurt you." He released the pressure and twisted to his feet with inhuman grace. Disorder offered his hand to help her up then. Emma scrabbled to her feet on her own, coughing and sputtering as she gulped in iron-smelling air.

"Okay, I will not ask so many questions. But, if there is a warning, I just want to know what I should be warned of." Emma held her hands in front of her, speaking as if she were appeasing a wild, unpredictable animal.

"Ah, fuck. You must think me insane." Emma didn't respond. "It's these fucking spectacles. That's why I prefer to send others. Let's start again. I'm from Recherche Oletta, or at least I work with them. I answer to higher authorities, as do they. As do we all. And, they are coming."

Emma wanted to ask who was coming, but feared that one more question might send Disorder over the edge of the precipice like a slight breeze. She needed to survive this. She needed to survive this and kill whoever had ordered this attack. And if this Disorder could bleed, then he could die. They all could.

Disorder sighed and slumped his shoulders, rubbing at his whirlwind eyes. His mannerisms smacked of familiarity, but Emma couldn't quite place it.

"Know that I do this, lady, to save lives. When they come, the only way to protect the people is to preempt opposition. To prevent people from taking up arms and fighting. For they will be slaughtered. I do this to protect them. To protect them," Disorder repeated, almost as if to convince himself.

"I understand," Emma said softly, leaning away. "It makes sense."

He snatched her wrist, hand inhumanly strong. His eyes dug into hers. "Don't patronize me. Now, you've saved me a trip, this night. For I would have visited you, too. You have this one opportunity. You will cease your hostilities toward Rostane. You will disband your army. You will leave this place and make yourself unknown." Disorder touched a finger to her chest, directly between her breasts. A warmth appeared at the surface of her skin. An irritating warmth, like a mosquito bite or a small scrape. But that warmth began to penetrate her body. She struggled against Disorder, but his grip was impossibly firm, an implacable iron shackle. The tiny ball of heat pushed through her flesh, through her bone, and lodged itself firmly into her heart.

It wasn't exactly a pain, but it caused her to panic nonetheless. Emma could feel it, this power, lodged in her heart. It was an alien presence, something that didn't belong inside her body. Something that didn't belong in this world. She began breathing heavily, panting, trying to fight the building dread.

"There will be no hiding, my lady. You must follow my instructions to leave, unless you wish to meet the same fate as Lady Breen." Disorder glanced over his shoulder, back toward Escamilla's corpse. "I want to keep people safe," he muttered. Then, he locked her gaze one more time and gave her a crooked smile—a smile that would have been charming in a different circumstance. In a tavern or ballroom; in a merchant's shop or on the road.

And, suddenly, it clicked.

"Aiden de Trenton?" Emma asked in a hushed voice. This man, this darkly insane, immensely powerful man, was Fenrir's brother. The resemblance was clear—in the corners of the eyes, in that smile, in his posture. This was the man who had sent a killer after Fenrir.

Emma expected another blow, an emotional explosion from Disorder. But, instead, he pushed past her. "I haven't used that name in a long time. As my little brother would tell you, Aiden de Trenton is long dead," he said softly. With that, he reached out, put his dark spectacles back on, and disappeared into the shadows.

Emma shuddered and nearly fell to her knees. But, she forced her weakened limbs to propel her to Escamilla. She laid on the bed next to the woman, cheek to cheek, and began to sob.

Chapter 15

Fenrir groaned and rolled onto his side. His muscles were bathed in fire, twitching impulsively like those of the recently dead. His hand shook like a feeble old man's as he brought it to his face to rub at his squinting, pain-filled eyes. Fenrir took a deep, shuddering breath which ended with a coughing fit, forcing him to curl up his body in order to lessen the tearing of his stomach muscles.

The fit passed, and Fenrir closed his eyes, hoping that the oblivion of sleep would help him through this torture. Before the next round began.

"Fenrir Coldbreaker, as I live and breathe!" A familiar voice. A… friendly voice?

"That's… Martis?" Even Fenrir's voice sounded broken, dry and cracked as the ashlands that supposedly peppered the continent. He forced his lead-heavy eyelids to rise, concentrating until his eyes focused on the face of his long-time friend.

Martis Aieres smiled, his eyes creasing as he approached. Fenrir could swear that there was more white in his braided beard and short hair than ever before, though it had only been a few months since he had seen the physician.

"It is indeed Martis, my friend. You've developed a fantastical ability to hurt yourself and wake up to my aging face. You must be some sort of magician."

"If I were a magician, I would magick away the pain," Fenrir groaned.

"Let's see what we have here." Martis began his typical poking and prodding, his powerful fingers ungently forcing cries of pain from Fenrir. Gods, was it more than twenty years since Martis' competent exam had yielded yelps of pain from a young Fenrir?

After he'd washed out of the Rostanian infantry? By Ultner's graying pubes, he wasn't young anymore.

He certainly didn't feel young right now. His knee, of course, felt like it was full of gravel. But, there were so many other pains plaguing his body that Fenrir was unsure how many other major injuries he had. "Why are you here, Martis?" he asked. "Not that I'm upset to see you.. erg… though you could be a bit lighter with the touch."

"Do I call him your father? No, certainly not, given that you have been disowned. And yet, here you are, housed in the servants' quarters of the de Trenton compound, languishing in the lower levels. Out of sight, it seems, but not out of mind. Now, why…"

"Rambling again." Martis had that tendency. The older physician laughed lightly, not at all insulted. He never was.

"Ha. I should know better than to indulge my penchant for serpentine conversation whilst entertaining Fenrir Coldbreaker. 'Fenrir the Impatient' could be added to your honorifics."

"So, Darian sent you," Fenrir said, attempting to reel Martis in.

"Calling him by his first name. Interesting. You both avoid mention of your relationship and acknowledgement of his high status in this country. Principal de Trenton. Councilor de Trenton. Perhaps King de Trenton, one day?"

"By Ultner, let's hope not. Ow!"

Martis gave his arm one last probing jab before stepping back from his examination. "My friend, you are intact. Bruises, no breaks. Cuts that will heal without intervention, aside from a cream that I will provide to avoid infection. And your muscles will continue to ache for days, although you are unlikely to receive any reprieve."

"My first march," grumbled Fenrir, straining to pull himself up into a seated position. He exhaled deeply, as if he had just shifted the earth in the attempt.

"What's that?" Martis raised a bushy gray eyebrow.

"My first march. I remember, when I… emancipated myself from Darian and joined the Rostanian military, Sergeant Alus sent all of the new recruits on a forced march. That old bastard rode a horse and forced us, double time, on a twenty-mile march. Full gear—backpack, spears, and so on—strapped on our backs. I lagged behind at times, but forced myself forward. I couldn't wash out in my first week, not without crawling back to Darian. And I couldn't do that. So, I ignored the pain and kept going." Fenrir felt a strange catch in his throat.

Martis simply watched, slightly askance, as he slowly fumbled around within his physician's satchel.

"The next day, I could barely move. I couldn't move. I thought I was dying, in fact. This…" Fenrir weakly gestured to his body, "…is significantly worse than that."

There was something sad behind Martis' smile. Fenrir couldn't meet his eyes, and glanced away.

"I can give you something for the pain, but you need to be drinking water whenever you have the chance."

Fenrir would have preferred an ale or a dozen, but no such luxury was available to him. No, Fenrir was still a prisoner, though his warden had changed.

Apparently, the shambling zombie that was post-incarcerated Fenrir was no use to his father. Instead, he'd been locked away in the cellars of the servants' housing in the de Trenton estate, though this was marginally more comfortable than his cell, he admitted. Namely, he had a bed. Too short, too narrow, but it was a bed.

And, three times a day, a Blue Adder would unbar his door and toss a heavy sack of food his way. Dried meat, dried fruit, dried… everything. Stuff fit for servants, but Fenrir tore into it with gusto. He'd gained weight, if not muscle, rapidly.

Fenrir spent a bit of time limbering up every day, moving his arms, stretching his injured knee. He'd even attempted to emulate his morning physical training regimen, from back when he'd been a guardsman. Not that he had much of an illusion of escaping his father's nest of adders. Just that, maybe, he figured that if he could regain some strength, he'd live a bit longer.

But he'd fallen out of the routine pretty quickly. Down here, where he was, it was too easy to lapse into lethargy. There was too much time to laze about. Too much time to ruminate about family.

Someone had also left a book in his little room. A thick, heavy fucker of a doorstop, the book was. Not something a servant would bother toting about, assuming that the servants in the de Trenton estate were literate. He knew his father preferred to employ the poor and unenlightened. It seemed charitable to some, but Fenrir knew that the less educated a person was, the less capable they were of stealing secrets. Regardless, no servant would be reading Trading Logistics and Logical Trading: Basics and Essentials for Domestic Trade by Eronean Envis. The very book that his father had shoved down his throat in his early teens.

So, even now, locked in a cellar and recovering from weeks of incarceration and malnourishment, Fenrir did not crack open the book. A tiny, useless rebellion.

A month, at least, he'd spent in this cellar, his only company being his dreary thoughts and the occasional silent Blue Adder. Interestingly, Ingla—his initial guardian, the woman charged with his safety and well-being—had never been among those who brought his food. No, it hadn't been until he'd recovered his energy that Ingla had made an appearance.

And put him into this sorry state that had brought Martis around.

"Here, take two of these every six or so hours." Martis handed a small cylinder to Fenrir, it containing several small, amber balls.

"What's this?" Fenrir asked.

"It's a concoction of my own design. Ground devil's claw root and innto flower, measured precisely and suspended in honey. These precise doses allow for standardized administration of the medicine, and prevent patients from overdosing or becoming addicted. I won't exactly call my tablets revolutionary—I have not the ego for that—but they certainly represent an advancement in modern medicine." Martis smiled widely.

"I am lucky to know such a brilliant man," Fenrir drawled. He popped four of the tablets into his mouth.

"Lucky to know me? No. Lucky to be alive after what happened to the little duke? Absolutely."

Fenrir grunted. "I'll drink to that."

"Only water. I would like to ask you for the details of that encounter…" The thick oaken door creaked open, "…but that will evidently have to wait for another time." Martis began to gather his things.

Ingla stepped into the room. Marched, was more like it. Fenrir stifled a moan. How could he fucking take more of this? There was nothing left of him. Nothing.

The small Sestrian woman, wearing her blue leathers, folded her arms and raised a single eyebrow. Fenrir struggled to his feet, straightening his back with a herculean effort. Even more of an effort were the crooked smile and the wink he offered.

"If it isn't the lovely sergeant, the sunshine of my life." Martis stifled a chuckle. Fenrir knew he'd pay for that, but he couldn't resist with Martis in the room. His friend always seemed impressed by his relentless prowess with women, and Fenrir did not want to disappoint.

"Physician. I expect that you will be needed by evening. And tomorrow. And the next day." She did not take her focused eyes off Fenrir. He tried not to shrink, though he felt much like a fly preparing to have its wings plucked off by a child.

"Indeed, Sergeant. Fenrir, my friend, I will see you this evening." He smirked, his braided beard swinging back and forth.

"And tomorrow. And the next day."

Chapter 16

Hackeneth was a marvel.

Hafgan had seen the seats of four duchies in Ardia. Florens, built upon a man-made island at the bend of the great Ingwine River, renowned for its arts and culture. Draston, wide and sprawling across the Singing Plains, called so because of the sound the wind made as it tore unheeded through the fertile farmlands. Hunesa, an amalgamation of a dozen cultures that had somehow formed its own identity. And, of course, Rostane, the city of stone that most closely tried to emulate life in the mountains.

And yet, none of them came close to the majesty that was Hackeneth. Though it contained less than half the population of any of those great cities, the largest Wasmer settlement was grand. Built at the throat of Limner and Phean, two of the highest mountains in the Tulanque Mountains, the surface of the city was a forest of sprawling stone dwellings that housed the lowest castes of the Carreg Da—the laborers, miners, and farmers. Most scraped together a living in the nearby fertile valleys or in the subterranean root farms. Others chopped and harvested the endless supply of trees throughout the mountains to create structures and warmth for the citizens of this place.

From the heart of Limner, Enorry Falls roared down from its heights, draining into the Fullane River. And though it wasn't evident to a casual observer, Hafgan knew that the power of the waterfall was harnessed in a dozen different ways to fuel the various enterprises of Hackeneth. Some was diverted into storage chambers that created running water for the more powerful castes, much of it heated in pipes from a constant burn of the coal found in abundance nearby. Waterwheels were used to power lifts and various mechanicals that helped the city run.

While half the city was aboveground, the other half—including the home of the warrior castes, the richer merchant caste, and the Dyn Doethas—was beneath Limner. In fact, most of the surface dwelling places were just visual shells, with many of the houses being connected by a series of well-marked tunnels. The Wasmer had excellent vision and preferred low-light areas, so the tunnels and caves of the mountains served them perfectly.

They were an underground people; thousands of years in the mountains had trained them to be that way. Yet, Hafgan knew that Wasmer had not always been bound to the darkness.

"Hafgan, Hafgan, light and tall." A hoarse voice, speaking the Wasmer tongue, scratching at Hafgan's ears.

Yurin peeled himself from the wall of a stone residence that lined the main street leading to the north side of the falls. He fell into step with Hafgan, who'd been walking vanguard of his budredda. They streamed behind him in even, regular ranks, having spent the night doing their best to clean up their appearances. They'd polished their weapons with snow and cleaned their clothes with rocks. They were still filthy and stinking, but a bit less so than the night before.

"You will be staying a step back from the lieutenant," growled Paston, gripping his spear with white fingers. He was Flam Madfall, born in the southern mountains and ever warring with the Carreg Da. Though his parents had left the clan years ago, Paston still retained his fear of Hafgan's birth clan. And, being budredda, he was doubly an outlander. A quarter of his men had never been in the mountains, and the other quarter wasn't Carreg Da. So, they were all on edge.

"You think to poke me with your little stick, budredda?" Yurin asked with a twisted smile. He placed a hand on the hilt of his sword over his shoulder; Hafgan knew that he could draw the giant thing with lightning speed.

"Paston, let it be. There will be those who wish us much greater harm than this man."

Paston relented with a grunt, though he retained his two-handed grip on his weapon.

"So, how do you find Hackeneth as an outlander? Does the beauty delight? Does the grandness fill you with awe? Are you terrorized by the sight of our temples?" Yurin gestured at a crumbling statue of Traisen, the god of war, that sat in front of a rough stone building signifying a neglected temple. Hafgan started at the disrepair; even a few years ago, the common folk would have clamored to get into that place. He remembered, on seventh day, his parents dragging him for miles to reach the temple, Yurin in tow, to pray for a safe lumber harvest. His family was of the laborer class, and cutting down trees was always a dangerous proposition. If Wasmer weren't crushed by falling trees, then limbs were destroyed in the transport of the wood. That was all, of course, assuming that neighboring tribes didn't raid the temporary lumber camps, killing or enslaving laborers for their own use.

"I find it... terribly dull," Hafgan said, letting himself speak the Wasmer tongue, the fluid language feeling unfamiliar on his tongue. "I find I missed it not at all."

"Nor has it missed you, my brother. So, it sounds like the humans suit you? Have you fucked any of their women? Have you become one of their little chiefs?" Yurin grinned his maddening grin.

"That's why I find myself here. I have become their king." Yurin narrowed his eyes, glaring at Hafgan before he realized it was a joke. Hafgan hadn't joked much when he had been growing up with his brother. There had been little to joke about.

They continued forward in silence. A strange silence, too. Hackeneth was typically as booming of a metropolis as the

199

Wasmer could sustain, with farmers, laborers, and merchants crowding the streets. Nothing compared to Rostane, of course, but nothing had prepared him for this echoing emptiness that filled the air. Hafgan saw perhaps half a dozen Wasmer going about their various businesses. One man was fixing his boots. A woman was dragging a sled full of sealed chamber pots. One child, a little girl, played with a stick doll between a couple of crates. But, they should have been fighting through crowds.

"Well, my king, perhaps you should not have returned," Yurin growled quietly. Hafgan wasn't sure if it was a friendly warning or a threat. Considering the setting, a threat was more likely.

"Like I said, no matter what happens, I serve my people first," Hafgan answered, scanning every person in sight, examining each of the windows.

So, when the attack came, it wasn't surprising.

The Wasmer stood up on the roof of a nearby building before drawing back his bow string. He was quick, this archer. But Hafgan attained his hedwicchen in an instant, feeling his anxieties and fears leaving him, the aches of the road and his injuries fading into an objective awareness. He was perfectly centered, controlled, and the world even seemed to slow around him.

The arrow left the bowstring and Hafgan heard the thwap of the string as it vibrated to a pause. The arrowhead was black, absorbing the light of the sun, and the feathers were a pure white that blended with the snow of the nearby peaks. The archer smiled, so certain he was of the course of his shot. He was probably the best archer they'd been able to drudge up, whoever it was who they'd sent to kill him.

It was a good shot, too. Hafgan was thinking that as he brought his spear around in a rapid blur, knocking the projectile aside with little apparent effort. His mind realized how dangerous that choice had been, how it would have been easier to throw himself flat, but, within his hedwicchen, he had few doubts about his prowess. Deflecting arrows had been part of his training. As had preventing assassination attempts.

So, he was also ready when the old man fixing his boot extracted a dagger and flung it at him. This time, he tossed his spear into one hand and batted aside the dagger with the back of his other, feeling the thing cut a hot line into his skin through his gloves. Enric and Alwyn rushed over to take down the man with a spear thrust. Two of his other men tried scaling the house from which the archer had launched his attack, but the man was already gone. Hafgan heard Paston shout an order for them to return.

Then he stood on the balls of his feet, waiting for Yurin to proceed with an attack of his own. But, though his brother had drawn his sword, he did not attack. In fact, his back was to Hafgan, looking for other attackers. So, apparently this attempt did not have the approval of the Dyn Doethas.

"Do they still travel in pairs?" Hafgan asked of his brother.

"You will find many of the old ways no longer hold," Yurin said, even as he rushed at the child playing with her stick doll. The girl had raised the thing to her lips, the hidden blowgun likely loaded with enough poison to stop Hafgan's heart in a moment. The poison's effectiveness never became a question, though, as Yurin's blade severed the girl's head from her shoulders. Even through his hedwicchen, Hafgan felt a surge of anger the likes of which he had never experienced.

"Peace, brother."

Yurin turned rapidly, seeing the look in Hafgan's eyes. "She intended to kill you."

"She was a girl. A child." Hafgan retained his hedwicchen, but just barely. This child, this girl, had had no choice in this matter, certainly. She'd been told what she needed to do, and now paid the price. But, that was Hackeneth. That was the Carreg Da. That was the Wasmer. Hierarchical to the point of sacrificing children in service of killing an unknown adversary.

When he'd been young, Hafgan had thought he could fix that. Now, he only sought to save it.

"Like I said, the old ways no longer hold. Remember your training. 'If one seeks your blood, they are the enemy. Even if they be a friend.'"

Hafgan remembered those words being intoned by Taern a number of times.

"I have no friends here," he said, resting his spear back over his shoulder and continuing forward toward Enorry Falls.

***

When he was young, Hafgan was idealistic.

Even before his parents sold him to the Dyn Doethas, Hafgan always had grand hopes for a better life. Working in the lumber camps—despite the danger of dismemberment and death—was fairly humdrum. The children primarily gathered kindling and stripped fallen trees of their branches before the trees were hauled off for processing. Yurin and Hafgan would tear through their work for the day and then go on adventures.

They would climb nearby peaks and swim through sub-arctic lakes, ever daring each other to greater feats of bravery. Yurin was the older, bigger, and stronger brother, and he could always climb higher, dive deeper, and jump further. Hafgan could barely count the times that he nearly died, plummeting off cliffs or nearly tumbling from the tricky point that was halfway to the top of Enorry Falls. But, Yurin would grab him at the last moment, and when the shaking terror passed, they would laugh in the manner of invincible, immortal children before mindlessly risking their lives again.

And, like an immortal child, Hafgan saw himself raising his own status. He would, based simply on his prowess and courage, raise his family from the laborer caste to the warrior caste and earn both glory and a comfortable life for his family. His mother deserved a life that was easier than group-hauling fallen trees through the snow, or cooking great pots of tuber-heavy stew to feed forty laborers. And his father deserved hands that were less calloused, cracked, and bleeding from swinging an axe day after day.

So, Hafgan thought to eventually raise himself to a warrior and then a war leader. Castes were fairly impermeable, but there were stories of great heroes doing so. Maybe, then, he could wield some authority over the Wasmer, gaining some influence and creating change. Maybe he'd even eliminate the caste system—a dream of his. Though Yurin was his better in all things physical, Hafgan was quicker and stronger than the other boys his age. They would gather at night and wrestle, the most common sport of the Wasmer. He rarely experienced trouble in subduing the other children, and always stopped just short of hurting them. His precision and control made him confident that he would, one day, become a war leader.

So, that day when Taern Llegyn, a gleaming Dyn Doethas warrior who was seemingly ten feet tall, showed up at their camp and purchased he and Yurin from his parents, Hafgan wasn't too upset. It was his chance to attain his destiny.

That had been a long time ago.

Twenty-five years had done little to change Taern. Instead of a pure black, his hair was streaked with silver. His facial hair was still trimmed fairly short with just a couple of braids flowing downward. Though the Dyn Doethas would never shave his face in the style of the budredda, he knew that fewer handholds meant less risk in a fight. His face was more weathered, certainly, and his bulky musculature had given way to a more slender, aged strength, but Taern, father of the Haearn Doethas, was hale and hearty still.

Hafgan, escorted alone to an isolated chamber deep in the Laenor—the palatial living quarters of the Dyn Doethas that sat deep behind Enorry Falls—held his hedwicchen as tightly as he could. He wanted to bury any emotions that he might feel at the sight of this man. He was rarely prone to rage or fear, but this man standing before him had the capability of eliciting both.

Taern surveyed Hafgan, his chilly blue eyes cutting through Hafgan like a mountain wind near the peaks. Hafgan carefully met his gaze, keeping his eyes partially blurred to avoid the intensity of his teacher and tormenter's attention. His hedwicchen was complete, but even so, some remnants of memory tugged at his consciousness, so strongly did Taern loom in his past.

There was a crushing sound behind him, causing Hafgan to instinctively bounce to the balls of his feet, ready for an attack. His head whipped around, one hand held toward Taern defensively and the other ready to fend off an assault. But it was merely the door slamming as the guards left the two of them alone.

Hafgan fixed his gaze back on Taern, who was now smiling a disarming grin, his arms spread wide in a greeting.

"Welcome home, my son," he said in the smooth voice of a practiced orator. It almost sounded authentic to Hafgan, though he knew better. This man could manipulate his own emotions and the emotions of others with as little effort as Hafgan would use to jump over a small creek.

"Arwein," intoned Hafgan, recognizing Taern with the Wasmer title of 'Master'. Whatever was between them, Taern had still earned that right.

"The people of Hackeneth have missed you. I have missed you," Taern said, his face growing wistful. Sad, even.

"I find that unlikely, Arwein," Hafgan said, switching to Ardian. Taern briefly frowned at the sound of the neighboring country's tongue before again adopting a grin.

"Well, perhaps the former is false. But I can honestly tell you… the latter is true." His Ardian was certainly rougher than Hafgan's, but his words were precise. Everything Taern did was a practice in precision. "Hafgan, I have known you since you were a pup, an impetuous boy of five or six winters. Twenty years, I worked with you. Twenty years, I taught you. Twenty years, I learned from you. With what we have been through, my son, I would consider you family. Or even a friend."

Hafgan remembered the Taern of five years ago on the day of his departure, covered in blood and quivering with anger, cursing Hafgan with the strength of every false Wasmer god. There was no love lost between the two of them.

"Twenty years, you deprived me," Hafgan corrected him, his voice carrying the monotone of his hedwicchen "Twenty years, you tortured me. Twenty years, you lied to me. You can pretend, Arwein, that there was a purpose to all of it. You can pretend that the terrors your forced upon me were in my best interest, for some greater purpose. But you would be lying, Arwein. For, when it came down to it, it was all for you. For you to command. For you to control." Hafgan was now in a state of relaxed readiness, prepared for any eventuality. The Taern of old would never suffer such insolence.

Instead of responding directly, Taern stared at Hafgan for a minute with a brief appraisal before sighing a deep sigh. He gestured to an austere, poorly-carved chair and took a seat himself in one opposite. Hafgan tentatively sat down across from him, wondering at the trick.

"You live too much in the hedwicchen, my son," Taern observed, changing the subject. "There are dangers in that."

There were, indeed, dangers. The dulling of emotions, even when not in the hedwicchen. The inability to feel strong emotions, even in times of great need. And a lack of self-preservation; when one did not feel fear, one might take unnecessary risks. Reflecting on his last five years—from the objective cocoon of the hedwicchen—Hafgan knew that he'd risked life on dozens of occasions, the most recent being his fight with Yanso. Or maybe his first encounter with Yurin... turning his back on his dangerous, unpredictable, quite possibly insane brother. No, it would have been deflecting an arrow with his spear when attacked by the assassins.

He'd been damned by returning to Hackenath in the first place.

"I am what you made me, Arwein," Hafgan said in his best monotone. Taern crossed his legs and leaned forward into his hands. It was not a defensible posture. Hafgan wondered whether it was a show of submission, disrespect, or just his older master getting soft and forgetful. Looking into his clear, azure gaze, however, Hafgan knew it wasn't the latter.

"Hafgan, release your hedwicchen. Look at me and tell me what you feel," Taern said, his voice sounding almost eager.

"No." Hafgan would not put himself at this man's mercy for even a moment.

"Please, my son. I know you do not trust me. But I swear to you, on my own life, that I mean you no harm." The only life that

Taern would care about would be his own, and Wasmer tended to take their oaths seriously. Even Taern.

Especially Taern.

Hafgan let his hedwicchen fade. The focus—on everything and nothing—left him. The vast emptiness that allowed him to remain objective, factual, and intensely focused was suddenly gone. The complete and utter understanding of his own capabilities, and the ability to weigh a dozen possibilities and calculate the probability of success, gone.

And his emotions slammed back into his brain.

He felt his teeth baring as he looked at Taern, a surge of burning anger building in his chest. He clenched his fists so hard that the bones audibly popped, and he tensed every muscle in his body, preparing to lunge. Apparently, his overuse of the hedwicchen had not dulled his emotions to the extent that he could no longer feel anger in the face of his Arwein.

In the face of the man who'd made Hafgan kill his parents.

"I... I..." Hafgan sputtered, lost in fury. It was almost as if twenty-five years of repressed rage and hate hit him all at once. Perhaps another side effect of living too much in the hedwicchen. "I should rip your throat from your body and fill the bellies of your victims with your blood. I... I should break each of your bones and toss you from the heights of Enorry Falls, polluting the water with your taint. I..." He almost felt lightheaded from restraining his urge, from continuing to voice his desires without acting on them. His discipline held, but just barely. He was here on a mission, he tried to remind himself. He still wanted what was best for his people, even if his people would rather not take credit for his existence.

Taern had the dignity to appear grim, though unafraid. "Before you kill me, I ask you to look deeper. Tell me, what have I experienced? What am I feeling?" Taern asked, his tone holding an unusual note.

The rational part of Hafgan fought back his burning desire to wrap his hands around this man's neck, the animal instinct to make him pay. His earliest lessons, before he had mastered the hedwicchen, had been focused on understanding emotions. People fought with emotions—anger, fear, joy—and understanding and using them was essential for combat. But so was reading the emotions of the common people, and knowing how to tug on fears and insecurities, as well as their faith in the gods, to manipulate them into becoming willing slaves.

Taern had tested them, the ten Haearn Doethas pupils, by forcing them to read the emotions and experiences of people brought into the Laenor. Merchants, laborers, miners, and even some warriors. The pupils had been asked to simply observe these people, alone or in a conversation with Taern, and then describe what each person was feeling. And not just through a 'This merchant seemed pleased,' but in a more detailed examination, such as 'The recent famine has the merchant anxious for the future of his family, but he is simultaneously excited that his biggest competitor is out of business.' There'd been leaps of inference that needed to be made, using a broad understanding of emotional tells and a deep understanding of cultural and environmental factors.

Emotions, Hafgan knew, could only truly be read outside of the hedwicchen. Part of understanding emotions in others was seeing what emotions they elicited within the self. One cannot truly understand rage or depression simply as an observer, bereft of empathy.

Taern's mouth twitched slightly upward, just on one side, as he observed Hafgan's war against his own anger. The brief smile, though, flickered and died; it was forced. An act.

Hafgan examined Taern's face in detail, top to bottom. He hadn't seen the man in five years. On the surface, Taern appeared largely unchanged, but Hafgan could see a growing crease between his eyebrows denoting an increase in general anxiety. He also noticed the six-inch-long scar—which Hafgan had put on Taern's forehead himself—and that it seemed to stand out against more worry-wrinkles. Taern had always been so confident, and though he'd sought to revolutionize Wasmer culture, he'd rarely appeared to worry.

His eyes, though, gave it away. The dark circles, illuminated in the low light, denoted little sleep. And, his eyes seemed... they seemed clouded, sad. He looked at Hafgan the way that a parent would gaze upon a neglected child after realizing that that child was filled only with hate. It was a guilt there. A shame. Remorse.

It could be faked, Hafgan knew. Taern was a master manipulator, able to simulate emotions as accurately as one of the great actors in the Ardian theater. The Wasmer did not have any sort of theater; the harsh conditions of the Tulanques lent themselves better to sports requiring physical prowess, and stone craft, than the fine arts that the humans likened to culture. Once, out of sheer curiosity, Hafgan had taken some of his ill-earned gains from The House and gone to the Penton Theater, built during the reign of Samuel Penton the Second. The building, meant to add culture to compete with Florens and some much-needed, curved architecture to the blocky Rostane, had been packed full that night. The great Manis Deon had been playing the role of the king in Thantos' Dream, and he always drew a crowd.

Hafgan vividly remembered Deon playing the titular King Barros Thantos. The man had commanded the stage, literally demanding attention. When Thantos' father had passed, breathing his dying wish that his son would hold the warring duchies together, Hafgan had felt the unfamiliar urge to cry. When Thantos had married Marin Thatcher, forming an alliance with the once strong Jecustan empire and finding love at the same time, his heart had leapt for joy. And, when Thantos had been assassinated by a pasnes alna, in a great theatrical conflagration, Hafgan had known real anger against the mages.

Taern was better than Deon.

He could make a mother smile as he took her child away for a few paltry garrs. He could deliver a sentence for execution, with the condemned thanking him before being speared through the heart to have the blood drained into the waiting mouth of his other victims. He could make warriors' hearts leap before sending them on a suicide mission against a rival tribe. He could convince a man to kill his parents in cold blood.

Hafgan, in his rage, wanted to believe that Taern was manipulating him. That he was faking this evident regret, trying to regain Hafgan's loyalty for some nefarious plot. But, somewhere deep within himself, he knew that Taern was telling the truth. He knew that Taern was truly exhausted, and truly regretful.

Hafgan sat back in his chair, the sharp edge of anger dulling for the moment.

"Tell me, Taern. What has happened here?"

Taern smiled wide, either relieved at not being bludgeoned or excited that his ploy had worked. "Little news reaches you people in Rostane, eh?"

"To Rostane, there is little of value in the mountains aside from iron ore and silver."

"Typical humans. Well, I suppose we don't make the effort at facilitating communication with our neighbors to the east, do we? No matter. It has been years since you vowed never to return. How do you find Hackeneth?"

"Aside from being filled with assassins?" Taern raised a questioning eyebrow at this. "It seems emptier. More...

210

dilapidated. I noticed a temple to Traisen that seemed to have fallen into disrepair, and there's refuse in the streets."

"Dilapidated? Your vocabulary has certainly improved, my son. But, that is an accurate description. Faith in the old gods has waned in recent years. Since you left, in fact."

Hafgan wondered how much he'd had to do with that. Plenty, he would wager. But there was more here to discover.

For the first time, Hafgan looked around the room where they were meeting, deep within the Laenor. It wasn't what Hafgan would have expected from a Dyn Doethas, from the de facto ruler of his caste and the founder of the Haearn Doethas, a new caste that blended together knowledge, faith, and military prowess. Taern's chambers were rough-cut rock, having none of the painstakingly-carved stone murals that graced the walls of most of the Laenor. Furniture was scarce; aside from the rough two chairs they occupied and a table, Hafgan could only see a small, lumpy-looking bed jutting out of an adjoining room. Most stunning was that Hafgan could not see Tarn's ornately cut spear, Torri Carreg—Stone Breaker—anywhere in the room. He had never seen Taern without the supposedly magical, but more likely creatively-named, weapon.

There was only one explanation.

"You lost control," Hafgan said, quietly.

Tarn barked a bitter laugh. "I lost control, yes, with no small thanks to you. Your proclamation at the Reckoning that day, made in anger and fear, sparked something within the people. It sparked something within Leyr Trystan. It may be the first time that he ever agreed with you."

Leyr had been one of the other Haearn Doethas, slightly younger than Hafgan and a constant rival. Where Hafgan was fast, Leyr was faster. Whereas Hafgan was strong, Leyr was stronger. Whereas Hafgan was clever, Leyr was brilliant. And so it had irked Leyr to no end that Hafgan somehow beat him in sparring as often as not, and that Hafgan had fallen into the role of Tarn's favorite. Of course, Leyr had never known that being the favorite left Hafgan with significantly more scars.

"What was it that you said that day, Hafgan? Do you remember?" Tarn asked, his eyes now burning with intensity.

"That the Dyn Doethas have no right to rule…" Yes, Hafgan remembered the rebellious words shouted during the Reckoning. Words echoed in the Cylch, particularly when the victorious fighter, standing tall and covered in blood, demanded attention. Taern had been on one knee, weaponless and furious, while Leyr had been sprawled out, seemingly unconscious.

"The Dyn Doethas have no right to rule," repeated Tarn, almost consideringly. "You know, they never really and truly ruled. That's why I needed you, Hafgan. That's why I needed the Haearn Doethas. Those war leaders were so petty, fighting one another and scraping together their own little domains within the Carreg Da, within the other clans. Starting wars simply to retain their tiny dominions. Certainly, we were able to guide and influence, but we never had truly ruled."

"You lied and manipulated. You changed the histories. You spoke with the voices of the gods to send good people to their deaths," Hafgan reminded him, leaning forward intently. He had seen evidence of these lies with his own eyes, when he had once had the daring to infiltrate the forbidden libraries of the Laenor. Books of histories that might as well have been children's stories or fairytales, so different were they from the supposed truths that Hafgan had heard all his life.

"And, for all that, we still never truly had control," Taern said sardonically. He rubbed at his temples in a practiced motion that belied his nerves and anxiety. "Hafgan, I say this to you now. You were right, that day. We never had the right to rule. The Dyn Doethas should never have been in charge."

"That is quite the admission. You finally believe that you cannot lead the people through lies and manipulation?"

"Hafgan, do you truly think me such a monster? I had always been appalled at the lengths the Dyn Doethas went to in order to eke out a little bit of extra influence, in order to rally the people behind a flawed common cause. Did you know that they had actually initiated a project to climb to the heights and create a gate to block Enorry Falls? To control the very life blood of Hackeneth as a sign from the gods that the people were on the wrong path? Three dozen enslaved laborers from the other tribes were even sent to climb to the peak and begin construction. Half died on the way up, and the other half were killed when the project proved unsuccessful." Taern stood up abruptly and began to pace. Looking at the polish on the floor, Hafgan could see this was a well-trodden path for his former Arwein.

"I would not put it past them, certainly. They have done worse." Hafgan thought of what he had read in the libraries. Dyn Doethas, hiding food and letting people starve in order to start a war with the tribes of Ardialos. Assassinating one of their most influential war leaders, Arwinyadd Anerin, for his hubris, and blaming a human expedition. Making up gods to be worshipped. Building the religion of the people around lies. Traisen, the god of war, was as real as the nighttime stories that humans told about Wasmer.

"It's why I created the Haearn Doethas. Trying to build a caste of Wasmer who could have the physical rule—through martial prowess—and also the knowledge to make wise choices with that power. Perhaps, then, we would not have to lie to our people and we could actually be something, besides simple mountain dwellers."

213

"With you pulling the strings of this caste, of course," Hafgan snarled. He had heard this diatribe before.

Taern paused in his pacing and turned to Hafgan. "Providing guidance. I am not so evil as past Dyn Doethas. I know the histories. I would not let us make the same mistakes."

"How many despots and dictators have said that in the past?" Hafgan asked, rising to his own feet so as to not be at a disadvantage.

"Every single one, I would imagine. But I would have been different," Taern said, not without some sense of irony. "But, as you said, the Dyn Doethas have no right to rule. We have confused our histories so that we barely know what is true and what is not. Sometimes, my son, I pray to Traisen or Oletta, actually believing that they are real, that my prayers could be heard! We are entrapped in a cycle of lies and mistruths; the people will never be able to handle the reality. I would have tried to erase our fake histories rather than contradict them, starting something new for our people. With your help."

Hafgan longed to attain his hedwicchen, and to eliminate this strange mix of rage and sympathy, hatred and love, that he felt toward his teacher and tormenter.

"Arwein, tell me what happened," Hafgan repeated.

Taern's face screwed up for a moment, taken with some strong emotion.

"You left Hackeneth, as was your right. I admit, I was furious at first, seeing it as a betrayal of me. A betrayal of our people. After all, you had finally achieved the first step of what we sought to do!" Taern clenched his fist for a second before releasing it. "But I realized that you were right. I had lied to and manipulated not just you, but everyone."

"What made you realize your mistake?" Hafgan asked warily.

"The fact that Leyr agreed with you, at least with the sentiment. That we should not rule. After you left, the people were stunned. Not because you were well-known, but for the very fact that you weren't. The fact that you seemed to emerge from the mountain, defeat all comers in the tournament, including me, and then turn down such power. It was an act of either insanity or divine intellect. Coupled with your proclamation, people began to lose faith in us."

The Haearn Doethas had largely been training in secret, and at the Reckoning within the Cylch, they'd emerged to battle with the other best-known warleaders and challengers. Almost to a man, the Haearn Doethas had won their matches, ultimately ending up battling each other. Which is how Hafgan had ended up facing off against Leyr, under the stone and sky of the great colosseum.

Hafgan shrugged. "I am surprised that I was able to have such an impact with a few words that I spoke, which were, like you said, spoken in anger and fear."

Taern chuckled. "You were just a piece. There were others working against the Dyn Doethas for some time. Strong-willed warleaders. The richest of the merchants. Embittered and jealous priests. Rian played a role."

Hearing Rian's name outside his hedwicchen brought a new surge of emotions to Hafgan. Luckily, shame and guilt were old friends.

"So, I initiated this avalanche, and others took advantage of it. The Dyn Doethas lost the respect of the people. They lost control of the people. And Leyr worked with them to undermine you," Hafgan concluded, guessing at the outcome.

Taern stared at the ceiling, exhaling deeply.

"No, it was worse than that, my son. At this point, I would welcome disrespect or lack of control. Either could be regained

215

with effort. By Traisen and Oletta and Ewen and the rest of the damned false gods, that would be preferable."

Taern leveled a look at Hafgan, and it was one that made him shiver. It was a sort of broken intensity in his former Arwein's face, like a shattered mirror reflecting the light of the sun.

"I am the last of the Dyn Doethas. There was a purge."

Chapter 17

Merigold was not well-traveled. Granted, she had finally left the Duckling and seen two of the great cities of Ardia. Hunesa, the ramshackle Crossroads of Nations, with a dozen different clashing styles of architecture matching the myriad nationalities walking the streets. It was a patchwork quilt of awful. Florens had been a beauty viewed from a distance, over fields choked with mud-covered bodies. Now, it was likely a shadowed ruin of itself, sacked by the voracious and undisciplined armies of Rostane.

Both, though, had been better than the shithole that was Polanice. Some cities could boast of having been great at some point in their pasts, retaining a bit of gold visible after a polish. Other cities could say that theirs was an industrial prosperity—not necessarily clean, but instead effective and productive. Polanice, the port on the southernmost point of the Rafonese peninsula, could say neither.

A victim of constant hurricanes and floodings, the city smelled like a sopping sewer. The roads, their pavement buried in mud and muck from years of shifting waters, were treacherous. The wooden houses stank of rot and looked to be in disrepair, and the people were a fit for their surroundings. The dark-skinned Rafonese dominated the streets, loitering or walking about as if it were more pleasurable to stand amidst the falling snow than amid the mildew of their homes, which perhaps it was.

But, the temperature and the weather were much harsher here than in Ardia, and Merigold shivered in her heavy coat. She glanced around for Lisan in the small market, acutely noticing that dark looks were being shot in her direction from the locals. Meri felt trapped, though they were in the open air.

"There is nothing," said Lisan, appearing from the crowd of suspicious Polanicers. Ill'nath, at Merigold's shoulder, held one hand on his club, eying anyone who came nearby. The cityfolk

217

were wary of them, sometimes glaring at the travelers with unadultered hatred. Their reactions did not reach the point of violence, but Meri thought that had a lot to do with Ill'Nath and his giant club.

"How can there not be a single horse and cart anywhere in this city?" Merigold asked, feeling distinct unease in this market square. They needed transportation for their trip to Agricorinor; walking would not be an option in this snow.

"Oh, there are plenty of horses and even more carts. But there is no desire to sell them to us."

"Why?" Merigold demanded. They were foreigners, but they had been nothing but respectful since landing in the city five days ago. There were dozens of ships at port, though few of these were from Saiwen, which Meri attributed to both the civil war and the fact that it was storm season. The Graceful Whale had just missed the worst of a weather front, but a couple of ships had limped in, ragged and lopsided, in the last couple of days. Even with that, Meri thought it strange that they had seen very few light-skinned Saiwenese around, Polanice being one of the only major ports for a hundred miles.

They called this place the Gateway to Rafon, though Polanice made a very poor first impression.

"Suspicions," said Lisan, turning at the sound of abrupt shouting and catcalls. She fingered the strung bow slung over her back and Meri gripped her dagger, looking toward the disruption.

A wash of white swept the road as the put-upon crowd began to disperse angrily. The only sight of cleanliness that Polanice could boast was their city guard, the Onelan, which translated roughly to 'the Sun Guard.' Two dozen men in pristine uniforms marched forward in white leather armor, white coats, and white helmets, all trimmed in silver. A handful of officers followed behind them on horseback. Some of the Polanicers flung mud at the Sun Guard; they were apparently not well-liked by the poorer, dirtier residents of the city.

Like many others, Ill'Nath, Lisan, and Merigold pressed themselves against the ice-rimmed facades of the nearby storefronts. Merigold covered her head with her hood as best she could; her platinum blonde hair made her stand out like a whore in a Yetranian chapel. Ill'Nath, though, took no such precautions, and stared at the guards with open hostility. Meri knew little about the man, but she had heard that Pintan islanders were generally resistant to authority, having no centralized government of their own. Ill'Nath did not appear to be an exception. His pale skin, and the fact that he kept his massive arms bare despite the cold, drew no shortage of attention.

Merigold held her breath, hoping the patrol would pass without incident.

"Bu nedi?" called one of the Sun Guard, speaking Rafonese. "Soluk derile." The column halted abruptly as the townsfolk continued to scatter, as if having a sixth sense for conflict—as crowds often did. The guard had a reputation for being brutal, and few would think to stand against them. Merigold had the same thought, but trapped as they were against the shoddy buildings, it was a simple matter for the guard to flank them.

An officer dismounted and pushed through—the only one of the Sun Guard lacking a helmet. He could only be described as pristine. White teeth were a stark contrast to his coal-black skin, a smile turning up the corners of his mouth. His beard was trimmed perfectly, and the hair on his head was perfectly greased so not a single strand stood askew. His young, handsome features were as symmetrical as a duck egg.

"Pintan, hand off that crude weapon," he commanded, speaking Ardian with scarcely an accent. "Thank you. And you,

Ardian, do not think you can draw that bow and shoot more than a couple before we skewer you."

Lisan subtly stepped in front of Merigold, trying to shield Meri's face with her broad body. A few other Rafonese were trapped by the guards, so Lisan may have thought to keep Meri yet hidden.

"No one need be skewered, lord..." Lisan said with a smile, not exactly brightening her ugly features.

"Captain, not 'lord.' Captain Curan Tinto, at your service. And you are, my light-skinned sister? What are you doing here?"

Lisan ignored the first question. "We are just visiting."

Tinto chuckled, a refined and calculated laugh that actually sounded authentic and would probably have been contagious given different circumstances. "No one would visit this shit-heap of a city, traveler. How did you get here? On which ship was your berth?"

"We arrived via The Graceful Whale just recently," Lisan answered slowly, as if she was trying to orchestrate a lie but couldn't quite get the music right.

Tinto pinched his nose dramatically and took two steps backwards. "Oh, so smugglers. And yet, I hear there were no goods offloaded from your boat. Few ships travel from Saiwen with nothing to offer but a few measly passengers. Why, then, do you find yourself in our particularly sodden asshole of the world?"

Lisan began to say something in response, but was cut off as a heated argument drew everyone's attention. Merigold glanced to her right, trying to be circumspect, but that was difficult to achieve when a man was being brutalized scant feet away.

A Sun Guard, his chubby but vicious features evident beneath his helmet, shoved an older townsperson against the facade of the buildings for a second time. The Sun Guard barked something, gesturing with violent hands, and the trapped townsperson only mumbled something in return. His fear was palpable, and Meri tried to edge away, but found herself with no room.

The townsperson's fear and meek response only seemed to enrage the guard.

Without any preamble, the white-armored brute yanked his knife from his belt and started hacking away at the townsman's raised arms. The victim howled, his voice echoing through the dirty streets as his face twisted in helpless agony. Before long, the man fell into a pool of blood—not quite dead, but crying and whimpering at his arms being gouged to the bone. The Sun Guard wiped his sword on the inside of his own blood-freckled white coat before moving back into a cluster of other guards, his weathered face twisted in disgust. A small group of these men started shouting animatedly at one another in an apparent argument.

Meri's own cloak was flecked with blood, but she dared not look up. She dared not make a move to help the fallen man, though he writhed at her feet. She was near panic, but could do nothing.

Tinto barked some orders in Rafonese and the men ambled back into formation. He didn't seem particularly perturbed by the horrid maiming of the man, who lay curled up like a dying spider. Rather, he frowned slightly at the lack of acuity with which his men responded to his commands. He turned back to Lisan, shaking his head and speaking as if she was a confidant.

"Things are going to the pit, lately. The men are keyed up and anxious, quick to anger and quick to strike. Only fear of punishment keeps any semblance of discipline, and, to be honest, I've barely the energy to keep them in line. And really, I can't blame them. War is at our doorstep, a war against an enemy we don't understand. An enemy we never can see."

"What does that have to do with us?"

"Well, if we don't know who we are fighting, how do we know we aren't fighting you?" The logic stank of paranoia, but Tinto's perfect face was deadly serious. "Our leaders have been found dead in their beds, bodies pierced by burning blades. Our ships—merchant and war alike—return as bits of lumber and the odd limb washed up on shore. Our people rise up in dissent, treating our noble order with disrespect and the occasional act of violence. We've had to become less tolerant to discourage such acts."

Lisan's mouth was open, and Ill'Nath continued to glare at anyone who thought to glance at him. Lisan glanced at the fallen man and licked her lips. "This has been happening for what—weeks? Months? We only just arrived."

"Yes, but—let us state the obvious—you are skinned differently from us, which makes you both suspects and targets. I'm afraid that, regardless of your nebulous reason for visiting this end of the world, you will need to come with us, as much for your protection as ours. You will be a guest at the Opal Tower." Tinto snapped his fingers, and four Sun Guards stepped forward with binding ropes held ready in their gloved hands.

Ill'Nath did not hesitate. He whipped his great club around with such speed that the hapless Sun Guard before him couldn't blink before his head collapsed with the sodden sound of a fallen pumpkin. Before anyone else could act, Ill'Nath crushed the ribs of a second man and was moving with purpose toward a third.

Lisan seemed shocked by the unexpected violence, but decided to follow Ill'Nath's lead by slashing at the throat of the white-coated guard in front of her with a frantic swing of her short sword. It created enough distance that she managed to find the space to launch an arrow at the face of the next guard. The man turned his head just in time, and the projectile was deflected by his helm.

"Damn," she muttered, grabbing another arrow from the omnipresent quiver at her side. She levelled her bow, but did not initially release.

The Sun Guard recovered and mobilized quickly enough, forming a semi-circle of bared steel facing off against the two warriors, a cloaked Merigold, a dying man, and a half dozen trapped Polanicers. It was then that Meri noticed she was gasping, sucking in air like a fish on the beach.

"That was poorly done, islander." Tinto spat from behind the safety of the sword wall. "Truly no harm would have come to you through detainment. Now, though, you have murdered three Sun Guard! Obviously, the result is a very painful, and very public, execution."

The dying man coughed and sputtered at Merigold's feet. A bloody hand grasped at her leg, contacting her skin. Without a thought, Merigold drew the maenen of the man.

In an instant, her breathing was calmed and she regained her control. The man was dying. What she was doing was a mercy.

And, to save their lives, Merigold Hinter needed to kill again. She drew more deeply of the man's lifeforce.

She played with three gorgeous children in the mud.

She saw one of those children dying of a wasting illness.

She saw a second slip off the roof of a building, breaking her neck.

She saw the third, a near-grown woman, leaving Polanice, heading north without a word of farewell.

Tears streaming down her face, Merigold unleashed the stolen maenen of the dying man. She shaped it into red, glowing plates and launched these into the crowd of Sun Guardsmen. The first plate cut halfway through a man's midsection, the hissing smell of burning flesh filling the air. It struck a second man in the leg, cutting the thing halfway off before losing its power and falling into the mucky snow with an explosion of steam.

A second plate was lost to her vision the second it left her hands, but the shrieks and screams told her that the thing caused an equal amount of havoc and death.

She propelled a third plate forward, straight toward the beautiful face of Captain Tinto. His reflexes were lightning, and he slashed the burning disk out of the air. But, unlike on The Graceful Whale, the plate did not shatter. Merigold had adapted her formula.

Knocked slightly off-course, the edge of the hardened plate caught Tinto in the cheek, sending him reeling into the ground with a bellowing howl. The spent plate killed at least one other man and injured a third before dissipating.

Still, a dozen or more Sun Guard circled, swords glinting in the wan light of day. Gritting her teeth, Meri drew to form another plate—but the maenen was gone. The well was empty. The old townsperson had died, either from her leeching, his wounds, or both.

Meri felt a shivering exhaustion take hold, her legs feeling as if she had worked three nights without sleep, but she dared not fall. These men, broken, bleeding, and scared, would be the end of them if she did. Instead, she hid her exhaustion like a predator, moving her hands to remove her hood and unveil her face.

This, like everything in life, was a test.

She stoically observed the path of destruction, the injured and dying. Tinto was being hoisted up by one of his lieutenants, while other wounded lay untended in pools of their own blood. Meri glanced down at the fuel for her destruction, the now dead man with the lost daughters. She narrowed her eyes at the Sun Guard arrayed before her.

"Flee," she said, softly. The men seemed paralyzed, some still holding swords raised and half preparing for an assault while others openly wept.

"Flee, and you will be spared." A little more volume. The Sun Guard, those still standing, shuffled backwards. Meri felt Ill'Nath at her left shoulder, and Lisan the Arrow at her right.

"Flee! If you linger or pursue us, your end with be inestimably worse than those on the ground. Flee, and return to your families!" She refrained a choking sob and bared her teeth like a predator.

"Flee or die!" Merigold howled then, in a voice that was nothing like her own. The Sun Guard, and any townsfolks who'd been trapped by them, scattered as if the demons of Pandemonium were nipping at their heels. In scant moments, only the dead and mortally wounded still remained. With a chill, Meri realized that she'd meant her words. If any had lingered, she would have found a way to end their lives. If they pursued, she would see them dead.

She dropped to her knees, further staining her coat and leggings with coppery blood and sickly brown mud.

"Ill'Nath, you are a dolt," Lisan muttered with little enthusiasm. "We had a path out without violence. You need to follow my lead, not vice versa." The huge islander merely grunted in return, busy wiping his club on the cloak of a fallen Sun Guard. "Merigold, that was… that was effective."

For a killer, being effective was at least a compliment.

"Are you… okay? We need to move," Lisan said, touching Meri's shoulder for a scant moment.

"Yes, give me a moment," she said quietly.

225

She knelt in the various slimes and tried to wipe her mind free of the memories of the fallen townsperson, and of her own feelings about what she had just done. It should have been getting easier.

Dear fucking Yetra, it had better not ever get easier.

The frantic neighing of a horse caught her attention. Meri rose on legs that felt like melting ice. Five horses, chestnut mares all, were lashed to a low fence nearby. The Sun Guard had left so quickly that the officer mounts had been left unattended.

"Well, at the very least, we have solved our transportation problem," Merigold said, forcing a wan smile onto her face. They'd have to move quickly and gather the rest of their party; it wouldn't be long until the Sun Guard gathered enough force and courage to come back for her. Merigold stepped over a severed arm, with her two protectors at her shoulders.

On to Agricorinor.

Interlogue: Wrath

"You are looking well. Your nerring has recovered far past what I had expected, and your maenen shines as bright as the stars in the night sky.

"Oh yes, it is a beautiful night. The leaves are beginning to vacate the trees, giving a clearer vision of the stars. Here, so far from any cities, the view is not obscured by man-made imitations of light. No, each constellation glows with power, and it brings joy to my heart. When you have existed as long as I have, it is a rare thing that can still elicit strong emotions. The stars, natural beauty, always stirs something inside of me. As do you, sweetling.

"It has been too long since I have seen you, and it has truly been my loss. But, I can see resistance in your eyes, and your muscles strain at your bonds. Your natural aggression may be beginning to surface as your nerring shrinks and decays, but I think not. I think that you begin to resent your presence here. You, who were so enthusiastic to serve me earlier.

"Wrath does not become you, sweetling. I know this is a vice of yours, perhaps your only vice. But, when wrathful, your intentions were always to protect those close to you, like your Merigold. In a case like that, is this truly a vice? I will leave that to the Taneos. I would believe that wrath can be justified, and perhaps even improve our world, so long as the instrument of such wrath does not lose perspective.

"Early on, I did lose perspective. When I left Aquine, I swore vengeance against those who had destroyed everything that I knew. Even not knowing who they were, and, of course, being completely unsuited to dolling out such vengeance. Who was I—a teenage girl who had never touched a weapon—to punish those who had the power to kill and imprison thousands of people? Nonetheless, logic was not a consideration. I was not in control of my emotions, so overwhelmed had I become in the aftermath of Aquine.

"Amorum was impressive, as ever. Though the vengeance was mine, it was reflected in his eyes. He gathered what survivors there were and armed them with whatever weapons were left. Many were afraid, but Amorum, the great orator that he was, doled out courage like an army cook doles out food.

"We set out, with a makeshift army of several hundred with no fighting experience… but with a great deal of resolve. We did not immediately pursue the attackers to Oagon, though a number of survivors had identified them as being from that region. It would have been a slaughter as it were. So, we traveled as a group to recruit others to our cause, as Amorum once had done on his own.

"Building an army from rubble is not an easy task, but nothing was too much for Amorum. He used me. Not for my body—as I refused to be touched after Aquine—but as a standard. A beautiful young girl, her family slaughtered and her world displaced, was a symbol that people would rally behind. In other villages and towns, such loss had become so common. My plight appealed to these people.

"Soon, I was giving speeches without Amorum, my words full of vengeance and violence and vehemence. Whereas Amorum was calm and appealed to something deep within his audience, I was all emotion. I could work a crowd into a frenzy, lusting for the blood of those who would commit sins without provocation. There was hypocrisy in this, but I cared not. I only wanted to make the Oagonan bastards suffer.

"It took almost a year, but we raised an army sufficient to stage an attack on Oagon. They had the weapons of Aquine now, and a siege would only lead to our deaths. So, we instead planned and plotted a way to drive the Oagonans to attack us outside the city. We camped outside the city for weeks, out of range of any of the death-dealing weapons of war. My army began to melt around me, men and women deserting as they saw the might of the enemy. Our army dwindled to a quarter of its original size, and then the Oagonans attacked.

"This was only a ruse, however. When they attacked the apparent remnants, our true forces—having been hidden in the forests—assailed the city. We visited the same torment on the Oagonans that they had wrought upon Aquine and so many others. We lost ourselves in the blood of our enemies and the blood of innocents. Me, especially.

"It was then that I discovered my powers. So few, in those times, could access miernes of any kind, and even fewer could sense those with the ability. It was neither frowned upon nor made illegal, such as in your Ardia, nor welcomed, such as is the case in Sestria. It was simply unheard of.

"I had become separated from my bodyguard and Amorum, lost in my wrath. I saw an Oagonan cut down one of my soldiers—a young, blonde boy—from behind. I flung myself at him, tossing aside my weapon. When my hands wrapped around him, my anger and wrath overwhelming me, I felt a force within him. Something that I could touch and take within myself. Something I could shape and control. And I did.

"None could touch me, that day. With a burning scythe and a thousand fiery projectiles, I rent all of those around me into bits of flesh and viscera—enemy and ally alike. Flesh was shredded, limbs were torn from bodies, and hearts were plucked from chests. I held that first man's power inside of me until I could find and restrain another. And then another. It was intoxicating, more so than the finest wines or the most potent opiate. I was overwhelmed with it, reveling in the power… reveling in the blood and death.

"If Amorum hadn't stopped me, I know not what would have happened.

"The Blood Maiden was born that day. What, you have never heard that moniker? Another convenient fact lost from the histories. I had begun the day wearing a white, silky dress under a silver breastplate. I was not meant for fighting, sweetling. I was meant for inspiration. The young beauty, fighting for justice and harmony, as Amorum put it.

"By the end of the day, everything was stained red. The fabric of my dress was stained crimson, and the blood had melded to the silver of my breastplate. Even my hair was hanging in wet, red tendrils across my splattered face. By the time I regained myself, people had fallen to their knees worshipping me. I lost my existence as a woman that day. My wrath had taken that away. Never again could I have a normal conversation about the weather or food or someone's hopes and dreams. Instead, people—friends and followers—only viewed me with fear and awe from then on.

"Ah, sweetling. So many strive for such power and for such respect. But, I recall a great feeling of loss. Of emptiness. I have enough experience in this world to know that my experience was not unique. Those driven by vengeance—upon attaining their goal—lose motivation for everything. For me, had it not been for Amorum, I would have also been lost. But, as always, he propped me up and kept us moving forward. To my destiny, many would say. Perhaps my wrath had bettered the world; we will never know what would have changed had I remained in control.

"Enough for today, though, sweetling. I already long to speak to you more, but, as always, pressing matters require my attention. It is time to do what must be done.

"Please hold onto yourself for me, sweetling. A good man, as you are, always listens. Even when he does not wish to. It has been so long since someone truly listened to me."

Chapter 18

Fenrir—the guardsman, the Bull, the Coldbreaker, the taker of fingers and killer of brothers—whimpered as he slumped to the dusty ground. He clenched his eyes shut, exerting all of his remaining willpower to restrain from dripping tears into the dirt.

"Get up, trash. I said, get up!" Ingla barked at him. Fenrir did not immediately move. He couldn't. His mouth felt like it was full of sawdust, his limbs like they were little more than flaccid bits of twine. A swift kick in the ribs didn't help the situation, although it did give him the slightest motivation to regain his feet, holding his side to lessen the pain.

"This is the man who broke the Lady Escamilla out of the Plateau? The man who killed Duke Penton? The man who was born of Principal de Trenton?" Ingla spat onto his boot, never breaking eye contact. Her deep hazel eyes, so often filled with anger, simply regarded him with disgust. She really was pretty, in a small, violent kind of way.

As in most cases like this, there was only one thing to do. Fenrir hung his head and let his shoulders slump, looking away— defeated. And then, in a sudden burst of motion and energy, he swung at Ingla with a right hook, twisting his hips to hit her as hard as he could.

To his complete and utter surprise, he connected.

A glancing blow, anyway. Ingla had begun to step backwards, so his meaty fist only caught her chin, but much of his strength had returned over the past weeks, and the brutal physical training sessions—running, calisthenics, weight training—that had left him whimpering like his ex-wife had given him back some speed. So, even that glancing blow sent Ingla reeling, spinning nearly a full circle.

Of course, she recovered like a skilled circus acrobat as Fenrir stumbled back into a clumsy fighter's stance. That one, last-ditch punch hadn't had the intended effect of putting Ingla out of commission, and his body was spent. He didn't even have the energy to sweat anymore.

Maybe he did need to drink more water.

Ingla wiped away some blood from where he had split her lip. She tasted it and smiled, which was an unnerving sight on a face that spent most of its time scowling.

The lithe Blue Adder closed the distance between the two of them in a heartbeat. She batted aside Fenrir's raised arms disdainfully, striking him in the stomach with a quick jab. As he doubled over reflexively, her foot flew up, catching him under the chin. Again, he was on the ground, spitting out blood from his skewered, bitten tongue.

Ingla crouched easily by his spinning head.

"There's some little fight in you, it seems. I made a mistake, letting you get close to me. I will not make that mistake again, trash."

"Women generally avoid getting close to me a second time," Fenrir said, slurring his words. He rolled to his side and gave her a bloody smile. "Sergeant."

Ingla squatted for another moment and regarded him. Fenrir braced himself for another kick, but she instead twisted to her feet like the titular blue adder. "That will be all for today. Clean up. You are free to walk the grounds until evening. Do not try to leave."

Ingla turned without warning and strode off. Such a strange and painful woman.

Fenrir did not immediately rise. There was no real rush, after all. He had nothing to do, nowhere to be. The sun was at its zenith although the day was cold—in the past weeks of his torment, Ingla had typically kept him busy until at least midafternoon before he'd be escorted back to his cellar-bedroom. Which had been fine with Fenrir—the training generally destroyed him so utterly than he could do little more than lie on his cot, twitching and wishing for death. The Spike would have been preferable.

At first, his torment had just been exercise. But, after losing his strength as a captive, and honestly not being in the best of shape to begin with since losing his job at the Plateau, exercise was the worst kind of torture. Running laps around the de Trenton compound before the sun came up. Swimming in the Fullane against the current. Lifting and carrying rocks from one side of the compound to the other. Whenever he slacked or started to slow, Ingla's fist or foot was quick to follow. Avoiding blows was his only motivation to keep moving.

Then, exercise had become punctuated with battle training. First, weapons training. Fenrir had expected that Ingla would be skilled—Blue Adders were the best. But, he wasn't bad with a blade. He'd typically placed high in guardsman tournaments at the Plateau, and he'd proved himself a warrior against those monsters in the ruins and in raiding the duke's inn stronghold. But, he'd either overestimated his own skill or he'd underestimated the training of the Blue Adders. Probably both. Ingla had made a mockery of him.

When fighting with thankfully-blunted swords, Ingla could disarm him in two passes. Fenrir had fought men who were about his size (or preferably somewhat smaller), but never someone so short. When he swung at chest level, the sword would glide over her head as she easily darted inside his guard. And, she was quick! Fenrir wasn't exactly young anymore, but she made him look like an arthritic shell of a man, a malnourished grandfather left to live in the streets.

It was worse with spears—he'd never mastered that weapon. And, bare-handed? That was just embarrassing.

Fenrir labored to his feet and glanced around. As always, the Blue Adders' barracks were bustling with activity: training, equipment and supplies being delivered, the blacksmith mending armor and forging swords. Adders, in their signature de Trenton-blue leathers and breastplates, prowled instead of walked, every one of them bristling with effortless martial prowess. As he watched, two Blue Adders sparred amidst a circle of calm onlookers, one wielding a great hammer and the other two thin swords. The hammer-wielder was a giant of a man, his skin as black as night. His opponent was tall and skinny, heritage indistinguishable beneath his shaggy black hair as he danced around with his two short swords. The hammer-wielder spun the giant gavel with bone-crushing force, and yet he could not land a blow. The raven-haired warrior dodged and parried, somehow knocking aside the oversized hammer with rapid, brutal blows. He seemed the superior warrior, until the black man—a Rafon native, it seemed—struck him down with a sudden blow from the handle of his hammer. And then his great weapon descended, raising a cloud of dust and denting the ground as it struck inches to the left of the shaggy-haired man.

There was a small cheer from the crowd of Adders as the Rafonese man offered his hand to the fallen warrior, who twisted up and bowed to the winner.

Meanwhile, Fenrir had just sucker-punched his own opponent, and felt great pride in having managed to do so. He hurriedly looked away from the scene of this training match.

The de Trenton estate was the largest compound in Rostane, consisting of over two dozen sprawling buildings. The Blue Adder barracks—the Adder's Nest—accounted for only a small portion of this, and it housed over four hundred of the elite warriors and their families. Like most buildings in Rostane and within the de Trenton estate, it was constructed of gray, Tulanque bricks. But, the four-story barracks were obviously of a higher quality than the rest of the city, though lacking any embellishment. Like every construction that Darian de Trenton payed for and authorized, the Adder's Nest was austere and eminently defensible. Darian always built for the worst-case scenario.

Fenrir took a long swig of water from a nearby tap, and then he spat blood. He left the area of the Adder's Nest and began to wander the compound, no real goal in mind. The entire place had a sickening tang of familiarity, like the taste of rotten fruit stuck to the roof of his mouth. Gods, he hadn't lived here for more than twenty years, and yet it still held some power over him. He felt the urge to hunch his shoulders and stay to the shadows, like when he'd been a kid. Hiding from his father, whenever he was around. Hiding from his brothers. But, in a small rebellion against his own tendencies, Fenrir kept to the center of the lanes, holding his head high and making strong, direct eye contact with those servants and workers, artisans and scientists, who huddled together and stared as he passed.

He knew what they were thinking. The failure son of the Principal, wandering the estate? What value could this criminal have here? Shouldn't he be dead?

Fenrir walked a little taller and fought his limp as he stared down any who glanced his way.

Almost without realizing it, Fenrir wandered to the main residence. The austere structure was the only one built solely of wood—an oddity in Rostane, a city built in homage to the nearby Tulanques. He'd never been certain why the house was so large; while he'd grown up there, it had been only him, his two brothers, his father (who was rarely around), and his mother, Astora. The place was cavernous, though, intimidatingly so to a child. But, it at least offered a host of hiding places, and Fenrir knew those places well.

Perhaps his father had built the structure simply to awe and impress his competitors. It was certainly large enough for several families. Or, maybe Darian actually had a soft spot. Maybe Darian had expected and hoped that his sons would marry, have children, and live together in this manor. Happily running the mercantile empire together, slowly choking out competitors as a family.

And here Fenrir remembered bashing in Aiden's skull as his brother had stood over Ethan's body.

No, there would be no families haunting these halls.

"Astora, come away from there!" came a shouted, authoritative voice from just ahead, cutting through his dreary thoughts. Cutting right to the bone.

Fenrir froze, his muscles turning to ice and then melting into water. He was covered in dirt and bruises, his collar ringed in drying blood. He hadn't shaved, and his hair was unbarbered and askew. His eyes were tired, as well, and he barely had the strength to stand still without his legs trembling in exhaustion.

And, Fenrir was simply not ready for this. He felt more prepared to face a horde of angry husbands, or a single Emma, than his daughter. He made as if to adjust his shoe and then ducked behind the stone, knee-high wall that ringed the yard of the main residence.

A coward, he was. A fucking, spineless coward. Punching unsuspecting women and hiding from girls.

"I need to harvest a bit of farelawn flower, first! It grows along the wall," came a young voice. A maturing voice, really, somewhere between a girl and a woman. Fenrir hunched lower.

"The Yarways will be arriving shortly for dinner. You must prepare to receive them." A tutor, maybe? A governess?

237

"The Yarways are dried-out old crypt keepers with less personality than the bodies they preserve." A smile tugged at the corners of Fenrir's mouth.

"Death is a lucrative profession, especially during wartime. Relationships must be forged; bonds must be solidified."

"And my daintily eating of a bit of bread nearby as the adults talk will forge those bonds? Pah."

"Nonetheless, you have duties, Astora. Duties that shall not be neglected because you would rather pick flowers."

"Flowers that, when mixed with warvine, will help me with the headache that you are rapidly giving me, Pona."

Fenrir caught himself grinning. He'd sometimes pushed his own tutors, though he'd been beaten for his insolence. Depending on the day, it had been worth it. Perhaps this girl was similar to him, after all, despite lacking his dubious influence in her life for the last ten years. Funny, how heritage worked.

There was a pregnant pause as the tutor collected herself. People wandered by, giving Fenrir strange, suspicious looks as he crouched and listened, but he made no move. His knee was screaming at him, but he didn't shift. Gods, he couldn't be seen.

"Astora, this is enough of your willful behavior. I am tasked with your education and the... polishing of sharp edges, but I will not be disrespected. I will not! Would you like the Principal to hear of your recent coarseness? Do you want the Principal to find you yet another governess? As it is, I understand not many wanted the job." A consistent troublemaker. His daughter indeed. "There are certain boarding schools that might be more appropriate for a young woman like you. Aron Academy, for instance, back in Draston." Fenrir hadn't heard of it, but Pona's tone was predatory.

A small sigh. "I'm sorry, Pona. I truly do have a headache setting in. Would you please allow me to gather a bit of farelawn before I prepare for the event?"

"You may." Pona's voice held a tinge of victory, though it was Astora who'd gotten her way.

Just on the other side of the wall, scant feet from his too-public hiding place, Fenrir heard scratching and shuffling as his daughter gathered her flowers. He didn't know anything about herbology— that was just another topic he'd ignored when growing up—but Astora's story sounded sketchy. It seemed unlikely that the farelawn flower, considered a weed by most, would have restorative effects. She was likely just pushing her tutor for the sake of pushing, playing the subtle and stupid power games that teenagers played. A beta dog seeing what it could get away with while the pack leader was watching.

The scratching grew closer, and Fenrir felt a cold bead of sweat running down the center of his neck.

"Come along now, Astora. You have quite enough. As it is, by the time we wash the dirt off your hands and knees, we will be late."

"Perhaps, by then, the Yarways will have died of old age," Astora quietly muttered, out of earshot of her governess but not her father. "Yes, Pona. I am coming."

Dry grass crunched as she moved back toward the house.

Sometimes, a man will do stupid things, knowing full well that they are stupid. Fenrir knew he should remain crouching, lest he be seen. But, he felt an instinctual, primal urge to behold his offspring. By Ultner, he'd spent years ignoring the fact that he had a daughter. Forgetting about her existence. Training his mind to avoid wandering down that particularly muddy path, which had been a real challenge when his primary mode of distraction during long shifts was thinking. But now, with her so close, he wanted to see her. He needed to see her.

So, knowing full well he was acting out of stupidity, Fenrir pulled himself up with a grimace as the bones continued to grind his kneecap into dust. With a catch in his throat, he looked across the yard toward his once-home. A tall, slender girl walked barefoot across the grass toward a severe-looking woman in her forties. The girl was dressed in a daffodil-yellow dress, which hung to just above her pale calves. Her hair stretched to below her waist in gentle waves, a chestnut color that Fenrir hadn't expected. Last time he'd seen Astora, she'd been clinging to her mother's shirt, no more than six years old, blonde hair blowing in the breeze as their wagon left for Draston.

All these years, when a stray thought of his would land on Astora, he'd pictured a blonde kid running about, hair the color of his own mother's. Time had darkened her hair. His archetype of Astora had been wrong for years, and it was dizzying.

"Move along, vagrant. I do not know how you entered the compound, but the Adders will not tolerate your presence for long. I would recommend that you find your way out of here before you get skewered." Pona stood tall fifteen yards away, raised voice oozing with disdain.

Fenrir turned to go, but not before Astora glanced over her shoulder.

Her eyes, even at this distance, were a clear, cool gray. The eyes of her namesake, Fenrir's own mother. He locked eyes with the girl, feeling his fists clench and his stomach twist into a sour knot. Astora's face was inscrutable. Was there recognition? Hatred?

Or was there nothing at all?

Regardless, Fenrir tore himself away from her gaze. With a strength he didn't feel, he strode back toward the servants' quarters.

Chapter 19

"And where were your men?" Emma screamed, advancing toward Captain Ezram, poking him in the chest with her mangled hand. She had to clench her teeth to keep from raising her voice even higher.

Ezram backed up against the wall of his sparsely-furnished, narrow chamber in the Sentael estate. He was half a foot taller than her and twice as wide, but he shrank back from her anger. It was an honest fear—the fear of a man who was avoiding being bitten by a wild animal, or standing too close to the edge of a cliff without a rail. It was not the fear of a man who had something to hide, and certainly not anything as dark as a betrayal of Lady Escamilla.

Ezram held up an arm as if to ward off a blow. Emma only sighed, anger seeping from her as quickly as it had appeared. Ezram was not her man.

"I, erm…. My lady, I have no knowledge of the changes to the orders. I certainly did not approve any change, and my lieutenants didn't, either." Ezram's eyes flickered to just over her shoulder.

Nail leaned on a crutch behind her, a reassuring presence despite the fact that he relied heavily on his support. The heat from Disorder's sword had cauterized the stump of his foot, and he had lost little blood. He insisted on being by her side now, though it had been mere days since his brother's death and the loss of his foot. He had barely spoken since, and his usually jovial face was filled with a chill, stony anger.

Havert hovered at her other shoulder. She'd recently promoted the dusty-skinned Sestrian to her personal guard as an Apple Knight. He lacked the swordsmanship of most knights, but Escamilla had trusted him, so Emma did, as well.

242

"I need you to launch a full investigation within your battalion, Ezram. I want the name and rank of everyone who has touched those orders. I want each one under observation. Any man who shows a hint of treason or treachery, or any suspicious behavior, will be immediately detained for questioning."

The five depleted regiments of her army had alternated as an honor guard for Lady Escamilla, sharing the duty with the Apple Knights. Each captain, and the men themselves, had wanted to hold vigil close to her side—a macabre escort to her grave. The logistics of the arrangement had been handled by her captains and their aides, and Emma had given it little thought. For who would attempt to assassinate a dying woman? But, somehow, the orders had been altered, for each regimental captain had thought that one of the others had had the duty at the time in question. The trail led in circles. The fact was, though, had twenty men been there on the night of Disorder's visit, Escamilla may have been allowed to pass quietly.

"The men won't like the investing—"

"I don't care what the men like!" Emma's anger resurfaced in an instant. "You will do as you are ordered or you will be stripped of rank and imprisoned. I'm certain Lord Unael would also like to know who betrayed us all." A fire in one of the stables had pulled his black cloaks away from their patrols in the tunnels beneath the hold. Unael was red-faced furious that his soldiers had abandoned their posts, but the stables being ablaze had been so unusual that word had spread quickly. Curious black cloaks had come running, all of whom were currently being sent to the Alganian borderguard for punishment after receiving a half-dozen bloody lashes. "And, I would expect that Unael would be less gentle."

"Yes, my lady." Ezram's expression was one of resignation.

Emma nodded to him, spun on her heel, and marched out of the room with an authority born of righteous anger more so than actual power. Some traitorous bastard in her army—and maybe Unael's retinue—had conspired to leave Escamilla defenseless, and she would find this person.

She would make them suffer.

***

"In any war of faith, there will be casualties," Ignatius Pender began, his hands resting on a podium that was too skinny to conceal his bulk. "We hope and pray that such causalities will be experienced by those who side with Pandemonium—the Rostanians and those who serve them. But, those who serve Harmony are not immune to tragedy. They are not immune to the dark powers that so often work to destroy us, both in overt and subtle ways."

His well-practiced sermon voice boomed across the Trins Grand Chapel, the seat of Yetranian worship in Jecusta. The opulence of this place was overwhelmingly hypocritical. The money to heat the great, vaulted ceilings could have fed hundreds over the course of the winter. The delicately-painted murals on the walls and stucco ceiling must have cost thousands upon thousands of hours of labor, which could have instead been used to build homes for the poor. A single, golden candelabra—of which there were dozens—would clothe half of the Farrow Hold's destitute.

But, in Emma's experience, that was always the way of religion.

She shifted in her seat, unable to get comfortable. Her head ached with a low buzz that hadn't left since that night in

Escamilla's chamber, as if a hornet had built a nest inside her skull. She could barely think straight at a time when she needed her head to be clearer than ever. There was no time to mourn, after all, until she found the traitor.

"We know that Yetra protects us. We know that Yetra guides us. And, even in tragedy, we know that Yetra often has a purpose that we cannot see. Lady Escamilla Breen, one of the greatest ladies that I have ever had the privilege to serve, was a champion of Harmony." Escamilla had never truly cared about Yetra, only using faith as a tool—a two-sided blade—for furthering this war. And it was questionable whether Ignatius had ever actually served her. He'd served himself, was more like it.

"The role of a champion is one of constant scrutiny. One of constant danger. Yetra, herself, before the Ascension, was the champion of Harmony, a figurehead around which the people rallied against the growing Pandemonium in the world. 'And, though she was at the head of the people, Yetra stood among them still. For great though she was, Yetra was from humble beginnings.' Yetra's very humility—her refusal to set herself aside from the common man—put her in danger. Many times did she face both insidious and overt threats to her life. And, though she always prevailed, the danger was very real."

Looming just behind Ignatius was Grand Taneo Endo Pious, the head of the Yetranian Church in all of Jecusta, and perhaps the most influential man of the Church anywhere in Saiwen. Lacking a single centralized bureaucracy, rank among the various Taneos was linked with the number of Yetranians in their regions. And, though Unael and the rest of the leaders of the country were lax in their observations of religious customs, Jecusta was very large, and very Yetranian.

Pious, in his deep purple robes and great, gold-trimmed miter, with steely gray hair and the lean features of a falcon, stood in stark contrast to the doughy Ignatius, who was dressed in his

245

simple orange robes which were still stained from the road. Ignatius being allowed to speak in the grand chapel was quite the honor for him. Emma would have expected him to clean up a bit; perhaps he was trying to make a statement. Or, perhaps he was just a bit lazy.

"Lady Escamilla Breen, however, was unable to protect herself from treachery. Her compassion led to her adoption of a small girl who later betrayed her. And, though she survived that initial attack, she was not to survive her wounds in the long term. But, even with the knowledge that she would soon pass, Pandemonium could not leave her be. An agent was sent to destroy her in her final hours. The agents of Pandemonium are strong, and two great men—Captain Ean Braston of Rostane, Hern Onnon, known to his friends as Hammer—died in her defense.

I do this to protect them. To protect them. Disorder's words rang in Emma's aching head. She blew out a long breath, trying to achieve some measure of focus.

Ignatius leaned on his podium, bowing his head in what looked to be a silent prayer. He visibly steeled himself before looking up, and his eyes scanned the crowd of gathered hundreds. Emma's officers, including the mercenary captains, Jecustan nobles, and local, high-ranked faithful. A daunting group, all in all.

"Lady Escamilla's body has been consigned to the flame in the customs of Jecusta," he said flatly.

An angry buzz in the crowd mirrored Emma's headache. It had ultimately been her decision on how to treat Escamilla's remain, but realistically flame had been the only option. The dark, magical spear—which had dissipated from existence within minutes of Disorder's departure—had done something to Escamilla's body. Sapped the remaining flesh from her, twisting her face into a grimace of eternal agony. None of the embalmers could have made her appearance acceptable for a viewing ceremony. So, it had been flame.

"Not as a punishment, as dictated by the faith," Ignatius went on, "but in a protest to Pandemonium. Pandemonium will not take what belongs to us. Anything touched by Pandemonium, from this day forth, will be burned, given to flame. For we must be hard, now, in our battle against Pandemonium! They seek to cow us into submission, creating fear and confusion among our leadership. If we are not safe in our beds, then where will we be safe?"

Emma's head continued its painful buzzing. She massaged her temples with the meat of her hands, noticing that her mutilated hand seemed to be aching more today.

Ignatius spread his hands, beseeching the audience. Behind him, Pious narrowed his eyes.

"But this does not weaken our resolve. In fact, it strengthens our need to fight!" Emma looked up. Ignatius, once the hypocritical peacemonger, suddenly finds his spine? Pious touched the chaplain's shoulder, but Ignatius shook him off. "I beseech the gathered faithful today. Will we live our lives in fear of Pandemonium? Or will we fight the growing darkness? Will we sit, idle, while good people are killed in Ardia, while our enemies use dark magic to—"

Pious made an imperious gesture, and two grim-faced Glories—Yetranian soldiers—came forward and pulled Ignatius from the pulpit. The chubby chaplain continued his proselytizing as he was detained, shouting to be heard.

"No, I ask you all to fight! To fight for Harmony, to fight for freedom from chaos! To fight so that we can sleep soundly…" He tripped down the stairs as the guards roughly escorted him forward.

A pallid silence filled the great chamber, the crackling sound of a thousand flickering candle flames the only thing to break the stillness. The sound of light was louder than one would expect.

Emma was awed that Ignatius would make such a spectacle of himself—in the favor of war, no less. In such a public place, at a likely cost to his career and potentially his faith. She had thought Ignatius a coward who hid behind his faith, but perhaps not. He would be ally. Escamilla had been right, even on her deathbed. Ignatius, who had preached against war while filling the men with righteous fervor, may have finally resolved his own internal conflicts. Perhaps, instead of being a hypocrite, Ignatius was a man experiencing a crisis of faith, torn between following Yetranian tenants and combating power-hungry rulers.

Grand Taneo Pious stepped forward to the podium with a practiced ease, betraying no hint of concern. He radiated an aura of authority, his glittering, intelligent eyes not dimmed by age. His voice, though quieter than Ignatius', seemed to fill every corner of the great chamber like a pervasive whisper.

"Chaplain Ignatius is passionate in his grief, which does him great credit. However, as we know, war only begets war. Yetra knew this, and only fought when the world was in dire peril. A civil war in our neighboring country does not constitute a dire peril, but rather the sad reality of a fractured society. My Jecustan flock, however, shall follow the path of peace. As is written in Pinquist, 'the most noble of wars shed not a drop of blood, and the greatest of peace can be attained with words, not arms.'" Pious had unconsciously mirrored Ignatius' own words in Brockmore, all those months ago.

"Now, let us bow our heads in prayer while we honor those who have fallen to Pandemonium. Lady Escamilla Breen, of course, as well as those who followed her. May their memories rest peacefully in our minds, and their brave actions fill our hearts.

248

The dozen men and women who were killed in the stables fire. May their service to their country be ever…"

Pious droned on for some time longer while Emma's mind drifted from crisis to crisis, never stopping long enough to come to a solution. At the top of her list was the investigation into who'd changed the orders on the night of Escamilla's murder. Her thoughts flitted away from that dilemma in short order, however. She also needed to promote someone into Braston's place as captain. Maybe someone she trusted, although that was a brief list. Good officers were in short supply; maybe she could work with the Florensians, with Eric Malless, to find someone to fill that role. Or might that person they chose be a traitor, as well?

Unael, too, was searching for traitors among his men, and he had pledged his full support in assisting with her investigation. He seemed truly appalled that such a tragedy could have occured within his very walls. He had surrounded himself with his most elite black cloaks, and he had put a number of pasnes alna on retainer after Iolen's stunt. Leeches and greenies, Ferl had told Emma. Those who could draw on the lives of animals and plants, respectively. None, aside from that cautaton woman, had been present in the hold when Iolen had arrived, and Unael was now taking no chances.

Lord Unael had been holding meetings with every territory head currently residing in his city, attempting to gain traction for the war. Emma had only been to one such meeting since Escamilla's death. She had described the killer in detail, but kept most of the conversation between Disorder and herself close to the vest. Her story, like when she shared her army's experiences with the Feral, had been met with disbelief, scorn, or occasionally fear. A man who disappeared into the shadows and wielded a burning sword? Preposterous, even with Nail's charred lump of a leg to provide support. A magical Pandemonium-laced spear that sapped life away? Where was this spear? Emma had no answer.

Her only real support had come from Unael and Evina Linstael, the de facto ruler of the Eastern Sweeps. The powerful woman did not look the part—she was bordering on obese, a second chin scaffolding the first. But, she was quick-witted and clever, able to talk circles around the much blunter rulers of Jecusta who'd been present. She'd questioned Emma throughout the telling of the story, focusing on specific details. What was the attacker wearing? Did she see where he was injured? Was there anything unique about his eyes? Evina had appeared troubled, but let the other rulers argue and fuss while she'd considered Emma and her story.

"It is customary to rise and sign the Ascension at the end of the ceremony. Sitting and scowling at your shoes is generally not recommended at such events." Emma looked up sharply. Savant Iolen was standing above her with a friendly smile creasing his face. He wore fine crimson robes of mourning, and two black cloaks stood ten feet back, along with a pasnes alna between them, an older woman with a splotchy red face and thinning hair. A cooing noise betrayed the fact that she carried a bird in her pocket to feed her magic. Though, based on her narrowed, frosty eyes, Emma did not doubt that she would leech one of the black cloaks if needed. The black cloaks were smart enough to keep a foot or two away from her.

Her own bodyguards, Nail and Havert, were seated at the back of the chapel, likely stuck behind the creeping mass of people, all attempting to exit the chapel simultaneously. Gods, if this place were to light on fire, they'd all be doomed.

"I'm not what you would call a devout Yetranian. For all I know, staring at one's feet is a time-honored tradition." Emma rose to her feet so as not to give the Savant an advantage.

"What religion do you follow, then?" Iolen folded his hands into his sleeve. A strange question. In Rostane, the only religion that Emma knew of involved the worship of Yetra. She had heard tell of a few religions across the Vassas Sea to the north, but nothing else in Ardia or even Jecusta. Jecusta, after all, was the birthplace of Yetranianism, and Jecusta was the negligent mother of Ardia.

"I can see from your eyes that my question puzzles you. You only know of Yetranianism, no?" Emma didn't respond. "No need to be embarrassed. You are a city woman from a Yetranian city. But, there are dozens of religions in Saiwen alone. Hundreds, once you travel beyond our continent. Yetra dominates, of course, but even within Rostane, you could find worshippers of other gods, other concepts."

"Concepts?" Emma eyed him carefully. This was a man who allowed no chance encounters. He was after something with this conversation. She resolved to give him nothing.

"Yes, concepts. For instance, in the Eastern Sweeps of Jecusta, the Cenors do not worship a god. They worship, or at least highly value, walls."

"Walls?"

"Yes, walls. The Cenors were historically persecuted by the Oshwon, a fierce tribe that you can now see wandering Farrow's Hold in bondage to the Jecustans. Safety became the most important commodity to the Cenor. Town walls were important, but also the walls of one's own house. A sturdy house that could withstand a blow from a great hammer without a chip was considered more important than any god. Even today, Cenor people are uncomfortable going outside into the world, where they are not enclosed by walls."

An Oshwon servant, wearing a white smock, was moving around the church and snuffing the many candles. Iolen noted Emma's questioning gaze.

"Oshwon have no gods that I know of, but they follow a path of freedom. A dangerous people to subjugate," Iolen said contemplatively, "but they have their uses."

"Why are you telling me this?" Emma asked bluntly. Of possible traitors, Iolen was high on the list. Escamilla had survived a journey of weeks to be murdered in Farrow's Hold. Coincidentally, Iolen—the former High Strategist of their enemies and someone with magical powers—had happened to arrive a day in advance of Emma and her army. The only reason Emma had not denounced the Savant already was that he was constantly supervised, though he seemed powerful enough that he may have found a way around that. Regardless, even if he was not guilty in Escamilla's murder, he had some inscrutable motivations. And, having fled or not, he'd been a high-ranking officer in the army that had unleashed the Feral, and he'd done nothing to halt that plan or warn her own forces.

"Because this war with which we are becoming increasingly embroiled is one that has its foundation in religion. Think of your own army. Yetranianism has been a cornerstone for rallying your troops. The Rostanians believe the same, that they have Yetra's blessing in the war they wage. When, in reality, their blessing comes from a darker place." Iolen's expression was black as tar. He was a consummate actor, if anything.

"And where is this dark place? Pandemonium?" Emma was sardonic. Though, thinking about Disorder's burning sword and swirling eyes, she felt goosebumps cover the back of her neck. And a slight burning in her chest, in her heart… the remnants of whatever dark magicks he'd left rooted inside her.

"Some may argue that is the case. There are powers in the world of which we have very little understanding. The learned, like me, have inklings. The unlearned continue to wander into things they do not understand, like a blind man steering a ship." It was clear Iolen was insulting Emma, but she ignored the barb. He

252

almost seemed disappointed that she didn't take the bait. "There are powers beyond what pasnes alna can summon, available to a select few. And these individuals grow in power in Ardia and elsewhere. Perhaps you have heard of Recherche Oletta?" Iolen observed her face like an eagle, waiting for her to betray some recognition.

But, Escamilla had trained Emma well. Not even an eyelid fluttered.

"The name sounds vaguely familiar. Tell me more," Emma said. Nail and Havert finally pushed their way through the exodus and began to approach. Emma shook her head slightly, keeping the men back a few steps. This was a chance to learn more about the people who may have ordered Escamilla's death. It was hard to visit vengeance, of course, when one did not know who to target.

"Oletta was… Oletta was worshipped as a goddess in a time long ago, when Yetra walked the earth. No matter what you believe about all this…" Iolen gestured to the various frescos and paintings in the grand chapel, all depicting the slender, blonde goddess throughout the stages of her life, from childhood to goddesshood. "There is no doubt that Yetra was a real person. There are too many historical documents to contradict that point, too many coincidental allusions across cultures and nations. Reference to Oletta, though, was largely wiped from human documents and histories. So much wisdom lost from that time…"

"Was she a goddess?" Emma asked, interrupting what she largely felt to be going in the direction of a condescending, philosophical rant.

"Are there any gods or goddesses?" Iolen picked at a stray thread on his sleeve. "Who knows? But we do know she was powerful, and was worshipped by the peoples who used to inhabit Ardia in ancient times, back before it was settled as it is today.

253

Primarily, the Wasmer. They didn't always live in the mountains, you know. They once inhabited most of Ardia, living in a hundred different clans, numbering in the tens or hundreds of thousands."

Emma had known few Wasmer, as the Plateau did not tend to employ any aside from the most skilled. But, from what she'd seen, the Wasmer were like humans—some were kind and friendly, and some were cock-faced assholes. She couldn't imagine seeing more than a couple dozen in one place at a time, though.

Iolen continued as if he were giving a lecture at the Enlightenment. "If we piece together old, crumbling documents—mostly those... borrowed... from the Wasmer—Oletta was destroyed in a great battle with Yetranian forces in her battles against Pandemonium. I would give this little credence, except that I have seen the ashlands south of the Tulanques. The power to create such devastation, still unhealed by our earth over the past four thousand…"

"Recherche Oletta?" Emma prompted him. She had too much to do to listen to a lecture. Irritation flickered across Iolen's face, and Emma felt a sudden flutter in her chest and a brief tremor in her hands. Did this man command fear just as he commanded magic?

"There are some who believe that Oletta was not actually destroyed, that she may yet live in some form, drawing upon her great powers to cheat death. Or, perhaps she does lie rotting and festering, but with great magics still lingering in her long-dead corpse waiting to be harvested. Recherche Oletta has been searching for her, covertly seeking power across Saiwen and beyond. And, I believe they are now moving because they have found her, or at least the key to her whereabouts." He examined his hands, as if in deep contemplation.

"What do they seek?"

"Were you not listening? Power. They seek whatever power Oletta has to offer. If she could indeed rival Yetra at the height of her power, then whoever has Oletta has whatever they want. The world, even."

This story rang false to Emma. If this goddess still existed in some form, and if she represented such power, why, then, would she remain unfound after four thousand years? Why and how would she be found now? Iolen was hiding something, some part of this story about goddesses and religion. A thread that, when woven into the fabric, would reveal the entire tapestry.

"So, knowing what they seek, how do we prepare? How do we fight them?" Emma asked.

"With faith!" Iolen laughed a bitter, mocking laugh. "I'm certain that your Ignatius fellow has spoken of this. The outnumbered, when faithful, have held strong against the many. And, you have no idea how outnumbered you are to be in this coming war. Now, if you would excuse me, my caretakers grow impatient, as do yours."

With a twisted smile, Iolen turned on his heels and strode to his pasnes alna sitter, arms wide as if greeting an old friend. Emma stared after him for a long moment, clenching her teeth against her frustration with the man. Against the emptiness she felt with Escamilla being finally and truly gone. Against the growing fear of what they fought, embodied by Disorder and the Feral. Against the compulsive urge to flee, to heed Disorder's warning and run to save her own life, maybe taking up the well-worn guise of a serving woman in some distant country.

And against this damnable headache.

"My lady, is everything all right?" Havert was at her side now, while Nail limped up quietly, his face pale and laced with a hard pain. But, he offered no complaint. The man merely stood, stalwart, at her side, resolve burning in his fevered eyes. There was no give in Nail. He would be avenged.

As would Emma.

"Yes, Havert." She eyed Nail and he met her gaze, almost as if they had an understanding. "Everything will be fine."

Chapter 20

The budredda weren't prisoners, strictly speaking.

They were assigned a wing in Sebiant Rhisfel, the Warrior's Respite. The bureaucrat assigned to them, Fel Jentin, had greeted them at the entrance near Enorry Falls, all politeness and politics, even praising Hafgan for his martial prowess all those years ago in the Cylch. No assassination attempt was mentioned, and nor was the fact that a human, Captain Rin Yanso, was a prisoner of the budredda. Humans weren't banned from Hackeneth exactly; they just rarely found a reason or had the fortitude to make the trip. Occasionally, traders would make the trek and brave their fears of the Wasmer people, hearing that there was wealth in the mountains, that Hackeneth was carved from gold. Upon seeing it, and finding out that garrs had no currency exchange to yets, the traders would as often as not just leave their goods and make the trip home with all haste.

After having seen his men settled and fed in relative safety, Hafgan had requested to see Taern. Jentin had raised a brow at that, but Yurin had taken him aside, whispering something in his course voice. Hafgan had thought, at the time, that Jentin was taken aback by Hafgan's insolence, expecting to see the highest-ranking Dyn Doethas in the city upon his arrival. As it turned out, however, Jentin had only been confused that Hafgan would want to see a man worth less than nothing to the Wasmer. The last Dyn Doethas was more insignificant than even the budredda.

The Dyn Doethas of the Carreg Da had guided the people for millennia. They may have lied and manipulated, but they were an institution. Above laborers, miners, merchants, warleaders, bureaucrats, and even priests, these men and women were the paragons of society, blending the ideals and strengths of all castes into one. Everyone bowed their heads upon seeing one of these wise and knowing leaders, the many hearts of society. They were the judiciary branch, hearing cases among the Wasmer and passing verdicts. They were religious leaders, guiding the priests in their devotion. They even led the miners and laborers, directing efforts toward the most beneficial public works.

The only segment of the Wasmer that the Dyn Doethas had never truly led was the military. Of course, 'military' was too strong a word for the Wasmer warriors. It implied that there was organization or a single direction for the warrior caste. Their force was more like an assembly of gangs, each led by a warleader. The Dyn Doethas influenced, but could never quite conquer.

And now, it was no matter. The Dyn Doethas, purged. The Laenor, raided and despoiled by common people and warriors who'd had enough of being manipulated by men and women who had no right to rule, no reason to hold themselves above others. When Hafgan had been young, he'd dreamed of a time when the caste system would be obsolete, when people like his parents would be able to expand themselves beyond being loggers. When a laborer could be a warrior and when a warrior could be a cobbler.

And, with his martial prowess, coupled with his proclamation, he'd made it happen. The blood of the Dyn Doethas stained his hands crimson whether he'd intended it or not. With such blood-slick hands, it was a wonder that Hafgan could still grip a spear.

He wandered the halls of Sebiant Rhisfel mindlessly, conscious that two guards dogged his steps but not caring. He had not yet retreated into his hedwicchen, but felt a numb emptiness nonetheless. Home was nothing like he'd expected. Certainly, the tunnels were unchanged. He could hear the echoes of warriors laughing and boasting, swearing and fighting. The familiar sounds of the Sebiant Rhisfel. But, everything seemed off. From the crumbling, disused shrines of Traisen that littered the broad stone halls to the near-empty streets above, Hackeneth felt wrong to him. And he could scarcely imagine a world where Taern was relegated to being a prisoner while Leyr held sway.

He and Leyr would certainly be meeting soon. There was no way that Hafgan would leave Hackeneth without a reckoning. This whole journey had been a mistake, however. He hadn't even bothered to give his warning to Taern. The man could do nothing with the knowledge, and that would only bring him greater shame and regret. It was but a wonder that Hafgan had thought to spare him the added stress.

No, he had to leave this place with his budredda. Leyr would never listen to him. Leyr would never heed a warning from the mouth of the budredda who'd shamed him in front of thousands. Though the gwagen had returned, being stolen from the very ranks of the Wasmer, his rival would assume that he was lying, making up a story to further shame him. He wouldn't believe Yanso, a human brought against his will to share his story of that night.

Without realizing it, Hafgan had wandered beyond the Sebiant Rhisfel to the Loch Creed, the religious district. It was the largest of the districts beneath the great mountain of Limner, its huge caverns hollowed out as if the rock had been eaten by great worms. It was also the brightest of the districts, screened vents honeycombing the ceiling to let in the light of the day or the shine of the stars. Mirrors were cleaned and maintained by laborers to ensure that light always graced the temples held within. Hundreds or thousands would cluster here daily, worshipping their god of choice and asking the Offeirs for divine blessings.

Basically, it was a district of false hope.

Now, it seemed nearly abandoned. Hafgan passed few others on the street during a time of day when you'd normally be barely able to walk without bumping another. He paused, taking a moment to consider another temple to Traisen, the stonework building in obvious disrepair. A lone Offeir, an old, old man, labored to drag away a chunk of statue that had apparently eroded. He was mostly unsuccessful.

"Let me help you, Father," said Hafgan in the Wasmer tongue, inclining his head with the respect due to a priest and an elder. Even if the man's beliefs meant nothing, Hafgan would never insult someone who had conviction.

"Pah, why bother? Traisen has fallen, and I'm unlikely to stand him back up on my own," said the Offeir, flinging up his hands in defeat and slumping against the façade of the temple. It was, indeed, Traisen's screaming, warlike face that the old man was trying to haul.

"What has happened here? Where is the respect for your god?" Hafgan asked. Stepping in front of the Offeir, he heaved against Traisen's head, righting the thing. At least the warlike god would be able to see his body, several feet distant, and remember what it was like to battle.

"Respect for my god? Where in the bleeding mountains have you been, boy? And what in the name of Traisen happened to your teeth?"

Hafgan clamped shut his mouth to hide his budredda dog teeth.

"I've been away," he said quietly. "Just returning."

"It's been at least two years since the purge. I'm assuming you know of that?" The Offeir eyed Hafgan warily. Hafgan nodded and gestured for the man to continue.

"Everyone has their opinion on the purge, these days. At the time, the people were behind it, having listened to that fool Hafgan Iwan at the Cylch, having gotten behind Leyr and his ilk in the months that followed. Now? Can't go far without someone swearing it was the best thing to happen to we Carreg Da, while someone two steps away would swear it was the biggest mistake ever made."

"What would you say, Father?"

"First, call me Ulin. And second, look at my bleeding temple! I'll let you use your imagination about what I think, boy, though I'll wager you are just as dumb as the rest of them. Besides, if I were to say what I was thinking, I might be liable to disappear like half the other Offeirs around here. Traisen still merits some respect among our warriors, though many just look to their new god." Ulin spat on the ground and gestured rudely at the cavern ceilings, revealing the passionate ardor that was so valued by worshippers of Traisen.

"New god?" Hafgan asked.

"New god. The god of stone and sky. The god of blood and metal. The god of feeding and fucking and fighting. It's like Leyr took all the gods that we've worshipped for centuries and blended them all into one in a sickening stew."

"And the people believe this?" It sounded like yet another fabricated story, even less believable than the rest of the lies the ancient Dyn Doethas had cooked up.

"The people are dumb. You point at a pile of goat shit, say it's a god, and they'll worship it! The god of putrid feces!" Ulin chuckled for a second before breaking into a coughing fit. He leaned against the wall of his crumbled temple, wiping sweat from his brow. The man was obviously in a slow decline, age finally getting the better of him. A bad way to go for devotees of Traisen. Likely, it wouldn't be long before he challenged some ox of a warrior to a duel and commited suicide in a very Traisen-friendly way.

"Does this god have a name?"

"No name. He's called the Flawless God, and Leyr claims to have met him atop Enorry Falls. People claim to have seen the clouds around Limner clear, pure light shining down upon the summit at the time Leyr was supposedly dallying with the gods. People claim to have seen their shadows stretching across the sky—our great and wise leader and his omnipotent god of shit. People claim that the falls ceased to flow for an hour, though I didn't see it. They claim when Leyr descended from the impossible climb, he glowed with a divine light." Ulin again spit, his saliva tinged with red.

"It seems things are changing in Hackeneth," said Hafgan. "Thank you for the information, Ulin. I would offer you help in cleaning this rubble, but I know you would refuse, so I'll not waste my air on the request."

Ulin smirked. "Maybe you ain't so dumb as you look, boy. Come by again if you're bored. Maybe I could get us talking about Traisen, eh? You seem like the martial sort; his blessing might do you some good."

"Maybe, Ulin," Hafgan allowed, knowing that he'd not be back to the ruined temple of an imaginary god. Part of him wanted to reach out and convince the man of this deceit, that his god was nothing more than a fairy tale. But, the larger piece of him knew that could only bring harm. It was precisely as Taern had said.

The people would never be ready for the truth.

***

Ulin's temple was representative of the state of Loch Creed. As Hafgan wandered, his guards still dogging his footsteps, Hafgan grew amazed by the state of this place. The figurative heart of Hackeneth had fallen into disrepair, neglected by both its disciples and its caretakers. The broad streets were filthy, almost as if the Wasmer had decided to use the religious center to store their trash. The hundred temples—ten to each of their ten gods—seemed empty and lifeless. Though he saw occasional Offeirs like Ulin, laboring in their yards to maintain what they could, or preaching to a few diligent souls, Loch Creed was not what he remembered.

Leyr had somehow subverted the gods themselves, fake though they may have been. He had replaced the faith in the many with the faith in one. The man had always been brilliant, his mind quicker than Hafgan's. Where Hafgan had been serious and stoic, Leyr had been witty and deriding, running circles around him with insults. Whereas a younger Hafgan had been content to grow as a fighter and perhaps eventually be a warleader under the tutelage of Taern, Leyr had always had greater ambitions. With his name on everyone's tongue in Hackeneth, it appeared that Leyr had risen to the challenge. But to what purpose? Had he deposed the gods to put himself—or this so-called Flawless God—in their place?

Lost in thoughts of both the state of Loch Creed and the machinations of his former rival, Hafgan almost missed the small rock that was hurdling through the air at his head. He reflexively twisted to one side, deflecting the small missile with his forearm and bracing himself for the inevitable attack. He fell into his hedwicchen with little trouble.

When he looked up and saw his attacker, he lost his grip on his hedwicchen. More precisely, he released it. Rian deserved that much, at least.

Rian, as small, compact, and lovely as he remembered, stormed up to him. Her shining black hair, seeming to contain all possible colors, bounced with her furious steps. He met her charge in silence, neither stepping back nor forward.

She twisted backwards and brought her hand across his face with a great, burning slap. She'd had to stand on her toes to reach his face, and lost her balance. Hafgan stuck out a steadying arm. Rian recovered, and then slapped him again. And a third time, even more fierce than the first two. At that point, she stuck her own stinging hand in her armpit, her gray, slim-fitting Offeir robes concealing the appendage.

Hafgan said nothing; he merely looked at her and battled away his shame. Or tried to.

"Hafgan Iwan. You should be dead," Rian hissed, her eyes barely more than furious slits. She leaned toward him as if she were ready to strike him again.

"Were there rumors of my death?" he asked, his voice quiet.

"No. But you should be dead."

The two stood for several long moments in the middle of the nearly abandoned street. Hafgan's guards, two hulking monsters from the warrior caste, were not anywhere to be seen; perhaps even they feared Rian's anger.

Her gaze was unwavering, cutting into Hafgan like the sharpest spear. She had every reason to hate him.

Though Hafgan had stared down the spear of Leyr, the sword of Taern, the daggers and blades of dozens of cutthroats, and the tearing claws of the gwagen, he lowered his gaze in the face of Rian. His to-be-bound.

"Rian, I..." he began, not sure where to start. He'd started to build his own pyre when he'd decided to return to Hackeneth.

Running into Rian was simply the torch to be tossed onto the dry kindling.

"You always were a fool, Hafgan. A great, hulking, bleeding fool," she spat, leaning back on her heels.

"The Offeirs of Oletta are wise," he muttered.

"The bitch be damned, we are wise! But it doesn't take an Offeir of the goddess of wisdom to see that you are a half-wit. You were given everything, you blood-soaked animal. You were given a chance to rule! A chance to actually change things, to address the inequities that plagued us. And what did you do?"

"Walked away," he said, answering her question as candidly as he could. "I walked away and left Hackeneth. I left behind the lies and the deceit, the memories and the pain. I left behind everything that I knew for the hope of something better. And, yes, I walked away from you, Rian."

She made a choking sound. "You did, and you know it. It was a singularly stupid thing to do. We were to be bound, you stupid, bleeding beast. Aside from your chances to change our world, you left me. You left me to pick up the pieces of the damage you had wrought with your little duals and your big fucking words."

"I know," Hafgan said, looking away. His bluntness and self-deprecation seemed to disarm Rian more than any story he could have woven. It wasn't a calculated move on his part. Though he'd been taught to read emotions and could do so fairly accurately, viewing Rian was like staring into the sun. She was bright as the ten hells and gave him a splitting headache.

Rian sighed. "Why are you here, anyway? What lingering head injury convinced you to come see me here?" She gestured at the small temple of Oletta he'd most recently approached, carved humbly from rock and illuminated by a seemingly stray beam of light. The effect was very intentional. The simple arches of one of Oletta's many homes within Hackeneth were clean and well-maintained. Rian, at least, maintained her vigilance, despite knowing the truth.

In truth, Hafgan had just been wandering and thinking, not realizing that he'd had any destination in mind. Or had he? Had Rian still been among the Carreg Da, of course she would be residing in this temple. His muscle memory, lingering despite a five-year absence, may have brought him here. Or, maybe it had been an unconscious desire to see Rian. If so, his unconscious was a goat-fucker.

He said nothing. She sighed again. Certainly a familiar sound to Hafgan. He never had been good at expressing his emotions, even before the hedwicchen had dulled them.

"Your teeth look stupid," she said with what almost sounded like affection, the forgotten remnants of a smile crossing her face. Maybe she was thinking of the awkward day when he'd asked her to be bound, where he'd stumbled over his words and actually attained his hedwicchen before he could finish in his monotone. He almost smiled at the thought, at the incredulous look on her face followed by her booming laugh, far incongruous with her small stature.

Half a year later, he'd left her.

"Rian, tell me what happened. I already know of the purge, of Leyr's new Flawless God."

Rian glanced around. Seeing only a few wondering Wasmer, lonely pilgrims or worshippers, she ushered him into the temple. Hafgan's guards kept their distance, neither seeming to care much about their charge.

The temple was unchanged. Rian, though only a couple years older than Hafgan, had been the Prime Offeir of a laborer caste temple for nearly ten years. Oletta had been the least worshipped of the gods among the Wasmer pantheon, especially among the lower castes. Her aspect was wisdom and knowledge, something that the physically-taxing and fairly routine lives of the miners and laborers had little use for. Why learn the histories and stretch the mind with logic when cognitive pursuits had so little do with swinging a pickax or clearing roads of snow?

Given the sparseness of any given prayer service, Rian's temple was small, containing only a dozen stone pews, a podium, and a couple of side chambers. There were no statues or intricate carvings of Oletta, nor any carved murals. It was as simple a temple as existed in Loch Creed.

Rian sat on a pew, the only one with a padded cushion. From the looks of it—a sack of clothes in the corner, bedding wedged under a bench, some toiletries and a bucket of water behind the podium—she had been sleeping there for some time.

"At least some things are unchanged," murmured Hafgan, glancing around the room.

"Yes, some things never change. Some people never change. They stay bleeding idiots," she retorted.

"If you brought me in here to continue insulting me, I might as well leave," Hafgan told her, not particularly enjoying her constant rejoinders.

"It's something you are good at, no?"

Rian looked fit to start attacking again, and Hafgan did remember... he deserved anything that she directed at him.

"Rian, I'm sorry. How are things? How are things, really?"

She sighed that familiar sigh, this one more regretful than anything. "That's a loaded question, you oaf. When you left me.... When you left Hackeneth, things went sour. Your arrogance was astounding, to leave after having achieved so much through battle. It was so... contrary to the beliefs of the people that they took to the temples. They came to me. They came to Shryn and Ineryn and Wrys and the rest of us. The thousands of

267

witnesses in the Cylch, and the thousands more that heard the story of your prowess amplified until you became almost a god in their eyes… it opened the door for doubt."

Rian's gaze was far away, remembering things almost fondly.

"For a while, I thought you actually changed things by leaving. It seemed, for a long time, that the people were questioning the caste system. It seemed that they were questioning how the right to live in comfort was granted simply because of the womb that bore you. The temple was full for the first time, Hafgan. I had people to listen to me… to learn of Oletta, despite certain truths that you sought to open my eyes to."

Hafgan slumped into a seat next to Rian. He remembered the day he'd emerged from his punishment in the pwoll, weakened, malnourished, and half-insane. He'd found books claiming that the gods the Wasmer worshipped had been imagined up by the Dyn Doethas, with the explicit purpose of controlling the people. The Dyn Doethas probably would have bled him, but Taern had been the one who'd discovered him. His time in the pwoll had probably been a fair trade for his life.

When he'd returned home, he had told Rian, in his fevered, fearful voice, what he had found. That Oletta, who she had dedicated her life to, was imaginary. That Traisen and Enyll and Feroh had all been dreamt up by the supposed wisest among the Wasmer.

She had railed against this, of course. She'd attacked his words with her own. She'd even attacked him in her anger, as she was wont to do. But, eventually, the logic that was so integral to serving the goddess of wisdom had led her to the truth. There was no Oletta. There were no gods. Hafgan's fear had been what convinced her.

And she'd hated him for it.

"That must have been fulfilling," Hafgan murmured. "Being able to guide the people toward wisdom."

Rian glanced up sharply, as if expecting sarcasm or mockery. Of course, Hafgan was being true to her. He'd always tried to be, for all the good it had done him.

"It was, you concussed oaf. Even the miners listened to my words, bending their ears toward the beauty of learning. Toward the beauty of knowing more than just what bashing a pickax against a rock could yield. For six months or more, Loch Creed was filled to bursting, all one hundred temples knowing more pilgrims during that time than the five years previous. But then things changed." Rian rolled her neck to the left and right. Left and right. She'd always had a nervous energy.

"Leyr?" Hafgan asked.

"Not yet. Or maybe so. Around that time, there was a great earthquake in Prineth, collapsing the great caverns and destroying the majority of the crops. Starvation was a greater threat than ever before, and the influx of pilgrims into Loch Creed continued. The people were fearful and looking for someone to blame, especially when children started dying from hunger and flux."

Rian's eyes had grown far away. Hafgan longed to hold her.

"And then, Leyr," he concluded correctly.

"And then Leyr, Rinx, and Wiscon. Three of your bleeding Haearn Doethas. They focused the people on the Dyn Doethas, elaborating on your message. You were a living martyr, having given up your place as grand warleader to find freedom from tyranny. Walking away while opening the eyes of the people. Leyr and the rest were seemingly everywhere, visiting each temple and spreading their message against the Dyn Doethas. They had failed us in so many ways. Hunger. Isolationist policies. Strangled trade. Constant war. Hoarding their own wealth. With their seeming devotion to the gods and the simplicity of their

269

message—of your message—the Haearn Doethas whipped the people into a hungry, righteous froth."

"And then the purge." Hafgan could picture the people, faces pinched in hunger and muscles hardened from continued labor, raiding the Laenor. The wide passages could be held by small, skilled groups of soldiers for days. Weeks, even. But a constant and concerted push from a desperate and frenzied foe could eventually gain passage. The few hundred Dyn Doethas would have been destined to fall in the face of that. But it would have been hard-fought. Maybe one of the reasons for the empty streets in Hackeneth.

Rian started to lean into Hafgan before hopping to her feet and turning on him violently, whipping him with her shining hair. Even with her standing while he sat, they were at eye level.

"The purge. It was less a purge than a war, as you can imagine. No one relinquishes power lightly. When the dust cleared and the bodies were tossed downriver, starvation was no longer a problem." Rian shuddered.

"What of the other clans? Did they not sense a weakness?"

"Of course, they did. These are the bleeding Tulanques, after all. But that's when Leyr really made his move. With so many dead, with Prineth destroyed in the quakes, with the Flam Madfall and the Yearer Inos growing ever bolder, he moved against the gods. The message was the same—they had failed us. Hackeneth, once the jewel of the Tulanques, had crumbled. First, through the corruption of the Dyn Doethas, and then through the inattention of the gods."

Hafgan thought of Rian's own reaction to his story of imaginary gods. "The people would not be so easily convinced."

"Of course not. But you must understand that Leyr had become something of a god himself. And that was when he introduced his new god. His nameless, single god."

"I heard there were theatrics," Hafgan said, remembering Ulin's story.

"You can't imagine. Enorry Falls halted its flow while shadows crossed the red-tinged sky. The earth shook, and avalanches fell to either side of Hackeneth, sparing the lives of all but a few goats. The walls of Loch Creed glowed red, emanating with a heat that I have never since felt! There was not a soul in Hackeneth that did not experience some impact of this god, the day that Leyr climbed to the top of the falls."

Rian turned away from Hafgan, walking slowly over to her podium. She leaned on the simply-carved wood, looking out over the benches. Hafgan knew her mind; she was wishing that her goddess could have instigated such miracles of nature. That her goddess was real, and that she herself could have been the one to kindle the faith. She had always loved looking into the eyes of a true believer.

"Do you believe in this god, Rian?" Hafgan stood, moving toward the podium. He felt heavy.

"Ha. Who knows? Who cares? With Leyr, anything is possible. Though, it was a bleeding convincing presentation. Really bleeding convincing." She dropped her head into her hands.

Hafgan reached out to comfort her, resting his hand lightly on her back. It had been so long since he had touched her; it could have been a different lifetime. She tensed under his touch, though, and he snatched his hand back. It was stupid, to believe that she would want comfort from him, from the man who'd left her and Carreg Da during their time of need. Some might even argue that he was responsible for much of this. He certainly felt as if it was his fault; the burning, sickening knot in his stomach told him as much.

"So, this god…" he muttered, moving away from his to-be-bound.

"The Flawless God," Rian said, straightening and turning away. Her posture bespoke of a renewed anger or a renewed grief. He shouldn't have touched her.

"The Flawless God… the people rallied around his banner, and Leyr, turning away from Oletta and the rest?"

"Aye, the bleeding Flawless God pulled people away. Seems that it doesn't take much for people to leave me. Speaking of, perhaps you should go. I hear you've a bunch of budredda relying on you." Her words were sharp, each one like a stab of a dagger.

"Rian…" Again, she'd left him speechless. Perhaps he should apologize, though what would that amount to? He would still have left, throwing away her chance at a happy binding, at a chance to transform Wasmer culture. She would still have been forced to live through the famine, the purge, and the subsequent desertion of faith. His words would ring hollow, and her pain would still be there.

Without a word, he started to walk toward the door. He'd hurt her enough; Rian was better without him. By Traisen, the Wasmer were better without him.

"Hafgan, wait," Rian said quietly.

He half-turned to look at her. She was looking at him now, her eyes shining with unshed tears, like ice glistening on a newly-fallen field of snow.

"Why did you come back? Why are you here, now, after so long?"

A warning, was all. A misbegotten warning that he had yet to even utter within the confines of Hackeneth.

"I'm not sure," Hafgan said softly, before heading back out into the trash-covered streets.

Chapter 21

Fenrir absorbed the blow with his flexed upper arm and surged forward, connecting solidly with his opponent's gut. With a whoosh of breath, the man staggered backward, but not without lashing upward with his foot to keep Fenrir from a quick follow-up.

His opponent today was a neolate—the derogatory term that the Blue Adders bestowed upon their new recruits. New or not, this friendly-faced young man was a giant from Rafon, much bigger than Fenrir. Hane was more muscular, too, though he still had some baby fat on his body. The boy certainly lacked the wear-and-tear that had weakened Fenrir's joints for nearly four decades.

But, over the past six weeks, Fenrir had not been idle. Ingla had insisted, of course, but Fenrir hadn't resisted her prodding. He'd found a core of motivation that he hadn't felt since joining the military as a teenager. As a result, Fenrir was feeling stronger, faster, and more coordinated than at any other time in his life. In the past, he'd often deluded himself into seeing himself as a fine, skilled warrior. He knew now that that hadn't been the case. Ingla had routinely beaten his ass, and he could barely hold his own against seventeen-year-old Hane.

No, he could hold his own against this giant, dark-skinned Rafonese boy, he told himself. In fact, he could win.

Fenrir began to circle to the right as Hane moved to the left. Without preamble, hoping to catch the boy off-guard before falling into a dance of feints and dodges, Fenrir surged forward, swinging a hard left hook. Hane anticipated the move and dodged it easily, agilely moving directly into Fenrir's right foot. Guards and brawlers rarely fought with their feet, but Fenrir was no longer a brawler. His wrapped foot connected solidly, once again with the boy's gut.

Hane fell heavily to the ground, to a mixture of boos and cheers from the onlooking Blue Adders. Fenrir smiled inwardly at their reactions.

Over the past two months, Fenrir had found himself with more freedom. Ingla either trusted him not to dart or otherwise expected him to get caught if he tried. Fenrir was often left to his own devices. Of course, he avoided the main manor and the stables, lest he see his daughter. He also avoided the great, steam-spewing brick of a laboratory—the Furnace—and the distribution centers, the heart of the de Trenton empire, lest he see his father. So, he'd fallen into the daily routine of the Blue Adders. He'd moved into the Adder's Nest, into a single, narrow apartment that resembled a crawl space. He shared mass-produced meals with these men and women, and had slowly built from exchanging pleasantries with them to actual conversations.

As a kid, he'd seen the Blue Adders as cobalt, untouchable gods, drifting around the estate as if they ruled the compound and beyond. Fenrir had been both awed and terrified of these warriors, particularly as the number and diversity of these guards had grown at the same rate as the trading empire. Those Adders from Sestria, Rafon, Poen—they'd seemed too foreign and brutal to the young boy, conversing and barking orders in strange languages as they did, eating odd foods and generally being different. Even as an adult, the Blue Adders had given him an uncomfortable feeling that he wouldn't quite have called "fear," but it was certainly far from "warm and fuzzy."

But, over the past two months, he'd learned a surprising truth: the Adders were human. They had thoughts and goals and fears and insecurities, as well as cliques and favorites. Granted, each one of these men and women were trained killers, but even killers had hopes and dreams.

Hane, for instance, in his thick, Rafonese accent, expressed a thorough homesickness, speaking of hurricane-ridden Polanice and its harsh winters as if they equated to the fields of Harmony. Eanor, a skinny Ardian from Hunesa, worried that his wife was cheating on him with his brother, and vowed to commit fratricide if he were to catch them at it. Ill'Polomo, a pale Pintan islander covered in a variety of piercings and tattoos, was lovelorn, as well, lusting after the daughter of one of Darian's mercantile partners. Of course, the father wouldn't countenance such a relationship, though Ill'Polomo was well-learned and well-spoken. Appearance, it seemed, could not be overcome by things as simple as love and intelligence.

Despite years of conditioning, Fenrir found himself not only liking the Blue Adders, but fitting in.

Ingla, however, was a cipher. The fierce, diminutive woman stood aloof, not joining the Adders for meals or engaging in the small talk and ribald joking of their masses. Rather, she simply spent her time training… and apparently resenting Fenrir. Even after abdicating some of her duties and allowing Fenrir to train with the rest of the snakes, she'd said little to him aside from insults and commands. Any flirting or attempts at conversation were met with chilly silence or a razor-sharp glare, and his attempts to learn about her from others were generally unsuccessful. Say what you wanted about the Adders, they were loyal to each other. Gossip was a behavior that simply didn't happen.

As Hane staggered to his feet, wiping grime and sweat from his brow, Ingla neither smiled nor grimaced. Instead, she reached into a nearby barrel and drew out two half-edged swords, tossing them to the ground between the man and the boy. Fenrir barely flinched as he twisted to the ground, grabbing the sword in an easy grip. His knee was feeling strong again; Martis insisted on a tedious array of exercises first thing in the morning and last thing before bed. And—damn him for being right—his joint was feeling decent because of it.

276

Hane was a bit more restrained, scooping up his blade more slowly, likely buying himself some time to recover. The blade seemed small in his dark hands, and Fenrir felt as if he should be intimidated. But, he wasn't.

Sword work was something that he was well-versed in from his time as a guard, and, though he had learned more in the past two months, he'd already had a strong foundation. Immediately, he came at Hane with a great overhand strike, forcing the boy to parry the blade with a teeth-clenching clang. Fenrir leapt back and then immediately lunged forward, his precise blade aimed at the boy's chest. It wouldn't kill, but it would leave a hell of a bruise.

Hane, though, was not as beaten as he'd appeared. He slapped Fenrir's strike aside with the palm of his great hand—which would have sliced him, had they been using real blades—and came around with his own sword. Fenrir managed to get his blade up in time, but not with the stability or strength to completely deflect the other weapon. Pain blossomed against his shoulder, and a numbness spread into the fingers of his left hand. By Ultner, this Rafonese boy was strong!

He wasn't out yet, though. He punched out with his pommel, catching the boy in the cheek and creating some space between them. The warriors eyed each other warily, both waiting for the other to make the first move. Hane—in the throws of youth—had little patience for such a contest, and sought to end things with the strength of juvenescence and giant arms. Fenrir parried his first attack. And the second. And he sidestepped the third, as parrying made his hands sting like gripping Ultner's spiked arms. Hane had some grace, but he was used to winning with muscle and tended to over-commit himself.

Fenrir used this. As Hane leveled yet another powerful swing at Fenrir's side, Fenrir dropped flat. Hane staggered at the lack of resistance and Fenrir managed his feet quickly enough to jab

Hane in the kidneys. Not too hard, but enough to score an obvious point.

"Ah, fuck!" the boy exclaimed in his Rafonese accent, to the laughter of all involved.

He smiled and winked up at Ingla, but felt his face drain of color upon doing it. Standing next to Ingla, arms folded across his simple but fine, silken clothes, was Darian de Trenton. His fucking father, overseeing the entire affair with his typical brand of disdainful judgment. His father, savior, and current owner.

Ingla raised her hand, and both Fenrir and Hane dropped their weapons. Still without even a splash of emotion, she reached into the weapon barrel and tossed out two spears. Two fucking six-foot-long practice spears with dull wooden tips.

Fenrir caught his breath for a moment and picked up his new weapon a few moments after Hane. The big Rafonese boy spun his spear a couple of times, the thing looking like a twig in his hands. The pointed staff felt awkward in Fenrir's hands; he'd spent years leaning on spears, at least during ceremonies at the Plateau, but he'd never learned to fight well with them. Ingla knew that, of course, from their training sessions.

She'd timed this nicely.

Hane darted forward with a couple of jabs, probably hoping to finally score a point lest he suffer the embarrassment of losing to the disgraced guardsman who wasn't even a real Adder. Fenrir managed to evade both with quick sidesteps, a bit surprised to find that training and muscle memory were taking over.

He struck back, finding only firm resistance from Hane, whose eyes showed a steely focus that belied his age. The boy probably saw his employer and wanted to impress. Fuck, everyone felt that way about Darian de Trenton. Even Fenrir himself, as he approached forty years of age. Even though he hated the fucker.

Hane and Fenrir continued to spar, neither landing a solid blow. Fenrir's hands were aching and growing numb, his fingers pinched and stubbed. His arms felt as heavy as thick, sodden ropes and it seemed he wore stone shoes that were pulling him down and slowing his movement. But, by the gods, he would not let Darian see him lose.

Fenrir leapt inside Hane's guard with all of his waning speed, accepting a blow to his aching shoulder in order to crack the boy in the face with the butt of the spear. Blood sprayed out from the boy's face as he kicked out at Fenrir, who turned his hips to deflect the wild kick. Hane lurched backward as Fenrir pulled back to jab the boy's chest, to finish the contest.

He happened to glance up for just a moment, catching his father's near-black, soulless eyes.

And then he was sprawling to the hard-packed dirt, ribs bruised or broken from Hane's last, powerful swing.

The gathered Adders probably cheered or hissed at the result, and maybe some paltry money changed hands at the outcome. Fenrir, though, could hear nothing but the sound of rushing water, and see nothing but hazy memories of a disappointed father.

Then he was lifted up and set on unsteady feet.

"Well fought, Coldbreaker," Hane said, a great smile creasing his bloodied face. He was jubilant in victory, of course. Any man would be.

"You, Hane, are the bastard offspring of a black giant." The boy gave a booming laugh that matched the width and breadth of his chest. Fenrir, despite everything, joined him. Several other Adders approached, smacking his shoulder and jibing him, mocking his appearance, moves, and personality. His ribs ached like he'd been kicked by a horse, and he overall felt like a three-day old corpse.

279

By Yetra's warm embrace, though, he liked being a surrogate Adder. If only, after the Adders cleared, he didn't have to deal with the king of all snakes.

"I sometimes wonder, boy, if I will ever be able to find you not covered in blood or filth," grated his father's voice once the others began to clear. Ingla stood by his side, hazel eyes flashing as she observed Fenrir.

"It is a bad habit of mine."

"I prefer conversing with cleaner individuals, but time is not with us. You will walk with me."

With that, Fenrir found himself two paces behind his father, hating that he had to do a quick shuffle to catch up. Now that the adrenaline had worn off, he felt like a tenderized hunk of chicken.

"I see that you are finally fit to do more than guard some meaningless hallway for some minor noble," Darian said, his eyes straight ahead as they marched through the compound. Ingla fell in five steps behind them, an angry ghost haunting their footsteps.

"It was usually the Enlightenment." The library, spanning most of the fourth story of the Plateau as well as the northernmost tower, used to observe celestial bodies. Fenrir had often been punished in this fashion, condemned to guard Scholars and Savants as they waxed ecstatic about philosophy and history.

"It is amazing, then, that you spent a dozen years guarding dusty books without accidentally learning something." Fenrir had, in fact, accidentally learned a great deal from the Scholars and Savants. The Enlightenment was far more like a university than a repository for old tomes. But, he supposed that argument was lost.

"What do you want?" Fenrir said bluntly.

"Can't a man simply speak with another for the sake of it?" Was that humor? From Darian?

"Some men might be able to."

"And I thought that you were a lackwit. Perhaps, in training your body, you have also been training your mind. Tell me, how do you find it, living among my Adders?"

It was better than being a guardsman, where the long, tedious hours were rarely broken by anything more exciting than a brief wardrobe malfunction by a visiting lady. Training at the Plateau had been rote and monotonous, a chore only to be completed. With the Adders, training was dynamic and purposeful, though far more dangerous. With both, there was companionship. But, whereas at the Plateau the relationships were more those of coworkers and acquaintances, the Adders had a deep brotherhood. No matter a person's background—son of a noble Rostanian, daughter of a Sestrian weaver—once they were an Adder, they had a new family. A new life.

"There are other things I would be doing," Fenrir said, voice carefully neutral.

"Of course. Drinking and whoring. Living the life of a wastrel. But it is not to be."

They were approaching the Furnace, Darian's laboratory and the best-guarded building in the compound, crawling with vigilant Blue Adders. Some were in full mail in case of a melee and others were in blue leathers in case of a pursuit. The Furnace itself was a huge slab of granite without a single window, steam always being emitted from great pipes atop the building, lending the monstrosity its name. Fenrir had sometimes wondered whether the steam was for show—what could possibly be going on in that building that caused these constant misty emissions?

He had never been inside this tower of scientific mystery, this place that inspired periodic infiltration attempts by de Trenton competitors, all seeking the secrets of burning ice and other de Trenton innovations. Invariably, these spies were caught, killed, and dismembered, if perhaps not in that order. Fenrir's brothers, Ethan and Aiden, had bragged about their visits to the Furnace, rubbing in the fact that Fenrir was never taken into their father's confidence. They'd given very few actual details, however.

"Tell me, boy. Have you happened across your daughter?" Darian asked, glancing at Fenrir ever so briefly.

"We haven't spoken."

"Hmm. If you were to speak, what would you say? Would you tell her of your life? Of your infidelities? Of your disgrace? Of your criminal dealings?"

Gods, what would he say to her? 'Sorry I forced your mother to leave by embarrassing her with extramarital affairs?' 'Sorry I didn't write?' 'Sorry I drowned thoughts of you with hard liquor and soft whores for these past ten years?'

'Sorry I didn't bother to be a father?'

"I'd warn her away from you, my lord," Fenrir answered. Darian looked at him then, just as the Adders swung open the weathered oak doors. Darian's abyssal eyes considered his son for a long moment before running his hands through his still thick, gray hair.

"That would have been good advice," he said, still meeting Fenrir's gaze. "It is a shame you did not give her that message sooner." If Darian were another man, Fenrir would have thought he heard a tinge of sadness in the man's gravelly voice. But Darian was barely a man at all, so Fenrir must have been hearing things.

"Come with me."

They entered the mythical Furnace. Fenrir didn't know what to expect. Viles of strange chemicals and jars of ground-up poisons and herbs? Well-guarded scientists laboring over mixtures as they added substances together to unpredictable results? Monsters roaming the halls? The reality was far less exciting. They entered into a bare reception room containing little more than a security checkpoint, this manned by a beefy Rafonese in de Trenton blues.

"Principal. Will you want an escort today?" asked the woman in a surprisingly mousey voice.

"No, Anna. We will not be in observable corridors today. Besides, Ingla will surely keep us safe." Fenrir had almost forgotten that Ingla still shadowed them. Dangerous thing to forget. He shot her a quick glance, but she didn't meet his eyes. Or had she looked away?

"Of course, Principal. I will open that door for you." Anna fumbled with something behind her desk and a small, blended-stone door on the far wall slid open. Darian had always loved his mechanics and his hidden passageways.

Anna handed Ingla a small gas lamp, and she led them into a dark, relatively narrow passageway, like those that were used for servants in the Plateau. Fenrir, having regained much of his bulk, felt entrapped by the cramped corridor. His father, a bit taller than Fenrir, had to stoop a little to avoid scraping his scalp.

Fenrir looked at the man's back, viewing this man who'd sired him. A sudden urge pulsed through him—a violent need to grab his father's head from behind and twist as hard as he could. With Ingla leading the way and Darian in between, she couldn't stop him in time. Would it be worth his own life to end his father's? Could he do it? Could he avenge his mother?

He clenched his eyes shut and shook his head to clear out these dangerous thoughts. He dragged a hand across his forehead, which had become sticky with perspiration.

After a couple of minutes, the hallway ended in a lift, similar to those found throughout the Plateau—they'd been added in the last thirty or so years so that obese nobles could avoid getting accidental exercise. Fenrir wondered whether there were workers locked in some dark room day after day, waiting for a signal to crank the mechanism that mobilized this rarely-used device. Must be a depressing job.

The three stepped into the cramped lift, its space so confined that they were touching each other, ever so slightly. The last time Darian had touched his son, he'd been jamming his fingers into Fenrir's shoulder wound. The last time Ingla had touched her charge, she'd been kicking him, barefoot, across the jaw. Fenrir imperceptibly shied away.

Darian pulled a lever and the lift began to move smoothly downward. There must have been some modern machinery at work; the lifts in the Plateau jerked around like an adolescent alone in his bedroom. Aside from some creaking, though, the relative silence of this lift was oppressive.

"Where are we going?" Fenrir asked, avoiding eye contact. His too-loud voice seemed to echo through the shaft.

Darian raised an eyebrow. "We are going to ensure that I can trust you."

"Isn't being of your blood reason enough to trust me?" Fenrir smirked.

"Being of my blood is exactly the reason not to trust you, Coldbreaker. Or do you prefer I call you the Bull?" Darian's sneer mirrored Fenrir's own. The thin veil surrounding his exploits with The House seemed to have been pierced. "Besides, this is a rite of passage. Your own brothers…" Darian trailed off, his brow furrowing.

Fenrir felt a stifling lump in his throat. Did he know about Aiden? That Fenrir had killed him? Or that Aiden had somehow come back from the dead and put out a contract on Fenrir's life?

After several minutes and an uncomfortable popping feeling in his ears, the lift came to a gentle rest with a discordant hissing sound, like the wind blowing through a thousand trees. They stepped out into another hallway, this one roughly hewn through the stone, coarse walls occasionally broken by strong wooden supports. Fenrir had heard that the Furnace was more below ground than above, burying the secrets of science within the earth itself. But he'd had no idea that the roots of this place ran this deep.

The tunnel emerged into a larger chamber, revealing the source of the hissing sound. An underground river was rushing through this chamber, dimly lit by gas lamps affixed to the wall. Several great waterwheels spun with the force of the water, turning gears and cogs, affecting nameless chains and pulleys that propelled various forces into the ceiling, likely powering the enterprises above. One wheel was sending barrels of water to the above, perhaps to be used as the source of steam in those great vents above the laboratory. Another was jammed with a bar of steel, being worked on by a small army of men wearing nondescript clothing. One noticed Darian, and shouted something to his compatriots over the roar of the water; all doubled their efforts.

"It fuels the Fullane, this underground river," whispered Ingla into his ear. Fenrir jumped; she was standing very close.

"I, erm… I've never thought about it," he replied, lagging a few steps behind Darian. He wasn't sure how to respond; this was the only thing Ingla had ever said to him without an accompanying insult, order, or blow.

"Most do not," she answered, her eyes on Darian as he paused to exchange a few words with an overseer. "Though the Fullane originates at Mount Limner in the Tulanques, there are many such underground rivers. It is said that you could follow them all the way to the center of the mountains, if you were strong and brave enough."

"I'm at least one of those."

"Or perhaps neither." A smile played on her lips. A joke from Ingla? They must have truly descended into Pandemonium.

"Why do you tell me this?"

"These places make me… uncomfortable." That was a revelation. Ingla's eyes lingered on his own in a strangely intimate way. For Ingla, an admission of weakness was likely the height of intimacy.

Fenrir wasn't certain how to respond, instead fumbling his words. "Um… why do they bother you?"

She snapped her head back and shot him with a glare like a crank bow bolt to the face. "You will not ask me questions, trash. Move." Ingla punctuated the command with a shove.

He shook his head. Yetra-damned women.

They followed the feeder river for a time, until they must have left the immediate vicinity of the laboratory. Fenrir thought they must be somewhere under the warehouse district, assuming the river was indeed heading straight toward the Fullane. They reached a small passageway guarded by two bored-looking Adders, older Sestrian men who didn't exude quite the reference for Darian that oozed from the younger Adders like Hane. Fenrir hadn't met these two. They mustn't stay in the barracks, though living down here didn't seem like a comfortable option.

"Principal," said one of them, this the thick-necked bastard with a slight sneer, as if he knew a joke but wasn't sharing the punchline.

"Lieutenant Yearon. All secure?" Darian had said the name with disdain. It was unusual for a man so clearly disliked by Darian to remain employed. There was a story there, certainly.

"All secure. It is time, again?" Still the sneer, though it bordered on open hostility.

"It is time. Ingla is with me."

"I see that." Yearon shot a look at Ingla, who seemed to shrink behind Darian. A story here, indeed. "Then, I will happily abdicate my place." Yearon stepped slightly to the side, as did the other guard. There was just enough room for Fenrir to scrape through after Darian. As they passed, Yearon grabbed Ingla's upper arm, whispering something fierce into her ear. She appeared to pale in the dim light before ripping free and following after Fenrir, who pointedly pretended that he hadn't witnessed the brief altercation.

A couple of minutes later, Darian pulled out a key, working it at the lock of yet another door. With the click of the tumblers, Darian turned and locked Fenrir in a fierce, almost feverish gaze. He gripped Fenrir's right shoulder, his powerful fingers digging into his shiny, pink scar. It hurt.

"I would spare you this, boy, despite everything. Despite what you think of me. But I need to trust you by whatever means, just like your brothers. So, I need you to know." His voice was low, as intense as his demon's gaze.

"Know what?" Fenrir whispered, fearing the answer.

"I need you to know the price of betrayal." With that, Darian pushed into the room. Fenrir hesitated, until he was encouraged by a sharp push from Ingla.

On a singular, wooden stool, a naked girl sat in the center of the small, fastidiously clean chamber. It wasn't a cell, then, as it didn't reek like Fenrir's had, and there was no evidence of a chamber pot. The girl's head rested in her hands, tangled brown hair shielding her from her visitors and providing a temporary refuge. She raised her head slowly, and Fenrir was suddenly sick upon seeing Astora's face looking back at him, old tears having left streaks on her smooth, young cheeks.

No, but this wasn't Astora.... This was an older Rostanian woman, probably a couple of years Fenrir's senior. Gods, being near his father was fucking with his mind. Though, the woman's eyes were a similar gray to his daughter's. The resemblance was perhaps a coincidence, but Fenrir knew, from experience, that nothing was coincidental with Darian.

"Peribel de Annos," Darian said, his voice as chill as his burning ice. De Annos–the woman must be of a merchant class, then, with his adding of the appellation "de" to denote new wealth. A younger Fenrir had tried to ditch the "de" from "de Trenton" to no avail.

"A woman with a brilliant mind. A woman with a bright future. A woman of unparalleled greed and stupidity." The woman flinched at each word as if they were tiny barbs tearing through her body. "We have had this conversation twice now. There will not be a third time."

"There is nothing to tell," the woman whimpered.

"Nothing to tell. Of course, there is nothing to tell. You are simply a woman, attempting to steal my secrets, steal my chemicals, because you are interested in expanding your knowledge of the world. Do you think I am a dullard? Do you think that all of this…" Darian spread his hands wide, "…came from a stupid man who believed the lies of a manipulative traitor?"

"No…" answered Peribel. "I tell you, I wanted to test a reaction with meldus, a new formula that I could not test safely in the Furnace. I wanted to take it outside Rostane in case… in case something went wrong. I didn't want anyone to be hurt."

"So you've told me," Darian said. "So, you take meldus out of this place under the darkness, expecting security to be lax. The Adders are very good, though, and detected your ruse. They followed you to that farm, where you simply read and waited. Waiting for someone."

"No! I was reading manuscripts on meldus so I could be sure before I risked my life." Peribel was openly weeping now, wiping at her eyes with trembling hands.

"Manuscripts that you stole from me." Darian leaned forward, his voice the hiss of a venomous snake preparing to strike. Peribel struggled backward, but had nowhere to go. Her ankles were bound to the stool, and the stool was bolted to the ground.

"I'm sorry! I'm so sorry! I made a mistake! I should have known better, but I needed to know!" Peribel cried, her eyes darting between Fenrir, Ingla, and Darian.

"Despite the consequences?"

"I wasn't thinking."

"A poor quality in a scientist. A worse quality in anyone who works for me."

Darian turned to Fenrir, his face as hard as the stone that encased them. "This is the unfortunate price of betrayal. Peribel stole from me and lied to me. The reasoning is inconsequential— perhaps she was, indeed, testing this formula on her own. Perhaps she meant to sell it to a competitor or enemy. It doesn't matter. The disobedience remains. The lies remain. The price is the same."

Darian carefully donned two thick leather gloves, and then he pulled out a small, clear glass bottle from an inner pocket of his black overcoat. He held it to the light for a moment, revealing a cloudy pink substance swirling around like a tiny storm. Was this a liquid version of his burning ice?

Peribel saw the bottle and renewed her struggles.

"Boy. Ingla. Hold her arms."

Ingla shoved his back roughly, forcing him forward.

"Do what he says, trash," she said, her voice filled with its typical anger. More quietly, punctuated by a small squeeze of his shoulder, she added, "Be strong."

Fenrir tentatively grasped Peribel's wrist, noticing, very acutely, her nakedness. Not in a sexual way, though she had a slim figure and near flawless, pale skin. No, he recognized the vulnerability of her nakedness. Fenrir wished, for a moment, that he could drape a blanket around her shoulders and take her from this place. He wished he had the strength to fight his father.

Darian dipped a tiny dropper into the bottle, extracting a miniscule amount of this pink substance. He held the dropper above Peribel, who was wheezing heavy, fearful breaths. Fenrir could feel the sweat beading on her skin.

"Peribel de Annos…" Darian began formally, "…in violation of your contract and in violation of the law, I find you guilty of theft and treason against the de Trenton family. It is with great difficulty that I will now carry out your sentence. You shall be put to death with the very chemical you sought to steal: meldus. Your family will not be paid your death pension, and will be made aware of your treasonous activities. If investigation reveals any culpability, they will be dealt the same sentence."

"No…" Perible moaned, straining against Fenrir and Ingla. "My son is innocent. Please…"

Darian cut in. "You will not be allowed a Yetranian funeral, but will instead be cremated and given to the Fullane." This was a deep insult to a Yetranian, only reserved for those who'd been damned or excommunicated. Peribel, like most Ardians, must have been Yetranian. Her struggles ceased at this condemnation, her head hanging limply in unrestrained defeat.

Without hesitation, Darian released a drop of the meldus onto Peribel's bare thigh.

Fenrir's eyes were trained on her exposed skin, terrified of what was to come. He'd heard stories, long ago, of the experiments conducted in the laboratory, of the mutilated sheep corpses that were fed to furnaces. Of the terrible, human-like howling of pigs that could sometimes be heard, late at night, emanating from the great, blocky building.

At first, nothing happened. Her skin remained pale and unchanged, and Peribel even looked up at Darian, hope thick in her gray eyes. And then she began to scream. It was a keening noise that cut through the small chamber like Fenrir's blade had cut through the little duke's body. Her flesh began to turn a soft red, color spreading slowly from the focal point of the drop. A deeper red bulls-eye was in the middle, and then that color spread, as well.

She bucked and pulled so strongly that Fenrir nearly lost his grip. Ingla, however, was granite.

The woman's thigh began to bubble and blacken, muscle seeming to melt below what was left of her skin. The flesh was dying by degrees, from below her knee to near her pelvic bone. Her calf, untouched by this spreading plague, twitched compulsively against the bonds. It only took moments for her leg to die, the effect of this chemical taking only a dozen or so breaths. Though, to Peribel, it must have felt like a lifetime—blue, straining veins were pulsing on her forehead, and her face was twisted in a caricature of humanity.

When it was clear that this first torture was over, Darian grasped Peribel's face in his leather grip and looked into her pain-filled eyes as she whimpered. His gaze was inscrutable, though a brief spasm of unrecognizable emotion flashed across his features before he let a drop of meldus fall onto her cheek.

This time, there was no delay. The thin flesh of Peribel's face began to redden and blacken, bubbling and blistering as she howled. Her mouth twisted in a terrible grin as her lips were eaten away, and her scream turned into a garbled cry as her tongue began to shrivel and melt. Her eyes, though, were the worst to behold. They began to bulge out of her head, seemingly larger than possible. The gray irises filled with crimson, and each eye simply popped and deflated, one after the other.

Fenrir fought the urge to be sick, but could not look away.

After a few more moments of struggle, the meldus finally spread to Peribel's brain. Mercifully, she was finally dead.

Darian de Trenton leveled his black-pool gaze at Fenrir without wavering, without a hint of empathy or guilt. Without humanity.

"If you betray me… if anything happens to me or my holdings as a result of your actions, this will be Astora's fate before it be your own."

Chapter 22

They would be safe in Agricorinor.

Meri clung to the idea like a woman slipping off a cliff would cling to shallow-rooted grass. Agricorinor would provide them with succor. Agricorinor would heal their wounds. Agricorinor would teach her to master her Yetra-forsaken powers, and then she would move on with her life. Whatever that looked like for her now.

There was no returning home. Even had Dunmore not been decimated, even had she not killed at least two townsmen— rapists, both—Ragen was gone. She has accepted her father as lost, and she had taken time to mourn and honor him. So then, would she pursue his kidnappers and murderers? The trail was colder than the harsh winter winds of Rafon. It would be like chasing a nightmare… impalpable, nebulous, and full of terrifying memories. She would be like Eramore, whose travels had launched a hundred stories.

Eramore, a Jecustan knight, had wandered the range of Saiwen searching for his lost wife. The stories said that she had been taken during a trip to the market in Farrow's Hold, and by a dozen men, each wearing a symbol of a crimson sword over their hearts. The Band of the Crimson Blades, as they'd become known, had disappeared into the night with Lady Raslin as their prisoner. Everywhere in Saiwen, there were stories of her husband Eramore's adventures in search of her. Once, he'd been in Nistling, and single-handedly boarded and destroyed a pirate ship on the Crown Seas, having gotten word that the Band of the Crimson Blades had an association with said pirates. In another story, this one from Thaul, he'd killed the lord of Yurinor in fair combat, thinking he had hidden information about his wife's takers. Instead of taking the city, as would have been his right, he'd then continued on his hopeless quest for a woman long gone.

He might still be hunting in his dotage; new stories popped up from time to time, though who could vouch for their veracity?

Merigold did not want to be an Eramore, a lost soul roaming the land searching for something that could not be found, saving and shattering lives in the process. She would not become a tragedy, a topic for roadside taverns and small town plays. "I've heard Merigold killed a dozen nobles in Farrow's Hold." "I've heard that she burned down a Yetranian chapel because they were hiding some knowledge of the men who destroyed Dunmore." No, that would not be her. So, what would she be, then?

Months ago, in her pain and loss following the Battle of Florens, Merigold had decided that it was her goddess-given role to exterminate the world of magic. It was a terrible thing, this ability that she had. The blood on her hands painted the appendages crimson. The memories that she had stolen rendered her confused about her own past. And the lives that she had ruined left her awash with a conflicting guilt and a feeling of righteous pride. No one should wield such power, but who was she to take it away? Cryden had said hundreds of people in every major city had some capacity for magic—would she have to hunt down and kill each of those people? And what would that do to her soul, assuming there'd be anything left of it after that?

The height of arrogance, to think that she—Merigold Hinter—would be chosen for anything by a higher power, by a goddess who probably didn't exist.

"Merigold!" A rough hand gripped her arm, yanking her near off her horse. "You were drifting off. It would be a shame to come this far and crack your skull on the road." Lisan shot Meri a wan smile that she flashed back, though unconvincingly. It was dark out; they had to ride at night to remain undetected, and the frozen night lulled Meri into the less-traveled reaches of her mind.

"Sorry, I've never been very good on a horse, and fleeing an army is a bit exhausting."

"Pfft. Hardly an army. Just a dozen patrols of Sun Guard bent on revenge after we maimed their highest-ranking and most well-loved captain. Tinto, with his formerly-perfect face, surely holds a bit of a grudge, as well," Lisan said wryly.

"Quite reassuring. You should have been a Taneo, advising people on how to overcome their challenges and find peace in their lives." Meri smiled in memory of Taneo Marsh, always lending an ear no matter how small the problem.

"Or I could just become a professional con artist and feed people the same number of lies," Lisan spat, and with enough venom that Merigold started.

"Whatever you believe in—Yetra, other gods, or nothing—you have to admit that the Taneos do a lot of good. They help guide the people, keep them on some moral path. Even if the book that spouts those morals may be flawed in some way, these people have given their lives over to others," said Merigold.

"I think we are considering different religions. Your average Taneo is just as greedy, corrupt, and manipulative as a noble. They just hide it under robes and behind a book."

"We may have to agree to disagree. I've little love, these days, for the Yetranians…." it was hard to say that, but it was true. Every time she found some sort of hope, again it was dashed against rocks like a ship in a storm. "But the precepts of The Book of Amorum are sound. The parables speak of love, patience, kindness, and charity. Certainly, some simply do lip service to that, but others live that, day by day."

"Those are dead values in this world. Love gets you betrayed. Patience gets you ambushed. Kindness gets you taken advantage of. And charity typically just helps line the pockets of people who don't deserve it." In the low light of the stars, Lisan's ungenerous features appeared nearly violent.

"Then in what do you believe? Who is the Day Mother?" Meri asked, remembering that Lisan had used this name like as both praise and curse in their time together.

"The Day Mother is a fake goddess who does nothing, much like Yetra. I've spent some time abroad, and I simply like the sound her name. She was, in fact, widely worshipped on an island off the coast of Menoga, a place where they spoke a bastardized Jecustan, despite the hundreds or thousands of intervening miles. She may even have been an offshoot of Yetranian myth, were I to make a guess."

"Tell me about Menoga. How did you find yourself there, in a country that barely anyone has ever heard of?" Merigold had been meaning to ask and learn more about their castaway attacker, but things had been so hectic, and frankly she had not been in the mood for conversation.

Lisan grimaced. "It was a long time ago, Merigold. I'd rather not..."

A painful half-moan, half-scream pulled Meri and Lisan away from their hushed conversation. Lisan whistled a piercing whistle to signal a stop, and their little party ground to a halt. Taking Lisan's lead, Merigold dismounted and nearly slipped in the icy snow, just catching herself by grasping the stirrup of her ornery horse, who she had named Grumpy.

Marius was driving the farmer's cart that they had stolen after escaping from Polanice. The simple brother had barely said a word since Remy had been sapped of his lifeforce. His eyes carried an emptiness that mirrored his comatose brother's. Merigold had expected—maybe even hoped for—some ill will toward her; she had all but ended Remy's life. But Marius treated her no differently from anyone else. That is to say that he ignored her. He followed any direction that Lisan provided with a mindless efficiency, but did little more than he was instructed. He had become an automaton.

Merigold nodded at him with the expected null response as she walked around to the back of the cart. Lisan loosened and rolled back the tarp, and the moonslight fell upon the two bodies within.

Remy did not move. He did not blink. He breathed, and that was all. He was simply meat, with no mind, no lifeforce remaining. The essence of humanity, the power indigenous to every living thing, was near gone. Merigold did not need to quest to see that his nerring was deflated and wilted, holding only a smidgeon of maenen. Cryden had told her that Feral were created by repeatedly draining a body of maenen, but that it was a careful process. Always enough had to be left in the nerring to prevent the ethereal vessel from collapsing, as he'd put it. Remy had been drained beyond that point when he'd tried to prevent Merigold from further staining her hands red.

They carried Remy with them on the slim hope that someone at Agricorinor knew more about this affliction, in case he could be healed. Lisan had argued against it as they'd readied their escape. An extra body would weigh them down, further slowing their flight from Polanice. Their chances were slim already; the Sun Guard had likely mobilized to find them almost immediately. Marius, though, would not budge without his brother, and despite his limited ability as a conversationalist, Marius was known as an unmatched warrior.

Besides, they had to cart Cryden along anyhow, so a second useless body wouldn't slow them down much more than one.

He was moaning again, which meant he might be close to regaining consciousness. The Menogan castaway had sliced open his abdomen, and Merigold again recalled how his guts had been visible through the gash, some even having tumbled onto the

297

deck. Combined with the blow to the head, the wound had left Cryden unconscious by the time Meri had ended the Menogan castaway. She'd been certain that Cryden had been killed—there'd been so much blood, such an awful amount of blood. But, he had still breathed, though laboring greatly to do so.

Of all people, Ill'Nath had tended to him. First, he'd cleaned the wound with the clean rags and whatever rotgut rum they could confiscate from the sailors. Then, he'd gently pressed any visible guts back into the wound, and begun sewing. He'd done so in layers—first, whatever muscles he could find, then followed by the skin itself. He'd proceeded to tend to all of wounded while still bleeding from his own chest wound. Merigold had supposed that a man whose face was covered with piercings, including a gaping cheek hole, would know a thing or two about body care. But Ill'Nath had gone to it like an experienced field surgeon.

Even then, the pasnes alna had not been guaranteed to live, if he even was now. He had lost a great deal of blood, and the threat of infection was almost a certainty. Ill'Nath had forced water and a thin broth down Cryden's throat. Most of this had been vomited up, but Ill'Nath had tended to him like a lady-in-waiting would tend to a princess. Somehow, the man had pulled through the worst of it, the first two days, without ever regaining consciousness.

By the time they'd landed in Polanice, the wound had begun to sour, first with a spreading redness and then with a running pus. Whatever god was watching over Cryden was unkind, as they'd chosen that time to allow him to regain consciousness. He'd been in a feverish agony, and they'd had to place a stick in his mouth both to keep him quiet, lest they be ejected from their inn, and to give him something to gnaw on, lest he dig his teeth into his tongue. As the hours had passed, he'd begun to settle, and his glistening eyes, awash in pain and recognition, had beckoned for Merigold to tell him what had happened.

She had, speaking quietly and holding his hand. She'd told him of the Menogan who had sliced his stomach open, who had killed and injured several others. She'd told him of how she'd killed him with a magical plate, and he'd shaken his head, either in humor that she'd used the most common tool of her former trade or in disgust that she hadn't kept the castaway alive to interrogate. She'd explained Ill'Nath's surgical treatment, though not in great detail—so as not to alarm him. He'd pushed her, though, with short phrases, for as many details as possible. Then, she'd told him how, when they'd landed, the Polanicers had greeted them with nothing but suspicion, how their boat had been under constant scrutiny by the Sun Guard and who knew who else. She'd told him how they'd secreted away, one night, to this inn run by a Sestrian who seemed honest and sympathetic, while they'd sought to find a cart to get them on the road north to Agricorinor.

He had gasped out to Meri, gripping her hand with a fevered strength and locking her eyes with an intense, heated gaze. "You must get us to Agricorinor. This is your greatest test. Even here, I feel it."

"Feel what, Cryden?" she had asked. He hadn't answered, though. In agony that rivaled a torture victim, he had prodded at his wound. He'd then closed his eyes, taking a deep, shuddering breath. And then, then... he'd screamed as if his heart was being wrenched from his body before again losing consciousness.

Two hours later, his wound had looked slightly better, and his fever had broken a bit. But, the reprieve from his illness had not lasted.

And so it had gone since they'd begun their journey. Cryden would wake from time to time, demanding to know what was happening with very few words. He would tell them to feed him, an almost beastial desperation behind the request. Then, he would probe and prod at his injury, and would howl in anguish before

299

losing himself for two or more days. It was obvious that he was using his powers to burn away whatever parts of his infection were most susceptible, but that he was also exhausting himself and doing an incomplete job.

His moaning now meant either that he was awakening or the fever was worsening. Regardless, they needed to keep him quiet; they still had some ground to cover until they passed into the place on the map where, as Lisan put it, Sestria was fucking Rafon. She was, of course, referring to the chunk of land to which Sestria laid claim, though it should have properly been Rafon's if one were limited by the unimaginative lines of real-world geography. It was one more step on their path to Agricorinor.

"Merigold..." wheezed Cryden, apparently awake and aware enough to notice her arrival. She took stock of his thinning body, weakly touching his pinched and drawn face. He could have been a corpse. "How..."

"The infection is again taking hold," she said, anticipating his question. Cryden squeezed shut his eyes. "Ill'Nath has been treating it with a herbal poultice, but it doesn't help."

"Where..."

"We are south of Sestria's grasp. We've still a ways to go," Lisan said, her brow furrowing as she peered out into the darkness.

Was there an echo, metal striking metal in the distance? Some shouts or screams? Or was it just their paranoia?

"Stop interrupting me," Cryden said. He sounded more coherent than he had since before his injury. "I'm just dying, not an invalid."

"You aren't dying," Merigold told him, grasping his hand. "Ill'Nath says that the wound is recovering. If only we could get this infection under control, you would be whole again. If you could simply rest in a bed rather than be jolted about in a poorly-built cart…"

"You have been feeding me? I require as much as you can force down."

"Yes, broth and soaked bread. You push up half of it, so we just keep shoving it back down," Merigold said in a weak attempt at humor.

Cryden took a deep breath and shuddered. He clenched tight his eyes and Merigold noticed a tear passively tracking down his cheek. She gripped his hand a little tighter as Lisan considered the pair of them and then walked away. Cryden took another breath and picked his words carefully, as if there were only so many remaining in his body.

"I will need to continue to fight this. I will lose myself again. Merigold, Agricorinor is a suspicious place. You, and those with us, will not be welcomed with open arms. Like Ardia, there are factions and divisions. I do not know the state of things, as it has been years since I last set foot in those halls."

"Why so long?" Merigold asked, adjusting herself to sit between Remy and Cryden. This was encouraging, him speaking so much, being so aware. She hoped it was a turning point.

"Let me talk, girl. I need to get something across. If I am still… unwell…. If I do not make it, you need to seek out Ellel Dietz. Speak to no one of what you have seen, save her. Refuse all others. They may threaten you. They may trick you. They may blackmail you. But speak… to… no… one… else." His words were halting now, and his mouth was beginning to slacken. Each word was a drooling effort.

"You need to rest so that I don't have to walk into this hornet's nest alone," Merigold said quietly.

He proceeded as if he hadn't heard her.

"Do not trust Enit Boran. Speak to no one but Ellel. Tell her that I... that I had to leave, but it was not her." The last word was slurred, and he stiffened, calling out as he summoned whatever powers he could muster to fight his infection. He slumped back into the cart. Merigold continued holding his hand for a moment, and then tucked the blankets back around him. She stood stiffly and looked to the north, toward that bastion of hope that was the seat of the pasnes alna on this side of the world.

They would be safe in Agricorinor.

Merigold knew it was a misplaced faith as much as her lifetime of belief in Yetra. Nonetheless, they plodded onward, their goal unchanged.

Interlogue: Envy

"Your nerring is beginning to decay more rapidly. I mustn't even quest—it is evident from your eyes. They still shine with intelligence and your innate goodness, but also with pure animal aggression. If this were not such a common sight for me, sweetling, then I might be afraid. As it is, this has become all too common during my long life.

"I have been sapping maenen from others longer than you can imagine. If only I could stop...

"But, there is so much that can be done with the maenen of another. It is far more than just raw power. Far, far more. It can be molded, shaped, sculpted... with the greatest practitioners being more artist than pasnes alna. With maenen, I can create light on a spectrum that you could barely perceive. I can fertilize crops with power such that a harvest could be yielded in a day. I can reinforce great monuments, allowing them to be greater still. And, I can destroy.

"I was the Blood Maiden, so long ago. In Oagon, I cut through hundreds of soldiers. Mostly enemies, but some allies. Even with my killing Amorum's people—my own people—they worshipped me. I was a god to them, a creature to be worshipped and feared. Even after I stripped myself of the blood-stained armor and began tending to the wounded, wrapping bandages around great cuts and tying tourniquets around severed limbs, men and women shrank back from my touch, refusing to meet my eyes. They gathered in small groups and whispered about my power.

"We had captured Oagon, though half of its population was killed in the attack and subsequent sacking. We had a town, again, to call our own. But it was not home. Home was gone.

"As people avoided me—the Blood Maiden—Amorum continued to operate as the brain and soul of the people, guiding

303

them with his powerful voice and persuasive manner. He would have made a great king, and the people began hailing him as such.

"It is with great shame, sweetling, that I tell you how I was overcome with envy.

"At the time, it seemed utterly wrong. These people had flocked to our side because of me. I was the banner, the figurehead. I had largely developed the plan of attack on Oagon, and I was the one who'd brought us victory, brutal though it may have been. Amorum may have motivated the people with fancy words, but I... I forced things to happen! I created victory with my own two hands!

"How foolish it seems now, sweetling, to feel this way. If only I could have known the future at the time. If only I could have known of the love Amorum had for me, that might have been the difference. The world, today, may well be different if that had been the case.

"But, my envy twisted me; it wrung my mind into a gnarled mass of jealousy. It seemed so wrong, unnatural even, that I was feared and he was loved.

"I began to cultivate my own group of followers, devotees who answered only to me. They worshipped the Blood Maiden as an idol... hung on my every word as if it were prophecy or the words of the divine. Amorum and I rarely spoke; he was focused on rebuilding the city and integrating the old and new residents, while I was focused on building my own influence.

"My followers spent a good deal of time interrogating prisoners, soldiers who fought for the Oagon and town leaders. Their methods were archaic and cruel, but they held such anger. I fueled that anger, sweetling, with my words and my very presence.

"That is when we found Intenu.

304

"Intenu was not an Oagon. She was from a country I had never heard of. Menoga, thousands of miles distant. My followers had begun to interrogate her and… it ended poorly. Like me, she was a metsika—a wild mage—though there wasn't a word for it in those times.

"After she slaughtered my men, I went to see her myself, and not without great trepidation. I had little understanding or control over my powers, and I feared the possibility of a rival or an attack. But, I also had an insatiable curiosity, a thirst for learning more about my unique abilities.

"Thankfully, Intenu had no intention of harming me. She had been taken captive before we had even arrived in Oagon, left in the care of the Oagonans by her captors. Sold to them, actually, to be used as a weapon. You see, in my region of the world, use of this power was yet unknown, and at least so rare that the people of my army were unaware of it. However, in other far away areas of the warring world, this power—though still uncommon—was harnessed, controlled, and used for war.

"Intenu was a victim of this—a weapon. In her country, they had a method for detecting who was born with this power, and a method for controlling it. She wore an ring in her lip, a beautiful, sapphire jewel. Whomever wore the matching bit of jewelry could control her powers, and she could not remove her own ring without it killing her. She had learned that she could only access her powers unconsciously when under duress, which explained why the blood of my followers painted the walls of her cell.

"Her captor had fled in advance of when my army had attacked, so, she could not be controlled, and could not access her powers.

"But she knew so much. So very much about maenen and maen, yenas and pearen. More than any great sage, it seemed. Though she could only access her own maen, the miernes armas—magic weapons, as they called Intenu and her ilk—were enslaved from childhood. Though their imprisonment was often plush, their needs met by servants and slaves, it was nonetheless a prison.

"But I digress, yet again. Intenu learned much from the other miernes armas, about all forms of power. She began to teach me of the artistry involved in what you would call magic, sweetling. And, she was a fantastic teacher, a maestro. And a lovely woman, as well.

"She also had the incredibly rare ability to sense the use of miernes in the wider world… all kinds of miernes. I had thought these powers so rare. We all did. But, in those days, she taught me that the powers were simply more buried. So many people had the ability to access miernes, but had no idea. I was the same way. I don't know if things are different, in these times, but people seem to be more readily able to embrace their powers.

"We helped awaken these powers. Most people had some idea that they were different, but were uncertain how. Intenu simply made them aware of their abilities, sweetling, and began to teach them, too. It was my own school of miernes, the only one for thousands of miles.

"While Amorum sought to integrate the peoples of Aquine, Oagon, and the many other small villages and towns that made up our army, and while he worked to forge peaceful alliances with nearby warring states and countries… I built my army of followers, my army of pasnes alna. I may have been feared, but at least I would be powerful. At least, I would be able to rival Amorum in influence.

"My envy, sweetling, was the beginning of the end of Amorum and me. It took years, though, for that schism to fully form. But the jealousy of the Blood Maiden was the origin of this split. He was a good man. Far too good a man for me.

"Just as you are, sweetling. This pains me, every time we meet."

Chapter 23

"You… you are a monster," Fenrir said to Darian, taking another gulp of Hunesian wine before emptying the bottle into his glass. His fourth glass, in fact. After Peribel's torture, they had left the laboratory in silence, retreating to Darian's office in the distribution center. Ingla stood silently in the corner, chin down and arms folded, while Darian and Fenrir spoke.

"If I be a monster, you fall into that same category. How many fingers did you take while in the employ of The House?"

"That was different," Fenrir said over the hollow feeling in his stomach that had remained since Peribel's death. Fenrir wasn't exactly a Martyr, but what had happened below… it was indeed different.

"Of course, it was different. You were doing as ordered, and you were doing it for money. Someone, though, has to give the orders. At least I have the fortitude to both give the orders and execute the sentences. At least I am there to witness." Darian took a sip of his wine, as well. His hand was steady, despite what had just happened in the caverns.

There was a sick logic to what Darian said. Tennyson never soiled his own hands on either the warnings or the assassinations, instead sending enforcers and eliminators on those jobs. Fenrir, himself, had carried out many such deeds, but been able to write his actions off as a part of "doing his job." These people all would have lost their fingers regardless, and, though Fenrir had bungled some of these jobs, he'd simply been a tool. Tennyson, or whoever he'd partnered with, had been responsible.

"As always, you serve as an example to us all, my lord," Fenrir said, carefully sarcastic.

"Usually, I would appreciate that you are hiding behind your sarcastic formalities. But, set that aside for once." Darian put down his wine glass and leaned forward over steepled fingers. "Have a conversation with me, boy."

Fenrir chuckled. "A conversation? I just witnessed you melt a woman with chemicals. It was as horrifying as being assfucked by Ultner in a Yetranian chapel. I'll likely not sleep for a month. And, now, after all these years, you want to have a conversation?"

"You think I relish murder?" Darian raised a bushy eyebrow, deepening the creases on his forehead.

"I think you are good at it," Fenrir retorted, leaning forward himself. He'd always known his father was capable of murder—there were enough rumors to that effect. But, now he had firsthand evidence.

"You know so little, boy, of how the world works. Success involves the protection of your assets. If you have something others want, very little will dissuade them from taking it. From the day that I began my work with herbs and chemicals, there were those seeking to steal from me. Those working to end me, in fact. Look at this." Darian rolled up his sleeve, revealing a long, uneven scar, faded from age and spanning the length of his forearm. Fenrir had seen it before, but never cared to ask. "When I first discovered burning ice, assassins were sent to kill me and steal the formula. I was nothing back then. I had a small workshop, funded by translation work and some meager trading efforts. I'd foolishly tested burning ice on a small shipment of beef, and the results were fantastic. It would revolutionize trade, boy." Darian's dark eyes were distant, fixed on his past, with a hint of a smile showing on his face.

"But, it was too soon. A killer came for me, caught me working late in my little laboratory. She didn't expect to find me awake, and I fought back. I caught her face with a gas lamp, but not before she gave me this scar."

Fenrir had never known that about his father. The whole thing sounded far too… human for Darian.

"When she was down, a container of newly-formed cubes of burning ice fell onto her face. The extreme differences in temperature—the sweaty heat of her skin and the intense cold of the burning ice—caused the substance to stick to her face, burning away her skin. That was the first time that I realized the… potential of these chemicals for alternate uses," Darian mused.

"Meldus," Fenrir concluded, shivering at the all-too-recent memory.

"Meldus came much later. But, first, I needed to discover who'd betrayed me. One of the teamsters, who shipped the beef, had taken some of the burning ice to a major shipping company in an effort to get rich. I confronted him, and he was penitent; did nothing but apologize. Boy, I was young and stupid. I forgave him. Then, more killers came for me. When I was at home, with your brothers and their mother. Before you were born." Darian abruptly sat back in his chair.

"I was prepared and had protection by then, and they were unsuccessful. But I learned an important lesson. Forgiveness begets treachery, and generosity begets greed. The only way to protect myself and my discoveries was to make it… strongly undesirable to cross me."

Eyeballs bulging and popping. Skin blistering and muscle melting.

"I found this teamster and made him pay for his actions. And, let it slip to my people the price of treachery. Just as Ingla will spread rumors about Peribel's demise. There are few methods as effective in protecting secrets as the threat of a gruesome death."

"You could have ended Peribel more easily than by using that fucking meldus. Why torture her? Why not end her more easily and tell others of a terrible death?" Fenrir rubbed at his temples.

310

"Because that would be a lie. Lies, of this nature, are always discovered. If Ingla were to lie when telling others of this tale, it would be detectable. In her body language, in her eyes. It must be a real threat to dissuade others." Fenrir heard Ingla shift behind him, and felt her gaze on his neck. She had been watching him too closely since they'd left that terrible place below the Furnace.

"It is a clear threat." Fenrir thought of Astora being strapped to that stool in the caverns, flesh withering at the touch of this chemical.

"Then it seems we have an understanding, boy." Darian's eyes glittered. Indeed, they had an understanding.

"Now that we are on the same side, it is time to talk about your task."

"Destroying The House," Fenrir muttered. The thought was ridiculous.

"Destroying The House," Darian repeated. "The approach will have to be different, now. Undoubtedly, your time with my Adders has been reported back to Tennyson. Turning you back into a decent warrior had to be somewhat public, however, and not even I can prevent every spy from entering a compound this large."

"But, if you catch them, you melt their faces."

"Melt them, cut them, burn them. Depending on the crime. But, since The House likely knows you are working for me, you will not be greeted with open arms, and you will not have an easy time getting close to Tennyson again." Darian stood and walked over to a wine shelf, where he stood considering for a moment before pulling a dusty bottle from the top shelf. Sestrian viognier, it looked like.

"You thought I could get close to Tennyson and kill him?" Fenrir laughed. "That was your plan? He would have murdered me. And, if I'd managed to kill him, there'd have been no escape. I would have been captured, and Peribel's fate would seem pleasant in comparison to what he'd have done to me."

Darian smirked. "I had thought the man who killed the little duke would be more skilled. Did I see a boy knock you to the dirt earlier today?" Darian sat, pouring Fenrir a glass of the viognier. It was sweet when he tasted it—far sweeter than he was used to.

"A big fucking boy," Fenrir muttered. His ribs still ached, but the emotional toll of the day (as well as the wine) distracted from the pain.

"Regardless, thanks to Ingla..." Darian nodded to the Adder, "...you are at least better able to defend yourself and less likely to embarrass me. You will begin serving your country by identifying agents of The House. The execution, tomorrow, will be a perfect opportunity. Agents of The House will be in attendance and will almost certainly attempt interference. You will point them out to us, as well as any nobles that you know have had dealings with Tennyson."

"The execution?"

"Events are moving, boy. Keep up. Tomorrow, Ingla and several others will accompany you to Amorum Square. You will do your task impeccably. You know the consequences."

"I don't know many members..."

"You know enough. Each one is a link."

"Aye, my lord principal." Back to the sarcastic formality.

Without any more discussion, Darian pulled away the bottle of viognier and opened a ledger. Evidently, Fenrir was dismissed; he rose, head swimming from all of the wine sitting in his empty stomach. He left the office with Ingla following closely at his heels. Fenrir's mind was reeling from the day—Peribel, the threat to his daughter, betraying The House…. Whatever had happened to a simple, predictable life?

Suddenly, Fenrir found himself pinned against the wall, Ingla's forearm against his neck and cutting off his airway, her face close to his. He grasped at her, but she increased the pressure on his windpipe right away, setting him to gasping. Her hazel eyes were aflame.

"Why do you disrespect your father?" she hissed through clenched teeth.

He gargled something until she loosened her grip. Then he took a merciful breath of air, sweet though it reeked of burning ice—like everything in the main warehouse.

"He's not my father. He disowned me, though you might not know that."

"I was there that day. I know all about you, trash. Lord de Trenton gave us very specific orders about you." Fenrir's brow furrowed—Ingla had been there that day? He'd seen a handful of Adders, but been distracted by shoulder pain and goading Sigmund Fitra. Wait… she had been guarding the back door into the warehouse. He'd flirted with no success; it didn't even feel like the same lifetime.

"To kill me?" he asked. His father had made that pronouncement the day of his disownment—death if he were to approach any de Trenton holdings.

"To restrain you and see you on your way," spat Ingla, scorn twisting her pretty features. It seemed unlikely that Darian would have granted him mercy, if even more unlikely that this angry Sestrian warrior would lie about this.

She shifted her grip for a moment and Fenrir's hand lashed out, knocking her arm aside. Briefly free, he struck upward with his knee at her pelvis, finding nothing there as she leapt backwards.

313

Then, he was again pressed against the wall, pain shooting through his ribs as her powerful fingers dug into his injury. Through pain-blurred vision, Fenrir could see a smile tickling Ingla's usually fierce expression.

Without precursor, Ingla's lips were unexpectedly locked with his own, her tongue hungrily searching his mouth. Despite the wound in his side, despite the fact that his father had just murdered and melted a woman scant hours before, and despite the fact that this angry little woman had tortured him over the past months, he returned the kiss with a fierce, rapacious passion. By Ultner's useless shriveled cock, it had been a long time since he'd had a woman.

His hands began searching her body, feeling her lithe, powerful muscles through her tight training blues. His left hand wandered to her lower back, lingering for a moment before gently touching her firm, powerful...

And her fist drove into his gut, setting Fenrir gasping for air again.

"Mind your father and preserve your daughter, trash," Ingla hissed at him before stalking down the hallway, a predator intent on her next prey.

Fenrir couldn't help himself, despite the pain. He barked out a laugh which set him to coughing, triggering more pain in his ribs.

Women. Godsdamned fucking women.

***

"And, yet again, I treat the noble warrior for wounds well-earned in fair combat," Martis said with his customary, omnipresent smile, beard-braids swinging as he began to wrap a tight bandage around Fenrir's bare torso.

"You sure nothing is broken?" Fenrir asked, wincing at the tightness of the bandage. The great, multi-colored contusion wasn't exactly reassuring. At the very least, Hane should have some of his own bruises that would be needing treatment.

"Bruised at best, slightly cracked at worst. Regardless, you will be fine to resume your training, though I recommend protecting the area with padding. Oh, and perhaps attempt evasion next time."

"Training may very well be over for now," Fenrir said with a strange pang of regret.

Martis pulled tight on the bindings, eliciting a grunt from his patient. "Does that mean you have an assignment at long last?"

Fenrir had been somewhat reticent with his friend since arriving at the de Trenton estate, leaving the exact conditions of his release a secret. It wasn't that he didn't trust Martis. In fact, it was the opposite. He trusted him implicitly and did not want to burden the man with his unsolvable problems.

"Aye, it looks like I have work to do. Tell me, what is happening in the city?" Maybe a delaying tactic would distract Martis. Besides, Fenrir knew little of what was happening in Rostane. The Blue Adders were insular, and seemed to actively avoid discussing news of the war.

"As far as I can gather, the mood is split, nearly in twain. Commoners, of course, are hurting the worst, with so many conscripted men having been killed in the Battle of Florens and subsequent skirmishes. Thousands of men are not coming home, and thousands more are not home right now to tend to their families and their work. There are daily protests, rallying around figureheads speaking against the war. The city guard, though, has been keeping order admirably. Barely any violence."

"Barely?"

"There's been a small riot or two near the docks, and one even in Little Town. A handful were killed, and a good deal of property damaged. One fire, but it was right beneath a great water barrel and was squelched before spreading. Few enough buildings are made of wood in Rostane, anyhow."

"That seems like enough to worry the Council," Fenrir commented.

"Certainly. There's some who suggest that The House is inciting these riots, that they are either empowering these figureheads or masquerading as anti-war idealists. But, Rostane is winning the War for Unification, as they are calling it. Many people, particularly the merchant classes, are ecstatic. A unified Ardia means that there would not be duchy-to-duchy tariffs, at least as the Council tells it. But merchants who deal with luxuries—silks, diamonds, spices—are railing against the war. It has been crushing their business for the last six months, and there is a call for peace, to leave Hunesa as an independent duchy."

"So, Hunesa stands?" Fenrir slumped into the sole chair in his little quarters.

"Indeed, but they cannot match the military might of Rostane, particularly after heavy conscription in Florens. The Drastonner army, small though it may be, has also been integrated, though they have not seen action. The Council, perhaps rightly so, does not trust the former Duchess Fraunt. Extortion, as it turns out, does not breed loyalty."

"No, it never does. Fear, though, can be a powerful tool." An image of Peribel's melting face flashed in his mind.

316

"Yes, it can, indeed," said Martis, a brief spasm of emotion crossing his face. "With the winter being so mild, I would expect the Council will launch the campaign against Hunesa any day now. They will fight, it seems, and may have some aid from Jecusta. It is unclear to we common folk."

"You are anything but common, Martis," Fenrir said with a raised eyebrow. "What of the Army of Brockmore? Or what is left of it?"

"They have sought shelter in Jecusta. That is all I know—the Council has quite effectively controlled the news of the war. Most of what I know, my students or I have overheard from our noble patients."

"Speaking of patients, how about some more of those pain tablets?"

"Certainly. After you tell me of your plight. I can see it weighing on you, a stone resting upon a frozen lake." Martis smiled reassuringly, pulling out his medicinal satchel.

"Can't be distracted, eh?" Fenrir asked wryly.

"You are too transparent, my friend."

"It has always been the case. It's a bit of a tale."

"I don't mind. I have a task of my own to avoid," Martis answered, breaking eye contact as he rummaged through his bag.

Fenrir didn't precisely start at the beginning, but he told Martis of his involvement with The House, and the rescue of Escamilla and Emma. How he'd become involved with the Army of Brockmore by Tennyson's order, and how he'd ended up killing the duke. He did not, however, mention anything about the strange paralysis that had taken him and his small command, about how his own ability had set him free for just long enough that he could plunge his sword into the chest of Duke Penton.

317

Strange that he hadn't experienced his phantom since then. He'd been consistently fighting, and these training matches weren't exactly safe. Such a useless, inconsistent ability.

And, finally, Fenrir told Martis of his current dilemma.

"So, you betray The House or lose your daughter? You believe your father would carry out that threat? Hurt a girl who is barely past her majority?" Martis fumbled with his braided beard, seemingly lost in thought. His eyes were far away.

"Darian doesn't make threats. He makes contracts. And not hurt, no. Kill," Fenrir corrected him, his throat strangely tight, feeling as if he had swallowed a handful of flour.

Martis stood and turned away, beginning to pace the small room, his measured, precise steps clicking in a soothing rhythm, arms clenched firmly behind his back. Fenrir knew it was part of the physician's process; many times, he had seen the older man march about a room, silent for long minutes while he attempted to work out a specific dilemma. The clack of his boots on the wooden floor was calming.

"What do you value, Fenrir?" Martis asked, abruptly stopping and leaning against the wall, his expression awash with a curious interest.

"Huh?" Fenrir asked. This wasn't exactly the breakthrough he had expected from Martis.

"What do you value? What drives you? I've been observing you, Fenrir, for over twenty years. I recall when you were a frightened, stubborn, teenage military washout with a broken knee, wanting little more than to escape from your father and stymie his wishes. Then, for years, you were a guardsman—never excelling, though certainly capable of doing so. You were often sucked into excesses of life, women and drink, though never lost in them like so many other men. It was enough to ruin your

318

marriage, though, and ensure that you never saw your daughter grow up. This was, perhaps, another attack on your father?"

"You are certainly speculat—" Fenrir began, not welcoming the intrusiveness of the line of questions, or the fact that Martis had apparently been analyzing his behavior for twenty years.

"And then you had your fainting episode, finding yourself unemployed and unemployable. You will recall that I had seen you less at the time, and knew not that you'd fallen in with The House. Again, no judgement," Martis added, seeing Fenrir's darkening expression. "I respect what you did. But, the major question is why you did what you did. Certainly, even after your disgrace, Darian would have offered you some sort of work. You are still his blood, after all, and it would have been safer for him to keep an eye on you if you were reliant on him for income."

"You don't know my father," Fenrir said, shifting in his seat. He was starting to feel the analgesic effects of the devil's root tablets. A shame that Martis doled these out so sparingly—they could solve a lot of Fenrir's problems.

"I know him better than you suspect. But, rather than seek out your father, you turned to the underground. And then more recent events unfolded. You rescuing Escamilla, becoming a criminal hero. You slaying Little Duke Penton, becoming a villain hero. It is quite the story, your past. But, it's not clear why you have done what you have done. So, I ask you again, Fenrir. What drives you? What do you value?" Martis rested on the bed, leaning toward Fenrir with his hands folded. Fenrir leaned away.

Regret. That was Fenrir's first thought. So much to regret. His mother and her ignoble suicide, goaded by the ostracism brought about by her domain blood. Followed by his brothers and their well-deserved deaths—or at least that of one of them, apparently. His wife… the only regret there was that Fenrir had had to marry her in the first place. And then, his daughter…. Perhaps, he could

319

have done more to keep the girl in his life. But, would that have made his life any better? Would that have made her life any better?

Likely not for either of them.

"Truthfully, I don't know, Martis," Fenrir mumbled. Martis smiled sadly.

"So, I suppose the question is, what will you do to protect your daughter? Astora, who you have not seen for most of her life?"

Fenrir sighed heavily. "I don't know."

"Would you risk your life to protect hers?"

"I don't know."

"That is what you would be doing..."

"I know!" Fenrir snapped, twisting himself to his feet. He ran his hands through his tangled hair, which was still shorter than he would have liked after its clean-cutting all those months ago. "Martis, this is enough. This isn't helping me."

Martis was infuriatingly unperturbed in the face of Fenrir's building irritation. "Some problems, my friend, can only be solved from within. Certainly, I could help you excise a bit of stray bone in your knee. Or, I could sew shut a shoulder wound. But, there is little I can do to help you with a moral conundrum such as this. Perhaps the Yetranian Church can provide guidance." Fenrir glanced up to see if his friend was serious. Martis' expression was a mask of earnest sarcasm.

Fenrir smirked. "I'd get more useful advice from a blind whore. At least she'd be more realistic." The two shared a quiet laugh, and Fenrir felt his irritation disperse. Martis was a friend.

"But, sincerely, my friend.... You need to decide what you value. I know you are not one for introspection, but such situations merit a deep look at oneself. And, I know you are not a man for emotions, but you need to decide: do you love?" With that, Martis retrieved his medicinal satchel in one smooth motion, pushing himself to his feet from the low bed. Fenrir moved to help him up.

"You're right, as always. I am not a man for those things. I suppose I will figure all this out in due course. At least this execution will be so crowded that I'm unlikely to be spotted or murdered amidst all of that. What is this execution about, anyway?"

"You don't know?" Martis' face lost any hint of joviality.

"I've been holed up here for months and no one tells me anything. And they aren't exactly posting the news on the corner in here. What? What's wrong?"

The physician was clenching his jaw. "I'm to help with the execution. I am making a potion."

"Poison?"

"No. It's to keep the man alive longer. So he… lingers. The Council demands it of me. Lord de Trenton demands it of me."

Nothing should have surprised Fenrir anymore. His father used torture to educate others. He might as well have a broader audience. "That's… unpleasant."

"Yes, it truly is." Martis stared at his hands, the nimble appendages clenching into white fists. "I am made for healing. Not this."

"A moral dilemma, it seems." Martis barked a forced, bitter laugh at the poor joke. "Who is to be executed?" Fenrir asked.

"I thought you knew, my friend. I am sorry."

"Who?" Fenrir's heart fluttered. Emma? Merigold? Did he have anyone else he cared about?

"Tilner Pick, your former companion and the retainer to the late Lady Escamilla."

Chapter 24

Trina Almark leapt forward with an impossibly fast overhand swing, spitting sparks into the air as her sword bashed into her opponent's. Her weapon was locked with Dien's, one of Ferl's best fighters, for a couple of seconds before they both hopped back in unison and fell back. Dien, a mongrel with blood mixed from Ardia, Rafon, Sestria, and Ultner-knew-where-else, was somewhat smaller than the warrior woman, but his strength was more than a match for hers.

But Trina fought with a fury that was impossible to defend against. Her long-standing depression over the loss of so many women warriors only washed away during these training bouts, which she held every morning. Anyone who wished to try their blade against hers was welcome, and, though she fought with a blunted sword, she allowed others to come after her with the sharpest of blades. Emma had forbidden her own men from joining the fight, but she had no such power over Ferl's Company or the Jecustans.

Trina had a dark reputation in Jecusta, Ultner's Fist having fought against the Jecustans in several skirmishes with Algania. There were many who sought to challenge her as a result, thinking that slaying the Silver Lady would grant them glory. But, not a soul could touch her.

Dien fought with a blunted blade, as well. Ferl had sent him as a friendly competitor and perhaps as an insult. You could never tell with those two. Yet, despite the man's obvious skill with a blade, Trina struck again and again, her weapon clashing against his guard like a she was a woodsman chopping down a tree. Dien began to tire after a time, his blocks and parries each a fraction of a second slower than the ones before. Soon, he found himself off-balance, flailing his arms as her blunted sword point stabbed into his chest after a fierce lunge.

Emma winced at the sight. That would leave a wicked, ugly bruise.

Trina, panting heavily from her exertions, her hair popping out of her tight, silver braid, stood over Dien for a moment as if deciding whether to jam her practice sword into his eye. Then, she sucked a glob from her nose and spat it onto the fallen warrior's boot, then striding toward Emma without a backward glance.

With the mercenary captain walking toward her with a drawn sword and a glint of violence in her eyes, Emma had to fight the urge to retreat.

"It's not like you, my lady, to sully your gown with the dirt of we filthy warriors," Trina said, digging the tip of her weapon into the dirt as she came to a halt. Emma was, in fact, wearing a gown of blue silk, worn under a fur shawl to shield her from the growing chill. Both gifts from Evina Linstael of the Eastern Sweeps. The lady had sent her many gifts, though they had yet to meet in private. Emma had ignored them up until this point, instead wearing her road-worn military outfits. But, today she'd attempted to look the part of a lady. Jecustan politics would be in her favor this day if she could win some hearts as a lady in distress. Harivor had informed her that her thick, shining red hair was even rarer in Jecusta than in Ardia, and highlighting that against—he had loudly "ahem'd" at this comment—what he called ladylike clothing might gain her war efforts some traction.

"Well-fought," Emma replied, ignoring a sudden burst of anger from Trina's caustic, insulting tone. Any fear she felt from seeing the captain dissipated. "I see your reputation is well-earned."

"Yes, some of us earn what we are given." A second flash of anger pushed against Emma's resolve like wine against a leaky cork. Trina knew just how to hurt her, almost baiting her to attack. But Emma wasn't stupid.

"And we must make the best of it, regardless. Tell me, I've heard rumors that your ranks are beginning to swell with new recruits, with Jecustan women anxious to work with the legendary Silver Lady."

Trina spat again, somehow well-hydrated despite her vigorous dueling all morning. From afar, she appeared to be some silver warrior woman out of legend, perhaps one of the Martyrs. Then, she spoke, sharp and uncouth.

"Dross. They are chaff." Trina began to stretch, spreading her legs wide and pressing her head well past her knee like some boneless sea monster.

"So, none worth salvaging? None to add to your ranks?"

"A handful might show some promise," she grumbled reluctantly from where her forehead rested on the cold ground.

"When do you expect to be back to a full contingent?"

Trina straightened and met Emma's eyes. "I will never be back to the strength I once had. I picked and trained those women myself. Some had been with me for near fifteen years, from the beginning. And they were killed for you. For your poorly led, pointless war against a force much larger than promised, and willing to use those goddamn... beasts." The last word was a choked hiss, Trina's eyes glinting with murder. Emma stepped back hurriedly before steeling herself. Nail and Havert were yards away, giving her privacy for her private discussion with the Silver Lady. By the time they reacted, the Silver Lady could slice her into eighteen equal parts.

But, Emma found that, aside from bracing herself, she didn't care. Death, it seemed, didn't hold the threat that it once had. Disorder's warmth flared in her heart, and she clenched her jaw with the strength to snap a walnut's shell.

"You are a mercenary. You choose a side and are paid for your work. And if that work requires that some of you die, so be it. You've lost soldiers before. I know for a fact you lost nearly the same number in that skirmish at Wenan. And, now, you are so broken? The Silver Lady, beaten into a depressed lump of wax after a loss on the battlefield? Even Ferl has more of a backbone."

Trina's mouth dropped open, her expression somewhere between astonishment and a sputtering rage. Emma began to imperceptibly stray her good hand toward the knife that she still wore at her side, despite her gown. It was unlikely the knife would do any good against this bestial woman, but she would not die without a fight.

The Silver Lady began to reach for Emma, her lips twisted back in a snarl. But, all at once, she seemed to deflate, all of her rage escaping her body like water from a shattered vase. Trina's shoulders slumped in sorrow, hard muscles suddenly turned to jelly, her eyes focused at Emma's feet. Emma reached out, touched the woman on the shoulder with her mutilated hand for just an instant before Trina stepped back, scrubbing hurriedly at her haunted eyes.

"I… I overstep, my lady. You are right. This is my own fault. It's just. I lost a… good friend that day." Ah, so that was it. A very good friend, Emma wagered. "This… all this…" Trina swept her hand to take in the drilling soldiers marching in formation, the blacksmiths hammering away at armor and filling molds for arrowheads, the cooks dumping unnamed slop into boiling water, "…it seems meaningless. I cannot bring her back."

Emma's mind, the twisted bastard that it was, summoned images of Escamilla. Her subtle teasing. Her precious, rare laughter. Her constant quizzing and training. A thousand good memories swarmed her like a disturbed nest of red ants, each memory's bite bringing a spot of pain that threatened to bring her to tears. She twisted her mangled hand with her good one, the

326

physical pain combatting the swirl of emotions she fought to subdue.

The tingling in her heart—Disorder's gift—subsided.

"Captain Almark, believe me, I understand. Though Lady Escamilla just left us, I have been feeling her loss for weeks. We were as close as two women could be." Perhaps as close as Trina and her unnamed friend. "But, though I never wanted this for myself, in the dark of night, I think about what Escamilla would want of me. What would bring her joy in Harmony…" Trina winced. Emma released her words, knowing they sounded hollow since she, herself, didn't believe in the Yetranian notion of a joyous, peaceful afterlife. "…Or what would honor her memory. Escamilla desired that I step into her shoes and continue to fight our battle. Fight against this great evil, for who other than utterly soulless, evil people would release the Feral or send a man to murder a dying woman?"

Trina clenched and unclenched her fists, her powerful forearms rippling with strength as she fought to control her own emotions. A hot anger? An empty depression? Something volatile, it seemed.

Emma pressed on through Trina's struggle. "I try to live the life that Escamilla wanted for me, even if it is… challenging. Even if there is a chance that I will be killed by those we oppose. But, I do it for her, and I do it because it is the right thing to do. Would your… friend want to see you having given up? Or, trying to fill your void with these dangerous duels? Would she see you dead for nothing?"

Trina once again seemed to relax, even smiling a weak smile.

"Alexa never liked fighting, violence. She always advised me to retire—'You have the coin,' she'd say. 'We could find a small city, somewhere, open a clothing shop for women…'; she had the eye of a seamstress. 'Why continue to fight? Why continue to help rich, powerful men grow richer and more powerful?' she'd ask." Trina's eyes grew unfocused, staring past the impromptu military camp set up in Landon, the long-abandoned western region of Farrow's Hold. She was probably seeing her own visions of Alexa. Her smile turned wistful, sad.

"Alexa was one of the reasons that we even contracted with Escamilla. Escamilla was different, she said. She didn't seek to absorb others. Rather, she sought to preserve something, something fundamental about Ardia. So, we took this job. My last job, I told Alexa; I told myself." Trina picked up her discarded practice blade, staring long at the dull, dirty metal. "But, that was almost certainly a lie. These things—they have a tendency to continue pulling you in like water circling a drain. I would, and will, always be the Silver Lady, Captain of Ultner's Fist."

She dumped the sword into a loop on her belt. "Alexa wouldn't want me to continue to battle. It seems, though, that I have little choice. That is my life. My lady, your leave?"

Emma nodded, watching as the lithe, beautiful, crass, and melancholy warrior strode away, her hips swinging in a way that would tempt men into a hopeless course.

She blew out a long sigh. She was no closer to determining whether Trina had anything to do with Escamilla's murder. She was one of the few who had no true alibi for the days preceding Disorder's infiltration of Farrow's Hold. No one—not even her own lieutenants—had seen her for days. Perhaps she'd spent that time forging orders, or meeting with agents of Disorder and this Recherche Oletta, making arrangements for their infiltration. Perhaps she had been planning this betrayal since signing on with Escamilla, or since their rout at Florens.

Or, perhaps she'd merely been set adrift on a sea of her own grief.

Emma did not rule out her involvement, but Trina Almark seemed an unlikely traitor. As did all of Emma's other suspects. Her captains each had clear alibis, what with moving her soldiers into Landon, clearing debris from the crumbling roads, and finding suitable quarters in the abandoned, blackened buildings. Landon had been taken by fire, years ago, and since the population had dwindled in Farrow's Hold over the past twenty years following an outbreak of the Black Tear, no one had bothered to fix up this part of the city. So, the task had fallen to the Army of Brockmore, and her captains were constantly in public view and far too busy to betray Escamilla.

Eric Malless had been less involved with clearing Landon and had disappeared briefly, here and there. But, as it turned out, he'd been sinking his dwindling resources into whiskey, a favorite in Jecusta. He had been found, robbed and stripped, in an alleyway near the Central District, reeking of vomit and the potent beverage. Eric may have been disgusting in his grief, but he also lacked the willpower to create a plan as complex as forging orders and tricking the rest of the military in the process.

Opine had been at her side for much of her own soliciting among the Jecustans, bored to tears at the intricacies and delicacies of politics. He obviously longed for another cavalry charge, like the one at the Battle of Florens. To see the bodies of the enemy trampled, bloodied and broken beneath iron-shod hooves. To rally the men for a daring rescue, defying odds and gaining worshippers in the meantime. That was what heroes did, after all. And a hero never betrays an old woman, consigning her to an unholy death.

That left Trina and Ferl. Though Trina's disappearances may have been attributable to her loss, she remained a possibility, if a vague one. And Ferl... Ferl was impossible. He was a slick-as-a-frog smooth talker who always had an explanation for everything. Emma glanced over to where he stood leaning casually against the burnt-out old cathedral which he had made the base of operations for his company. He was chatting with Dien, slapping the beaten warrior on the shoulder with a good-natured jibe. He somehow noticed Emma's gaze, met her eye, and shot her a quick smirk.

The mercenary captain very well could have betrayed her. On a number of occasions. He could have simply ordered his greenies to stand down at Atwater. He could have unleashed Ashland's power into the command tent while they'd been on the march. Or, he could have simply left after the Battle of Florens. They would have been chewed to pieces by the Rostanian Cavalry along the march. So, as much as Emma wanted to condemn Ferl for Escamilla's murder, it seemed unlikely that he would go to the trouble to ensure Escamilla's demise in such a way, given that he could have accomplished their defeat so much more easily at so many points.

But when there was no one to suspect, one must distrust everyone.

"My lady." Harivor shuffled up, buried in his furs against the morning chill. More furs than were strictly necessary, it seemed, but the emissary had a chronic cold. "The hour grows near. They will start without you, so you would be best to begin the trek. I've prepared a carriage, if you will just follow me." He sniffed, twisting his nose in such a way as to keep the protuberance from openly running.

"Of course. Let me gather my escort and I will be with you shortly," she said, distracted. Her gaze was still fixed on Ferl. Strangely, he frowned and shied away as an Oshwon servant ambled by. Shirtless, as they often were, and painted with tattoos. This man was writhing with snakes, the scales appearing to move along his body as he walked.

"My lady, might I be so bold as to say that you are dressed quite appropriately for this event? Quite, ahem, ladylike.

Although, I might point out that there is now a smidgeon of dirt along the fringes." He gestured at her hem, which was now slathered with a generous portion of mud. Emma checked a sigh.

"Thank you, Harivor. I would change but, as you said, we have little time to waste. Let us head to the hold."

***

Emma wasn't sure whether she had arrived late or whether the Jecustans had started early. Regardless, as Harivor led her into the meeting room—another unnecessarily massive, drafty room, but with a magnificent view of the city through an impressively large glass window—she found herself in the midst of an argument.

"...do not have an absolute rule over this country," spat Marc Ervis, magnate of the Upper Plains, the region most directly bordering Algania. The magnate was a horror to behold, half of his face little more than mutilated scar tissue that had resulted from an Alganian assassination attempt fifteen years ago. More of a thwarted torture session, really, as the attacker had plucked out Ervis' eye with a fork and covered one side of his face with a criss-cross of precise cuts. The result was a scaly mess that gave the man the permanent scowl of a freakish school teacher. But, the scowl wasn't just a mask—Ervis had been well-known as a curmudgeon even before his disfigurement.

Unael leaned forward, his forehead resting against his hands. Clearly, this was not a new topic of discussion. "You made me the democratic leader of Jecusta, which means very little in the actual governing of this country, as no one can ever fucking agree on anything. But, in times of war, my rule is absolute. There

331

wouldn't be a democratic order without me, remember?" He met the eyes of each of the gathered rulers of Jecusta. Ervis of the Upper Plains, returning the firm look with a cyclops glare. Clem Linstael, the obese pedophile who did little to actually rule the Eastern Sweeps. Evina Linstael, who was not afforded a seat at the table, but instead watched from her perch, leaning against the wall, her great weight likely a strain on her ankles Rential of the Low Plains, the whip-thin man who had spoken harshly of Emma and Iolen at that first fateful meeting. And a handful of other heads of house from around Jecusta, whose votes were beholden to one of the four aforementioned men for some reason or another. Blackmail, protection, money…. The usual.

A democracy, indeed. Emma and her small entourage—a hungover Malless and a bored Opine—took their places at the table while her knights found a place along the wall and Harivor scuttled off, sneezing and coughing.

"Why would you think this is a time of war? We've reports of a nearly united Ardia for the first time in nearly a century. Certainly, their military has been mobilized, putting down minor rebellions in Florens and Draston, and in readiness for the final push on Hunesa. But, we've no expectations of hostilities directed toward Jecusta." This from Lord Linstael, speaking around a goblet of wine. He was known for his excesses. The obscenely rich often were.

Evina folded her arms, her expression dark. Unael clearly took note. "As I've said, and as you know, there was an attack in this very hold," he commented. "A guest under my protection, as well as two others, were killed. I–"

"But no Jecustans," interrupted Lord Linstael. "Just foreign visitors, who brought this trouble across our borders. Send them back, and the problem is solved. There is no threat of war."

Emma felt the urge to scrape the smug expression off the jowly face.

A pretty noblewoman leaned forward and spoke up cuttingly. "Of course, the Eastern Sweeps cares little for the prospect of a war hundreds of miles away, when half of the country acts as a buffer between possible hostile forces and your own fat ass. You'd have to send your share of soldiers and conscripts, your share of wealth to purchase supplies and equipment. When you never really expect a threat to reach you," she said from between her teeth. Emma didn't recognize her, but from her positioning at the table, she was loyal to Unael.

"You will watch yourself, little girl—" Lord Linstael sputtered, his paunchy face splashed with an indignant red.

"If she were truly just a little girl, she would certainly have to watch herself around you," sneered Rential. Emma could see Evina scratch at her face to cover a grim smile. "Even worse were she a boy."

"I did not travel all this way to be insulted by you imbeciles! These rumors were planted by my enemies—"

"Your only enemies are obesity and children with sharp teeth…"

"Enough!" Unael roared, surging to his feet, his eyes flashing with the hot anger of a man who had fought—and killed—in battle. Even Emma felt a flutter of panic at the sight. "Lista, you will not insult a magnate. And, Linstael, have some godsdamned pride for once in your life. We are here to discuss the protection of our country, not squabble over all of your various indelicacies. We are here to determine the best way to address the growing threat to the west!"

He gestured at Emma. She opened her mouth, not certain whether to say anything. Harivor had counseled silence on her part while these leaders reunited for the first time in six months.

The reunion always hit a few potholes, Harivor had said with a wet cough, each one mirroring the bumpy ride of the long carriage rides that it took for the magnates to reach this capital city.

Luckily, the decision was made for Emma as Iolen strode through the double doors, flanked by his usual escort of pasnes alna and black cloaks. The drafty room was suddenly becoming quite crowded.

"My apologies, my lords and ladies, for my tardiness," said Iolen with a small bow. He was clothed as Emma remembered him from the Plateau, in the plain, maroon robes of a Savant. His simplicity almost seemed outlandish among this crowd.

"You weren't invited," muttered Lord Rential, his lined face dark with disgust.

"I invited him," Unael said, lowering himself back into his seat with much more effort than he'd needed to rise. "He's not likely to spew fire this time around, and he has insight into this unique threat."

"As does the Lady Breen." Iolen nodded to Emma. "You have knowledge at your disposal from both sides of the conflict. I would advise that you not waste it, as is your wont."

General grumbling ensued. Iolen, ever the politician.

"Now, can we move to the topic at hand? Our own intelligence has confirmed that the Ardian military is still mobilized. In fact, the army has nearly doubled in size from their conquered territories and the addition of the Drastoners. They are currently massed near Hunesa, with a smaller but still sizable force near Draston."

"Yes, establishing order and consolidating their hold on the duchy. Not massing to attack," Rential said.

"Does it take thirty thousand soldiers to maintain control of a broken city?" asked the young noblewoman, Lista. She twirled her auburn hair in a ladylike way, but spoke with the confidence of a general.

"It is easier to flex a muscle than to use it. It is simply a tactic to stop any rebellions before they begin. You should know more than anyone, Grand General." Lord Lintael was obviously still smarting from before.

"If I might interrupt," began Emma, looking to Unael.

Unael was almost pleading as he answered, "Please do."

Emma had been thinking about this moment for weeks. A chance to address the leaders of the nation, gathered in haste via pigeon messengers. Jecusta was technically run by this democratically-elected council, though in reality all votes were bought and sold like any other commodity. Unael held his position through his immense popularity with the military, while most of the others simply tended toward being the wealthiest and most historically powerful individuals from their regions. As such, trying to get the rich and the powerful to agree was like getting an irate mule out of the stables.

However, they were bound to attend a war council, lest they miss a chance to issue their vote regarding the war plan. Though Unael held absolute power in times of war, the council could declare peace, or put to question whether war was ever even declared. Given that no true blow had been struck against Jecustan flesh, that was a very likely outcome of this meeting.

So, Emma had a brief chance to convince these magnates of the peril represented by the Ardians.

However, her tongue stuck to the roof of her desert-dry mouth as she attempted to swallow. Maybe a sword-wielding warrior woman could not make her feel fear, but addressing this august crowd, with all of her hopes of revenge, of her future, on the line, transformed her blood into ice.

335

She took a deep breath and steeled herself, placing her mask firmly into place and obscuring Emma, the handmaiden. Emma, the spy for her mistress. Emma, the lover of stupid, brutal men. Emma, the frightened, lost, lonely woman.

Instead, she was every inch the Lady Emma Breen, the woman who'd once led an army to a decisive victory against a well-organized superior force with barely a casualty. The woman who'd kept an army together with her strength of will, and a bit of brutality. The woman who could face down lords and ladies, who could convince people with her words. The woman who'd once been called a friend by Lady Escamilla Breen.

"My lords and ladies. Most of you do not know me, and you would have no reason to. I am Lady Emma Breen, recently fallen into this role, the leader of the homeless thousands of soldiers currently residing within your great city. Some will tell you that I came from nothing. Some will tell you that I am still nothing. I say to you, what I am doesn't matter."

Emma surveyed her audience. She barely had their attention. Lintael was simply drinking, with Rential fingering a filigreed dagger hanging from his belt. Even Unael seemed distracted, muttering something to himself.

"Rather, I am a messenger. I have seen what awaits Jecusta, should the country be taken unaware by the Ardians. By those who control the Ardians."

Harivor had emphasized—she must be a lady. Use her shimmering hair to her advantage. Convince them with her smile, her pliability. Pretend to be in distress. That was what these men responded to. In Jecusta, ladies influenced through manipulation. Being direct and forceful—like Escamilla and other successful women in Ardia—would not be well-received here. Rather, feminine subtleties were needed.

Emma did not like that approach.

"Blood, my lords and ladies. Death. Men and women raped and tortured after seeing their children slaughtered. Villages and towns burned, the ashes scattered to the wind and covering the land with a pallid fog. And that is before they unleash their demons."

Now, Emma had their attention.

"The Feral came at us in the night, with a shrill howl that will make any one person realize just how insignificant they really are." Even through her mask, Emma shivered. She remembered the night she'd first heard the Feral, down in the ruins beneath the Plateau. She recalled the blood washing over her in the deepest dark.

"They tore through our soldiers with unparalleled violence. They killed men in their tents and bedrolls, ripping off faces with their bare hands. Tearing through flesh with their teeth, and leaving men—the few who survived a wound, that is—with gaping holes in their bodies. Other Feral wielded weapons, striking with the strength to leave men's hands numb, to send seasoned warriors' weapons spinning into the night. Even pierced by steel, the Feral would continue coming. It isn't that they do not feel pain. It is that their rage and hate is stronger."

At this point, even Linael had set down his glass of wine to watch her. Evina, standing behind him, gave Emma a grim nod. Keep going.

"These Feral killed six times their number during that attack, putting down trained soldiers who were high on recent victory. And not just soldiers were killed. Camp followers—launderers, cooks, messenger boys—were found torn to bits. Only a few hundred Feral did this. You could discount this as rumor or the ravings of a mad woman. But, I know you have interviewed my soldiers. All tell the same story. You cannot deny the fear still in the eyes of these men. The Feral are real," Emma said, her voice holding a solemn finality.

"Let's say that these Feral are real," Rential remarked, with some skepticism. "If your reports are accurate, then you already killed them all. What is left to fear?"

"'Why grasp with the hand when a finger will do?'" quoted Opine, likely from some obscure military story. "The enemy only needed a few hundred of these Feral to scatter our army. We would expect that they have many more at their disposal."

"Speculation," Ervis said, his twisted face betraying scant emotion.

"Even if their reserves are a matter of speculation, we would expect that the Rostanians could always create more. As our distinguished Savant has informed us, the Feral are created by pasnes alna, leeching people dry of what makes them human. A forbidden rite, it seems, but one which is condoned by those who entreat with the Rostanians." Emma folded her mangled hand with her good one, drawing the gaze of some of the rulers at the table.

"What do you mean by 'those who entreat with the Rostanians?'"

The obvious question had been asked by Rential, who eyed Iolen with mistrust.

"The night that Escamilla was killed.... The night that the black cloaks were misled and my forces were betrayed, I met her killer. I spoke with him."

Unael raised an eyebrow at this. Emma had been quite reserved about that meeting, telling him very little and giving no excuse for why she'd been spared when two men lay dead and the third crippled.

338

"He commanded terrible powers, blinking in and out of the shadows and wielding a terrible burning sword. You saw the results of that blade all too clearly." Nail shifted behind her on his prosthetic foot. "The killer summoned a spear of black power to kill... to kill the Lady Escamilla. It sapped her life away, and she had to be given to the fire." Emma's lip betrayed her, quivering for a moment.

Luckily, a group of servants entered the room bearing covered trays of food, the clang of the servant's door drawing the eye. Unael waved them away for the moment, but Emma had attained the cover needed to recover her composure.

"What did this man say to you, Lady Breen?" Evina asked, speaking out of turn. Her husband looked miffed, chronically so, but no one else seemed to mind. Evina was the real power— unfortunately, Clem had insisted on making this trip anyway.

"He spoke... erratically. His emotions were barely under control. But, he spoke of a power behind the Rostanians, something called Recherche Oletta." Evina looked up sharply, and Lord Ervis narrowed his eyes. His eye, rather. The name was familiar, then. "He implied that he answered to a higher authority, as did this Recherche Oletta. And that whoever commanded him was coming... coming for us all."

There was a hush in the room at those last words. Unael was grim, and Ervis seemed thoughtful—though it was difficult to tell with that face. Clem Linael, for his part, had forgotten to shut his mouth, while Evina smiled a small, prideful smile. Rential, though, continued to finger his filigreed dagger.

"And since when do we trust the words of our enemy? It would certainly behoof him to spread fear among us with lies," Rential said, leaning back in his chair, obviously unconvinced. "Assuming, that is, that this conversation even took place. Strange

that these details only surface now, my lady. Seems quite...
convenient."

Emma felt a flush in her cheeks, as if she was a child caught
sneaking sweet meats. Somehow, telling the truth could feel like a
lie when reality was unbelievable. "Lord Rential, I understand that
my story may push the boundaries of the imagination. I wouldn't
believe it, myself, were I sitting in your seat."

She had to convince all of them, though. If even Rential held
out, it was unlikely that the Jecustans would mobilize their
military. Rential could subvert the others, casting enough doubt in
an already doubtful situation that it could shut down any chances
of aid. Rential, too, was the magnate of the low plains, and those
endless fields of wheat, corn, and peas—supplies that would be
essential in supplying an army during the winter. He owned the
stockpiles, vast towers of unused food, and would not part with
them cheaply. That might be enough to dissuade the other
magnates.

Escamilla said there were two things that drove men. Cocks
and coin. Maybe a passionate entreaty was not the way; maybe
she had to appeal to these baser needs.

"But this is surely the truth. Isn't the possibility of a threat
enough to muster a piece of the military to come to Ardia's aid?
To ensure your own protection? Certainly, this action could only
have extreme benefits for each of you."

Rential's boney expression assessed her like savvy skeleton.

"Lord Rential, I'm certain this army would have need of your
stockpiled food. I understand that twenty percent of your excess
went bad, unused, by the end of last spring. Countless tons of
food, rotting in your towers. You know, marching soldiers require
a great amount of bread and meal. I would be willing to wager
that the cost of sending out a few thousand troops would be less
than the gain from emptying your stores."

Rential released his filigreed dagger and leaned forward onto his elbows. His face was still awash in scepticism, but it lacked some of the hostility of earlier. There was some level of calculation in his sharp eyes now. Rential knew he was being played, but in a way that might end up with him still being somewhat the richer.

"My Lord Ervis, you have been in a hundred skirmishes with the Alganians. Everyone here is well-aware of the military aid that you have requested from the state over the years. Aid requested, but often denied. This would set a precedence of aid in the case of a possible foreign invasion. And perhaps accrue a favor or two."

Mentioning the Alganians made the functional side of Ervis' face tighten. Emma expected that one reason Ervis opposed a possible mustering was because his own requests had been denied over the years—he was actually said to be quite warlike, advocating invasion of their coastal northern neighbor on several occasions. Danby had been quite thorough in his information-gathering with the magnates.

Like Rential, Ervis said nothing. But she felt him loosen, just a bit. Perhaps just enough.

"You do not need to give a speech about the Eastern Sweeps and how this could benefit us. I know what you are saying is the truth. The Feral are no rumor. Recherche Oletta is no rumor. The Linaels are with you, as are our forces," Evina said, her voice sharp with command. She was larger than her husband in both body and spirit.

Clem twisted in his seat, staring back at his wife. She made some gesture with her fingers, perhaps a stabbing motion. Clem paled and turned back around, once again becoming absorbed in his wine.

"And, at this time of year, an army would need warm clothes. Tents. Blankets. And, we all know the greatest supplier of textiles in the country is Farrow's Hold." Thanks to Harivor for that hunk of gold. Unael likely didn't need any convincing, but it never hurt to appeal to everyone for the sake of appearances.

"Basically, my lords and ladies, a muster makes sense. Whether you believe my story…" Emma nodded gratefully to Evina "…or wish to stimulate your economies, this is the right path. There can be no harm in gathering together a few thousand men each. You are either showing the foresight of great leaders in the protection of your country, or each of your regions end up a bit more financially viable."

Glances were exchanged. Postures were altered. Brows were furrowed. Eyes were narrowed.

Emma could see it. She could feel it. She had them. Fear of wailing beasts and mad assassins was nothing compared to potential gains. Look like heroes, or get rich in the process. There would certainly be more discussions and arguments, as well as negotiations and dealings. Emma would likely have to commit the remainder of Escamilla's fortunes—those not seized by Ardia—to supporting the military. But, she knew that they were convinced.

It was a shame that, just then, a black cloak captain rushed in the door, his face red with either cold or exertion.

"My lords, I apologize for this…" he gasped for a moment, catching his breath. Unael gestured impatiently with his hand. "I apologize. But, we have a problem. The Brockmore forces—they are rioting outside of the Trins Grand Chapel."

Emma felt her heart drop out of her chest. At the moment of her first major political victory, something had to go wrong.

Because, why in the fuck not?

Cocks, cocks, and godsdammit.

Chapter 25

They all expected to be caught at some point. You could see it in Ill'Nath's wary, shifting eyes. In Lisan's slight hunch. In how Merigold could never sleep, save when she needed to be awake. The only person unaffected was Marius, staring straight ahead as he drove the cart, following explicit instructions and only occasionally checking on his brother.

But, though they'd expected to be caught, it was still a surprise when it happened.

"What in the name of Yetra..?" A bright, silent flash filled the night sky like a thousand bolts of lightning bursting through the air. Merigold covered her eyes, but too late to escape temporary blindness. She stumbled through the snow disoriented as she tried to find Grumpy, her horse. She yanked the nail from around her neck and brandished it in front of her as she moved, as if swinging the weapon wildly might protect her from whatever was out there.

"Merigold!" Lisan's voice guided her. "Merigold, Ill'Nath, to me! Marius, draw your sword and kill anyone who isn't us!"

She blinked away the flash and reached for Lisan, feeling herself pressed against Grumpy. Through squinted eyes, Merigold could just make out Lisan the Arrow fumbling for her bow with cold fingers.

They were amidst a small forest of evergreens on a path that was hardly travelled, still slogging through heavy, wet snow. Their party had traveled off main roads, avoiding cities, towns, and even villages. Throughout, they'd hardly encountered a soul, and yet occasionally Merigold had still heard metal ringing in the distance, or the slight sound of a cry carrying on the wind. As if they were being haunted by the sounds of battle. It had kept them all on edge, though they didn't speak of it. Marius and Ill'Nath, of course, spoke of nothing.

Lisan sent an arrow sailing toward a black shape. No sound, and the shape stood firm. A tree. Merigold heard crunching snow all around them as heavy, booted feet moved toward their location. A lot of booted feet. Merigold pressed against her horse and quested out. Even in her blindness, she could see the nerring of a dozen figures glowing with a warm light. And the nerring of a thirteenth glowing distractingly brighter, a sun amongst stars.

"Remy!" the voice split the air like a war cry.

The sounds of battle rang out, the sharp report of metal clanging against metal. The suddenly sweet, coppery smell of blood mixed with the eye-watering stench of turned-out guts.

"Remy!" Meri's vision was beginning to clear, and she could see Marius fighting with the skill of a master and the fury of a berserker. He was taking on two opponents simultaneously, not at all impeded by the heavy snow on the ground. Both wielded strange spears that each had a large point on one side and a serrated blade on the other. Marius did not wait to see how these men fought with the weapons. With his short sword in one hand and a dagger in his other, he batted aside a weak attack from his first assailant and slashed at the unguarded hand of the other.

"Stay away from my brother!" he roared with the fury of Ultner.

The second man dropped his spear in surprise and took a foot of steel in his chest as a result. The blade was stuck, though, and Remy abandoned it as he leapt back from the first attacker's spinning attack. Remy drew a second dagger and feigned throwing it, causing the attacker to raise his guard. Remy flung his second dagger, point first, into his opponent's gut and finished the job by hammering the dagger home with a well-placed kick.

Lisan had also begun to recover her vision, but found that her bow string, abused by the cold and damp despite her care, snapped under the pressure of a draw. With a curse, she fumbled with her pack and pulled out another string. Ill'Nath stood in front of her, waving his club about with abandon and forcing distance between the attackers and the cart. One man lay dead at his feet.

One brown-cloaked man.

Now that Merigold had regained some of her senses, she realized that these weren't members of the Sun Guard—not one of the many patrols that had been pursuing them. The cloaked men all wore dark cloth masks, and their faces couldn't be seen. Were they simply bandits? Was her party in the wrong place at the wrong time? But their spears were outlandish, and they seemed to be far too skilled for the average bandit.

And then there was that woman of power, standing near the fringes of the battle.

She alone did not wear a mask. Silver-blonde hair like Merigold's own fluttered in the moonslight, and her sharp-featured face was of an even lighter complexion. A lithe man, perhaps her bodyguard, stood at her side, his hands concealed in the pockets of the robe he wore. Her nerring was near blinding, and so much different from what Merigold had seen before. It felt wild—fit to bursting, even. She approached one of the evergreens and leaned on it, her bare hands caressing the rough bark as one would a lover. The needles of the tree began to turn to ash, blowing in the direction of Merigold's party.

Meri remembered Dunmore then, and the ashy mist that filled the ruined cities. The dead and dying trees, including her and Sandra's willow. She remembered Ferl's Company, and his band of mages who'd cut down the front ranks of the Rostanian Army. This woman was a greenie, and a powerful one at that.

"Merigold, if you plan on doing something, now would be the time," Lisan hissed. She had finally managed to restring her bow with numb fingers, and shot an arrow at the woman. Without any visible motion, the metsika created a green, glowing barrier that jumped into existence just long enough to disintegrate the missile.

In retaliation, the woman launched a flurry of tiny, glowing needles in their direction. Merigold and Lisan both threw themselves flat while Ill'Nath managed to position an attacker between him and this mage. Remy, however, did not see the magical attack, embroiled as he was with an equally-matched opponent, a small and agile man wielding one of those dual-headed spears. Both were knocked off their feet by the needles and fell to the snow. Neither rose.

Ill'Nath's assailant also fell, pierced from behind by the needles, and Ill'Nath took a wound in the shoulder. He grunted in pain, but kept his feet. Behind where Meri lay in the snow, she could hear her horse scream in pain and panic before it tumbled to the ground, flailing its legs and kicking Meri hard in her leg. It hurt, but Meri had lived through too much worse pain to let something like this distract her.

"Monga!" screamed the bodyguard in an unfamiliar language. "Monga! Endo feren!"

The woman flinched and directed her attention at Ill'Nath, Lisan, and Meri as they scrambled to form a defensive perimeter. Though only five spear-wielding attackers still stood, they had no chance of fighting off another spray of needles or worse. Merigold gripped the leg of the injured Grumpy and began to draw, her head throbbing.

She had never drawn from an animal before, not that she remembered. The maenen was similar—surprising similar—to what she felt from humans, and yet incredibly distinct. There were fewer memories and more sensations... impressions.

She felt a fearful sensation of being confined, though her spirit would soar. She felt the weight of an ungrateful burden. And she felt a driving need to be free and a drowning fear that prevented her from trying.

On instinct, Merigold shaped Grumpy's maenen into a great red plate that she placed in front of her party. A second later, the disc shuddered as a wave of needles crashed into the other side, sounding like a furious rain splattering against a tin roof. Merigold gritted her teeth, straining to maintain the shield. She reshaped it; instead of a plate, she created a triangular cone like the beak of a bird.

Another spray of needles, these ones more like nails, connected with her shield. Instead of it fully absorbing the blows, it sent the nails ricocheting off into every direction, crashing into trees and skidding through the snow. Lisan ducked around the shield and released an arrow with the happy sound of a death cry. She took cover again as another, more direct and powerful barrage struck the shield.

Merigold exerted herself to reshape the barrier, repairing the chipped and damaged pieces. More than before, she felt stretched as she served as a conduit of maenen, drawing it from the horse and into her nerring, and then shaping it directly. She felt like the transition hallway in the Yetranian chapel—stomped on by a hundred feet with a constant shifting of temperature as people entered and left. It was exhausting.

Another barrage, and Merigold fell to her knees. Her whole world was this shield, was maintaining it and keeping them alive. Her body was the incarnation of pressure, of tension. Her nerring was pain, and the instinctual sensations of Grumpy became stronger and stronger. She knew true fear, a sense of learned helplessness and of inescapable fate. The smothering feeling urged her to give up, to stop the fight. Her death, the end of a useless and servile life, was imminent, and it would have no impact on the world one way or another. Dropping the shield would be easy. So easy.

But something within Merigold fought this sensation. She'd known despair before. The hollow, dark despair of a cellar. The foggy and disbelieving despair of losing her friends and family. The personal and bloody despair of a lost child.

This would not break her. Merigold rose back to her feet as the launched nails transformed into a concentrated beam of power, drilling through the center of her barrier. Her efforts were focused on bolstering her shield, and she held. By Yetra's fucking perfect tits, she held against this woman, this skilled and powerful metsika of unknown origins.

However, holding was not enough. Her fuel was rapidly being depleted; there was little maenen left in Grumpy, and he was bleeding profusely from his wounds. Either his nerring would deteriorate or his heart would stop. And then they would be defenseless.

There was no shortage of trees to fuel this woman's own assault.

Abruptly, just as Grumpy was about to give out, the attack halted. There were screams and the sounds of battle from behind her opaque barrier, and Merigold had no choice but to release the shield, her legs quivering as she lost her connection with Grumpy's maenen. She took a few fumbling steps and leaned against the cart.

The woman of power lay dead, a white-fletched arrow sticking from her ear and somehow focusing attention on a bright green gemstone in her ear, standing clear against the flowing blood. Two other arrows were lodged in her side, making her resemble the pincushion that Merigold kept in her room for mending Ragen's shirts. A Sun Guard stood over the woman, driving a sword into her chest just to confirm her death.

Their pursuers had caught up with them, at last.

The woman's bodyguard ineffectually fought off two Sun Guard soldiers, each one of them swinging long swords in practiced unison to dismantle their target. Several other Sun Guard battled their assailants in a pitched battle. The tide had turned in an instant, with the Sun Guard outnumbering the attackers two to one. Ill'Nath, with little hesitation, jumped into the fray, blindsiding a Sun Guard with a club to the side of the head and then taking on another, a huge man near his size. Lisan, on her last arrow, carefully took aim and caught a Sun Guard in the mouth, sending him reeling backwards in a spray of blood.

Behind the Sun Guard, Merigold could see a familiar face. At least, half of a familiar face. The right side of Tinto was familiar; he was a graciously handsome man, his delicate features drawn in a firmly serious line. The left side of his face, though, was a disaster of flesh. Even in the low-light, Merigold could see the damage she had done to him—melted flesh poorly sewn together, pulling tight the skin around his eye and mouth and giving him the grotesque look of a child's nightmare. He barked orders at his men, trying to coordinate an assault on two separate forces. The battle was largely turning into a free-for-all.

Merigold took the opportunity to check on Marius, who lay in the bloodied snow a few feet away. Merigold could not help but cover her mouth. His body was a ruin, punctured by countless needles in his chest, stomach, arms, and face. The needles had dissipated, but every inch of Marius was covered in welling, oozing blood which was made worse by the cold. Worst of all, he still lived, gasping and wheezing for breath through his pierced lungs. Helpless to aid him, Merigold dabbed at his face with the edges of her coat. She started when he spoke.

"You are my brother's killer," Marius wheezed and gurgled.

"I am... yes." Why lie to a dying man? Why lie to herself?

"It was not your fault. It was an accident."

Merigold gripped his blood-slick hand, feeling warm tears flow down her face in stark contrast to the freezing night. "I am so sorry."

"You must protect him…. He might recover…" Marius said in barely a whisper.

"I will. I promise," Merigold said with quivering lips. There was no hate in this simple man, this peerless warrior. No accusation. Only love for his brother.

A great bellow pulled Merigold's attention away from the dying Sestrian. Just as the Sun Guard had mowed down the attackers, Ill'Nath and Lisan had cut a bloody swath through the Sun Guard. There was only one man left standing: Captain Tinto.

"Ill'Nath, stop this!" Merigold commanded him, her voice carrying a strength that she did not feel. The big islander hesitantly lowered his club while Tinto remained in an easy fighter's stance, the tip of his short sword resting in the snow. Lisan stood back, her own sword bloodied from the battle.

"You." Tinto glared at Merigold with the face of a devil. "You! Do you recall me, Ardian? Because I will never forget you." His voice, so firm and cultured before, was lispy and nasally, betraying a lack of teeth in half of his mouth.

"How can I forget? You were the officer who was trying to unjustly arrest us after your guards sliced up an innocent man," Merigold replied, as if that story would assuage her guilt over the massacre.

"An innocent man? How would you know? You know nothing of our lives, of our people. It could have been an innocent man who ran his mouth. Or, he could have been a serial murderer, finally caught, if only by happenstance. The fact remains—you did not know. You have no context with which to judge us."

"Tell me now, then, Captain. Clarify this murder for me," Merigold said, recalling the man's memories, the loss of his children. Tinto chuckled without humor, his features twisting with the pain of the simple movement.

"You are a persistent one, aren't you? Persistent and carelessly powerful. I imagine you have left many dead bodies in your wake, wild one. My men killed that civilian because they are scared. Every sideways glance, every bitter word under their breath, could be the face of rebellion. We have being whittled down, and now we finally have found our enemy." Tinto slogged through the muck and crouched down next to the body of the metsika's protector. He ripped off the cloth mask, revealing a pale, feminine face. More than pale, the skin was near white, much like the small patches of untouched snow around them. The woman's features were pointed, harkening back to the castaway who'd gutted Cryden.

She was Menogan.

"Who are these people?" Merigold asked, though she knew part of the answer. Tinto shook his head wryly.

"I do not know. They are from far away, to the west, and they do not speak our language. They are the ones who have been sinking our ships. They are the ones who have killed our nobility in their sleep, who tried to burn the Opal Tower. They are the ones at the heart of our unrest. As we sent our patrols out… to find you… we began coming across bands of these people. They have been burning towns and villages, ambushing the good people of Rafon. We've been hunting them as much as they have been hunting us." Tinto kicked the fallen metsika with a sudden flash of anger.

"And where are the pasnes alna through all this?" Tinto kicked the woman again, snapping the arrow right out of her ear. "Gone. Fled. Supporting them. Who knows? Agricorinor within the borders of our country and yet silent, taking no action and turning away our messengers! Even Telidian, advisor to the monarch, tucked his tail and ran like a fearful mongrel. The only way we can fight these magic-wielding demons is to catch them by surprise or get lucky."

His teeth were clenched as he held back this avalanche of just-contained rage. He was furious, clearly, but not at her and not for himself. Not even because he'd been maimed. It was because his people and countrymen were in danger. This man cared, Merigold could tell. He was not a bad person, despite the murders his men had committed in fear.

"So, it wasn't us, then. Your xenophobia was unfounded," interrupted Lisan, who was busying herself collecting arrows from the fallen bodies nearby. Ill'Nath remained cautious and ready to strike, should Tinto make a move.

Tinto sighed and shook his maimed head, almost sadly. "It doesn't matter, Ardian. You killed a dozen of my Sun Guards. Not just killed, but you cut a scar into the memory of Polanice. Even would I call off the search, the Sun Guard would not listen. I understand our mistake—that you have nothing to do with this threat—but you could not convince the Sun Guard otherwise. If only you had simply accompanied us to the Opal Tower without resisting, you would be free on your journey by now."

Lisan's eyes flung daggers at Ill'Nath, but the big islander either didn't notice or didn't care.

"Speaking of, we should be on our way," Merigold said, laying a hand on Ill'Nath's arm. The islander did not take his eyes from the captain. His thoughts were clear. Cut off the head, and the body dies. Merigold knew otherwise. Cut off this head, and the body would just get stronger. And, she would not have yet another death on her conscience.

"Agreed," Lisan said, her voice as calm as a bird gliding on thermal rises. "Captain, I apologize for your losses here today. And for your losses in Polanice. But, know that if you continue your pursuit, we will fight you. There will be more death, and we both know you do not want that. Ill'Nath, come now. Let's be away from this bloody place."

The three turned their backs on Captain Tinto and his mutilated face, leaving him standing alone amidst the bodies of his friends and enemies. Ill'Nath stopped to gather Marius' corpse in his arms and add yet another body to their wagon.

"If you strike out for Agricorinor, which is what I suspect…" lisped Tinto, "…tell them to please send help to Rafon. The monarch knows, we need it."

They would be safe in Agricorinor.

It was about as likely as Yetra dropping down from Harmony and giving Meri a hug and a plate of Ragen's stew.

Chapter 26

"Well, I be thinking it's a big fucking mistake," Paston said, grinding his teeth. He'd been doing that lately, in the time that they'd basically been confined to Sebiant Rhisfel.

"I'm not seeing another choice," Alwyn argued. "If we ever want to get out of this fucking rock, you're going to have to meet with him. I have no doubt it will be a spectacle, from what I've heard whispered about you."

"It will be a fucking trap," grumbled Enric, working at his skull with a dry razor. The blood streaming down his scalp did little to deter the man from sheering the hair from every inch of his head, however. People leaned into their habits even more when stressed, Hafgan knew. It was probably why he himself had been training so hard, ten hours a day. Driving his men like a slave master, pushing them beyond their capabilities for weeks now.

His budredda, all three dozen of them, had been made hard during their march with the Rostanian Army. They'd be made lean during their march through the Tulanques. And they were being made strong through their time in Hafgan's Anvil, as some of the newest budredda called it.

It was an apt name, given that their little assembly chamber was lined with a blue-specked iron ore that gleamed throughout the day as light flickered through the vents, reflected by mirrors. Each morning, he lined them up for increasingly-complex calisthenics—practicing balance and strength, stretching their muscles and expanding their reach. Then, they practiced formation fighting and more human tactics, fighting together as a unit and responding to commands. Most seemed bored by this style, but Hafgan knew that the Wasmer were generally unfamiliar with formation fighting. Not that he expected things to come to arms, of course, but it always helped to be prepared.

Then, they would move to sparring, one-on-one battling with padded spears. They would form three circles, with the winner staying in the center. Paston never lasted long, though Enric was one of the best. Jenyn was his greatest fighter—a short, slim Wasmer who seemed to instantly memorize a new move or tactic after only seeing it a single time. He'd joined up after the gwagen attack, simply wanting to return to the mountains. But, though he'd yet to shave down his teeth, he'd found himself a happy home among the budredda. He rarely spoke, but often smiled.

The men encouraged Hafgan to spar with them, just like he had back when they'd been marching with the Rostanian Army. He refused, though. He did not want to discourage them. Though they were better than they'd been——much, much better—they still didn't hold a candle to his abilities. Beating them senseless would have been effective to motivate them initially, but at this point it would crush their egos. That, and with Carreg Da warriors wandering through their training sessions, Hafgan did not want to give away anything about his style. At least half were spies.

"Like Alwyn said, we do not have a choice. Leyr summons us, and we must answer," said Hafgan.

Enric shifted on his feet. "There will be a battle, Lieutenant. Why else would they be summoning all of us to meet in the Cylch?"

"Since when do you be balking at a little battle?" asked a smiling Paston, nudging Enric with the butt of his spear. Enric batted it aside irately.

"Ever since I fought in one."

The sobering statement shut up the good-natured bickering. Hafgan sighed. They were all afraid of what would come. He couldn't really blame them.

Just then, the bureaucrat Fel Jentin, flanked by some nameless Wasmer and Yurin, entered their chamber with little fanfare. The

356

man greeted Hafgan with a smile and his arms spread wide. He was nothing but cordial, and Hafgan had no reason but to trust the man. He had provided the budredda with ample food, safe if not particularly comfortable lodging, and a frequent line of communication updates about their status in Hackeneth. And yet, there was something about Fel that Hafgan couldn't pin down. Something odd.

Something that gave him an instinctual feeling of unease.

"Brother, brother, brother boy. How treats you this place?" asked Yurin in his hoarse voice.

"As well as it ever has. Which is to say, like cold shit," Hafgan said, sticking to Ardian. Yurin laughed, the sound like gravel falling down a chute.

"I forget just how funny you are. It's always so nice to see you."

"Dogs always do get excited to see their master," Hafgan said, dismissing his mad brother and turning his attention to Fel with a nod. "Rensa Fel."

"Hafgan, I hope the day finds you healthy and well."

"Of course. Our lodgings are quite adequate." It seemed like an accurate enough statement, if not a compliment. Fel raised an eyebrow and tilted his head, his braids jingling the bells and bits of metal that decorated them.

"We strive for adequacy in all things. Now, as we spoke about last week, Leyr would like to stage a welcome within the Cylch, for you and all your men. As you know, he has been busy securing the southern border against the violent remnants of the Flam Madfall. Thankfully, the Flawless God stands with us." Yes, their god had stood with them, Hafgan knew, as they subjugated a clan of hiding people who had been ravaged in previous wars, a bully kicking a downed and helpless child.

Paston stiffened at the reminder that his people were being systematically destroyed and enslaved. He made a move as if to say something, but Hafgan waved him back with a flick of his wrist.

"Praise be to the Flawless God," Hafgan said, his voice as slippery as the peaks above them. Fel smirked at that, showing an authentic humor.

"Now that he has returned, Leyr would like to honor you for your sacrifice during the Reckoning, helping the people see the truth through your words and subsequent departure. He would also like to honor your men for having stood firm against the rebel, Siarl Llywelyn, the disgraced warleader of the Yearer Inos."

Hafgan flinched, recalling Siarl's death at the hands of the gwagen. "It will indeed be a great honor to be in Leyr's presence."

Hafgan glanced back at his budredda. They stood firm against his scrutiny, betraying none of the fear that they had shown earlier. The budredda were strong. The budredda were confident. The budredda were his.

"My men are ready."

***

The mere existence of the Cylch boggled the mind.

The weight of the earth was acute in this place, this impossible crater inside the mountain. It was as if the gods had hurdled a star

358

into the earth and, embarrassed by the damage they had wrought, constructed the mountains to conceal the wound. The entire crater was not concealed, however. A single, great hole at the peak of the cavern ceiling let in the light of day or the glow of the moons. The Wasmer called this hole the God's Eye, as it had a very peculiar ocular appeal when blue Glasas superimposed itself in front of white Gwyna. Tonight, though, only half of Gwyna was visible, shooting a stream of light into the Cylch.

To Hafgan, it almost looked like some fake god was winking at him gleefully, delighted to see how this would unfold.

The crater itself was ringed by slopes that had been carved into seating for over ten thousand souls, and the benches were now packed with laborers, miners, merchants, and craftsman. Not to capacity, but there were certainly at least a few thousand present. And, they sat silently. Carreg Da warriors were scattered throughout the crowd, ensuring their good behavior and silence.

Leyr always had wanted to be heard, particularly as Taern had never seemed to hear him.

Leyr, the god-finder himself, stood in the center of the arena, ringed by a handful of warriors. Rinx and Wiscon, two of Hafgan's compatriots from his days as Haearn Doethas, were standing slightly behind their leader. Rinx was fairly unremarkable, aside from the fact that one eye was blue and one was brown. His dark hair was cut much shorter than typical and his face held his customary grimace. Wiscon had the unusual affectation of being overweight. With food always being fairly scarce and expensive, it was difficult—and frowned upon—for any Carreg Da to carry extra weight. However, even during the intense training of their upbringing—that same training that had turned Hafgan into stringy, solid muscle—Wiscon had never shed his extra padding. His reddish, unkempt beard only seemed to emphasize his adiposity. However, he was not a man to be trifled with; he was surprisingly swift and had the strength to match.

Leyr, though, drew the eye. He was immaculate, his dark brown hair held back in a loose ponytail, his facial braids short and tight. His eyes were a piercing black-brown, the color and depth of the caverns that honeycombed these mountains. His smile gleamed, his dual dogteeth sharper than was natural, and perhaps even filed to a point. The only flaw to his handsome face was a slight, almost imperceptible twist to his smile. Hafgan remembered the crunching sound as his own elbow had broken a couple of Leyr's teeth and dislocated the warrior's jaw. In this very chamber, nearly five years ago.

"Hafgan Iwan, returned to his people," boomed Leyr, the acoustics of the Cylch carrying his voice to the ears of each Wasmer in attendance as if he were standing at their shoulders. He stepped forward, arms spread wide, approaching Hafgan and his assembled budredda. Hafgan's loyal men stood behind him in a tight, staggered formation. A Rostanian formation; not the typical loose ranks of the Carreg Da warriors.

"And his brave warriors, who fought against the rebel Siarl, the man responsible for the deaths of so many Carreg Da warriors in the shadow of Findyn Peak, fighting with treachery and guile. We, the people of Hackeneth and followers of the Flawless God, thank you for your service and welcome you back to your home."

"Ain't my home," grumbled Paston just behind Hafgan. He had recently expanded his vocabulary to include the word "ain't," the slang word adopted from Captain Yanso. Though Paston was proud of having picked up the colloquial term, Hafgan was not pleased at the dialect. He preferred his men to speak proper Ardian.

Luckily, the people cheering in the seats—at the urging of several dozen warriors—drowned out Paston's comments.

"We are pleased to be returned to Hackeneth, though brief our stay will be," Hafgan proclaimed in Ardian, the foreign language echoing discordantly through the Cylch as an unwelcome guest. He could hear the crowd murmuring, uncertain of either his words or his intent. Ardian was not well-taught among the laborers and miners, though higher castes tended to know it with at least passing fluency. Mixing with humans was fairly rare these days, but not unheard of.

"Then we shall savor the time we have together. Tell me, I hear you have news for us from that war-torn land to our east," Leyr said, stepping toward Hafgan. He walked easily, effortlessly, displaying a combination of his warrior instinct and an act for the watching masses.

"My men and I come bearing a warning, Leyr."

The man's face twisted in interested concern, a worry painted on his face—as if drawn by a skilled artist. Fake, of course, but Hafgan couldn't see any clear signs of his perfidy. "Please, tell us. The Carreg Da have been through much since you left us. This warning may spare us yet more suffering."

Hafgan examined the faces in the crowd. The people seemed many things: frightened, subjugated, and resigned. It was not a mix of emotions that would be easy to alter, and Hafgan knew that he would fail before he even opened his mouth. Nonetheless, he spoke. Not to Leyr, but to everyone in the stands. It had been so long since he had spoken to a crowd of more than a handful of people. His mouth was cotton, and the Wasmer tongue felt heavy and awkward.

Nonetheless, he cleared his throat and began his plea, slowly turning as he spoke to include the entire crowd.

"Our history, the history of the Carreg Da, the history of the Wasmer, is fraught with peril and hardship. Warring with each other. Warring with humans. Warring against the elements and scraping a harsh living out of these unforgiving mountains. War, it seems, is in our people's blood. Battle is our birthright. Conflict is our purview. And, though it has been a challenging existence, we have grown strong!" Hafgan, speaking Wasmer, paused for the cheer. Only a handful of people thought to respond to his words, however, either cowed by the warriors or just uncaring for what he had to say.

"In my journeys, in the journeys of these brave men behind me…"

"Budredda scum!"

"Traitorous, human-fucking wretches!"

The words rang out from the crowd at random. Hafgan fought the urge to achieve his hedwicchen, which would eliminate the anxiety, but also eliminate any passion that might infect his voice.

"…brave men behind me, we have faced a new enemy. An ancient enemy, in fact, of the Wasmer. Preceding most of our written histories, Wasmer once occupied Ardia proper, before being driven away and forced to live in the mountains." That caused some grumbling, some confusion. The taught histories— the false histories—said that Wasmer had always been in the mountains. They were born of the mountains just so much as the rock, the peaks, and the snow.

"We fought an enemy, incalculable in number and driven forward by pasnes alna. They were manlike, driven by a need to kill and kill again, their shrieks echoing to the highest peaks. They fought with a ferocity that precluded survival; they cared only to trample our corpses, to eat of our flesh and drink of our blood. They fought, even when mortally-wounded, just to inflict more pain before they passed. They were utterly without soul." Hafgan paused.

"They were the gwagen, and they have come again."

The crowd was silent. Contemplative, perhaps. Or scared.

Or just stunned stupid.

The silence was broken by a chuckle coming from Wiscon, the big man almost jiggling with barely restrained glee. Leyr glanced backward, harshly, to stop this laugher. Again, it might have been an act, but it seemed authentic even to Hafgan's trained eyes.

"The gwagen, Hafgan, have been long recognized as a myth. Perhaps the humans tricked you." Implying he was dumb. "Or, perhaps some pasnes alna manipulated the minds of a handful of humans, driving their weak minds into a raw insanity." Implying that humans were dumb. "We, of course, appreciate your warning, but you can see that the worries within Hackeneth are greater than whatever you witnessed."

"We saw throats ripped out in front of our eyes! We speared them and watched them fight us, even as their lives bled from their bodies!" Enric shouted from behind Hafgan. His face and perfectly hairless head were red with barely-kept anger. He never took well to insults, and he'd never really understood, or come close to mastering, the hedwicchen.

"Sounds like you speared them wrong," snorted Rinx. A skeptic to the core. In fact, Hafgan was surprised that Rinx would have thrown in with Leyr and his Flawless God.

"Let me show you just how I impaled them," riposted Enric, shouldering his spear and stepping forward.

"Enough!" Leyr shouted, now playing the voice of reason. "There shall be no Wasmer blood shed in the Cylch on this day!"

Hafgan wondered whether that was true.

"With respect, Leyr," he intoned. "We witnessed these creatures ourselves, and we brought an additional witness with us to lend credence to our story." Hafgan had spoken in Ardian, and gestured back to his ranks.

Yanso, his ankles and hands bound together, was guided forward from the center of the budredda. He had been diminished, somewhat, during their stay in the Sebiant Rhisfel, his muscular frame waning into a more slender strength. They'd been giving him some freedom over the past weeks, knowing as well as Yanso did that leaving the stewardship of the budredda was a quick way to be publicly executed. Though his injuries had healed, he had not tried to leave.

"Tell them, Captain Yanso, what you witnessed."

Humans were immeasurably easier to read in comparison to Wasmer. They had a thousand tells—fidgets, twitches, cracking voices—that Wasmer were trained to restrain, from a young age on. However unintentionally, the Wasmer lifestyle just didn't leave room for visible weaknesses. Taern would easily be able to detect the truth versus lies from a human. Leyr would be able to do the same, though he might not choose to listen to the signs.

"Aye, I'll tell them what I fucking saw," Yanso growled. Hafgan had promised him freedom for speaking the truth, and he hoped Yanso would remember that. Yanso stood tall, staring Leyr straight in the eyes, almost as if challenging him. "We were guarding some fucking twisted compound, listening to howling day and night. The kind that made your blood run cold and your stomach twist in knots. My men were deserting or disappearing. Some of your fucking goa…" He cleared his throat. "…Wasmer disappeared throughout the nights, too, maybe fleeing from that place or maybe otherwise taken. Well, one night, I was given a message to enter the compound, to prepare whatever was in there for the attack on the southern flank of the Army of Brockmore."

Leyr folded his arms, apparently displeased that a human would be in the Cylch, a place sacred to the Carreg Da. Though, he must have known that Yanso had been in Sebiant Rhisfel, a canker in the mouth of the Warrior's Respite. Rinx spat on the ground in Yanso's direction, and Wiscon frowned, an unusual motion for his typically cheerful features. It was a testament to

364

Yanso's desire for self-preservation that he didn't charge Rinx over his disrespect.

"Inside, there were tunnels carved into the ground, but not with shovel or pick. The walls were smooth, as if melted. The pasnes alna inside gave me a tour of the facility, where these demons were chained up in the dark of the caves, slavering and struggling to escape. There was nothing fucking human about them. Nor was there anything Wasmer about them, for there were a number of your people who had been reduced to the state of these monsters. The lead pasnes alna—Swenter, was his name, a Sestrian—sent them forward as my men and me left the compound. My soldiers were slaughtered, and I only survived after I killed four of the fuckers and hid under their bodies. Their Wasmer-fucking bodies!" Yanso shouted, his voice echoing through the Cylch.

The crowd was hushed, all eyes turned to Leyr; frightened children watching their abusive father for courage. Leyr considered the lone human for a long minute, his face inscrutable even to Hafgan's eyes and his features tinged opal by Gwyna. He could thank Yanso as a savior, or he could condemn the man to death. He choose the latter.

"Rostanian, you come here, to this sacred place, and tell me that you killed four of my people, defiling their corpses to save your own life. You tell me lies about what you witnessed, mistruths written as clearly on your face as a pox! The Wasmer with you, they may have been duped by your pasnes alna, but you seal your own fate by knowingly fabricating a story. Rostanian, I sentence you to death, to be carried out immediately and visibly. Let the people know that the Flawless God will not broker with liars." Around the Cylch, several bureaucrats translated Leyr's perfect Ardian. Hafgan had always been so jealous of his diction.

The crowd cheered, two thousand maddened voices joining in unison like coyotes gone wild for blood. The Carreg Da warriors did not need to urge this cheering.

He nodded to Rinx, who smiled a rare, rusty smile as he stepped forward, pulling his ornate, silver spear from where it had been strapped to his back. Yanso stood stunned, an animal trapped by a hunter. Rinx's multicolored eyes gleamed as he projected a perfect thrust without preamble, aimed at the bound human's heart.

It would have struck true, too, had Hafgan not knocked it away with his own weapon. As it was, the blow still parted the skin on Yanso's upper arm. He staggered backwards and the budredda's ranks opened to receive him, providing shelter to their long-standing prisoner.

"This man is under my protection!" Hafgan shouted in Wasmer. "I promised him safe passage and release if he shared his story. His true story! If he killed Wasmer, it was because they had become gwagen. And he tells no lies, Leyr. We tell no lies!" He squeezed his fist twice in quick succession, and heard his men forming ranks, a circle bristling with points that would protect them from all comers.

"You choose a human over your own kind? Is that how far you have fallen, budredda?" asked Leyr, pulling his own spear from his back. Not his spear, but rather Taern's weapon—Torri Carreg, the Stone Breaker. The silver hilt was carved with tiny scenes depicting various mythical stories from all of their gods. The blade, sharp enough to split a bolt of cloth dropped upon it, glistened in the moonlight, its single emerald seeming to glow of its own accord.

"I choose the truth! I choose to protect my own people rather than enslave them. I choose to raise them up rather than murder them under the pretense of a new god. A false god!" Hafgan yelled, once again lost in idealism within this place.

There was an audible gasp from the crowd, followed by a sick silence.

Leyr slung his spear over his back, smiling wide.

"You think the Flawless God to be false? You think to renounce the new religion of your former people? Let me show you just how false the god is."

Leyr stepped into the center of the God's Eye, mere paces from where Hafgan and the budredda waited in formation, bristling with spears like a hedgehog. He whispered something, chanting words unfamiliar to Hafgan before holding Torri Carreg straight above his head, pointing it directly at the sliver of white Gwyna.

For a moment, nothing happened. Hafgan, though he knew in his heart otherwise, hoped that nothing would come of it. Also, briefly, he considered piercing Leyr's unguarded heart with his spear. It would spell his death, of course, but it might free his people.

Then, a dim red light began to filter through the Eye, subtle and almost inviting. It grew in intensity until it was a bright, slender beam, fully engulfing Leyr and bathing the man in crimson. His white grin became bloodstained. Like a cancer, the red slowly emanated from Leyr, first encompassing Rinx and Wiscon, and then touching Hafgan himself.

It was a warm light, filling him with both strength and pleasure. Hafgan suddenly wanted to reach for his spear and twirl it, showing off his strength to the world. He wanted to find Rian, and kiss her and make love to her on Oletta's alter. He wanted to go back five years and take up the mantle of leadership, showing the Wasmer what they should truly be, and how they should truly live.

But then the feelings began to twist. He should silence the voices of any who dared to challenge his ideals. He should rip out the hearts of the warriors who would pose a threat. He should murder the boys who showed too much potential and could one day challenge him. His sudden pride was becoming paranoid, toxic.

Leyr continued to smile his bloody smile.

Behind him, he heard Paston sobbing quietly. Enric was shouting something at the Eye, his voice ferocious with rage. Jenyn was vomiting up the contents of his stomach, having fallen to his knees and crawled to Hafgan's side. Alwyn was bashing his spear against the ground again and again, like a miner picking away at the stone.

His men were going mad.

Hafgan fought through the impossible pride and conceit he felt as if it were a stone wall, reaching for his hedwicchen. It was a thousand miles away, over mountains and across oceans, but still he struggled. Still, he reached for the emptiness, releasing his defenses until he could feel an omicron of solitude, a piece of emptiness. Through some force of will, or perhaps through intense practice, he managed to achieve his centered state.

He found he was already clutching his spear, realizing dispassionately that there was no chance to leave this place intact. Leyr was unmoved, but Rinx and Wiscon had both obviously achieved their hedwicchen, as well, and were bathed in red but otherwise unaffected. They watched, outwardly disengaged, as the budredda went insane with grief and fear, pride and anger.

Hafgan stabbed at Rinx with a perfect lunge, his spear straight and true as it pierced the man's thigh. Though he was in his hedwicchen, or perhaps because he was in it, he had deemed a emotion-maddened Hafgan as something less than a threat. And, because Hafgan knew he would react to a center mass lunge, he went for a disabling attack. It was effective, and the ever-scowling Wasmer fell to the ground, gripping his bleeding leg hard and letting out a piercing scream. Long unchallenged, he had forgotten his lessons in bearing pain.

Wiscon, though, was now alerted, and he brought his great axe around at Hafgan's head. He dodged low, feeling the breeze as the crescent swept by inches away. Hafgan dashed forward to land a kick, but Wiscon was ready and punched outward. Hafgan pivoted, pushing off the man's fist and balancing easily, landing several steps away.

Hedwicchen battles were always so much like a dance, had the Wasmer practiced such a frivolity.

Hafgan knew he was fated to win this battle. He knew Wiscon's deficiencies; his weak left knee from a fall during a climb in his youth. His tendency, even when in the hedwicchen, to let his eyes dart to his intended area of attack. And the fact that Wiscon was at the bottom of the Haern Doethas class, having being beaten by each of the other nine students. That was, if he and Wiscon were to dance alone.

"Hafgan Iwan! Enough of this!" Leyr, free of his revelry, pointed Torri Carreg at him. The red light still shone down from the Eye, and the spear seemed stained by it. The emerald shone as a ruby.

Leyr sprinted forward. There was none of the control that Hafgan had seen Leyr demonstrate thousands of times in the past. There was none of his calm, cold calculation or his devilish precision. A pure rage, a hatred evident in every motion, fueled Leyr's muscles. His face was twisted back, and he looked like nothing more than a rabid animal, his lips bared and revealing a mouth hungering for blood.

He struck Hafgan with a two-handed blow that left his hands stinging after his parry. Leyr didn't pause, but rather attacked again and again, faster than he had ever been. Stronger than he had ever been. And he had already always been faster and stronger than Hafgan. Hafgan could not dodge a single attack; he was forced to parry in a near desperate state. That desperation didn't reach him in the hedwicchen, however; what he experienced was only a realization that he was likely to fall. Nonetheless, he dug deeper into the hedwicchen, searching for weaknesses, seeking to slow the world around him in order to read Leyr's movements. But there was no way to read a madness.

Wiscon struck from his left and Hafgan managed to duck the blow, allowing the axe to whistle past. Leyr followed up with a powerful overhand swing that Hafgan blocked, his spear held out before him in a two-handed grip as he pounced to his feet. Nearly blocked, anyhow, as the blade of Torri Carreg split the wood of his spear. Hafgan's weapon was nothing special; he'd picked it up at a market in Rostane, and it was a seemingly sturdy and well-made weapon. He'd had it for five years, and it had survived axes, swords, and bludgeons. But, it could not survive Leyr's maddening might, nor his perhaps magical spear.

Hafgan stumbled backwards, wielding a broken piece of wood in each hand. Leyr paused, frowning as if he'd expected more. There was little more to give, though. Wiscon, though the least of the Haearn Doethas, was one of the best fighters in Hackeneth. And, the only man to have ever bested Leyr was Hafgan himself. With a broken weapon, the battle was over.

Leyr knew it, too.

"Hafgan Iwan!" His voice projected to every corner of the Cylch. The audience seemed utterly stunned by the events in the ring, by the insanity born of the Red Eye. "You have betrayed your people. You have lost your way. You have led these proud men astray in your dalliances with humans. You bring lies to the very heart of Hackeneth. As I teach, none of us is without flaw, save the Flawless God. But you, Hafgan, are a cancer. You are only flaw. You are the bruise on the potato, the rot in the meat. Our Lord is forgiving, but only to a point."

370

Leyr looked oddly despondent to Hafgan's eyes as he brought around the butt of his spear, connecting with Hafgan's temple. Hafgan made no move to resist, but instead shifted slightly to minimize the damage. It still felt as if his head had been kicked by a rearing horse. But, unlike Rinx, he remembered his lessons in pain.

He was on the ground, dazedly staring up into the Red Eye. The crimson dazzled, as if it were born of a star that had strayed far too close to the earth. He let his hedwicchen fade, but felt only a calmness take him. None of the rampant pride from before… just a resignation, perhaps. An acceptance. Even a welcoming of what was to come. It was appropriate that his blood be shed here, in the place where his life had been upended.

"Imprison the budredda with the human. We shall see if they can be rehabilitated, for, even diminished, a Wasmer is a Wasmer." Leyr's voice was sad, playing to the crowd. "And Hafgan Iwan, for your many betrayals, you are condemned…." It was time. "To ten years in the Pwoll, to consider and repent. Perhaps, then, you will come to know your own insufficiencies. Perhaps you will come to accept the Flawless God."

A panic took Hafgan, and it was a fear like he had never known. Not the Pwoll…. Not again—a week in the place had nearly broken him when he'd been younger. Death would be preferable. By Traisen, he would invite death with open arms; fling himself on the blade willingly! His breath came in panicked gasps and he felt his body shaking uncontrollably. The low moan that he'd thought had come from his maddened men actually creaked from his own throat.

He took one last look up into the Red Eye and, though maddened with fear and pain, thought he could see a silhouette in the distance, someone standing on the surface and looking down upon him. There was a sense of presence to that figure, a heaviness that pushed down upon his throbbing head. But also a sense of the divine. It was too much. It was all too much.

Hafgan closed his eyes and began to weep.

Chapter 27

Trins Grand Chapel was one of the wonders of the world.

While much of Jecusta was crumbling with age and exposure, the chapel stood strong against time and the elements. Flying buttresses, each painstakingly carved into the likenesses of suffering sinners or noble martyrs, jutted from the main structure, supporting the great internal vaults. Stained glass windows peppered the walls in a gleaming spectrum of color that reminded Emma acutely of the scenes at Brockmore Manor, showing the life and time of Yetra. An unnecessary number of sharp minarets topped the chapel like a thousand daggers tearing through the flesh of the sky.

The great structure was a writhing mass of holiness and pretense. And, right now, it was beset on all sides by a horde of shouting, furious soldiers. Emma's own soldiers—maybe half of her forces.

The market square in front of the chapel had been destroyed, wooden pergolas pulled to the ground and carts toppled, their food trampled and ground into a pasty mess. The tide of soldiers struggled to reach the top of the broad thirty steps leading to the main entrance of the church. A wall of white-armored Glories exhaustedly strained against the Brockmore soldiers, each bearing tower shields adorned with the Yetra's Ascension symbol in a crimson red. Occasionally, when the Ardians pushed particularly hard, a club, spear butt, or even an aspergillum—typically used to spread Yetra's Tears about, but a passable bludgeon—would lash out at the offenders. A few men at the fringes of the mob nursed bruises, broken bones, or cracked skulls.

Luckily, steel had not yet been drawn—even in the midst of whatever madness was taking her men, there was an unspoken understanding that blades would spell disaster for all of them.

Along with Unael, Rential, Ervis, and an armed escort that included one pasnes alna, Emma pushed through a wavering line of uncertain black cloaks, cordoning off the mob from the rest of the city. They had taken little action to control the Ardians yet, though the mob had apparently been building for a few hours. The city watch captain likely had no idea what to do in this situation. Attacking and subduing the Ardians could be seen as an act of war, but doing nothing could also cause great damage to the city.

Emma spotted Captain Quentin milling about with some Apple Knights who periodically pulled a raucous man or two from the crowd, penning them in with armored bodies. It seemed like a half-assed effort, to be honest. Here and there, she could see other officers attempting the same thing, some with more fervor than others. Ferl, surrounded by his greenies and a line of his cutthroats, leisurely sat atop an upturned cart, watching the events unfold with a carefree smile. Either he had some part in this or he simply found amusement in chaos.

Emma couldn't help but feel a fierce rage at the sight of this disaster. She had been close... so fucking close.

She outdistanced her escort, aside from Havert, and approached Quentin, noticing that his thinning hair was dusted white with flecks of snow. She hadn't even noticed the lazy flecks that had begun drifting from the clouds.

"What the fuck is going on here?" Emma snapped. Not exactly ladylike, but her rage needed a vent.

"My lady, the Yetranians... it's Ignatius." Quentin gestured helplessly at the top of the stairs.

Since the funeral, weeks ago, Ignatius had been a 'guest' of the Yetranian Church. Obviously, his stunt—calling for war against the wishes of his superior in the great vaults of Trins Grand Cathedral—was not appreciated. Though Emma had had little insight into the morale of her men, lately, it had been impossible for her to ignore the grumbling about their missing chaplain. He was well-loved among the men, his sermons giving them a carrot to amble after, and his simple manner and clothing giving him the appearance of a common man.

Emma's eyes had been drawn to the shield line of Glories, but now she could see, over their shoulders, Ignatius kneeling in the light snow atop the stairs. He was stripped naked, his body red from the cold, with his pudge providing a bit of modesty. From this distance, she could not see his face, though it seemed as if he held his head proudly and with some defiance. Ropes tied to his wrists and pulled taut by a couple of Glories forced his arms out to the side in a "t."

Behind him stood a towering Glory, a bulky man who must have been close to seven feet tall. He wore a white, dual-pointed hood, his wavy brown hair, speckled with gray, running down from the disguise. A poor disguise it was, though, as a man that size wasn't exactly easy to obscure. Behind the huge Glory stood the Grand Taneo Endo Pious himself, his head apparently bowed in prayer.

A gleeful bell rang from somewhere atop the chapel, sounding the hour across the city. As Emma watched, the giant twisted, his arm whipping across his body to bring a lash down across Ignatius' shoulders. The chaplain howled, the echo of his pain audible over the din and acting as a stick being jammed in an ant hole. The Ardians found renewed courage and once again struggled against the wall of Glories.

"What is this?" Emma asked in a hushed voice, her fury at her men dissipating. Though Ignatius was not on her list of friends, he did not deserve to be tortured like this, his life made a spectacle for the masses.

"The Trials," said Quentin, his eyes fixed on the chapel's landing. "The Trials of Yetra."

Another Taneo stepped in behind Ignatius with a slow, measured stride. He was mouthing a prayer as he swung his aspergillum, flinging some substance onto Ignatius' wounds. And judging from the bound man's sudden straining, this was more than just the blessed water, Yetra's Tears.

"The Trials?"

Quentin looked at her, not quite aghast at her lack of knowledge, but with his face betraying a slight frown. He was fiercely Yetranian, and expected the same of his men. He must expect the same of his liege lady and employer, as well, she guessed.

"Yetra went through much during her mortal life, trials of pain and suffering. Her first trial was the loss of her family to the fires of—"

"I don't need that much detail." Quentin narrowed his eyes at her. "Tell me enough to understand what is happening here."

"Yetra is commonly believed to have faced fourteen trials spread across her mortal life, before Ascending to Harmony. The Trials of Yetra are a... punishment for those who are excommunicated for treason against the Church. Every thirty minutes for seven hours, an excommunicant is inflicted with some sort of torture, in Yetra's image. You have witnessed a simple lash, which is one of the lesser Trials, almost a respite. They spread lemon and salt on the wounds as a method of purification." The aspergillum. "Other Trials are more damaging and permanent."

"What did Ignatius do, aside from call for war during the funeral?" A pair of Apple Knights were dragging an unconscious or dead soldier just a few feet from Emma. Blood gushed from a crack in his forehead—somehow, the crimson wash highlighted the soldier's youth. Emma felt a warmth burning in her chest as her rage began to build anew.

"They say he betrayed the Yetranian faith, that he condoned a heathen army to vent destruction against the people he was supposed to serve. He allowed—encouraged, even—the use of magic to kill men, and laughed during the deaths of hundreds. That he broke his vows of chastity while on the march. That he is, himself, a heathen, an agent of Pandemonium." Quentin's voice had become more and more distressed as he'd spoken, and a hand unconsciously gripped his sword hilt, fingers white with the effort.

Quentin knew these denunciations to be lies, and it was rending his faith to pieces. Should he believe the upper echelons of the church, the church to which he had given his whole life? Or, should he believe his eyes—believe that a man whom he respected and had followed—was doing the right thing by fighting these Rostanian armies, including the Feral? Maybe this was why Quentin was doing a half-assed job at controlling the mob. He thought his furious, rioting men were right.

And so did Emma.

"What happens after the Trials?" she asked through gritted teeth, her voice barely audible above the crowd.

"Typically, once a heathen is excommunicated, he is never allowed in a church or chapel again, and is loathed by worshipers of Yetra. He is marked by the Trial, his scars as much as beacons to any of the faithful. His soul is consigned to Pandemonium, of course. But… but… Ignatius has been sentenced to experience the Trials five times. No one has ever survived more than three." Quentin examined his gloved hands, expression blank.

Unael was nearby, furiously conversing with his own captains, trying to make sense of this mess. Ervis and Rential both stood off to the side with their own guards, the magnates no doubt eager to witness any missteps that Unael might make with the escalating situation. Lords and ladies were always like that, in Emma's broad experience, gleefully waiting for a mistake just so much as buzzards awaited the death of a starving man in the desert.

Unael gestured Emma over with an impatient wave. Nail and Havert helped her force her way through the milling throng, picking up some other Apple Knights as they went and forming a protective wall around her.

"You need to disperse your men. Now," Lord Unael said bluntly, his brow creased in frustration.

"Of course. As soon as my chaplain is freed of this public torture and released into my custody," Emma replied, meeting his eye without flinching.

"This is a matter of the church. I have no authority over the Yetranians."

"No authority? This is your city!" Emma snapped. Unael's face tightened, emphasizing the harsh lines that came with a lifetime of command.

"The Yetranian Church has historically been run independently of the state. They are outside of Jecustan law." His voice was as cold as winter.

"And that includes public torture?"

"We let them deal with their own traitors. If you don't remember, I recently lashed quite a few of my own soldiers after the death of your lady. We deal with our own, and they with theirs."

"Lash, yes. For dereliction of duty. And then they were patched up and sent north. This is prolonged torture, a spectacle. And, this is an Ardian who is being tortured in your city. One of my followers, under your protection." Emma clenched her hands in front of her, the ache from her mutilated hand barely keeping her rage in check.

She was losing control. Her head buzzed so much it might have been vibrating.

Rential mumbled something to Ervis, who nodded and continued to watch, askance. More black cloaks were marching into the square as they spoke, acting as a caution against further violence. Some of the guards had clustered on the roofs of nearby buildings, stringing short bows and training them on the mob. If one got spooked and released an arrow, this square would become a blood bath.

Unael leaned toward her, speaking in a hushed voice that smelled slightly of wine. "You know the outcome of this, do you not? If you do not withdraw your men, and if I interfere in any way, you lose the support of the Jecustans. You think Rential or Ervis won't use this as an opportunity to stay cloistered in their little keeps? Let your man die. It is for the greater good."

"If I let my man die, I will not have an army for your support to matter. We need him." At least a third of her men were here. How many others lacked the fortitude to approach the chapel, but would nonetheless be devastated at the loss of their spiritual heart?

Unael sighed a cold mist, his eyes distant as if he were watching a memory. "I truly want to help you, Emma. Escamilla was an… unmatched woman. Long ago, I promised that I would do anything to help her in the event of a disaster, and she made the same promise to me. She saved my life fulfilling her promise. I owed her this much, at least."

Escamilla had never mentioned the extent of her relationship with Lord Unael—only that he was a staunch ally, someone who she was certain they could rely upon. How had she put it? "If I were to trust my life in the hands of one man, it would be Brox Unael. But only him." She had provided no additional context; she'd been dying, after all.

"If we must save your man, though, I will not be able to raise an army. Pandemonium, girl, this would pit me against the church and could spell the end of my rule in Farrow's Hold. I could lose my position in the military, even." His voice was a snake's hiss. "But, I follow through on my debts, even to the dead. Especially to the dead. This is your choice, Emma."

Her choice. Again, her fury flared like a stab in the heart. How dare Escamilla put her in this situation? How dare Unael give her this ultimatum? She bit her tongue and looked to the steps, to Ignatius and the Grand Taneo dwarfed by the huge Glory, who was, in turn, made an insect by the majestic Grand Chapel. Her soldiers had pushed the shield-bearers back a step, but there was a fresh contingent of Glories approaching from a side street, bristling like a pearly hedgehog. Someone threw a fist-sized stone into the mass of white-armored soldiers as they pushed their way through the crowd.

This was going to get ugly, and quickly. Emma forced back her rage as if she was straining to close an overstuffed trunk. There was no choice to make, not here. They needed to act now.

"Stop this, my lord. Whatever the cost."

Unael winced, as if he'd already known her answer. But his face hardened with resolve, a judge about to give a reckoning. Emma felt a brief surge of pride in knowing this man, the Lord of Farrow's Hold. There were good men left, after all, in this stricken world.

"Senco, Dinael, to me! Spire formation. No blood. To the stairs." His voice was sharp with command, and his men responded in an instant. His captains mobilized fifty black cloaks into the proper formation—a hollow triangle with her and Unael in the center. She hadn't precisely expected to go with him, but, looking at the black wall surrounding them, Emma realized there

380

was little choice. At the very least, Rential and Ervis were outside the wall, but so were Nail, Havert, and Opine.

Unael's elite black cloaks parted the mass of buzzing Brockmore soldiers like a leper in a market. It was strangely quiet in the wedge, and the odd silence seemed to amplify Emma's omnipresent migraine. Unael's face was steel—a cold, hard cypher. Emma tried to don her own mask, but, as the shielding wall of Glories parted and revealed the damage done to Ignatius, she could not hide her anger.

The chaplain's head was now drooping after that last lash, blood dripping down from his double chins from some unseen wound. His stomach and chest were carved with a thin "Y," a mockery of the Yetranian Ascension, and likely the first Trial, as the wound was scabbed over with dried blood. Around his feet, the scattered snow was stained red, though, as with his facial wound, the cause was not obvious. Missing toenails? The toes themselves?

"Lord Unael? This is not your place," said the Grand Taneo, his sharp features betraying no emotion, his voice loud but not unfriendly.

Then, Ignatius raised his head.

A metal bar, the width of one of Emma's thumbs, protruded from both of his cheeks, running through his mouth cavity and held between his teeth, small weights hanging from each side forcing him to clench his jaw, lest the bar do more damage. Blood oozed from the twin wounds, streams running down his cheeks and converging at his chin. His lips were quivering with the effort and tears ran freely from his eyes.

His face was twisted in the grin of a child's nightmare, his eyes were glossy with a tired fear.

"All of Farrow's Hold is my place, your eminence. Particularly when an act of such violence is sparking a riot in my very streets."

381

His voice sounded calm as a frozen pond as he ascended the deep steps, Emma struggling to match his confident stride.

Endo Pious arched a bushy eyebrow at that, looking down upon them both literally and figuratively. "Indeed, my lord. I have more Glories on their way, but your assistance in dispersing this rabble is greatly appreciated. Harmony favors those who assist the church."

Ignatius grunted and spat, trying to say something around the iron bar.

Unael folded his arms across his broad chest, his fingertips barely brushing the pommel of his sword… almost as if it were an accident. A game was being played here, Emma knew. A subtle game of gestures and hidden meanings. A game that Escamilla had taught Emma well over the years. And one that was comfortable and comforting to play. Though, she was going to change the rules.

"You will release my man immediately," Emma said, her voice as calm as she could force it to be. Meaning that it had some bite behind it. The huge, hooded Glory stepped forward, still holding his thick leather whip.

"Your man? Do you claim ownership over this excommunicant?"

"I claim no ownership. But I do pay his wages and help keep him plump." Emma heard a snicker from a black cloak behind her, this followed by a barked order for silence.

"Troubling that you put such faith in a faithless man," Endo said, his voice solemn with condemnation.

"I put faith in no one. But I will not see a loyal follower be tortured without just cause," Emma said, avoiding looking at the mess that was Ignatius.

"From a woman who brutally ordered several of her own men dragged to death, simply because they were fleeing for their lives?" Emma's throat was tight, her tongue glued to the roof of her mouth. "And, this excommunicant vowed to uphold the standards of Yetra when he was sworn into our order. These are not arbitrary standards, nor is this an arbitrary punishment. Yetra's mortal life and time were fraught with strife and warfare, resulting in nearly the end of humanity. The very face of the earth was changed by these battles, much of that land still unable to sustain life, near to four thousand years later. Because of war. Because of the unchecked use of power."

Pious stepped forward, the giant Glory flanking him. Emma noticed that the huge, pale hands of the torturer were covered in a criss-crossing of scars, the pattern so consistent that they must have been intentional. Perhaps a penance for his sins. Emma felt an urge to reach for her knife, though it would do little good against any of them. Even Unael seemed shaken by the size of the Glory, amplified by the fact that they were two steps from the top of the stairs.

"If we of the Yetranian faith allow such power to be condoned by one of our own, we are in turn blessing the end of the world." Pious' expression was solemn.

Just then, a bright bell tolled from far, far above the gathered masses.

"Flame, your Holiness," said the scarred Glory, his voice surprisingly rich—a clean spring running through the woods.

"The Trial of Flame," intoned Pious, raising the volume of his voice. "Yetra endured so much during her time on earth, suffering for us, for humanity. One of Her most arduous Trials was also one of her first. Yetra witnessed the death of Her family in the burning ruins of Her home, a city of great good destroyed by the betrayal

383

of the few. Though the flames did not touch Her skin, She felt the searing pain of every charred victim, so great was Her empathy."

Pious gestured to a brazier, and a pair of lesser Taneos reached into the smoldering flames with twin tongs. From the brazier rose a glowing orange half-oval of iron, glowing brightly in the misty afternoon. A heavy chain linked the ends of the oval in a twisted piece of jewelry. The lesser Taneos approached Ignatius, heads bowed and expressions blank.

"Yetra was forever bearing the weight of these sights and experiences, the flame hanging around Her neck as a constant reminder of Her lost family. It symbolizes, of course, Her anger at the atrocities that She witnessed, as well as the light that opened Her eyes to the awfulness that was… that is… humanity." Pious lowered his head, raising his arms in prayer. The lesser Taneos began to lift the macabre necklace.

"Don't," growled Unael.

"Don't?" Pious was almost incredulous as he lowered his arms. One, apparently, did not speak to the Grand Taneo is such a way.

"Don't. Or my black cloaks will tear through your Glories, killing those who resist. The Magnates will put you to trial for inciting a riot by torturing a man who is under the protection of the Hold, like all of the Ardians gathered before you."

"You wish to do this, Unael?" whispered Pious, voice heavy with threat.

"I honor my promises." The Lord of Farrow's Hold was all regret, but he continued. "You will release this man, immediately, to the custody of Lady Emma Breen. You will disperse your Glories, as their gathered numbers are in direct violation of Wantael's Concord. And, you will pray for the quick recovery of these injuries that your minions here inflicted."

Pious was a hawk, regarding Unael as a defensive rabbit, his mood reflected by his predatory gaze. It was the gaze of a hard, hard man—a man who was both comfortable addressing great crowds and condemning men to death. The gaze of a man who had both been the witness to, and bringer of, numerous atrocities. The gaze of a man who, it was said, had heard the voice of Yetra.

Then, all at once, he stood tall, posture relaxed.

"Very well. Release the excommunicant. These Trials have ended. This man is not even worthy of Yetra's suffering."

The lesser Taneos tossed the scalding iron necklace into the snow with a hiss while the Glories roughly untied Ignatius' wrists. The huge Glory removed the weights from the iron bar that speared the chaplain's face and yanked the metal out of his face, Ignatius whimpering with disbelieving relief.

The Grand Taneo had already turned and retreated, without hurry, through the great arched doors of his grand chapel, to be followed by his various underlings. The hooded Glory lingered for a moment, watching Ignatius being carried down the stairs by a pair of black cloaks before turning with the grace of a tiger and disappearing into the center of worship in Farrow's Hold. Yetra's perfect face stared down at them from an intricate stained-glass window. She seemed to be frowning in condemnation, Her expression punctuated by the burning scythe that She held in her hands.

Amidst the cheering of her men, Emma met Ignatius' gaze. Despite his shattered cheeks, the paunchy man managed something that approximated a wan smile.

He mumbled something before his head fell forward, limp, as black cloaks dragged his bloodied feet behind him.

Emma couldn't be sure, but it sounded like he'd said, "I never lost my faith."

Interlogue: Gluttony

"Sweetling, I know not how many more of these visits you will be able to bear. I see the beast within you beginning to surface. I can hear savageness in your voice, utter instinct in your movements. This happens, every time. You have listened to me tell you of my life while I take yours away. It has been many, many years since I have felt such guilt.

"I think your goodness is rubbing off on me.

"There was a time, another time, when goodness was an annoyance. For years and years, it was a fierce inconvenience to me. The embodiment of that goodness, of course, was Amorum.

"He continued to preach of love and Harmony, of joining together instead of living a fractured, battle-ridden existence. Our town—Oagon—had grown into a great city in a few short years. Amorum was still loved and respected, and I was still feared and powerful. Even then, I was not fully comfortable with my role, and continued to be envious of the great orator. We spoke very little, and only met when absolutely necessary… in council meetings and such. Our relationship grew ever more complicated. We never spoke of our tension, but the schism was growing.

"As was my power, sweetling. Both in terms of my influence and my own maenen.

"I learned that I could call upon my own maen as well as maenen. So many pasnes alna who draw upon the maenen of others do not realize that they can draw upon themselves. It is a dangerous balance to maintain, converting one's own life force into the corporeal. Many also do so and destroy their nerring, and they can never recover.

"I thought to expand my maen, essentially giving me a deeper well to draw from—so to speak—in the case of great need. Drawing maenen from others also has a small cost to your own maen, but a skilled practitioner understands how to apply that maenen to her own maen, keeping the nerring full. I thought to hold in as much maenen as possible within me to expand my nerring. It is an incredibly uncomfortable feeling, sweetling; one I cannot accurately describe to one who has never experienced it. It is as if one has overindulged on the finest foods, reached far past satiation, and then continued eating. A mixture of incredible pressure, desire, pain, and pleasure.

"It is gluttony.

"I truly became a glutton in those early days. I drew more and more maenen whenever I had the opportunity, and held it within myself for as long as I could bear it. Where did I get it from? That's an excellent question coming from one as far gone as you, sweetling.

"My followers. Men and women threw themselves at my feet, begging to serve as donors of power. They had begun building a religion. Nothing like the Yetranianism that you see today. Regardless, to sacrifice one's life force in service of the Blood Maiden was the ultimate honor. I did not lack for donors, though I had to keep this practice as secret as possible.

"Amorum suspected, but he never knew for sure, I think. He never accused. He simply spoke to me of Harmony and unity. Kind and inspiring words that, were I not the Blood Maiden, may have touched me.

"But, instead, I continued to expand my nerring, and continued to master maenen and maen at the cost of my followers. My school began to flourish under Intenu, and I had a small army of pasnes alna. Several emerged as my captains—Yinra, Pinetoe, and Wantran. These people also gorged themselves on maenen, but they preferred animals. Yinra preferred birds... particularly great, predatory birds. He felt as if drawing from great birds—once, an eagle—granted him great freedom and allowed him to call upon his maenen faster. Pinetoe drew, most strangely, from goats. He always suffered from guilt, drawing maenen, and he felt that drawing from goats, which were very common in our region, was the least evil he could do.

"Wantran was the most unusual. She drew from cats, which she also kept as pets. But, that in and of itself was not unusual. Rather, she also had the incredibly rare ability to draw yenas, the life force of plant life. Even now, it is so rare to find a pasnes alna or metsika who can draw multiple types of miernes, but Wantran could. She was skilled beyond belief, and dangerous beyond belief. Of my followers, it was her who I most feared.

"As time passed, I felt the urge to draw even more. My expanded nerring almost demanded it. And yet, I did not want to further deplete my followers, as they could be put to other uses.

"I worked out a plan, a hideous, devious plan driven by my gluttony. Amorum had forged a strong alliance with one of the closest cities—Feriline. We had open trade agreements, protection pacts, and even blood swaps, where the son of their leader was sent to live in Oagon, and the son of one of our councilmen was sent to live in Feriline.

"I conspired to break the blood swap. Along with Wantran and Yinra, I infiltrated Feriline and killed the son of our councilor. I killed him in a bloody fashion, leaving his remains—only his head intact for identification—in the great fountain, gracing the market square of Feriline. The water ran red, sweetling, and that liquid was a precursor of what was to come.

"Oagon made war on Feriline. Amorum frowned and disapproved, but the people were on my side. The side of violence. The side of killing. With my pasnes alna, with the remainder of the weapons of war from Aquine, we easily took Feriline.

"And, from the prisoners, I had an entire new crop to draw from. My gluttony would nearly be sated, for a time.

"Sweetling, I have regrets. With your goodness flowing through me, these regrets are more... pronounced than usual. I feel the need to explain that I no longer draw maenen simply to draw maenen, simply to experience the power. Rather, I must for many reasons. Since what people call my Ascension, my own maen has been draining, slowly, leaking from my nerring. I have no explanation for this. Perhaps I have drawn too much in my time, damaging myself beyond repair. But, my nerring appears to be whole. Or perhaps I have simply lived too long in this world. Though I appear as a beautiful woman to you, sweetling, I am older than you can imagine.

"Were I to stop drawing from my donors, such as you, my sweetling, my nerring would dry up. I would turn Feral, as they call it.

"And, eventually, I would die.

"I fear death, sweetling. I experience such terror when contemplating the subject, the thoughts of emptiness and simply... not being. I cannot allow that to happen. Oh, the Taneos' views on the afterlife, living in paradise with me? All fabricated to give hope to the masses. I know not what happens after this life, and I refuse to find out.

"I feel as if I still have a place on this earth. That I am needed. And, even if I am not... I will not die.

"I do not know whether I am a goddess, as they preach. But... I am close enough that the difference matters not."

Chapter 28

The stiff odor of mold was evident as she brought the wedge of cheese to her lips. Its texture was slimy, as if the block of whitish yellow was perspiring at the thought of being consumed. But, as Morgyn's teeth sank into the soggy, old bit of cheese, she couldn't recall having ever tasted something so wonderful.

"Hey, shit-stealer! Get away from there!" shouted a voice—an angry guardian of old, rotting food. Morgyn darted away, licking her fingers and shouting "pig-fucker!" She'd never understand why people were so protective of their trash. It was being thrown away, for Ultner's sake! It would be buried somewhere west of town, eventually to be covered in literal shit, and then the area would be repurposed as a farm. Rostane was fed on trash.

It had been weeks since the Patriarch had sent her back into the wild. Morgyn had resumed her life of scrounging and parasitism without missing a beat. She hadn't sought out any of her acquaintances or friends. There was only one person she trusted, and she couldn't find him without potentially revealing herself to others. And she didn't want to take that risk, lest The House catch her. That certainly wouldn't end well.

So, she slept in filth, ate refuse, and sheared her hair short again to combat the lice. She kept her face coated in muck so that no one would recognize her, and she even went barefoot like the truest of street urchins. Perhaps her time with Escamilla had not made her soft, after all.

But even her desire to remain anonymous could not keep her from the first public execution in Rostane in eighty years.

She emerged from her alley and was immediately caught in the roaring flow of a human river. Well, not entirely human, as she was firmly wedged in front of two huge, well-muscled Wasmer.

Probably porters, but no less intimidating for the simplicity of their occupation.

Most of the city had turned out for this—the death of a traitor to the duchy, to the country. Maybe people had a stronger sense of nationalism than Morgyn would have thought, wanting to see the treasonous bastard pay. Certainly, judging from the laughing group of Taneos nearby, some had turned out with a sense of religious and moral righteousness, hoping to see a sinner pay for his crimes, seeking the validation of their Yetranian concept of universal balance.

Maybe, like Morgyn, some were also going out of a sense of morbid curiosity.

Or, maybe they were just bored.

The veins of the city began to clot as the people converged on their goal—the great Amorum Square at the foot of the ramp leading to the Plateau. That was where the Spike had stood for years and years, largely ignored and sometimes even decorated for the Ascension Festival.

The scene was much like that of a festival. Wherever people gather, so do merchants and salespeople, much like flies attracted to compost. Every few feet, food or drink vendors had set up shop, hawking their various meats and pastries with deep voices accustomed to being heard over a crowd. Of course, there were entertainers—torch-jugglers, sword-swallowers, exotic dancers— all of them trying to capitalize on a free audience. She even saw one man selling miniature carvings of the Spike as souvenirs to mark this joyous day.

It wasn't all carousing and celebration, though. Not far from her chosen path, a well-dressed bald man perched atop some stacked crates, shouting and gesticulating with passion. His audience responded with angry hisses and shouts. Morgyn couldn't hear the words, but she knew this must be a group of objectors who opposed the civil war. She had almost been caught up in a riot a week ago, near the docks, and that ruckus had been ignited by the same hairless bastard. She'd lost a perfectly good hiding place in the resulting fires. Now, she skirted these anti-war fanatics.

Morgyn's size played to her advantage in the crowd as she squeezed between bodies and even crawled between legs to get closer to the scene that would soon play out. She managed to get to the square proper, and then made a brief climb to sit on a window ledge of one of the many stone-faced storefronts ringing the square. It afforded a great view over the heads of the gathered thousands while offering her an easy escape route if she got caught. One does not survive long in Rostane without the ability to quickly scale the often rough-faced stones of Rostanian buildings, and this storefront was rough enough that Morgyn could easily make it to the wooden awning and henceforth escape across the rooftops. Thus feeling as secure as possible, Morgyn examined the square.

In the center of the massed people was the Spike, ringed by fully-armored Knights of the Wolf, with crankbowmen right behind them. The thin, silver spire seemed to glow in the reflection of the sun; it had been freshly polished for this occasion. Near the bottom of the fifty-foot-tall device, it was only as thick as her thigh, getting narrower closer to the top.

Bleachers had been constructed on one side of the Spike, well-guarded from the common population by the personal forces of the dozens of gathered nobles from around the duchy. Adorned in colorful silks and likely nibbling on delicacies and drinking fine wine, the nobles were set quite apart from the rest of the Rostanians. Morgyn had faint hopes that the bleachers would collapse under their ample weight.

Surrounding the tip of the Spike in a u-shape was scaffolding, with a platform built specially for this occasion. Most of the

Rostanian Council was there, flanked by six Wolf Knights. Morgyn recognized a couple of the councilmen, primarily from her work with The House. There was, of course, Lord Faris, the advisor to the late duke. His silvery-black hair blew in the wind, and he seemed among the least perturbed to be standing atop the world, about to dole out justice. Similarly unbothered was Darian de Trenton, his weathered face showing not a single emotion. Baronness Farah Erlins, still wearing black in mourning for her husband, clutched the railing in one hand and the arm of a guardsman with her other. Publicly, her husband Baron Theran Erlins had been murdered by the Florensians, sparking the war. But, Morgyn knew that the man had been tortured by Duke Penton and the Rostanians. She had found him herself, chained and mutilated, laying in a pool of his own putridity and leaning on the burned stump of his amputated hand.

She wondered, briefly, if his Farah knew the truth or if she was simply a pawn.

A few more council people were on the scaffolding, but Morgyn didn't know them as well. Pereway de Ingus, a Nistling merchant who had holdings in Rostane that were only second to de Trenton, himself. Count Aron Witton, the man with the most productive farms in the country. And so on. A mix of the wealthy and powerful, nobles and merchants, ten in all. People who would generally only give Morgyn a second glance, and then only to see where their boot struck.

Finally, there was the prisoner himself, the man destined to be impaled. Tilner Pick, Lady Escamilla's closest confidant.

He was well-groomed and clean, his silvery hair tied in a ponytail. An interesting and theatrical choice, as the man had been rotting in the Plateau's prison for weeks. Morgyn figured that there was some symbolism in his cleanliness, but she didn't strain herself to figure out what it was. She had met the man a couple of times, finding him to be relatively insufferable in his devotion to

Lady Escamilla. Morgyn had wondered what that would be like, to command the emotions of others. It was almost a foreign concept.

"…peoples of Rostane. Peoples of Ardia." This from Lord Faris, speaking into a great, curved cone in order to project his voice across the square. The crowd was surprisingly compliant, and quieted instantly.

"We are at war. Florens, our southern neighbors and ostensibly our allies, invaded our country in the heat of summer, slaughtering our fellow Rostanians. Breaking the tenants of Yetra by harming their fellow man for the sake of power. For greed. Perhaps, for envy." Faris seemed to survey the crowd as he touched on both nationalism and religiosity.

"And envious they should be! Rostane, the city and the duchy, is the pride of Ardia! We have the greatest technology, the most intelligent scientists. Ours is the strongest navy and we keep the most skilled soldiers. Our farmers are the most stoic, our merchants the most savvy. Though their aggression is a tragedy, it is a great compliment. Rostane, my countrymen, my family…" Wait, wasn't Lord Faris clearly Alganian? "…we are the jewel of Ardia. And, this tragedy is an opportunity to finally take what is ours. Ardia, Rostanians. Ardia shall be ours."

A resounding cheer came as the gathered crowd was taken by Faris' words. But Morgyn noticed a subset of people, here and there, who did not cheer or shout. Some merchants, some commoners. Mostly women and older men. As like as not, their sons and husbands, their laborers and skilled workers, had been conscripted into the army. Even now, the conscriptions continued, and the ranks of the army swelled while the population of the city dwindled.

"However… However, my people, there are those who would see us fail. There are those who would fight us, who would betray us. Those who would support our enemies against us." He gestured to Escamilla's retainer.

"Tilner Pick is one of those men. He tirelessly worked to slaughter our families, our parents, our husbands, our children." The guards holding Pick forced him to stand upright, and a third grabbed his face. The prisoner struggled, but he was weak and outmanned. A sad-faced man with a braided beard stepped in from behind the guards, procuring a flask. The guards forced the potion into Pick's mouth, clamping shut his nose and covering his face so that he'd swallow. Pick slumped backward, defeated.

Morgyn had heard gossip about the Spike, and of the plans for this traitor. The potion forced down his throat numbed the pain and slowed the heart, keeping the man alive as he was lowered onto to the tip of the Spike. He would be suspended by his wrists and ankles, parallel to the ground, and the needle-sharp tip of the Spike would be inserted quite precisely into his stomach, avoiding major organs and blood vessels—allowing the victim to survive while impaled, perhaps even for days. The ropes impaling the man would be slackened or cut completely over the hours, with his body sliding down the length of the Spike a little at a time. Some, stories said, survived until they reached the ground. If that happened, people would line up to spit on the body.

The guards readied the ropes to tie down Pick, to suspend him like a fish snagged by four lines.

"Thousands of our soldiers were killed at Florens, but we were ultimately victorious! With our allies, we fought back the combined forces of Florens and Brockmore, led by the traitorous Lady Escamilla Breen. The Army of Brockmore and the Florensian forces were routed, the Lady Escamilla killed in the counterattack. Tilner Pick…"

"What?" roared Pick, ripping free of his guards in a burst of wild strength. The Wolf Knights worked to subdue him, but Pick was quicker. He darted under the grip of one knight and kicked him in the side of the knee. The man's leg buckled and he fell heavily to the platform, rolling toward the Spike. Where there was no railing.

The other knight ignored Pick and dove toward his companion, catching his armored leg. The first knight dangled slackly for a moment, in the open air, held only by his comrade-in-arms. Morgyn realized that her mouth was hanging as slack as the knight, and she popped it shut.

Then, the hanging knight realized his plight and began struggling, but this was the worst thing he could possibly do. His struggling savior was jerked forward a few inches, and kicked in the face. He began to topple into the gap even as he lost his grip on the first man.

Both tumbled into the air, the first knight headfirst and thrashing. The second guard flailed against the body of the Spike and even managed to grip the great impaler for a moment and slow his fall. But, somehow, he knocked himself away from his salvation and Pick's doom. Both guards slammed into the ground with an audible clanking. There was no way that their armor had saved them at that height.

Some of the Wolf Knights surrounding the Spike rushed to the men as Tilner Pick faced the council and the remaining guards. Even though the man was malnourished, he appeared to be in control. He'd managed to pick up one of the fallen guard's spears, and he used the pointy stick to hold the other guards at bay. Because the platform was so narrow, the guards couldn't flank him. A standoff, it seemed. Morgyn had been in one or two of those in her life.

The crowd growled and barked like alley dogs fighting over rancid meat as they tried to make sense of the falling of the Wolf Knights. It soon grew quiet once again, though, as a collective

Rostane strained to hear. Luckily, the echoing cone was a powerful tool.

"You lie about Escamilla. She lives, and the army fights on," Pick shouted, his spear leveled over the gap at Lord Faris.

"I gain nothing from lying, prisoner," Faris said, his voice calm and his arms folded.

"You seek to disillusion the crowd, to make them believe in your right to Ardia." Even half the square away, Morgyn could hear the faith in his voice. She wondered what it would be like to have such blind faith in anything. She glanced down for a moment then, and swallowed.

"No, prisoner. The people know the truth."

"Your truth!"

"The only truth. You want to know how she died?"

Morgyn stiffened. Tilner Pick made no move, either.

Faris' voice was calm. "We had someone close to her, prisoner. A dark-haired girl." Morgyn touched her shorn hair and glanced around. "She put a knife in Escamilla's back weeks ago." Morgyn remembered the warm blood washing over her hands. Her face and chest burned with the memory, and she felt like every eye was on her. Realistically, the crowd was near silent, every ear on the echoing conversation.

"No!" boomed Tilner Pick with the call of a slaughtered pig. He launched his spear directly at Faris' chest. There was a flash of red light, and the weapon was deflected, flipping end over end into the crowd below.

The Wolf Knights rushed Pick, but again he was too fast. He flung himself off of the platform.

And directly onto the Spike.

Morgyn felt a sudden urge to run as the great spear pierced the heart of Escamilla's man, but found herself unable to move. A paralysis seemed to permeate the gathered thousands like a plague for a solid five seconds. And then, someone screamed, breaking the pregnant moment. Some surged toward the Spike, pushing back on the ring of Wolf Knights. Others attempted to leave the square by whatever means necessary, even if it meant trampling the fallen.

It made no sense to Morgyn. The crowd had come to see the blood of a traitor. But, after seeing two guards fall, and that traitor impale himself of his own volition, there was a general, irrational panic. The Wolf Knights beat the frenzied crowd back, spear handles and pommels cracking bones and even a few skulls. Morgyn, perched on her window ledge, thought twice about joining the mob as the pandemonium grew in pitch and violence. She glanced over her shoulder—she could still climb to the rooftops at any time.

Her eyes were drawn back to the Spike. Pick's body was inching down the spire, limbs hanging downward like he was a spider impaled by a toothpick. His lifeblood outpaced his corpse, bathing the silver monument in a dark crimson already reaching the ground. The councilors were at each other's throats. At least, de Trenton and Lord Faris were harshly gesturing at each other, an occasional shouted word audible above the cacophony. The other councilors were either watching their apparent betters, cowering on the scaffold, or descending a ladder to the ground. Apparently, a wall of soldiers was preferable to the heights, though the danger was much greater below.

As she watched, a stray thought picked at Morgyn's brain. She'd caused this. Because of her, Escamilla was dead or nearly so. Because of her, Pick had flung himself to his bloody death. Because of her, Rostane was panicking. A girl who had no true power. She could barely get a stray dog to share a pile of trash with her. And yet, her actions had set in motion a chain of events that had led to... all this.

A weird mix of feelings came to her as a result. She was appalled, certainly. Though this city had treated her as an unwanted daughter, and though Tilner was a pompous kiss-ass, she wouldn't have wished rioting on one and death for the other. She wasn't heartless. And yet, she couldn't deny a loud, rhythmic pounding in her heart that could only be interpreted as a fearful excitement.

Maybe murdering Escamilla had been the biggest thing she would ever do.

A two-toned, ear-splitting whistle cut through her revelry. That was a signal call from The House!

"It's the girl!" roared a deep voice from the crowd, somehow audible above the sounds of disarray and panic.

"Aye! Go left!"

Morgyn came instantly on guard, seeing four men battling across the flow of people toward her position. Two, she recognized—Yarem the Head, known for his shiny, perfectly-shaped bald head, and Minks, a tall, wiry Sestrian, said to be a master knife-thrower. The other two were big, meaty protectors, if she were to guess their rank.

Stupid, stupid. She should never have come here, curiosity be damned. Of course, The House would have agents among this gathering. Recherche Oletta likely patrolled the crowd, and maybe there were even some agents from the now-defunct army of the nearly-slain Lady Escamilla. Thousands of people were here, so someone had been bound to recognize her. Living with Escamilla had made her both soft and stupid.

There was no time to hesitate. Morgyn twisted nimbly from her ledge and grappled up the stone facade of the shop as the men approached. The rough-hewn bricks scraped her fingers—she'd lost her callouses—but she ignored it. Just as the men reached the store-front, Morgyn pushed off the wall, leaping the last few inches to the wooden awning. For a terrifying second, she was in open air, but her hands managed to grasp the slightly-damp wood. She'd done this more times than she could count, and it wasn't difficult.

Except that the wood was rotting, and her fingers tore through the moldy wood as if it were made of cheese. And then she was falling, spinning slightly in the air before her shoulder and then her head connected with the paver stones. Black and red filled her vision, and her skull was bathed in an intense fire. She squinted open her eyes and tried to roll to her side, though it felt as though she were swimming in mud. Dizzily, she slumped back to the ground.

"…Tennyson will be pleased. He's been looking for this one."

"Thank Ultner she fell. She'd've been off if she got up there."

"Nah, we've got agents on the roofs. They have her description."

"But now we get the reward."

Morgyn couldn't see who was talking, but she felt rough hands wrap around her ankles. She willed her body to fight, but it only struggled weakly. There was a crude laugh.

"Don't know how this one got Escamilla in the middle of that army. Look at her—she's skin and bones." Morgyn felt herself being lift by one leg and shaken, a demonstration of her diminutive stature.

Bastard. He'd die first.

"Stop messing around. Let's get out of this crowd. Look, more Wolfies are showing up."

"Aye, we'll head ba…"

A furious roar came, and Morgyn, head first, was suddenly on the pavement again. She squinted against the brightness just in time to see one of her captors barreled over by a huge blur. Both went flying out of her sight, and her head swam when she attempted to follow the action. The meager contents of her stomach rose into her throat and Morgyn worked to retain that bit of cheese she'd eaten while the world spun around her.

There were more shouts behind her, and the sounds of a battle. As Morgyn made a final attempt to rise, something struck her skull with a glancing blow. Her brain had taken enough knocking around, and she mercifully lost consciousness amidst the scuffle.

Morgyn's last memory of the scene was of vomiting up the old cheese.

Chapter 29

Fenrir had to look away.

He'd seen gruesome things before. Pandemonium, he'd done gruesome things before. But Tilner's death was too much—both the circumstance and the manner. It was... a shame... that he'd had to be broken before ending his own life. Fenrir wished he could slap the man's mustaches straight off for his stupidity.

What could have driven him to do that? He wished he could have heard the words, but Ingla had been too busy barking in his ears for him to catch what Faris had said to Escamilla's retainer.

Fenrir took a long, subtle pull from a near-empty flask of Sestrian rum that he'd managed to purloin from one of the warehouses. He coughed and sputtered; the shit burned, and it had been a long, long time since he'd had a drink. But by Ultner's serrated cock, he needed it.

"Trash! Focus on the mission!" Ingla hissed, slapping the flask to the ground and cuffing him. She and the Blue Adder Eanor stood at his shoulders, making hand gestures to the few other Adders who were just out of sight. Fenrir had only spotted two associates of The House so far, none of them rabble raisers or inciters. He pointed out one of them to Ingla—Canor, an asshole from Algania who had once spilled a beer down the back of Fenrir's shirt. The man was dragged off by a couple Adders a few minutes later.

The mission had been a disaster, as were most that Fenrir became involved in. He hadn't seen anyone meaningful—and hadn't expected to, considering the people of note within The House tended to conceal their identities behind masks. And, now that Pick's body slowly drooped down the Spike, the crowd was in a panic. There'd be no finding any other associates amid this mess.

"Wait… there!" He saw four of them, clustered together. Yarem the Head, the sick bastard who was said to have a penchant for children, and Minks, who made a living by sticking knives in people from a distance. Dern, a hulking bastard who grinned while he broke the fingers of hapless merchants who couldn't pay their protection charges. And Enen, a man known for just being a bad guy. All scum. Dung beetles. Worthless, sadistic fucks, like most of those attracted to The House.

They were only steps away, and standing over the body of a young girl. A girl that Fenrir recognized, and not necessarily with fondness.

Nonetheless, he found himself shoving through the crowd and slamming his shoulder into Yarem, bearing him to the ground. He slammed the man's shiny, cracked egg of a head against the cobblestones—not with enough force to kill, but certainly with enough to take him out of this little altercation. He bashed the man's bald head again, too, just to be sure, before snapping to his feet.

Durn approached him, the hulking giant grinning the grin of a madman, tossing a wicked little dagger from hand to hand in the manner of a wannabe pirate. Fenrir reached for his own sword before remembering that Ingla hadn't allowed him to be armed, lest he try something funny. Durn's grin grew wider.

Fenrir started to feel disconnected, his vision wavering and becoming separated from his consciousness. His fucking phantom, finally resurfacing to hover above him as he faced death. He hadn't felt this way since that day when he'd run through the little duke, and in a detached way, he reflected that it wasn't a good sign. But, his consciousness didn't stay separate for more than a moment.

Without any preamble, another huge man—this one even bigger than the protector—slammed into Durn and tumbled over

404

the fallen Yarem, who was very much dead at this point. Maybe the second head-bashing hadn't been necessary. Fenrir, his consciousness again merged with his body, looked away.

Their little battle seemed to have triggered a riot state nearby, with Rostanians shoving, screaming, and trampling all comers. Eonor, their lone back-up Adder, lay writhing in the street with one of Minks' knives wedged in his throat. Ingla was fighting off the remaining two members of The House with a fluidity he had never seen before. Then, as he watched, Enen pressed Ingla hard while Minks backed up to throw another deadly blade at her.

Fenrir doubted she would be as pretty with a knife sticking out of her eye.

Without any other weapon, Fenrir used the only thing at his disposal to stop another knife toss—he shoved an angry and bewildered Wasmer at Minks with all of his strength. The merchant went flying, hitting Minks hard just as he threw his weapon. The projectile disappeared into the crowd behind Ingla, its path followed by a hideous shriek. Minks himself disappeared beneath a throng of people who must have seen him with the knife.

With a simple and unhurried jab, Ingla finished Enen before turning to Fenrir with a furious look.

"You trash! You were to point them out—not attack them! Not kill them! What good is a dead prisoner?" She gestured at the fallen Yarem. Fenrir just shrugged and walked over to the fallen urchin, the little girl who had once bashed his head in with an iron baton, beginning a desperate escape through the ruins beneath the Plateau.

"I already regret this," he mumbled as he made to toss her over his shoulder.

"Don't lay a hand on her, brother," said a deep, articulate voice. He'd forgotten about whoever had borne Durn to the ground and taken the protector out of the fight. Fenrir turned to assess this new threat. It took a minute to recognize the man, but when he did, Fenrir couldn't help but grin.

"It is great to see you again, brother. Just curious—fuck any women lately?" Fenrir asked. The big man's toothy grin was unaffected.

"You will find that I am fully capable of fucking whomever I want, brother." Toothy, the man who had, along with Morgyn, attacked Fenrir all those months ago, held a knife dripping with blood. "Now, move away from the girl."

There was no reason not to move away. Fenrir couldn't think of a single, compelling reason to want to stay anywhere near the treacherous little snake. And yet…

"No, I'm good." Fenrir bent down to lift her over his shoulder, secure in the fact that Ingla now stood by his side to discourage any attack.

"What are you doing, trash?" she hissed at him through clenched teeth. She was rapidly losing control of the situation, and her stoicism—weak in the most predicable of situations—was slipping. Fenrir studied her face, and then something behind her drew his attention. And not in a good way.

"Um…. You said I should point them out if we come across any other members of The House, right?"

"Yes?"

"Well, there they are."

"Where? And how many?" She glanced around, and immediately sighted the two dozen men, each wearing a mask of a different animal, insect, or demon, all of them extricating themselves from the crowd.

"Right there. All of them."

***

Discretion being the only part of valor that really mattered, Fenrir shouldered Morgyn and shoved his way through the crowd. He assumed that Toothy and Ingla were following, but truthfully didn't care at the moment. When a nightmare gave chase, you kept it to your back regardless of who followed.

The crowd was thankfully thinning in front of him, and Fenrir barreled down a few people as he sought to create distance between himself and The House. There were enough side streets and alleyways that he might be able to lose them, and maybe find his way back to the de Trenton compound. Where in Ultner's asshole were the rest of those Blue Adders, anyhow? They were quick to jump in and drag trash off the street, but where were they when blood started flowing?

Fenrir found his way to a side street, seeking out a long, unobstructed stretch to create some distance. Morgyn, the little ruffian, bounced on his shoulders, but she barely felt like a weight. He hadn't spared the girl a thought since his imprisonment; he'd seen her a bit amidst the Army of Brockmore, and she'd usually had some smartass comment, and he'd retorted the best he could. Truthfully, they'd developed a bit of a clever back and forth, but she was really nothing to him. He wondered how she'd become separated from the army. Escamilla had taken a shine to her, so maybe, upon the lady's death, she'd simply fled. Or, maybe she was still working for that Recherche Oletta—she obviously wasn't an ally of The House.

Breathing heavily, Fenrir glanced backwards before making a sharp left, knocking over a stack of empty crates in his inattention. He didn't see any masks just behind him; maybe they'd gotten caught in the rioting crowd. Ingla and Toothy, though, were right on his tail and keeping up fairly well. Ingla passed him with a burst of speed, taking the lead and pushing them to a street on their right and then an alley on their left.

Toothy shot him a dark look around his desperate gasps for breath. Fenrir gave him a smile and a wink before stumbling to a stop, lest he crash into a skidding Ingla. There were a dozen masked faces—grotesque birds, animals, and Pandemonium-knew-whats—lining the far end of the alley.

"Ultner's rotten testicles…" Fenrir mumbled as he spun around and saw a similar group closing in behind him. Glancing up, he saw the spotters hopping across the rooftops; hence, no close pursuit—they could easily have found where they were fleeing. He should have known that.

Toothy shifted on his feet, adjusting his grip on his knife. He was looking about ready to charge the group behind him. Fenrir placed a hand on his shoulder.

"You'd better not, brother," he said quietly.

"You'd rather be tortured to death? I've seen what they do!" His eyes were wild, his breath coming in gasps. The masked men just stood there, blocking their path.

"You used to have no problems opposing The House, as I recall."

"Things were different, then. We need to get out of here." His voice was desperate.

"Agreed," Ingla said, her voice calm. She showed none of her characteristic anger. Her eyes were clear, her jaw set with the determination of one who expected to die, but not without taking a few enemies with her. And she was fully capable of that much.

"Ingla, look at me." She turned, and he grabbed her chin and gave her a rough, passionate kiss. She held on for a second before slapping him away, to the discordant laughter of the gathered associates, protectors, enforcers, and eliminators.

"The Bull always knows how to treat a lady!" called one voice. Fenrir had hoped he'd recognize one, and he did. Unfortunately, it was Garrett, a cocky young enforcer who'd been a constant thorn in Fenrir's side. But, unmasking one was a way to humanize the rest of them and remind them of their once comradery.

"Ask your mother how I treat a lady, Garrett. She would be the one to know," called Fenrir.

"Ha, well, she is about your age, Old Bull." The younger man took off his mask; he was practically a baby, barely twenty. And yet, he had collected enough fingers to build a house with.

"I doubt she's so old." He made as if to rub his knee. "Garrett, I need to talk to Tennyson."

The boy laughed a charming, infectious laugh. He might have been a noble instead of the son of a whore. "He's not much interested in talking with traitors," he said, pointedly looking at Fenrir and Morgyn, still slung over his shoulder. "Nor members of rival organizations." Glaring at Toothy. "Though, he might be interested in having a conversation to find out what that one knows." Ingla effortlessly spun her blade in her hand and stepped toward Garrett. He backed up, despite the assurance of a couple dozen helping hands.

"Nonsense, Garrett." The crowd parted as Tennyson, the leader of The House, glided into the circle. His own mask—the blistered, silver visage of Ultner—always seemed to grin, but especially now. "Fenrir and I are old friends, and what old friends wouldn't want to speak?"

Fenrir grinned while repressing a shiver. He spread his hands wide, taking in his little party and all of the surrounding animals, demons, and insects. "Exactly. My friends and I would love to join you for dinner."

Chapter 30

"We need to hurry. We have no choice. We must do it. We must do it. We must do it," Yurin mumbled to himself, knowing full well that Hafgan would hear him. That was his nature, avoidantly aggressive. And, as always, a little odd.

"Shut up, Yurin. Why haven't you learned to shut your mouth?" Hafgan growled, trudging through the snow in utter misery. He had a choice to make, a critical choice. The type of choice that sets the course of a man's life. The type of choice that sets the course of an entire people's future. The type of choice that never should be given in a sane society.

The choice of whether to kill his parents or flee his country.

"My brother knows we must do it, though he may lie to himself. Leyr already did it. Rinx already did it. Prineth could not and his place was forfeit," Yurin continued to mumble. Hafgan was not sure at what point exactly his older brother had snapped. When he'd been young, Yurin had seemed so strong, practically invincible. And yet, his mind was now unhinged. Everything about him spoke of a dangerous unpredictability. Unlike the rest of the Haearn Doethas recruits, Yurin had not mastered the hedwicchen. He had no need to do so, however; his particular battle style was irregular and random, so much so that, even in his hedwicchen, Hafgan could not read what was coming next. It was a limitation in so many ways, but somehow Yurin persevered. He was third ranked in the class, only behind the rotating spots of Leyr and Hafgan. It was almost as if Yurin, himself, had no idea of his next move.

"I know damned well what Prineth faced." And that Prineth had freed his veins of blood afterward, caught between this oath of ultimate loyalty to Taern and the lingering love and obligation he felt for his family.

The logging camp was sprawled before them, unchanged from the previous fifteen years. Maybe a little more run-down, a little more dingy. And, to Hafgan, seemingly much, much smaller. How had the entirety of the first few years of his life been spent in this place? A few log cabins tossed across the hill, as if the snow was taken with a pox. A longhouse used for mealtimes, festivals, and gatherings. And a diminishing supply of lumber in every direction. One day, soon, they would be forced to relocate, traveling even further from Hackeneth and relative safety. But they would cling to this gods-forsaken patch of mud until the last possible moment. For, as humble as it was, it was home.

His parents, Lifna and Harran, still lived in the same wooden hut, the garrs gained from selling their children having been traded for food instead of even the basest luxury. Times had been hard fifteen years ago. Times were hard at this moment, too. Times were always hard in the Tulanques, truth be told, and an injection of temporary wealth would do nothing to change that.

And his parents would pay a price, this night, for trying carve out a better life for themselves by sacrificing their children.

"The only way to truly master the art of war is to master the hedwicchen," Taern had said to the gathered Haearn Doethas. "And the only way to truly master the hedwicchen is to fight a grief beyond reckoning, a grief that would destroy the soul unless repressed behind a barrier of emptiness. You must cut all bonds with your previous life in order to create this grief. But, you are strong. You are the Carreg Da. You are Hackeneth. This will make you stronger than all who have come before you, and with that strength, there will be change. We will guide our people from their mistakes, from these mountains. And we will carve out greatness through your actions." There had been no cheering at his words. Most of the Haearn Doethas had been in their hedwicchens.

Leyr had gone first. He had no parents left to him, so he'd had to slay his sister. Rinx had taken the same route that Hafgan and Yurin were asked to take. As far as Hafgan knew, neither Leyr nor Rinx had left their hedwicchen in the week since.

"Yurin…" Hafgan grabbed his brother's shoulder, and the man tensed up. He could have spun around, swinging his fists, and Hafgan wouldn't have been surprised. But instead his shoulders slumped and he took a great shuddering breath. Not for the first time, Hafgan wondered at how much of his brother's mild madness was real, how much feigned. His opinion was that it was somewhere in between.

"Yurin, my brother… we need to choose. We have been asked to do an unspeakable thing this night. Something that is intended to break us. Something that will break us, unless we dig so deeply into the hedwicchen that we can suffocate the grief. And you, my brother, have not the ability. We must leave this place together, and start a life elsewhere. With a different clan. Or in a different country. Ardia, maybe. Or Algania."

Hafgan had little hope of convincing his brother. Hafgan had pitched this idea twice already, first half-heartedly and then more forcefully. What was Hackeneth to them, anyhow? Couldn't they live better elsewhere? Couldn't they have an impact on the world outside of this barren place without… doing this?

Yurin said nothing. He didn't turn around. He didn't breathe. The snow continued to fall, forming a sheet upon his head for the long minutes where nothing happened. Perhaps he really would be convinced, and they could abandon this grotesquery.

And then, he spoke quietly. "We must do as Taern says. We must follow his orders. We must."

The snow continued to fall, heavier and heavier, like a white, leaden blanket.

"Yurin…"

His brother turned and stared at him, his eyes not shifting for once, not darting about with uncertainty. Clear as the stars peeking through the clouds.

"I will do it, little brother. You need not stain your hands." With that, he turned and walked toward their parents' cabin.

Hafgan gripped his spear with white, shaking hands. His parents would die this night at the hands of his brother, or his brother would later slit his own wrists if he failed. There was no leaving the mountains.

But he might spare his brother further madness.

"You bleeding dog of Taern!" Hafgan shouted, his words consumed by the blizzard around them. "All you are is a bleeding dog, less than a man. And, like a dog, you should be beaten." He launched himself at his brother, spear spinning.

Yurin put up a small fight, but he'd been surprised. Truly stunned by Hafgan's single-minded, hedwicchen-driven attack. By the fact that his brother would attack him, here and now. His unconscious body lay in the snow within moments.

Hafgan felt no grief while driving his spear into the sleeping bodies of his parents. Nor any joy at saving his brother.

He felt nothing.

***

A week had passed since Leyr had had Hafgan thrown down here, into the impenetrable and inescapable darkness that was the

Pwoll. Maybe had been a week. Maybe it had only been a day. There was no way to tell.

The Pwoll was a cylinder bored straight into the ground, deep within the hallowed halls of Limner. The walls were smooth and unscalable, and a bit slimy from whatever moisture permeated this place. With his broad shoulders, Hafgan could barely turn around, let alone sit or lie down. Every bone in his body, every muscle in his body, ached from the lack of movement, from the awkward angles. His back was on fire, his neck and shoulders feeling as if they were being crushed by stone. And, though his legs wanted to give out, they had no choice but to hold him up.

His hedwicchen had failed him, down here in the Pwoll. His only company was himself and his gods-forsaken memories, being relived without the protective ability to strip his emotions. For whatever reason, he relived the night of his parents' murders over and over again in his head. He recalled exactly how easily the spear had slid into the chest of his father, followed by that of his mother. He remembered how the blood slowly spread across their threadbare blankets. Hafgan had turned and walked away without a backwards glance. He need not look, for in his hedwicchen, he had objectively acknowledged his success.

When Hafgan had tried to leave the hedwicchen, days afterward, he had almost been torn apart by grief, guilt, and anger. But, he was strong enough to handle it, and he could return to the hedwicchen when the pain became unbearable. The emotional torment would have been worth it, too, had he been able to save his brother from madness.

But, as it was, Yurin had not been saved. When the brothers had reported back to Taern, Hafgan shared how they had each blooded their blades, Hafgan on their mother and Yurin on their father. Yurin, however, could not or would not lie. He had fallen to his knees, telling a story of cowardice, how he had run from his fate like a goat might flee an avalanche. He'd begged and wept, asking to continue serving Taern.

And, Taern had acquiesced, allowing him to serve as an errand boy, scout, and assassin. Though he'd seen his brother little since then, Hafgan knew that Yurin's hands were stained red with blood. Almost as much as his own.

Unable do anything but ruminate, Hafgan could not help but consider the what-ifs. What if Yurin had allowed them to flee Hackeneth instead of killing their parents? What if Yurin had stuck to their story rather than telling Taern that he was a coward? What if his brother had been less of a coward?

Within his own madness brought on by his isolation, Hafgan cursed his brother's name, screaming it to the unlistening gods. He swore to make his brother bleed for forcing his hand. He called his brother every name he could think of, condemning him every way that he knew how. And then, he wept and sobbed, losing whatever moisture was dropped for him into the Pwoll by his caretakers. He begged his brother for forgiveness, calling out a hundred different decisions he could have made that night. But, his brother never responded.

The Pwoll was already breaking him, and it had only been a week. Or maybe just a day.

***

The gwagen were near.

Soulless and furious, the gwagen lurked deep in the caverns of Limner. He could picture them, hunched over with their heads tilted to best hunt for the sounds of their prey. They were near silent in their hunt, predators to the core. And, when they would sense some movement, maybe a rodent, or maybe a lost and wayward Wasmer, they would burst into violent action, shrieking and sprinting toward blood.

Their howls cut through the stone walls of the Pwoll, the echoing such that their yowling seemed to come from every direction. Hafgan, half-awake—always only half awake—tried to spin around to fight them off, but he could barely turn around. He could feel their damp breath at his shoulder, and smell their stale, flaking skin. The sharp pain as their teeth began to tear into his throat…. He would flail out with a fist, instead cracking his knuckles on rough stone.

The pain would bring him back.

It was a dream he was experiencing. A nightmare. He was alone in the Pwoll. Completely and utterly alone. There were no gwagen, not here. They were a hollow, dark memory from a time when he'd had the ability to defend himself. When he'd had the ability to stretch his legs or have a clean glass of water or look up at the sky. When he had been free.

But even awake—as awake as one could be in a place like this—Hafgan could swear he heard the howls of the gwagen, somewhere in the distance.

***

More time passed. Hafgan's body acclimated to the Pwoll, somehow unknotting and finding ways to become more comfortable. The smell and feel of his waste, drained into a small hole in the center of the Pwoll, no longer bothered him in the slightest. His kept his face clean and free of hair, pulling out each hair individually daily with his fingernails, the small pain of each extraction becoming almost a song to him.

His caretakers would come twice a day, or maybe once a day, and toss food down to him. They were not cruel to him; they would rap their spears five times to let him know that they were tossing down strips of meat and a small, disposal bladder of water. They were ordered not to talk to him, of course, per the rules of the Pwoll. It was meant for intense contemplation of one's wrongs, depriving a person of senses to enlighten the mind, and the caretakers were only meant to provide food. That did not keep Hafgan from speaking to them.

"My friends," he had said one night, in Wasmer-tongue. "Did you witness the Cylch, that day? Do you believe the power of your Flawless God to be good? Look at what it wrought upon our people. Look at how weak and cowed our people have become! This god has destroyed us, turned us into cowering shells of what we once were. Has it done the same to you?" Of course, there was no response.

Another night. "I believe in your Flawless God. I believe in my folly. Bring Leyr down here and let us speak. I'm certain we can reach an understanding."

A different night. "My friends, you bring me a feast again, already. You are my saviors. But, please make no noise. I want to be left to my solitude."

The worst thing was that he was not being sardonic. He truly wanted to be left in the Pwoll.

Chapter 31

Her head feeling as if it were in a vice, Morgyn slowly regained her senses without opening her eyes.

Last she remembered, she'd been bouncing off the ground, carelessly failing to flee from The House. Now, she was… here. Wherever here was. She didn't appear to be bound; she moaned and moved her limbs as if having a fever dream, not finding any resistance at her ankles or wrists. It seemed like she was reclining on a chair, in fact—something cushioned. She could smell roasted chicken and garlic, which made her nauseous stomach churn, and she could hear several voices speaking calmly.

"And, aye, I followed your vague orders. I did everything that Escamilla told me," said a deep, familiar voice. It seemed wrong that Fenrir would be here; maybe her brain was actually damaged.

"Yet, she is lost to the world. You were to protect her above all else, and you simply and obviously failed." Morgyn had to repress a shudder upon hearing Tennyson's high-pitched voice. So, they had brought her to The House. She would not leave this place alive.

"She wouldn't have been protected if an army of forty thousand overwhelmed her much smaller force and she'd had a sword buried in her throat. The best thing I could have done was slay the little duke—which I did, by the way."

"He oozes heroism, this man."

Morgyn's eyes shot open and she moved instinctually toward the voice. Barin sat just across from her, over a laden table, his voice bringing a surge of joy that she couldn't restrain. He saw her move and his face melted into a warm, toothy smile. Despite her pounding head, she smiled, too, and made to stand up before she realized that there was a knife at her throat.

"Ah, the urchin awakes," said Tennyson, sitting at the head of the table with no plate of food before him. "I didn't expect that I would ever see you again. Frankly, it boggles the mind to try and understand why you would ever return to Rostane."

"It's my home," she mumbled. She could feel her ogra against her chest, practically burning a hole into her skin. "We always return to our homes."

"It is an unusual dinner party I am hosting. I have you, Morgyn, a turncoat and traitor. Barin here is one of your friends from Recherche Oletta, a rival from the lowest rungs of society. One of de Trenton's Blue Worms, of course, simply observes from afar." Morgyn followed his gaze to a powerful, but bound and gagged, Sestrian woman under heavy guard in the corner of the room. Fenrir's eyes kept straying towards the woman. "And, of course, I have my old friend Fenrir. Who very well may have betrayed me, as well."

"I would never do that. Remember, I am just a dog that follows orders," Fenrir said with a rueful smile. He seemed calm, collected, and confident, as if there was no danger here to his life. Yet, danger was omnipresent when Tennyson was involved.

"A dog can follow the command of many voices."

"When that dog is a survivor, it's a good policy."

Tennyson laughed. "I have so missed your company, Bull de Trenton, Coldbreaker and Duke-Slayer. The House is diminished without you among our ranks."

Fenrir smiled disarmingly. "Why would you have thought I'd left your ranks?"

"Come now, Bull. You forget to whom you speak. Even hadn't you been seen training among the Adders and in the company of this one, it was particularly damning when you pointed out Canor during the execution, considering how he was carried off by a couple of your Adder friends." Tennyson was relaxed and sure. Morgyn felt the opposite, particularly since a blade still rested on her shoulder. Behind Barin and Fenrir, each, were also a pair of guards to ensure good behavior.

"I was just waving to an old friend." Fenrir's voice had cracked.

"And were you overwhelmed with emotion, having to violently embrace Yarem the Head because you missed him?" Tennyson's hand went beneath his cloak.

"Would you believe 'yes'?" Fenrir asked, a quaver in his voice even though he continued to smile. The man was a cunning moron. Tennyson laughed.

"Should I just take him out back?" Garrett asked, he being one of the men standing behind Fenrir. His hands were twitching at the dagger he wore at his belt.

"Nonsense, Garret the Quick. Sometimes, a little good humor goes a long way. For instance, the Bull knows some brilliant jokes that are sure to brighten anyone's day. Why don't you regale us?"

Fenrir paled, and swallowed deeply. "I certainly couldn't, not with a lady present." He nudged Barin and raised an eyebrow, the implication pretty clear after the bastard had disabled Barin with a switch-kick to the sack. Barin wasn't baited. God, she had missed her surrogate brother.

For as long as she could remember, Barin had been there to protect her. She'd met the older man one day when trying to pick his pocket. Stealing from a thief is never a good idea, and Barin was no exception. Yet, instead of beating her and tossing her into the gutter, he'd consoled her. He'd advised her. He'd even given her shelter.

He'd smiled at her. And, he'd simply loved her, treating her like family.

When she had been buried in debt and constantly threated by loan sharks, it had been Barin who had cleaned her slate. When she'd been apprenticed to the abusive Roal, Barin had been the one who'd broken his neck in a back alley. When she'd simply been scared and alone, he'd held her and told her that it would be all right.

She loved her surrogate brother more than anything. Which was why she had been avoiding him for such a long time. Recherche Oletta couldn't know that she still valued his life, lest they continue to use him as collateral. On the surface, he was a member in the lowest rungs of the organization, but in truth, he was just there to ensure the more talented, connected, and versatile Morgyn would stay honest and aligned.

"What about you then, man of Oletta?" Tennyson turned his attention toward Barin, and man paled in response.

"I'll tell a joke," Morgyn said, taking the focus off of Barin.

"A joke from a traitor. This should be fun," Garrett said, still fingering his weapon.

"Let's hear it, girl." Tennyson leaned forward. Morgyn glanced at each person sitting at the table, her eyes settling on the bound Sestrian woman. She did have a good one, after all.

"An Ardian, a Rafonese, and a Sestrian walk into a bar. All women. The Ardian asks the bartender for a drink, and he pours her a glass of beer. She smiles her thanks and walks away. The Rafonese woman asks the bartender for a drink, and he pours her a glass of fine wine. She's pleased, and finds a seat."

Morgyn had everyone's attention. It was entirely unnerving; even through her cloudy, beaten skull, the fear was too much. Her heart was pounding like the fluttering wings of a hummingbird, and she froze.

"Finish the joke," said a parrot-masked monstrosity sitting to Tennyson's right.

Morgyn tried to swallow, but couldn't gather the saliva. She took a deep breath and continued.

"Then, the Sestrian asks for a drink. The bartender spits in a glass, pisses in it, and tosses in some kerena butts. He slides it across the bar to the Sestrian woman. She looks at the drink, looks up at the bartender, shrugs, and takes a deep drink. 'Better than I'm used to at home,' she says." Morgyn paused after the punchline, insulting both rotgut Sestrian ale and their misogynistic culture. It was greeted with nothing but silence as all eyes turned toward the head of The House.

Tennyson tilted his head like a dog trying to understand a command. He leaned forward and placed his fingers together in a steeple.

"Kill her."

Cold fear sliced through Morgyn as rough hands jerked her head back, baring her naked neck to a curved dagger. She struggled, but more hands grabbed her and easily pinned her arms to her side.

"No!" shouted both Fenrir and Barin as they surged to their feet, both men finding their advancement blocked by sword blades at their own throats.

Tennyson laughed—a hideous and gleeful sound.

"You are all so predictable! Everyone, sit down and perhaps no one will die. Perhaps."

The protectors grasping Morgyn released her. Her heart was in her throat, choking her, and she wiped away tears before gathering herself enough to focus on whatever horrors would come next. She sat on her shaking hands.

"So, Bull, you apparently care for this girl."

"I just don't want blood on my meal." He gestured toward the laden table, taking a bite of a bit of chicken as if to prove his point.

"Right," Tennyson said drily. "Well, perhaps I will just end this one." He pointed to the Sestrian.

"What do I care about a filthy Adder?" Fenrir asked, washing down his chicken with a swig of wine.

"Right," Tennyson said again. He nodded to a steel-haired protector in an eagle mask, who punched the Sestrian across the face, knocking her chair over. Then, the man kicked her once. Twice. A third time. She only grunted through her gag.

Fenrir was stoic at first, but flinched more at each blow. "Fine! Enough of this, Tennyson. No need to torture women and girls. Just tell me what you want of me, this time."

Tennyson sat back in his chair. "I assume your father has something over you. It's unlikely that paternal love drove your father to free you from your death sentence."

"I am well-loved," said Fenrir. Morgyn was surprised how calm the oaf of a man was. Her own heart had failed to slow.

"Certainly not well-loved enough to enjoy the goodwill of a notoriously stingy Darian de Trenton. Tell me, Fenrir de Trenton. You once asked me to punish your father. Do you recall that?"

Fenrir was silent for a moment, and then he nodded abruptly.

"If I were to tell you, now, that I have changed my stance on that issue, how would you react?" Tennyson's devil's face appeared to grin even wider. The Sestrian Blue Adder, having been propped back up in her chair by twisted, animal-faced monsters, began to struggle at Tennyson's proclamation.

Fenrir, of course, didn't react. "I would say that it would be a difficult thing to accomplish, particularly as he is now known as a lord around these parts."

"Not particularly difficult if one has someone on the inside."

Morgyn shivered at his tone. The implication was clear.

"I can't imagine you have a person close enough for that to work." Either the big man was intentionally daft, or purposefully acting that way to delay the inevitable request.

"I think that I do." Tennyson nodded at his men again. Morgyn felt a blade tickling her neck and saw that the Sestrian was in the same position. Nonetheless, Fenrir didn't immediately move. He gazed at Morgyn, eyes inscrutable. Then, he shifted his gaze to the Sestrian woman. He sighed deeply, the effect like steam escaping an overfilled kettle.

"Why now, Tennyson? You know you have me. You know you've had me for years now. So, just tell me. Why now? Why couldn't you have offed the man twenty years ago and saved me some pain? Or, hell, why not when I asked you?"

Tennyson barked a very wry, very human laugh. "I've put a lot on your shoulders these past months, Bull, so I will share some of the reasoning. Ardia is a changing place, and not changing for the better. The duke was an incompetent, but at least he was too strong-willed in his incompetence to not entirely be a puppet. It was our role to oppose him, but you killing him set off a chain reaction. The Council now holds power. Your father. Faris. De Ingus. Witton, Erlins. Things are becoming far more... deviant than I expected. Events are moving in the wider world beyond Ardia—events that are, for various reasons, meeting their lines of convergence here."

"Why here?" Morgyn asked, her desire to know briefly outweighing her fear. For the second time, she was the center of attention in this terrifying, stuffy room.

"Shouldn't you know, given who you serve?" Recherche Oletta... Morgyn could feel her ogra against her skin. She was doomed once they found that little artifact, the thing that let her gaze into the nethers between worlds, or whatever the fuck it did.

"I only serve myself," she said, quietly. Barin smiled sadly at that, as she'd known he would. Tennyson waved at the men behind her, who began to haul her to her feet. Apparently, she was no longer welcome amidst this group of men. A second pair started to haul Barin from his chair. The conversation continued while she went limp, passively resisting her captors to learn just a bit more—anything that might help her with Recherche Oletta on the off-chance that she lived through this.

"Regardless, it is why the members of the Council must die. They make deals beyond their understanding, creating an... unfortunate situation that has already affected our neighbors across the Vissas. Things are going to get bad here, Fenrir. Know that what I ask of you is actually for the betterment of this country. Believe it or not, I do not relish torturing girls and women—nor men, for that matter. But, I do what must be done to ensure your loyalty in this matter. I do what must be done to preserve this place, to preserve what must be protected."

"There's one problem. I can't do it," Fenrir said, his voice quiet, wrenched with pain. Morgyn was almost to the door, and she couldn't see his face, but he sounded... he sounded lost.

"What, you suddenly have qualms about killing a man who once buried his fingers into your flesh as a punishment? Like you said, I have you," said the devil in the silver mask.

Morgyn suddenly jerked forward, out of her captors' grips for a split second, for just long enough to hear Fenrir's words before she was dragged out of the room by her feet.

"I would love to end him. He deserves death ten times over. But... if he dies, so do I. So does my daughter."

427

Interlogue: Pride

"Unfortunately, sweetling, we have reached a point where your maenen can no longer nourish and sustain me on its own. I cannot begin to describe the disappointment. Tasting your goodness has been the only delight in my life, of late. I am surrounded by incompetence and narcissism, and, though I appreciate my tools, I cannot help but grow frustrated as I begin, yet again, to make my presence felt in this world.

"My Erudites have brought me another man, but he is not so good as you. He has done some terrible things, though you would not have known it from the way he lived his public life.

"I should not be upset, my sweetling. We all have done terrible things. Few greater than me.

"I told you of my gluttony, how I betrayed a trusted ally to instigate a war so that I could continue to sate my inexhaustible need for maenen. After that victory, my influence waxed as Amorum's waned. My people had grown rich from the rapine of Feriline, and most were unwilling to accept Amorum's message of Harmony. His efforts to make peace with those surrounding tiny kingdoms and countries lost traction. As I told people—what was to prevent others from betraying us, as Feriline did?

"Truth be told, I barely had to convince the people that war was the right path. They had tasted wealth and victory, and the idea that all should be united under our rule—my rule—had an innate attraction.

"Without even speaking to Amorum, I could sense his defeat from a distance. He had dedicated his life to spreading words of peace and Harmony, attempting to bring people together during a time of chaos and war. And yet, here he was, a leader of a people who ached to subjugate those around them.

"It embarrasses me to say that I felt the urge to gloat. So great was my pride that I wanted Amorum to recognize that I had taken control of the people.

"One day, in a great council chamber in our Feriline, one of my followers insulted Amorum, calling him a dusty old relic, laughing at his continued efforts to sway the people toward Harmony.

"I lost control. At that time, my nerring was unrivaled and I was swollen with maen. Without the need to draw from others, I sealed my followers in the council chamber and disassembled the man, piece by piece. I kept him alive far past his endurance.

"I learned that I still had love for Amorum, despite everything that had come between us.

"Instead of gloating, I went to mend my relationship with the great man. I will spare you the details—I would rather not recall the details, in fact. Suffice it to say that it went... poorly. My pride, after all, could not be overcome, and Amorum, after all, had a touch of pride, himself.

"Nonetheless, despite this confrontation, he did not leave me. I am uncertain, to this day, why he stayed.

"With my army of pasnes alna, and my growing conventional forces—conscripted from Feriline and flocking to the victorious Blood Maiden from outlying regions—I was near unstoppable. We did not pause to gather our strength, as before. Rather, we immediately set off to make war.

"Twelve years. Twelve years, we struggled against a thousand warring countries. Some capitulated without a fight, our reputation spreading more quickly than our army ever could. Others, however, fought harder than I would have thought possible. With each tiny kingdom and country we took, Amorum set to trying to peacefully integrate the countries into my growing empire. Others of my officers and leaders—Wantran particularly—dealt with our conquests less civilly. There was too much for me to keep track of, so as long as Amorum was not insulted or threatened, I gave my people free reign.

"It was my pride, sweetling. As we continued to take what you now know as Siawen, the southern continent, I began to feel invincible. Untouchable. I began to believe the stories of the Blood Maiden, that I must be a god. How could I not be? I had power unrivaled, even by my strongest officers. Even than Wantran, though she had access to yenas. People pressed their foreheads to the ground when they saw me coming; took care of my every want. I had the finest foods from every country. The most beautiful, exotic lovers. I wanted for nothing. I was like a goddess, then. Unrivaled.

"Eventually, I owned most of Saiwen and even a portion of Imsal. The lands were different, back then, millenia ago. Bigger. The wars—both my war for dominance and those that followed—changed the face of the world. Although Ardia, long before it was your little country, was a challenge.

"The Wasmer lived in this mostly unsettled land. They had traveled from the west, somehow circumventing the Great Barrier, and settled many years before my dominance had spread to western Saiwen. I had seen a small number of Wasmer in my life, but had not realized that they had the numbers—or the intelligence—that they later showed me in your Ardia.

"They had their own goddess, it was said. Oletta. Goddess of wisdom.

"In my pride, I assumed she was a fraud. That she had simply confused the superstitious Wasmer, taking a figurehead place as their leader. I did not realize, at the time, the hypocrisy of my assumptions.

"I also assumed that she would be weak. Pride, sweetling, causes us to underestimate those around us. In this case, I was quite wrong.

"With my empire stretching far to the east, my conventional army—and even many of my pasnes alna—had been left behind to keep the peace. It was surprisingly challenging to exert control over a city thousands of miles away, one who had not seen its goddess in years. So, when fighting the Wasmer, who were more numerous than now, we were hard-pressed. We did manage, with reinforcements, to slowly push them back toward the mountains you now call the Tulanques.

"They fought our pasnes alna with miernes of their own, their so-called sibrowd gwintan—Wind Whisperers—to great effect. However, we had our own weapons that I had not yet unleashed upon the world.

"The Feral. The Soulless. The Empty. Your unfortunate fate, sweetling. Gods, if I could have known you in my youth…

"Your goodness continues to fill me with guilt. But, guilt keeps me from repeating my sins.

"I had never killed any of my donors over the years. In turn, I had forbidden others from murdering their own donors. Some had given in completely to their animal instincts… unable to wear clothing, carry weapons. Others—as I learned—if you left them enough nerring, would retain enough of their instincts to have some sense of self-preservation. They could bear armor and wield weapons, though blunt weapons were often safer.

"These Feral were easy to control. They never attacked those who had drawn from them, and it only took a tiny bit of power—a suggestion of it, really—to point them at an enemy and say 'attack.'

"The Feral were brought to the frontline, and leveled against the Wasmer. These fought with a ferocity unknown by men, their

432

basest emotions unrestricted, needing only to kill. The Wasmer retreated across the country as our forces tasted victory again and again. It was a slow march, as it did become more difficult to restrain the Feral following a battle… after they had developed the taste for blood and killing. We had to use them sparingly.

"Not far from what you now call Rostane, my forces were handed their first real defeat! I lost thousands of men and even more Feral. Even a number of pasnes alna. This Oletta had joined the fight, and she brought her might to bear upon my forces.

"For years, I had rarely taken part in the battles, content to allow my captains and army to put their own lives at risk while I simply reaped the rewards. Wealth, of course, but more importantly, an ever-flowing supply of maenen. But I was needed here. It would not do for men to lose their faith in me, and another rout could do just that.

"So, the armies—my own and the Wasmer—again joined, just south of today's Tulanque Mountains. I did not utilize the Feral there. Rather, I wanted to focus my own powers—and the powers of my pasnes alna—on the enemy magics. Most specifically, this Oletta.

"The conventional forces battled. The Wasmer were excellent warriors, but my forces were veterans, hard from years of war. We also had great creatures from the Imsal, the northern continent. The lithros, beasts with six legs that could brush off arrows with their tough skin, and provide my officers with an increased line of sight, allowed them to more easily control the battle. My pasnes alna also rode atop the lithros, although they held back during the beginning of this battle.

"Soon, our experience wore at the Wasmer, and they brought forth their own weapons, the sibrowd gwintan. My pasnes alna met that threat, and the battle was at a standstill, neither side gaining dominance. Until Oletta joined the fray.

"She was magnificent. She wielded pearen with such acuity, such artistry, that I was amazed. She drew from deep within the earth itself and called forth great waves of power, selectively slaughtering my soldiers while preserving her own. She had such utter control.

"Nonetheless, I was the Blood Maiden. How could she hope to stand against me?

"My forces retreated as I stepped forward, surrounded by my guard and my donors—followers who were ready to sacrifice themselves for the honor of my touch. I unleashed my own powers, which were more potent than Oletta's, but less discriminating. Waves of flame and blades and death cut across the battlefield, killing some of my own but more of hers. Before long, the battlefield was clearing, and Oletta and I strained against each other.

"My donors were emptied by the dozen, made husks in an instant. I began drawing from my bodyguards, sending many of them running. Around Oletta, the land crumbled and split. Today, these Ashlands are still uninhabitable south of the Tulanques.

"I will never know how she made it past my defenses, sweetling. But, a tiny bar of power—the width of a finger— pierced my body, sending me to my knees. I still have the scar."

"At the same time, I drew of my own vast maen, sending a wave of power at her. Her assault ended, though I know not what damage I did to her. Her forces retreated, carrying with them their wounded goddess. Not killed, I learned later. At the time, however, I could only think of my own wound.

"Fatal, it would have been. And my powers were not good for healing... not at the time. I had not bothered to learn of the human body, how to fix or how to mend it. How to translate maen and maenen into physical manifestations of the body.

"I would have died. I should have died. My followers wept and looked away. Killed themselves, in some cases. Many were unable to bear the thought of their immortal Blood Maiden dying. Unable to comprehend that I was not invincible.

"Wantran came to me one night. She somehow incapacitated my many guards, managing to reach me undetected. She stood over me, the nearest thing I had to a rival. I was at her mercy. With her power, her ability to draw maenen and yenas, she could have set herself up as a goddess, just as I had. She could have ruled over these men, these countries, this world, just as I sought to. She could have ended me, weak as I was.

"But, she did not. Her eyes were sorrowful as she beheld me, and she reached out to touch my hand. I shied away. Of course, I shied away—she was pasnes alna, likely to suck me dry. But, I had no escape. She grasped my hand and held it for a long while. Looked into my eyes. And, she healed me.

"It was excruciating. I thought it was my end; my screams must have echoed throughout all of my domain. But, with the damage to my organs, the pain of the healing was worse than the pain of the wounds. Sweetling, I cannot describe it adequately. It was as if my tissue first had to die before it could be reborn.

"But, I was healed. Weak for days. Months…. Sweetling, sometimes I still feel the pain. In speaking of it, I feel the pain right now. Here, in my left side and in my back. I do not know whether Wantran left a bit unhealed, or even left the scar as a reminder of the cost of pride. She was lost to me soon after, and it is too late for me to ever know.

"You, sweetling, are beyond pride. Soon, you will be beyond pain, as well.

"I could almost envy you, but we know the cost of that sin."

Chapter 32

They buried Marius with his brother.

It was not an easy task. Even after they'd thawed part of the ground with a huge bonfire, the ground remained mostly frozen. Lisan and Ill'nath used Marius' sword to hack the chill soil to pieces, with even Merigold taking a turn, despite her empty exhaustion. Even so, they were barely able to dig deep enough to cover the bodies. It was ill-suited to their sacrifices. But, this was all their diminished party could do.

When they'd woken up the morning after the battle, Remy had been dead, lying between Cryden's feverish body and the blood-soaked corpse of his brother. Merigold had had nothing to say. Ill'nath never said anything. And Lisan hadn't said anything. They'd just proceeded to bury the twins as best they could.

There were no honorariums nor tears. Neither would serve a purpose, not now.

Marius had implored Merigold to take care of his brother. Several hours later, his brother had been dead.

Perhaps, somewhere, beneath his broken and fragmented nerring, some piece of Remy had still existed. Perhaps the presence of his brother had bound him to the world, even given him some sense of hope that he would be restored. Perhaps, had Marius survived, there would have been a chance to heal him. Certainly, someone in Agricorinor would have known, and would have researched this very problem. And yet, they would never know.

The cart was lighter now, with just a single, near-dead man inside. Merigold hoped, at least, that they would be able to save this one person. She had not broken yet, but losing one more of her protectors—a man who had kept her safe and treated her with respect, a man she even considered a friend—would mean she very well might. Just when she'd thought she had reached the very depths that guilt could take her to, she stretched the emotion even more.

In the cold light of midafternoon, they continued their journey north through the perpetual, pearlescent snow.

***

Sestria's Grasp was a strange place. Not a good strange, either, as in trying a new foreign dish and being delightfully surprised. Sestria's Grasp was a bad strange, as in finding that such a new dish was full of scorpions, razor blades, and horse cocks.

As Lisan would say, the Grasp was where Sestria was fucking Rafon. And so it would appear on a map if one squinted and had a bit of a dirty imagination. And, even in person, that appeared to be the case. Almost at once, they rode from a pine forest into a field of lonely stumps. The trees, though, had not been used to build any meaningful structures. Rather, the logs formed a low barrier as far as the eye could see. Not a wall, but a marker of the border between this strip of land and Rafon. Even as Meri watched from her horse, she could see a group of two dozen bundled-up Sestrians rolling one of the established logs out just a few feet. Then, they ambled over to the next great log, dug in their heels, and heaved that hunk of wood so that it would be in alignment with the first.

"They are self-styled expansionists," explained Lisan. "Rafon lost this piece of their country in a wager gone awry, and the Sestrians gladly moved right in, outright ejecting the former residents. The exact borders of this misbegotten deal weren't clear, so the Sestrian squatters created their tree wall. Over the last dozen years or so, Prince Albun has declared that the Rafonese lied about their scope of the wager, and has ordered a slow expansion of the borders."

"And the Rafonese just... allow it?" Merigold asked, watching these men work.

Lisan smirked. "It's a useless game of tug of war. The monarch declared that this incursion needed to be halted at all costs. So, each night, a group of Rafonese laborers roll those logs back into place." Merigold had noticed that the logs were being rolled along a well-worn muddy path. "Neither ruler will yield, of course, so the common folk get to enjoy the back-breaking labor for a barely livable wage." One of the men slipped in the mud, causing a chain reaction as a second slipped and the log began to roll backwards. Shouting ensued and the group restored order, but not before the log had squashed the legs of the first fallen man.

"A cruel place," Merigold murmured.

"You have no idea." Lisan kept her eyes straight as a column of maroon-cloaked Sestrian soldiers marched by, giving them stares colder than winter. Even Ill'Nath, from his place driving the cart, kept his head down. Perhaps the big man had learned something in Polanice, or in the flight and battle that had followed. Or, maybe with his shoulder injury, he just realized that there were only so many heads he could smash before becoming overwhelmed. Regardless, the line of soldiers passed without incident.

"Do you think they know about the Menogans?" Merigold asked, feeling her mouth dry at the sight of so many hard-eyed soldiers. She had been stumbling from war to war, and was growing sick of the sight of weapons.

"I expect so, with incursions so close to the border. We need to find out what is going on here, and we need to find out what is happening in Agricorinor. I don't want to wander into another ambush. I'd rather we kept our hands clean on the rest of this gods-forsaken journey." Lisan had spat the last words, her tranquility finally beginning to crack. Her unpleasant face was rendered even less palatable with her frown.

"I am thankful for it, Lisan, but I need to ask. Why are you still with us? This has to be far worse than you could have expected. Yetra knows... I couldn't imagine a worse journey if I tried," Merigold said. She cupped her gloved hands around her nose and breathed out, savoring the moment of moist heat on her face. She could barely remember what warmth felt like after these weeks of trekking through the snow.

Lisan considered Merigold from the corner of her eye. "I've already told you the origin of my name. Arrow."

"Yes, but this is more than keeping true to your name. We have been through pandemonium."

Lisan laughed quietly. "My life has been pandemonium, stumbling from one fire into another. I have been hunted by mercenaries in Algania in a case of mistaken identity. I was caught in the great fires of the Eastern Sweeps, where the sky was black with smoke, so much so that day appeared to be night. I was enslaved in a galley and brought beyond the Great Barrier to Menoga, where I fought and stowed away to get free. I have stolen and I have killed and I have done some terrible things. But, through it all, I can say that I have never lied. I have always kept my word. It is worth braving all of this... horseshit... to be able to maintain some sense of self, some semblance of honor. This world wants to strip you away. So, you must choose what to give up, and what to hold onto."

What to hold onto. Merigold wondered what she still had left to cling to, to protect, at this point. Not much, it seemed.

"Lisan... thank you."

Merigold's simple thanks brought a soft smile to Lisan's lips, though she said nothing in return. They rode in silence for some time, reaching more populous areas for the first time since their flight from Polanice. Though they were clearly foreigners, and though war was at their doorstep, no one really gave them more than a glance. Farmers continued clearing snow from fields, harvesting root vegetables, and working on their various winter tasks, like mending fences and feeding livestock. Laborers cut down trees and hauled lumber while traders choked the roads with wagons from Yaraban, the capital city of Sestria, to feed this appendage. They were not the only light-skinned travelers from Saiwen on the road, either so maybe they were not so unusual a sight. The lack of reaction seemed promising, suggesting that they would not have a repeat of Polanice.

Merigold could see towers beginning to show in the distance, through the mist of the gentle snow. Each glowed slightly, lighting the way for weary travelers. Behind these, there was the shape of a walled town.

"What is that place ahead? Should we skirt it?" Merigold called.

"That is the prize of the wager between Prince Album and Region Lord Merinto. The city of Terranice. And, yes, we need to stop. We need supplies for the last sprint, and, like I said, we need to figure out what we are walking into, and what has been happening in Agricorinor. Though I plan to stay my course…" Lisan smirked, "I do not intend to do it blindly."

"How will we learn about it? No one will want to talk to us foreigners."

Lisan's smirk cracked. "Luckily, or more precisely unluckily, I know someone in Terranice. And, the Day Mother-fucking bastard is a pasnes alna."

***

It hadn't been the border tug-of-war that had made Sestria's Grasp bad strange, in Meri's estimation. Rather, it was the display at the gates of Terranice that turned peasant-abusing-bad into stomach-turning-sickening.

The stone watchtowers that Merigold had seen through the fog were not, in fact, meant to light the way for travelers. Rather, they were devices for torture. Above each great flame was a floorless cage holding a naked prisoner. Without a floor, each prisoner was forced to wedge their arms and legs through the bars to hold themselves up. Each tiny prison was low enough that the person's genitals likely blistered when fuel was added, but far enough above that they would not cook like a hunk of pork. And above each cage was a torturer wearing a black-as-night hood.

As Merigold watched, one torturer dumped a thick substance onto one of the men, a Menogan.

"Honey," murmured Lisan, her voice tinged with disgust.

"Honey?" Merigold asked, somewhat boggled. To make the prisoner lose his grip?

"For that." The torturer, who was completely encased in a protective suit, held a strange, papery ball with a long set of forceps. He reached down and bashed the ball against the cage, and it began to crack like a stubborn duck egg. The Menogan began screaming then, howling and shrieking. He was in clear and utter agony. But Merigold could not see anything that might be causing it.

442

Lisan answered the question in Merigold's eyes. "Rilling ants. That was a nest. The little flying bastards are attracted to the honey and, well, the bite is incredibly painful. I've been bitten once; it feels like the skin is melting right off the bone. And…" she rolled up her sleeve, showing a deep brown, puckered scar the size of a yet, "…it scars. The Black Hats get their jollies from trying to shock people into the fire, either from the pain or through inducing suicide. Sometimes they hold contests to see who can get their victims to tumble into the fire first."

The Menogan, though his shrieks pierced the air, did not relent. He clung to the cage, either through blind determination or in hopes that his comrades would stage some sort of rescue. From other torture towers, more voices joined the Menogan's in a choir of agony. Merigold was surprised that she felt nothing for these men. No sympathy, no sorrow. It wasn't that she supported the torture, but rather she just had no pity left to give.

"Tell me of Menoga, Lisan," Merigold said abruptly, speaking loudly to be heard over the shrieks and a sudden cheer as one of the men fell into the fire a few towers down. They had not much spoken of the country of the man who'd disemboweled Cryden. Caring for Cryden and Remy, and then fleeing for their lives, had not offered the opportunity. And, even on the quieter trail, conversations had stayed fairly surface-level. Presumably, neither wanted a reminder of that night on The Graceful Whale, and it had seemed almost sacrosanct to breach the topic. But now, seeing these men being burnt and tortured, Merigold wanted to know.

Lisan apparently understood. She remained silent until they had passed the towers and entered the city gates, receiving only a disinterested nod from a Sestrian soldier. "Menoga is… Menoga is both a much better place and a much worse place than Ardia. Art and culture flourish, and the ruling class allots resources to such pursuits. Medicine is more advanced than you see here, with some exceptions, and there is far, far less crime. Common people live a higher quality of life. But, it is brutality that prevents crime. There are rarely second offences because the punishments for first offences tend to be violent and public. And, slavery is the backbone of the economy. Menoga has taken the entire continent, bringing the Reanoners, Ellenese, Pen, and a dozen other peoples into their empire. Each of those vassaled countries—the Silver League, they call it—offers a yearly tithe of slaves for use around the continent. Labor is never an issue when you consider the availability of backs to break."

"You were a slave?" Merigold asked, shivering at the reminder of her own captivity.

"Aye. They took my ship, where I was working as a deckhand for a time. They had some of those magic-wielders who easily subdued us. Weeks I spent in the hold of a galley; tumultuous weeks." Lisan's eyes were distant. "We passed through the Great Barrier, called so because it is thought to be impassable. Thousands of miles of oceanic mountains and reefs that no Ardian captain would dare to brave. But we survived. For four hundred and seventy-nine days, I lived the life of a slave, working on the docks and in delivery. I was an oddity—a Jecustan amidst the Menogans. Frankly, some of the attention was nice." There was a gentle smile on her unattractive face now, but it suddenly hardened into a tight frown. "Some of the attention was not so nice."

"How did you escape?" Merigold asked, frowning along with her. She could empathize with being a slave.

"I rarely left the docks in Mannamut, the capital of the empire. Mostly I worked as a porter, unloading ships, doing back-and-knee-breaking labor. I feigned being broken like the rest of the conquests and, over time, my overseer became lax. I slit his throat and tossed him into the Red Bay, and then I managed to stow away on a ship heading back across the Great Barrier. At least, I hoped that to be the case; the captain and his mates spoke Ardian. For weeks, I lived in a crate, foraging for supplies and water. I twice had to kill when I was discovered, but the ship was large enough, and the storms were severe enough, that any missing persons were just assumed to have been fed to the sea. They never docked, but laid anchor west of Rafon. I swam for it, one night, and nearly drowned, too. Washed up on shore and so on." Lisan's lips tightened like a door to a safe. She was done sharing.

Merigold used the lapse in conversation to take in Terranice. Though they were in Sestria's Grasp, the city was Rafonese. Well, mostly. Polanice had no architectural embellishments, considering that the city was constantly destroyed and rebuilt from the yearly hurricanes. But Terranice had more of that Rafonese style which Meri had read about. Buildings were constructed of brick of varying shades, the bricks used in alternating patterns of color and shape. The result was that the typically three-story buildings had a striped look, reminding Merigold of a cat that had once lived near the Duckling. It was well-built, organized, and utterly efficient in the use of space. But Sestria was not content to take a city and leave it as is. The Sestrian dome, the cornerstone of Sestria's architectural identity, was growing out of these Rafonese buildings at random. As a result, the city appeared almost tumorous.

Guards lined the roads, maroon coats appearing like drops of blood around the city in contrast to the colorless clothes favored by the Sestrians and Rafonese who lived there in pseudo harmony. There were light-skinned folk from Saiwen all over—merchants, laborers, artists. No one singled them out or seemed to treat them any differently. All things considered, Terranice seemed like a pretty decent place... aside, of course, from the Menogans being tortured at the gates.

Merigold glanced back at Ill'Nath, who met her gaze directly. After a moment, he gave her a wink and a half-smile, light shining

445

into his mouth through his cheek-hole. Meri raised an eyebrow and glanced away. Even after all their trials, she could not quite get used to the sight of his teeth and gums, highlighted by the metal-ringed hole in his face. The Pintan islander was such a weird man, and this was somewhat out of character for him. Lisan, to her credit, seemed unaffected. She led the party unerringly down one side street and then another, each perfectly perpendicular to the last. The Arrow led them straight, as always, to their destination.

"Is this… is this a bakery? Are you hungry, Lisan?" Merigold asked.

"Aren't you?" Lisan dismounted and tied up her horse, raising an eyebrow at Merigold. The sweet, yeasty smell of bread and cakes filled the air, and Meri's stomach growled.

"Of course, the answer is yes. But this seems to be a strange choice, considering how close we are to our destination. Plus, don't we need to see this pasnes alna friend of yours?"

Lisan glanced through the wall of glass lining the front of the building, squinting to see through the reflection. She stiffened her shoulders and clenched her warrior's fists.

"We are about to."

Chapter 33

"Well, what do we have here?"

The adonis of a baker, wiping his flour-clouded hands on a clean rag, raised an eyebrow. The man was Sestrian, his olive skin near flawless despite him being Lisan's age, or maybe in his early forties. His short-cropped brown hair and tidy beard framed a handsome face with a strong jaw, and his short-sleeved shirt, covered by a baker's apron, betrayed a fit and well-muscled body. Merigold felt her heart flutter just looking at the man, and it was a feeling she'd never expected to experience again.

"Mane, it has been a long time," Lisan said, her voice cautious as she pushed her way into the shop. Merigold followed, while Ill'Nath tended to their horses, cart, and near-dead passenger.

"Longer for you than it's been for me, it appears." So handsome was his curved smile, so calmly casual was his tone, that you could almost forgive the insult. From the way Lisan flinched, though, Merigold knew that she did not forgive it.

"And who is this beautiful, albeit dog's feet-filthy vagabond that you have with you?" He turned the full force of his smile on Merigold, and she knew he was ribbing her. He spoke Ardian flawlessly, too; Meri realized that, though he was Sestrian, he'd likely been born overseas. Interestingly, signs around his shop were in both Ardian and Sestrian.

"Merigold Hinter is my charge. I would ask you to leave her be, but I might as well try to keep the moons from rising or sailors from fucking whores," Lisan muttered, averting her eyes from Mane.

Hesitating for a moment, he walked around the counter and embraced Lisan, murmuring something soft into her ears. Merigold could see her shoulders tense, as if she was about to

447

strike or hurl the man through his glass front, but, instead, she relaxed and sank into his embrace.

The strange moment was interrupted when Ill'Nath stomped into the building, Cryden cradled in his arms. Without giving anyone a second glance, the big islander pushed aside a few potted plants, gently laid his charge on the table, and grabbed a loaf of bread and started chewing. Mane raised an eyebrow.

"I trust you can pay for that, vagrant?"

Ill'Nath paused his mastication, yanked out a tiny pearl piercing from above his eye, and tossed it at the baker with disdain. Then he returned to his meal.

"The company you keep, Lisan, is revealing, to say the least. Now, tell me, what brings you, a lovely, filthy waif, a rude giant, and a probable corpse to my humble bakery amidst this humble town, all amidst a fucking cesspool of treachery, murder, and war?"

Lisan sat heavily in a chair and Merigold joined her, running her fingers through her tangled hair. She was, indeed, embarrassingly filthy. Dear Yetra, what she would do for a bath. Lisan sighed next to her, perhaps coming to the same conclusion. "Trust me, Mane, when I say that none of us would be here, in your bakery, in Terranice, if we could have avoided it. Per my contract with my employer, I am escorting Merigold and her companion to Agricorinor."

Mane's calm mask slipped. Shattered, for a moment, really. "Are you fucking kidding me, Lisan? You're traveling to Agricorinor right now? Have you not taken heed of what is going on in Rafon? In Sestria? Have you had a conversation with a merchant? With a soldier? Are you daft?" He gestured with the passionate expressiveness that Sestrians were known for.

Lisan lowered her eyes. "We have had to travel less populous roads for a reason or two, and we weren't exactly on speaking terms with the guards."

Mane paused, scratching at his beard. He walked over to the table where Cryden lay, stroking the potted plants that Ill'Nath had pushed aside. They were yellow lilies, beautiful and likely extremely difficult to maintain in this cold. They reminded Meri of summer in Dunmore.

"And who is this half-dead man you've dropped on the counter in my bakery? Should I assume he has been taken with a plague, and…"

"Merhaba, asik misin?" A chubby Sestrian women pushed into the store, ignoring the 'Closed' sign hanging from the door. Lisan bounced to her feet, Ill'Nath hefted his bread, and Meri grasped her nail-knife under her shirt. The Sestrian woman looked at the apparently fierce customers, blanched, and stumbled back out the door. Mane sighed as dramatically as the star of a Rostanian play.

"Lisan, alone, could scare away my business, let alone with the rest of you. Now, who is this?" He pushed aside the hood that had painted Cryden's wasted face with shadows. "By Pilene's watery teets. Cryden Renshaw? What's wrong with him? I think it's time for some explanation." The charming, enthralling smile vanished from his face, to be replaced with the familiar, confident authority of a pasnes alna. "Now."

Merigold glanced at Lisan out of the corner of her eye. The warrior woman stood with hunched shoulders, looking for all the world like a beaten child. Meri was stunned that this Mane could disarm a woman who had killed, assassinated, or otherwise skewered Yetra knew how many people. Merigold, though, had gained some level of comfort around pasnes alna, and she felt surprisingly unintimidated by the handsome and powerful… baker.

"The story starts in Ardia, Mr. Mane. You have heard of the civil war, by now?" He nodded curtly. "Well, the Army of Brockmore… the rebels… were decimated at Florens. And, there was…" How to describe it? Rage. Anger. The chorus of fearful cries as the Feral had torn through their exhausted army. Cryden had said not to tell anyone of these demons, though, save a pasnes alna named Ellel Dietz. She fumbled her words. "And Cryden had recently found me; he wanted to recruit me as a pasnes alna. He decided to enlist Lisan, Ill'Nath, and a couple of Sestrians to protect us on the journey."

"The cautaton is not welcome in Agricorinor," Mane told her, his tone like an armored boot stamping on an insect.

Merigold felt herself blush. "What?"

"The cautaton is not welcome in Agricorinor," Mane repeated more slowly, as if she were a dullard. "Why would he bother trying? There is something you are not telling me, someone who Cryden recruited to be a pasnes alna." The sarcasm lacked some of the previous goodwill. Merigold did not appreciate his tone, either, and Lisan still said nothing.

Meri gritted her teeth.

"Listen here, baker. I don't care if you are a pasnes alna, a baker, or a Yetra-fucking king. I keep my own counsel, and…"

"Asik misin?"

Again, a man had pushed in, also ignoring the fact that the bakery was closed. The grizzled Rafonese warrior wasn't wearing a helmet, but his muddied white coat, trimmed in silver, betrayed his allegiance. A Sun Guard, here, in Sestria! The warrior paused, meeting the eyes of each wary occupant in turn. His eyes widened when he saw Lisan's distinctive, flat face, and they expanded even more when he noticed Merigold's platinum, albeit greasy, hair.

450

"Mamatay!" roared the man, hand on his sword. Merigold did not speak Sestrian, but the meaning was clear. Killer. Slayer. The Sun Guard didn't draw, though. Ill'Nath spat out his bread, grabbing a nearby rolling pin as he did. More conventionally, Lisan drew her own sword. The man took two resistant steps back, and then spun to flee.

Lisan shook herself from her stupor. "Get him!" she shouted, and began to give chase. But it was a futile effort, as a finger-thin beam cut through the air, piercing the man in the back of the head and sending him sprawling against the bakery door. Ill'Nath quickly grabbed the body, dragging him out of sight of the glass store front, leaving a trail of blood and brains like an arrow pointing to the murder.

Mane withdrew his hand from one of his beautiful yellow lilies, though it was now little more than an ashy gray stick. He frowned, first at his plant and then at the body. Then he strode over to the door and drove home the bolt with a harsh click.

"I hope you will tell me why I just killed a Sun Guard for you, Lisan."

She cringed at his arctically cold tone and even colder stare. He leveled that same withering gaze at Ill'Nath.

"And put down my godsdamned rolling pin."

***

Cryden lay moaning on a decorative carpet, as Mane refused to allow the cautaton to rest on his bed.

The others reclined on comfortable chairs in Mane's fairly lush apartments, which were built above the bakery and certainly not impervious to the sweet smells indigenous to such establishments. Closing her eyes and breathing deep, Merigold could almost pretend that it was early morning at the Duckling, with the scent of warm, rising bread filling her nostrils as she woke from her comfortable bed. Ragen had always risen before first light to get the day's bread going, knowing that his daughter loved to wake to the scent.

But, he was gone, and Mane was here. The pasnes alna baker had regained his earlier calm, and he sat comfortably, one leg crossed over the other. He sipped from a small porcelain cup of tea, though he'd not offered such refreshment to the others. Merigold supposed she couldn't blame the handsome man for a touch of rudeness; he had committed murder—quite casually—on their behalf.

Amazing, how he had shaped the life of that single flower into a beam strong enough to kill a man. Merigold, when creating her own weapons of death and destruction, drained entire human lives, ending hopes and dreams to summon a handful of colorful, burning discs. Though the Sun Guard had died in an instant, and that was a terrible loss of life for a man who had not really wronged them in any way, Meri had really just felt a sickening pang of jealousy at Mane's power and precision. She still felt shameful in remembrance of that jealousy.

Ill'Nath continued chewing on the hunk of bread that he had squirreled away. Complementing the crackling of a fire, the annoying, sticky mastication split the air, made louder by the hole in the islander's face. Even so, a memory of warm bread filled Merigold with a hollow hunger. And yet the handsome baker made no offer of food.

"Why do you bake?" Merigold asked abruptly. Cryden had said pasnes alna tended to be in positions of influence. Advisors

452

to kings and wealthy merchants, or at the very least researchers who would be widely consulted in matters of politics and war.

"Why do I bake? That is the question you ask? You are in an unfamiliar country, being pursued by the authorities of another, and I just killed a man twenty feet below us and chucked his body into the basement. Not to mention, the strangling noose of war is drawing ever closer to our necks. And you ask why I bake?" Merigold felt her cheeks redden at Mane's words, but she didn't relent.

"Yes, why do you bake? Someone of your obvious talents should undoubtedly be having some impact on the future of this country, helping in preparation for this war, or helping its people. And yet, we find you standing behind a counter, rolling dough and wearing a lady's apron."

"Lisan, your little hopeful pasnes alna must learn some manners and boundaries." Mane gently stroked the leaves of a red-vined plant that grew from an ornate pot next to his chair. The whole room, in fact, was full of well-kept foliage, with bursts of color coming from a dozen varieties of lovely and exotic plants. "Merigold is a lovely name. Perhaps you should seek to emulate the grace of your namesake flower rather than adopting the coarseness of a whore."

Merigold found herself on her feet, striding toward the cocky, arrogant man. He gripped his plant more firmly as she grasped her nail-knife. She would kill this man. Whore? She was not a whore!

Before anything more could happen, Merigold was brought down by powerful arms and dragged off into the corner of the room. She fought the rage that boiled just beneath the surface, struggling mightily against the need to draw the life from her assailant. It would only lead to more death. And, Yetra's fucking asshole, she needed to learn control.

Ill'Nath slowly released her, holding the hand that gripped Merigold's charm. She squeezed shut her eyes and released her weapon reluctantly. The big islander placed both his hands on her shoulders in an odd and seemingly intimate gesture, as if between siblings. His eyes, the color of swirling oceans, met hers.

"The past cannot control you. You are more than what has happened to you. You are more than the things that you have done," Ill'Nath said in a hoarse whisper, his voice barely more than a steamy breeze on her cheek. The fact that he'd spoken at all shocked her out of her rage.

"Ill'Nath, you speak?"

He simply grinned back at her with a mouth full of metal. She might well have imagined the words. He led her back to her chair and went to kneel beside the ailing Cryden, beginning to prepare a mixture of broth and herbs to force down the unconscious man's throat.

"Are you under control now, want-to-be-a-pasnes alna?" asked Mane, his voice as condescending as that of a mother responding to an emotional child. He sipped at his tea like a Yetra-fucking Rostanian count, holding his pinky at just the right angle.

She did not like Mane, but they still needed information. She could be pleasant, if needed. She would just treat him like a rude customer at the Duckling.

"My apologies, good sir," she began. "That particular phrase resonates poorly with me, but it is no excuse for my actions. Can I ask you a better question? Why would the Sun Guard be here, in Terranice?" Lisan nodded at her, encouragingly. It made Meri angry, but she kept a smile on her face. Mane set down his tea, wiped his mouth with his sleeve, and shrugged disarmingly.

"For you, of course. Everyone in Terranice has heard of the Polanice Massacre, where a petite Ardian blonde slaughtered dozens of the Sun Guard in broad daylight. A contingent arrived not two days ago, seeking permission of the prince to conduct an informal search and remain stationed in Eneral, the old barracks that Sestrian forces refused to man. The prince acquiesced, although not without a vow of loyalty, that these Sun Guard would have to stand in defense of Terranice in the case of an attack or siege."

"The Menogans," Lisan muttered. She was still not herself, behaving as if she were small and insignificant.

"Yes, your friends, the snow-skinned Menogans. They've found, or created, a consistent way past the Great Barrier, and here they are. It seemed fairly insignificant at first. People going missing, ships dashed upon the rocks, occasional farms burned. Pretty common around here."

"The Rafonese would blame the Sestrians," Lisan said, sitting up and leaning forward.

"Yes, and vise versa. In the twenty years since the Grasp was taken by Sestria, things have been tense, to say the least. It was a wager poorly made, and a wager poorly lost," Mane said with a shake of his head at the stupidity of kings.

"What is this wager everyone has been talking about?" Merigold asked, leaning forward in her chair. It would be just like nobility to wager the lives of the less-worthy in pursuit of their own gain.

Mane laughed, and it sounded like the soothing strumming of a harp. "Prince Albun, then a young man, publicly wagered with Region Lord Temps Merinto that he would fuck his wife, Lady Garns. Merinto, of course, was confident in the fidelity of Lady Garns, a storied beauty and fierce politician. He blustered, quite publicly I might add, that he would give up his very holdings to the man who could bed his wife. In front of international ambassadors and domestic lords, the laws stated that this was a binding contract, witnessed by too many persons to be discounted.

Lady Garns, of course, was already sucking the cocks of Albun and half a dozen other lords for political favors. It took little effort for Album to make her a deal—substitute the cocks of many for the cock of one. And Sestria's Grasp was born of that infidelity."

Lisan shook her head at the stupidity of it. "They say Lord Merinto took his own life after the Sestrians moved in, but I'm reasonably certain Albun ended him as a loose end. Or perhaps Lady Garns did, removing the source of her shame. But the Grasp is ever a troubled place."

"And more troubled now, since your Menogans landed." Mane stroked his plant with a frown.

"What do you know about them? Why are they here? Why hasn't anyone stopped them?" Merigold asked, thinking of the group that had ambushed them. It had been a fairly small number of men, though they'd had power. "Surely, the Rafonian army, or the Sestrians, would be able to fight them off."

Ill'Nath snorted loudly, rose from Cryden's side, and went to stand by the window overlooking the street. Apparently, he had a poor opinion of the military here. Mane agreed.

"The powers-that-be have been so busy pointing fingers and undermining each other that no one mobilized any real combative force. And now there are enough Menogans on the mainland, scattered all over like fleas on a dog, that there's about as good a chance of dislodging them. They are outmaneuvering the standing military at every turn. Yet, even now, Prince Albun assumes the monarch is partnering with them in a ruse, and certainly the monarch assumes the same, so any truce between the two countries is loose at best."

"So, will there be war?" Lisan asked, massaging her temples. "Are these people that stupid?"

"They're scared," Merigold interjected. "Captain Tinto spoke of fear, and the common folk are looking for an enemy they understand."

Mane gave her an appraising look. "Yes, and the Menogans are inscrutable. No one knows why they are here or what their goal is. Few even know of the empire, on the other side of the Great Barrier, since it takes a great deal of testicular fortitude to even approach the western stretches of the Vissas Sea, let alone seek a gap in those thousand-mile reefs. Even fewer speak Menogan or have any concept of the language." He stared at Lisan, bright intelligent eyes seeming to strip her down to whatever lay beneath the skin.

"I only know a few words and phrases," she muttered, glancing at her hands as if remembering her servitude.

"Where are the pasnes alna? These Menogans fight with miernes, but the Rafonese told us that the pasnes alna have fled. Why are they not helping the people?" Merigold asked.

"A father must feed his own children before sharing food with the village. They are looking after themselves." Mane, despite his confidence, almost sounded ashamed. He brought his teacup to his mouth and found with a frown that it was empty.

"But you are still here…" murmured Lisan.

"I am still here."

A silence permeated the room—a thick and sickening lack of sound. Lisan continued to rub at her head, fussing up her hair but not seeming to care. Mane considered his empty teacup, a wry smile newly drawn on his face. Ill'Nath stared out the window, standing like a great marble statue. And Cryden lay on the floor, making no noise aside from some ragged breaths. Yetra didn't give a shit about his fate, or any of theirs.

"Mane… can you help Cryden? He's been unwell. A wound soured…" Merigold said, expecting very little, but feeling obligated to ask.

"Yes, the smell makes that evident." Mane wrinkled his nose in disgust. None of them could smell good at this point in their journey, but Cryden did have a tang about him. "But, no, I've no affinity for the health of men. I doubt he would survive my touch, and I've little desire for another death on my hands—for today, at least."

Merigold hung her head, letting her dirty hair cover her face. It was a girlish, old habit that was ill-suited to her life these days, and she knew it. It wasn't like she could hide away from the reality of her life through a tangled knot of filthy locks. And it wasn't like Ragen would feel guilty and soothe her, complying with whatever she needed. Aside from her bodyguard, she was alone, without friends and without family.

She could feel Mane's eyes on her, but refused to look up. The weight of everything seemed to be settling more deeply onto her weary shoulders. They would not be safe in Agricorinor. They were unlikely to even survive the journey. Cryden, potentially her only remaining friend, if he was even that, had not showed signs of consciousness for days. Mane could not or would not help. Remy had fallen to her own uncontrolled and disordered mind, releasing his tenuous grasp on life when Marius had succumbed to his own wounds. Their group was already shattered.

They would fail. They would die.

Mane sighed deeply, and Merigold glanced through her hair at the impossibly handsome man. There was something like empathy gleaming in his eyes. "Cryden may yet survive, should you get him to Agricorinor. There are a few who might be able to heal him, if fewer still who might be willing." The pasnes alna rose to his feet, heading toward his stove to heat more water for tea. He spoke over his shoulder.

"I've some business to tend to in Agricorinor. It's a short trip, so I suppose I could tolerate your company. I might be willing to shield you from some of your pursuers and help avoid other… chance encounters with the Menogans." He fumbled with his teapot. "Besides, I imagine that the powers that be would be displeased if I let the Slaughterer of Polanice walk free."

Meri didn't say anything, but she took a deep, shuddering breath and felt a warm relief spread through her chest. An ally, someone else who was willing to help her. Again, in her time of need, the world offered some sort of balance. Maybe Yetra had not fully forsaken her, though she and the goddess were far from being on speaking terms. She quickly wiped at her eyes before shining her very best smile at Mane's back, though Lisan seemed to have deflated even further at the suggestion.

"That sounds lovely, Mane. I thank you for the offer, and we would find your company agreeable. If the Sun Guard is lurking around here and looking for us, we will need disguises, and…"

Ill'Nath spun around from the window with a forceful grunt, gesturing wildly toward the window. He reached for his great club and rumbled toward the stairs as Merigold, Lisan, and Mane all headed across the room. Merigold clutched her nail as she rubbed at the fogged windows to get a better look.

"Yetra, you bitch…" she murmured, losing semblance of calm afforded by a brief bout of safety.

Assembled outside the bakery, amidst the swirling snow, milled two dozen Sun Guard, their number supported by another dozen maroon-cloaked Terranice city guardsmen. There was some confusion to be seen, as officers from each factor appeared to be arguing about their approach. Apparently, the Sun Guard they'd killed, who Mane had dumped into the cellar, was missed, or

459

someone had seen the whole thing through that damnable glass window.

"Nanvora should know better than coming here," Mane said, gripping the sill with white hands and staring at the Sestrian officer. The officer was a stocky woman with short-cropped hair and a scowl that seemed very at home on her face. Two Sun Guard officers—thankfully, not including Tinto—were arguing hotly back while one stuck a sheet of paper in the officer's face. She threw her arms up and thundered away, though her men remained. The Sun Guard assembled by the front door while the Sestrians lofted light spears... the type that would be appropriate for chucking through a man from a distance.

With a curse, Lisan spun to grab and string her bow. Merigold glanced around for some weapon other than her knife, but there were only bushes, scrubs, and flowers of various shades and sizes. Ill'Nath was positioned at the top of the stairs, club draped over his shoulder in readiness. She knew he must still be in pain from the battle with the Menogans and their metsika, but he did not show even a drop of weakness.

Mane grabbed her shoulder and hissed into her ear, and she felt a thrill at the feel of his warm breath on her ear. "By the time this is done, you will have cost me my bakery. Somehow, you and Cryden will repay me for this, you know. I don't know how, but you will." There was a shattering noise from below. "You know something, would-be pasnes alna, something you are refusing to tell me. Something that is crucial to this war. Cryden would not be back in Terranice just to escort his little protege to a place where he is forbidden entry."

There came a loud shattering sound from below. Mane yanked a miniature tree from its ornate clay pot, sprinkling soil everywhere. He did the same with a bush, and wrapped a vined monstrosity around his neck. Suddenly, he was transformed from a well-groomed baker into a beast that had just staggered its way out of a jungle. He would have looked ridiculous, except that Meri had just seen him blast a beam through a man's head. He locked eyes with Meri one last time.

"I'll take care of this."

"Mane..."

"But, when you get to Agricorinor, tell them... convince them to get off their asses and do something."

***

"Charlamane de Merin, under the order of the crown prince, you are to release the fugitives into the care of the Sun Guard!" called an authoritative voice in heavily accented Ardian. Merigold could hear clearly from behind the cracked door as Lisan and Ill'Nath rushed down to the cellar with Cryden and whatever meager supplies they'd managed to shove in their bags. Meri should have been with them, but she needed to listen, if only for a moment. The pasnes alna was protecting them, after all. Protecting her.

"Since when does Albun take orders from the monarch?" asked Mane with a wry tone. She could almost picture the sneer on this face, goading the Sestrians into anger.

"It is a partnership, and in this partnership, we are hunting the little Ardian girl and her ugly companions. I trust the rumors are false, but a passerby witnessed a Sun Guard being attacked through your window. And, what's this? A recently-washed, dark stain on the wood. Blood, perhaps?"

461

"It is the right of any baker to spill a bit of cherry filling. But, worry not. If you are hungry, I do have the pastries for sale at three flins each. I might even have enough for everyone here. Although, I will expect reimbursement for the broken window."

Merigold peaked around the edge of the cracked door. Mane stood tall, draped in plants and supremely confident in the face of three dozen soldiers. A number were crowded into the bakery, Sun Guard all aside from the Sestrian officer exchanging words with the pasnes alna. Beyond the broken window knelt soldiers with large tower shields, spear-throwers positioned behind them. Merigold licked chapped lips, knowing that she should be following Lisan and Ill'Nath. Nothing good could come of this.

"Enough of this, Mane. We know that you have the girl. If you make a move to fight, we will cut you down and find her nonetheless. Prince Albun would surely favor you, should you cooperate, whereas he will damn you if you do not." The Sestrian officer spoke with the easy assurance of someone used to being obeyed. Strangely, he was holding a small cat beneath one arm, as one would carry a parcel. The animal was preening, unaffected by the tension in the room. "Drop your plants or else."

"Come now. I am merely a simple baker. A baker with a love of fauna and a unique fashion sense." Mane was stalling, giving his charges more time to escape. Tunnels beneath the cellar were connected to a warehouse several blocks away, outside the city walls. Few pasnes alna would leave themselves without an escape route in the case of a torch-bearing mob. Or, a steel-bearing horde of guards. "There are no girls here. So, leave, soldiers, unless you plan to buy a baked good."

The tension was palpable. The soldiers were tense, though Mane made no move, and nor did the Sestrian officer. The two Sun Guard officers glanced at each other with uncertainty, while one other, a slender Rafonese man, stepped forward, snapping shattered glass beneath his feet. The guards jumped at the sound.

"See here…" the officer began as a spear whipped by him, flung by an on-edge Sestrian. The projectile flew straight and true toward Mane's vine-encumbered chest. A yellow flicker, and the weapon was deflected back toward the Sun Guard. With that, pandemonium found a home in the bakery.

Mane shot a green beam of light at the officer, who raised a shield of his own as the cat drooped in his arms. A metsika! The beam deflected toward a Sun Guard, cutting through his shield and his armor, and losing power only after it burrowed partway through his stomach. The man next to him surged forward toward Mane and a misthrown spear took him in the back. The next guard in line whipped around, looking for the source of the spear, and was rewarded by a small disc of power severing his head from his body. The disc, not quite spent, took out another man before fizzing out in the snow.

Gray, dead leaves flew from Mane as he deflected a magical attack from the officer, this one appearing to be a simple ball of fire. On impact with Mane's shield, the fire flew back upon the floor and began to take hold, here and there, on the dried wood. Mane continued to fling discs and beams into the crowd, pausing every so often to deflect a thrown spear. No one could approach him, and he was without care. He turned toward Merigold for a moment, reaching for one of the flowers on his counter, and she shivered at the gleeful gleam in his eyes and the joy reflected in his wide smile. He lived for this, Mane did.

Merigold prayed—to no one in particular—that she never fell in love with killing.

The flames spread and the Sestrian metsika fled, leaving behind the corpse of the cat, as well as that of a rat, to litter the floor. Smoke began to fill the room, making it more and more difficult to see. As Mane reached for another plant, his ammunition supply having turned into desiccated ash, a stray spear caught him in the thigh. With a cry, he spun around and hit the floor. From the ground, he spied Merigold watching from her vantage point.

"Flee, you idiotic girl!" he shouted through gritted teeth. He twisted around, knocked a potted plant off of the counter, and grabbed a pink flower from amidst the shattered ceramic. He crafted a deadly yellow beam to pierce the eye of a Sun Guard who staggered out of the smoke, holding his hands in front of him to find his way. "Flee, girl! Make Agricorinor listen!" Merigold jumped back, torn by her impotence but finally heeding his warning. Coughing from the spreading smoke, she took the steps two at a time to head into the cellar.

She sidestepped the body of the first fallen Sun Guard, the man who'd been in the wrong place at the wrong time, and headed toward the half-open false wall. It was dark within, and she had no lantern. With a deep breath, she stepped into the tunnel and closed the pivoting door behind her.

The darkness devoured her, and her blood froze. It was cool and damp in here, just like her prison in Dunmore. She gripped her knife, feeling the comforting grip dig into her palm. With a deep breath and a hand on the wall, she started forward with faltering steps.

Every stray sound, every echo in this tunnel, was one of her demons. Saren, creaking his way along the planks above, preparing to retrieve her bucket and lower the ladder to whatever horrors he had planned. A wisping echo of the ashes that swept a decimated Dunmore. A chuckle of a mercenary as he brought her to the back room to 'negotiate.' And a small cry that would have been the voice of her unborn child. A wracking sob tore through her body and she fell to her knees.

She would rather face a dozen soldiers in the light of day than this darkness all alone.

464

The past cannot control you. You are more than what has happened to you. You are more than the things that you have done. Ill'Nath's quiet voice and words of supposed wisdom echoed in her mind. Easy to say, hard to live. She was alone in this. No one could truly understand what she had been through. Dear Yetra, she could barely comprehend how her life had changed. Since then, she had fought in a war, traveled hundreds of miles to another continent, dealt death to soldiers seeking to imprison them, fought off a magic-wielding Menogan, and bandied words with one pasnes alna while protecting the life of another.

Merigold took a deep breath, rose, and continued forward.

She reached a hand forward and swept it in front of her as if she could part the darkness like a curtain. Her steps became more competent, and she even began to hum a little tune that Ragen had taught her. The cheery notes seemed to chase away a bit of the blackness. A quarter hour later, she could see lantern light outlining two figures—one shorter and muscular, and one much larger and bearing a great burden on his back.

"Merigold! You lagged for far too long!" hissed Lisan as Merigold squinted into the light.

"I'm sorry... I needed to see what happened."

"And what did happen. Mane, is he alright?" Merigold could see the abject concern in her eyes; the sickening, unreturned love that Lisan had for the handsome, abusive pasnes alna. If she knew the truth, Lisan would go back. She would return to her death and doom the rest of them.

"Mane is fine. He stalled them for quite a while before I left. They were too afraid to attack." Lisan considered Merigold for a minute, searching her face with the eyes of a warrior. Merigold did not move a muscle, and met her gaze without a twitch. Abruptly, Lisan nodded, just slightly slumping her shoulders.

Lisan appeared beyond exhausted. Merigold had been so focused on her own aches and agonies that she had forgotten the toll that this had taken on her protector. Whatever twisted relationship she had with Mane had only exacerbated her fatigue. Merigold decided to tell another lie—a small reassurance. She placed her hand on Lisan's powerful shoulder.

"Don't worry, Lisan. We will be in Agricorinor in just a few short days. And… we will be safe in Agricorinor."

Chapter 34

Rap. Rap. Rap. Rap. Rap.

"My friends!" Hafgan shouted through cracked lips, his voice dry and hoarse. "Would you like to join me this night for dinner? The accommodations are sparse, but I'm sure I can spare some room."

There was no answer, of course. Perhaps his caretakers were mute.

"Hafgan?" asked a quiet and familiar voice. Hafgan shuddered at that voice; hearing it almost caused greater pain than what he had experienced in the Pwoll. Rian had come.

"Hafgan? Answer me…" Rian called softly into the darkness.

"Rian." His voice was heavy with emotion. He'd never expected to hear another voice aside from his own, let alone hers.

"Can you climb? Well, you don't have a choice."

A heavy rope crashed into his head, and he groped at the thing. There were thick knots every couple of feet. Almost on instinct, he began to lift himself up, arm over shaking arm. He had such little strength; twenty feet felt like climbing to the summit of Limner.

He crested the rise and felt himself being pulled the last feet by a few willing hands. He didn't see any of them, though, his filthy and aching body being immediately embraced in a fierce, familiar hug. Rian's shining hair tickled his nose, but he welcomed the discomfort.

She pushed him away, and he began to make out his surroundings in the wan light of a lantern. There were fourteen Wasmer surrounding him, none of whom he recognized. Wait, there was one… Hafgan stared at him dully, with a vague recollection.

"I told you I would tell you more about Traisen, boy," Ulin said with a wide, toothy grin. The old Offeir who Hafgan had met in Loch Creed all those weeks ago held a bloody spear. Hafgan guessed it was stained with the blood of his caretakers. He felt a surge of grief over that; they had been good to him, or at least not cruel, and he felt like he'd known those men, though they had never seen each other or spoken.

All of the people who he could see now were Offeirs, men and women in gray robes, the medallions of their various gods hanging around their necks. Despite their different deities, these people were united and moved with a unified purpose.

"What's happening here?" Hafgan asked quietly, his eyes darting around. Even the confined and crowded hallway felt like too much for him. Too much space. Too much... everything. He felt a sick urge to return to the Pwoll.

"We're rescuing you, you bleeding dimwit!" Rian said, but without much real rancor. She had blood on her mace, too.

"We've gotten to be a bit bleeding tired of this Flawless God," said Ulin. "There's little more sickening than using the powers of the heavens to drive men to madness. The people are terrified into submission, but we faithful don't fear a good fight."

"You rallied and united Loch Creed?" Hafgan asked slowly, trying to process this change in circumstance. He hoped to all the false gods that this wasn't a dream.

"By Oletta, you are stupid. Yes, hence the weapon-wielding Offeirs in front of you. Now, eat this." She handed him a bag of dried meats and potatoes, a veritable feast. "We will be safe here for a little while, but you need to get your feet underneath you." Rian, her eyes glistening, reached out and squeezed his hand for the briefest second. She smiled silently.

Then, her face grew hard.

"We are getting you out of Hackeneth."

***

Restless activity turned into silent inactivity as they took their succor with few words. After dressing in some fresh war robes, Hafgan paced; what was the point of sitting after spending such a long time enclosed? One of the Offeirs handed him a spear—an ancient, beautifully-crafted blade meant for a warleader of great repute. Traisen's symbol, a raging beast of unknown type or origin, decorated the blade. This haft, of a hard steel alloy as opposed to oak, would not split under pressure during battle.

There was something special about this spear, too, which was evident by the way the Offeir handled it. He cradled it with the care someone might show a newborn, gifting it to Hafgan with a slight reluctance. Maybe it was a sacred artifact, blessed by a pantheon of false gods. But, really, it did feel so very natural in Hafgan's hands. He had trouble putting the thing down. It made him feel… it made him feel much stronger than he should after his imprisonment.

Rian was off scouting and attending to her little rebellion, having left him with the dozen or so Offeirs. Most were dedicated to Traisen, though there were an Oletta and Denzo mixed in. This handful would be able to do little against the Leyr's warriors, let alone Leyr himself. In Hafgan's prime—meaning, before he'd been shoved into the Pwoll—he could have bested all of them single-handedly. There wasn't a true warrior among them.

Hafgan caught himself muttering about how easily he could have slain the men around him, even orchestrating what he would

469

do with his spear, step-by-step, as if he were composing a dance. He shut his mouth at their alarmed stares.

At some point, Hafgan fell asleep against the hard ground and woke hours later, finding nothing changed. Some movement, actual food, and real rest had been enough to help him regain some of his strength. He went through some of his exercises with the spear, gaining an impression of the weapon's weight and balance. Though he still lacked his old energy, it felt good to strain his muscles and do something familiar. This spear was an extension of himself, seemingly crafted just for him. Just holding the weapon seemed to bring him an unusual vigor. He continued to push Offeirs to see where the spear had come from, but no one would tell him. In fact, no one would say much to him at all. Strange, considering they were sacrificing their lives to free him.

The Pwoll lay deep within the Laenor, where several of the cruel prisons were isolated—far enough away that penitents could not communicate with one another, but close enough that they could easily be monitored. Hafgan knew the place, at least from years ago, and began to plan for their escape. There were some tunnels that led to the surface city of Hackeneth, but also a few that spilled out on all sides, and elevations, of Limner. Some of these pathways were known only to the Dyn Doethas, meaning that there were few left living who knew of them.

A loud whistle split the air and the Offeirs began to stir, grabbing their weapons. Ulin, who had been napping loudly for some time, snorted, blinked his eyes, and leaned over to Hafgan.

"Make ready, boy. It's time."

Down the passageway, a few shouts echoed out, these followed by a brief clashing of arms and some muffled shouts. And a death cry, as well—a sound that Hafgan was very familiar with.

Rian appeared from the shadows, accompanied by two more Offeirs. And, behind her, some familiar faces.

"Lieutenant! We be worried!" cried Paston, looking far worse for wear himself. Alwyn smiled a tired smile, revealing newly filed-down dogteeth. Enric nodded, his face and head covered with a stubble that Hafgan had never seen. His hair was an unusual orange-red color.

"We were worried," Hafgan corrected, almost automatically. He was suddenly surrounded by his budredda, each one of them slapping his back and giving him salutes. One or two even hugged him. It was almost as claustrophobic as the Pwoll, but Hafgan didn't want his men to step away. He felt a sudden wet pressure behind his eyes.

Rian shoved her way through, her small, lithe body scattering the larger fighters like an upturned sack of marbles. She strode up to Hafgan, staring at him in a way that made her seem just as tall.

"It is time for us to all get out of here. We will seek refuge to the south. There are some left among the Fflam Madfall who continue the fight against Leyr. We will assist them, build up a force, and eventually return to Hackeneth to fling Leyr from his perch."

"And his bleeding Flawless God, too," coughed Ulin. He didn't look particularly well, but he stood as straight as the spear clenched in front of him.

Hafgan observed Rian as she began to usher her Offeirs forward, touching each one on the arm and saying encouraging words, smiling that authentic smile. She would have been an excellent leader, and an excellent life partner. Had his life been different, he could have been happy. As it was, he didn't deserve happiness.

He cleared his still-sore throat. "Rian, what path are we taking? I know of some back ways."

"The back ways are blocked, choked with rock and rubble. We head to the falls." She pulled at her medal, an unadorned copper circle worn by the followers of Oletta. Her hand clenched the rough circle and she yanked at the chain. It snapped, and she tossed the thing aside with a dull clang.

"There will be blood."

***

And blood, there was.

Though the Pwoll's chambers were fairly isolated, deep in the Laenor, and guarded by only a few Wasmer who were being punished with undesirable duty, the closest path to the surface took them through the heart of Sebiant Rhisfel, the barracks for the Carreg Da warrior class.

As Rian had hurriedly explained, most of the seasoned Carreg Da warriors, along with Leyr, were out on campaign against the Ineyth, securing their northern borders. Meanwhile, Rian had coordinated a raid on a small Carreg Da village to the south with some of her Fflam Madfall allies, effectively drawing attention away from Hackeneth.

However, even with the distractions, there were always warriors on hand in Hackeneth, and it wasn't long until their way forward was blocked by Carreg Da fighters. As was their way back.

The budredda fought as a unit, just as they'd been trained—a bristling hedgehog of spears. Captain Yanso had been freed along with the warriors, and while he refused to even look in Hafgan's

472

direction, he fought as fiercely as the rest of them, rallying them with Rostanian war cries and coordinating their offense with practiced orders. In the close confines of the tunnels connecting the main chambers of Sebiant Rhisfel—where there could be only eight men fighting abreast—the discipline of his budredda continued to win out against the less disciplined, more individualistic fighting style of the Carreg Da warriors. Nonetheless, within the first twenty minutes of fighting, two budredda were lost, pierced by the spears of their enemies.

Hafgan left his men to their own devices as they pushed forward, directed by Rian. He rather tended to the rear guard, where the Offeirs managed to hold their own, but just barely. He darted to wherever he was needed, blocking fatal blows from falling on the less-trained religious men, or landing a killing blow to an unprotected side. He was weak from his imprisonment and had to make each move count. In the confusion of the melee, though, he managed. Even malnourished and half-maddened, he was better than the best of the warriors around him.

It had been so long since Hafgan had truly fought outside of his hedwicchen. Battle, in that void, was the calculation of a thousand probabilities, an intense focus on the most important details, and a mechanical but flexible reaction to any possibility. Outside of his hedwicchen, it was a thrilling and terrifying experience—a constant scrape for survival while numberless choices warred in his head as equally important. There was no detachment from those around him, and a persistent fear scraped inside his skull, particularly as he saw friends and acquaintances fall while he could do nothing.

Ulin was the first of the Offeirs to die. Battered by the passage of time and slowed by whatever sickness slogged through his veins, the aged Offeir of Traisen took a spear to his belly. He smiled a red smile as he clenched at the length of wood protruding from his gut; Hafgan felt a sickening pang of guilt, knowing that the man would not be joining his imaginary god in the afterlife.

After seeing the old man die, he again sought his hedwicchen. But whether from his madness from the Pwoll, or from being touched by the crimson light of the Red Eye, it was like trying to capture water with his hands. It kept slipping away; he could feel it, but couldn't quite grasp it. His emotions—fear, anger, confusion—flared every time that he tried.

"Hafgan, down!" shouted Rian from over his shoulder. He dropped to his stomach as an arrow whistled overhead. They had entered a larger chamber, a training yard, and one or two of the young Carreg Da had bows and vantage points. One Offeir and one more budredda fell before they fought their way into the next tunnel, and Paston caught an arrow in the meat of his left arm. Hafgan pulled him into the center of their little circle of warriors.

"Sergeant, this is going to hurt," he said, gripping tight the arrow before pushing the thing through. To Paston's credit, he didn't lose consciousness, though he screamed enough to shake the mountain. The men rallied and fought hard as Hafgan cut off Paston's sleeve and bound the wound; his second was well-loved among the budredda, and they would do anything to keep him safe.

In fact, each one of them was well-loved, and each death was a great loss.

"I'm fine," Paston said through gritted teeth. "I be leading from the back for a bit."

"I will be leading from the back," corrected Hafgan, grabbing his ornate spear and pushing forward. The rage at seeing his first budredda hurt, and the loss of several more, boiled his blood, bringing to the surface every scrap of hate that he felt for Leyr. For Yurin, and for himself.

474

Using his gifted spear, he vaulted over his set-upon men, stepping on the head of a Carreg Da warrior to propel himself forward and behind the line of Carreg Da. Before a single fighter turned, three bled from fatal wounds to their major organs. In Ardian culture, striking from the rear was said to lack honor. Seeing the eyes of the man you killed was supposed to somehow elevate you. But, for the Wasmer, killing was killing. Even having spent five years among humans did nothing to change Hafgan's opinion on the matter.

Four more warriors rushed at Hafgan, and he curled his lips back as he met their attack with a primal scream. He ducked a clumsy lunge from one, laying him out with a rib-crushing shoulder to the chest. Another drew blood on his shoulder with a quick jab. He bared his teeth, jumping into the man's guard and slitting his throat with a choked-up grip on his ancient weapon. Without a pause, he next used the fallen warrior's dying body to catch the spear of a third attacker, disemboweling him with a swipe of his spear. The thing seemed to cut through their war leathers like butter. The final warrior stared at Hafgan, took two staggering steps backward, and then began to flee. Hafgan shouted something wordless and heartless at him, flinging his weapon and catching the man in the back. He fell into the earth, writhing for a moment until Hafgan ripped out his bloody spear.

Hafgan did not feel any weakness. The weapon seemed to glow in his hands. He wanted more blood.

He whipped around, looking for another enemy with wild eyes. Breathing heavily, he saw a group of Wasmer pointing their spears at him. He readied his own weapon, leaning into his back foot, ready to leap forward. Until Rian pushed through, shouting his name.

"Hafgan! Hafgan, you bleeding dimwit! You're going to get yourself killed, after we went through all this trouble to heave your dirty bones from that hole in the ground. Hafgan… what's

475

wrong?" Her hair was matted with blood, and she seemed to weave on her feet in exhaustion.

He took a deep, shuddering breath. "Nothing. We must continue on. The falls are not far; I can hear them." He spun abruptly and strode out ahead of his men.

And he tried to forget the urge that he'd had to pierce Rian's heart.

Chapter 35

"Where the fuck is she, boy?" Darian demanded, slamming his fist into the desk.

"I told you; she fell behind fighting off those masked bastards. I have no idea," Fenrir said, finding the inside of his glass easy to look at compared to his father. They were secreted in his father's office above Warehouse Six, Fenrir having been ushered there when he'd returned to the compound—limping heavily on one leg and dripping blood from a half dozen shallow cuts. Tennyson's masked goons had been very thorough in making Fenrir's escape story seem plausible.

"So, I am supposed to believe that Ingla, one of my most seasoned and best-skilled Adders, fell behind while you, a mess of a man with a shattered knee, managed to fight your way free?" Darian's anger did not appear to be focused on Fenrir. Even with this, however, his head seemed to be elsewhere.

"That was the point of the training, wasn't it? I've gotten better. And, I know more than anyone—it only takes one lucky shot. Or, one unlucky shot." He finished his second glass of wine with a gulp. Local stuff, from one of the small wineries on Vineyard Way. He hated it, to be honest, but it was strong. And, with everything in front of him, he needed something strong.

Darian sighed, and moved the wine bottle away from Fenrir as he reached for a third glass. Apparently, additional fortification was not on the menu.

"No matter. I've little doubt that she will turn up. She is stronger than you know." Darian looked up, his eyes tired but intense. "It was stupidity to publicly attack these people, boy. There were not enough Adders nearby to deal with something like that."

"Things would have gone better had your Wolf Knights managed to keep their balance near the Spike."

"Not my knights, boy…" he muttered. Then he pulled a small book out of his desk and began to write something down in his bold handwriting.

Fenrir only observed. His father was much the same man as in Fenrir's memory, a powerful tyrant always looming larger than life. He had always seemed so unstoppable, imperturbable, like a mountain or the Plateau itself. And yet, lately, he seemed preoccupied, disengaged. Maybe his mental faculties were slipping. Maybe the stress of running a mercantile empire, coupled with his new lordship, was getting to him.

It would be so easy to reach across the desk and grab his father's throat. He might even be able to close off Darian's windpipe before he managed a noise to alert the Adders outside the office. If Fenrir played his cards right, perhaps he could trick the guards and make his way out of the compound, maybe even finding a way to get a likely unwilling Astora out of this Yetra-forsaken place.

Maybe. If. Perhaps.

Darian rose abruptly, his face and mannerisms nothing if not decisive.

"Well, boy, you had better suit up. We have a long night ahead of us."

"Ahead of us?" Fenrir asked, realizing how dumb he sounded.

"Yes, boy. You are to accompany me, as an Adder, to the fete and council meeting this evening. I've little manpower to spare this night, and you with your… having gotten better skills… should bolster my personal guard nicely. And, I know I have your loyalty." Darian's eyes flashed, and thoughts of meldus flitted through Fenrir's mind. He grimaced at the reminder of both that poor woman's gruesome death and his current dilemma.

Fenrir nodded to his father. "I will protect your life as if it were my own." Basically valueless, in other words.

Darian rolled his eyes. "And, actually pay attention, boy. Events that will influence the future of our country will take place tonight."

Fenrir pulled himself to his feet and winced. The House had done a thorough job, indeed. He creaked toward the door, looking forward to escaping the burning eyes of his father, even just for a bit. And, to taking some of Martis' devil's root pills.

"Oh, and Fenrir…" Fenrir paused, glancing over his shoulder. "Make sure you are well-fitted with a helmet."

"Why, so no one will see your shameful spawn?"

There was a pause.

"No, I just didn't think that you'd want Astora to recognize you."

***

Thankfully, Darian did not spend much time at the fete.

Fenrir had to stand at his shoulder, along with two other Adders named Mel and Kenpin—the latter being the same Rafonese man he'd once watched fight in a training battle wielding a great hammer. He sweated beneath his helmet, watching a hundred visiting nobles from around Ardia feasting, and then dancing, all to celebrate a war that was thought to be won. Against their own countrymen.

The nobles had even commissioned some players to recreate Escamilla's murder and Tilner Pick's demise. Of course, Escamilla was depicted as a decrepit old hag who was apparently stabbed in the back by some little boy while meeting with her group of drunkard, hick captains. And Tilner was a clear pedophillic fop, ordered to jump onto a ten-foot pole that ended with the actor falling into a cake. The player playing Lord Faris was none other than the great Manis Deon, handsome and powerful beyond reality. So, Faris must have been the one to commission this insulting, dishonest play.

But Fenrir could barely spare a thought for any sort of outrage. First because he knew that, in a previous life, he would have cut off any of these men's fingers for a sack of yets. Second because he knew, in his heart of hearts, that these depictions were not the reality. And third, and probably most importantly, because he couldn't take his eyes off of Astora.

She was just… well, she simply drew the eye. She wasn't the prettiest of women there by a long shot, though she was lovely in her own way. Luckily more like his mother than her own mother. Her chestnut hair didn't have the silky smooth look that was popular among the noble ladies; it was interrupted by unruly, unpredictable waves. Her face resembled Fenrir's, perhaps a bit too much, with a strong chin and a broad nose. But her eyes, they captivated. Her manner, too. All of these ladies were more refined, more polished. But they didn't shine like Astora. They only reflected her brilliance.

His daughter flitted from conversation to conversation, easily and effortlessly weaving in and out of groups. He could hear her lilting, authentic laugh carrying across the ballroom. Among Rostanian nobility, it wasn't polite to laugh so loudly, but Astora didn't care. And Fenrir smiled every time he heard it.

Once she came to the table nearby, talking with two noblewomen from Draston who appeared to be longstanding partners of Darian's. In Fenrir's mind, the conversation was the embodiment of who his daughter had become.

"Ladies Lillian and Gregoria, how simply pleasing it is to see you!" Astora said, her voice all silk and smiles.

"Likewise," said a dark-haired powdered harlot, her waist hardly larger than Fenrir's forearm. Likewise certainly didn't seem like an accurate statement based on the tone. The long pause beckoned for Astora to leave, but she didn't take the hint. Or maybe she just ignored it.

"How goes the fur trade, Lillian?" Astora asked, placing a hand on the chubbier one's arm. "Have you recovered from your losses?"

"Losses? I, uh…" Lillian stammered.

"Yes, losses. I heard that you will be selling half of your holdings by Ascension next year. I imagine that will have put a strain on your father, the poor man. Has he started drinking again? That stuff is simply toxic for him."

Lillian's mouth hung open, either from the surprise at her family's plight, or because she was being reminded of it.

"And your father?" asked Gregoria archly, in a reminder of Astora's dubious parentage. Fenrir shivered, unbidden, even though he knew his face was hidden.

Astora did not miss a beat. "Sadly, killed during the war, fighting for our country."

Did she believe that? Did she know who he was, what he had done? What had Darian told her? What had her mother told her? What did she remember?

So many fucking questions, and here he was, unable or unwilling to answer them. Instead, he stood stiff as a board, sweating beneath his blue leathers.

"Yes, but on which side? I've heard he was a traitor."

Perhaps his slaying of the little duke had been kept quieter than he'd thought.

"He fought on the same side as Lord Aser. Have you or your husband heard of him? I hear he is quite dashing." Gregoria paled, huffed, and walked away. Astora had the grace not to appear overly pleased before gliding off to cause havoc elsewhere. Fenrir had to bite his lip to keep from grinning.

Not long after, though, Darian abruptly excused himself as some rich merchant groveled for attention from the merchant king. Fenrir flanked him, along with Mel and Kenpin.

They convened in the Great Hall, now strangely bare compared to what Fenrir remembered of it. Never a bright room, it at least had the benefit of a huge Yetranian Ascension mural, which added a bit of color and a near-naked picture of a goddess. When standing guard, one could use their imagination to fill in the details. Now, though, the walls were completely and utterly empty—just cold, hard stone stained by the shadows of what once had been.

The attendees, at least, added some color, garish though it might be. The entire Rostanian Council—all ten of them, including Darian—was present around an oval, oaken table. Lord Faris, of course, was at the head of the table, a calm pillar of stability. Aron Witton, a count from northern Florens, lazed in a chair, his chubby cheeks poorly concealed by a patchy beard. Pereway de Ingus, Fenrir remembered well from his youth. The merchant had seemed to be an inattentive and doting old man, even thirty years ago when Fenrir had been a child. But, he was canny and sly, creating an empire to rival that of the de Trentons.

He was an enemy of the family, and Fenrir wanted to clap him on the shoulder with a thankful hand, though he feared he'd break the skeletal old bastard if he tried it.

Then there was Baronness Farah Erlins, her raven-black hair standing in stark contrast to her pale skin, betraying at least a hint of Domain blood. She sat solemnly next to Faris, inspecting her folded hands. She was probably little more than a figurehead, used to incite the masses after her husband had been tortured and killed at the hands of the Florensians when they'd invaded Rostane unprovoked. In reality, Fenrir knew that he'd been tortured by the little duke and locked beneath the Plateau, tormented by someone before falling victim to madness and those monsters. Theran Erlins had even seemed like a fairly decent man; it was a shame, really.

"Good of you to finally join us, Darian," Witton said around a gulp of wine as Darian took a seat opposite Faris.

"I care not for your petty politics and little maneuvers, Witton. The time for that has passed," Darian said dismissively. Surprisingly, de Ingus and another one of the council members, a merchant by his clothing and bearing, nodded their assent. Cliques in the council, apparently.

"Let's get this over with," de Ingus suggested, his voice distracted as always, as if he had somewhere else to be. "You already know my answer."

"Pah, your answer is always no," mumbled Count Pentis, a man Fenrir could barely recognize, so much had he aged in the past year. He coughed into his kerchief.

"Your wife can't say the same," retorted the merchant councilman.

"Gentlemen, please. We are better than this," Lord Faris said, his calming voice cutting through the rising racket. "I believe we should hear what our potential allies have to say."

"Aye, let's hear them," Witton said, pretending as if it had been his idea. Fenrir got the impression of a bootlicker.

"Call them in," Faris said, beckoning to one of the dozen Wolf Knights ringing the room. Fenrir didn't see any familiar faces, but it was difficult to see what lay beneath the helmets.

The knight obliged, ducking into a small adjoining chamber which was most often used for visiting dignitaries. He emerged two minutes later, two people in tow. He cleared his throat.

"Lord Proctor Finn Lo'Argeen and Lady Immis Si'Abrill of the Menogan Empire," announced the knight, chosen as the herald thanks to his booming voice. Fenrir remembered the knight, after all. Reman always had a driving baritone, and was known for starting rousing ballads at Yetra's Arms during his off time.

The visitors were unusual, to say the least. Finn Lo'Argeen seemed fairly normal, though sickly looking. Maybe he was some bastardized Alganian mongrel, though that name was unfamiliar—nothing like any family names Fenrir had heard of. He was pale, too, and it wasn't clear if he was ill like Lord Pentis, had never seen the sun, or just had a strange pigment. It certainly wasn't the ruddy white of the Domain. What really made the man stand out, though, was the fact that he wore black, opaque spectacles that seemed to suck up the nearby light. There was no way this Lo'Argeen could see through them, but he seemed to be aware of the room, glancing about. His teeth were gritted together in a vice of a smile. `

The Lady Si'Abrill, though, was unlike anyone Fenrir had ever seen. She was also pale, again not like his mother or others of Domain blood. They were a dirty snow whereas she was like a field of ice. Pure, unsullied…. Perfect. Her eyes were a stark contrast, a piercing green brighter than those of anyone from Jecusta's Eastern Sweeps, where such eyes were common. They were almost alien emeralds shining in her face. Her lips were small, and either painted a light blue or colorless. Her hair was a deep, soft brown, and cut just above her shoulders and her plainly adorned black dress.

"My lords, I am honored to again be given the gift of your time," said Lo'Argeen, his voice sounding like his nose had been oft broken. Other than that, there was nothing odd about his way of speaking; he could have been born in the shadow of the Plateau. And yet, he was a lord of the Menogan empire?

"You are always welcome to our time, if not our yets," Witton said. There was a forced chuckle from the gathered council members. Faris sat back down after a brief bow.

"My apologies, esteemed guests. It has been a trying day, and the evening's festivities can be draining."

"We are not without humor, my lords," said Lady Si'Abrill, with one raised, perfectly manicured eyebrow. "It appears, however, that Lord Witton is." More authentic laugher from around the room.

"Perhaps we will get to the point, then," said Lo'Argeen. He seemed like an impatient man—a coiled spring just barely restrained by the bonds of decorum.

"Let's hear it, then. I've ladies demanding my attention," said de Ingus, the moldy old man being self-aware of his rotting state. Darian shot him a glare, betraying their old rivalry.

"Yes, give your speech," Darian said, his voice tinged with disdain.

Lo'Argeen stepped forward and took a breath, a sneer on his mouth. Si'Abrill, though, put an arm on his shoulder and began to speak. She spoke near perfect Ardian, but pronounced each word so precisely that she almost sounded like a translator, speaking without processing the words being emitted from her mouth.

"Lords and ladies of Rostane, of Ardia. Again, and for the last time, we come before you to propose the alliance between our two great nations. Menoga, as you know, stretches nearly across a continent, west of the Great Barrier." Fenrir had not known that; he'd never heard of Menoga, and had had no idea it was possible to cross the Great Barrier. A sailor acquaintance of his had described it as an endless wall of towering waves caused by a convergence of tides over thousands of miles of shallows and reefs. The sailor had been well-spoken for a man with fewer teeth than fingers.

"We have sought contact with Saiwen for hundreds of years, our sailors either coming back unable to pass the barrier or not at all. But, now that we have established a consistent passage, we seek to ally with you. We have the military might that can aid you in consolidating your grip on Ardia and expanding beyond. We simply seek our own footholds, some coastal cities, to…"

"We do not seek to expand beyond Ardia," Darian interrupted. "And we certainly do not lack the might needed to consolidate our own country."

Lo'Argeen cracked his knuckles and spoke through gritted teeth. "You have farmers and laborers, half of them holding their spears the wrong way, as likely to stab themselves as others. You have dissidents raising the population against you, or have you already forgotten your riots earlier today? And you have the ire of the underground, which is slowly eroding your authority."

"Nonetheless, we can handle our own affairs in this small matter of civil war, as we have over these past months," said Darian, his manner as calm as in any negotiation.

"Right, and what will you do when your farmers are killed and your lands grow sallow? When you have no laborers left to haul ore from the Tulanaques, or to unload your ships and carry your goods? What will you do when one of your neighbors—Jecusta, perhaps, or Algania—senses your weakness and comes knocking on your doors with armies of their own? We have thousands of trained Menogan killers…"

"That sounds distinctly like a threat to me, and why would we welcome thousands of trained killers into our lands?" This from de Ingus, suddenly as savvy as a horse salesman. "In my experience, it would be difficult to expel those who do not want to leave."

"Come now, de Ingus; Darian. Our Menogan friends have already shared quite a bit of wealth, not to mention other gestures of goodwill to show their intent," Lord Faris commented.

"Aye, we've already some marriages on the books," said Witton with a grin.

"Your Menogan whore means nothing to me," Darian said, to the gasps of half of those present.

"Darian, you overstep," Faris warned.

"I overstep? You, Faris, overstepped by allowing these persons here, allowing them insight into our internal strife. We will not subdue Hunesa with thousands of foreign invaders and further fracture our country." Darian's hands were balled and white, and Faris, usually unflappable, seemed ready to spit in his face.

"Ha!" Lo'Argeen barked, his sneer morphing into a real smile. "I love those who speak their minds! Lord de Trenton, I will do the same. Without us, you will fail. Already, armies are forming over the borders, ready to strike at you where you are weak. You have made many enemies across Saiwen, some of which you do not even know of. You need us, Ardians, like it or…"

Lady Si'Abrill put her hand on the man's shoulder and stepped forward, her alien eyes entrancing Fenrir's. He wouldn't have minded seeing himself reflected in those gems. "My apologies. Finn can become… passionate. Know that he speaks true in all things, however. Jecusta is on the verge of being swayed to stage an attack, and they will not allow any of your freedoms to persist. We simply seek to help and establish our own profitable strongholds outside of Ardia proper. We do believe it will come to war, and we desire to assist."

"My sources concur with that," Lord Faris said. "The Jecustans know of our strife…"

"Probably because your friend Iolen defected…" mumbled de Ingus, only half under his breath. Faris gave him a hard look.

"…and the remnants of Escamilla's army is still sheltered in Farrow's Hold. A combined force, even with half of Jecusta's standing army committed, could pose a true threat to a newly united Ardia," Faris finished.

"This alliance makes good sense if we want to continue to rule Ardia as a council," said Witton, with some solemnity.

"I second that. It will save the needless death of our own people," said another council member, one Fenrir didn't recognize. Judging from his pudgy cheeks and fine clothes, he'd probably never met any of his own people, or ever even had to wash his own cock. Likely, he had a servant for that.

It was quiet in the Great Hall—the sort of quiet that fills a room when a decision is about to be made. When the conclusion is foregone, and when those who disagree finally cease their protests and give in to the inevitable. The quiet that is marked by self-satisfied smiles and grim jaws being set as wishes are fulfilled and snuffed. As some men make piles of coin while others lose more. As life is decided for some, and death for others. Fenrir had seen it all before, standing in rooms like this. Which was why he felt surprised by what came next.

"This isn't happening. I won't allow it," Darian said, his voice the hardest steel. He refused to bend, apparently.

"You don't get to decide!" Witton spat. "Your money only goes so far."

"Fine, let us have a vote. That is why we have a council, is it not? So that the man with the biggest army doesn't get to make the call," Darian commented.

Faris nodded grimly, rising to his feet. He wasn't a particularly large man, and his looks were middling. But, his calm and his confidence controlled the room.

"My fellow council members, it has come to a vote. Our alliance with the Menogan empire, for the duration of our internal conflict, is up for final consideration. As is our standard, each person among us casts one vote, and the majority rules the day. White, yes. Black, no."

This process seemed to be well-practiced for this group. Each council member was given two pebbles—one black, one white— from a servant decked out in the green and gold livery of Rostane. Darian didn't hesitate before casting his black stone into the center of the table. De Ingus, crotchety to the core, had to huff at Darian before doing the same. Witton tossed his white stone into the center, as did Faris and two other nobles, including an older woman with sharp features. She vaguely reminded Fenrir of Escamilla, though Escamilla never would have supported a foreign force stepping onto Ardian soil.

Darian glanced at the other merchant council member impatiently, and the man took the cue to add his vote to the 'no' pile. Darian's pitiless gaze next fell onto a noble—Count Torin, Fenrir remembered, from years ago, was an asshole. He was a stick of a man with a penchant for being caught in the wrong place at the wrong time. It wouldn't take much for Darian to buy him out, and that played out as a black stone rolled into the center of the table.

Four to four.

Baron Pentis, with a wheezing, wet cough, tossed his white pebble into the mix. He had seemed hesitant until Witton had cracked his knuckles audibly. A fair, balanced council indeed. Five to four, but Faris needed the majority to win the day.

Darian shifted his gaze to Baroness Erlins, the final, unspoken voice in the room, her pale complexion somehow seeming whiter beneath his scrutiny. She clutched both stones in tight fists as if she was trying to squeeze water out of them. Darian tapped his fingers on the table—the sound of heavy expectations weighing down the room.

She peered up at him from under long eyelashes, and her lips twisted in a sudden, definitive smirk. Her white stone rolled into the center of the table like a human skull grinning up at Darian. Fenrir's father stiffened, and the son heard a sharp intake of breath.

"Sorry, my lord principal. You won't be getting your way today." Erlins' voice was soft, but intense. Witton wore a wide grin. "Don't think I do this for you, either, your corpulence." Witton rose to his feet, knocking back his chair.

"You overstep, you plumped-up whore!"

"Stop this! Be gracious in victory, Witton," Faris said. "The votes have been cast, and we are bound to the story of the stones. Lord Lo'Argeen. Lady Si'Abrill. We welcome the alliance with the Menogan empire."

"Superb!" Lady Si'Abrill pronounced. "We will immediately inform our proximal, seaborn forces and send for the others, and if you would be so gracious as to arrange for the lodging that we discussed, we can…"

"You fucking bitch!"

Fenrir started at the commotion, which had not been directed at Si'Abrill. From one of the staging rooms, there echoed the sounds of an argument and another shouted curse. And an angry woman's voice. A man rushed into the room, with Wolf Knights, retainers, and even Fenrir finding their hands on their blades.

"My lord principal. There is a matter that requires your attention," Sigmund Fitra said, his voice vitriolic. Fenrir noticed that he was no longer wearing the silver Wolf emblem signaling his generalship. Perhaps it was just a wardrobe omission, but the fact that he was back in de Trenton blues instead of the Rostanian green and golds spoke volumes.

"What?" Darian's voice was a snarl, that of a wild animal barely restrained.

"I'm more than just a matter," came a voice, slightly wobbly. Fenrir shivered and smiled simultaneously. Astora pushed her way into the room, flanked by a helpless-looking Blue Adder. Evidently, it only took a slender teen girl to disarm a weapon's master.

Sigmund spoke through gritted teeth, and Fenrir noticed that he had three lines of blood across his right cheek. That was his girl, right there. "Lady de Trenton struck Count Mern Seenly across the face with a stone chalice. And, when Lady Gregoria tried to intervene, she yanked down her dress, exposing her…"

"I know what woman keep under their dresses," Darian growled. Witton barked a laugh while Faris frowned at the whole affair. Lady Si'Abrill, to her credit, was unaffected, though her fellow Menogan grinned a sly grin. "We are done here."

Darian stood abruptly, motioning for Fenrir, Mel, and Kapin— the other Adders—to follow him. He roughly grabbed Astora's wrist as he went, and she grimaced in obvious pain.

"Principal, let me explain!" She yanked her arm back to no effect. There was tempered steel in Darian, Fenrir knew, of the type that was nearly immovable. "The count grabbed me; he…"

Darian backhanded Astora without releasing her wrist. She reeled back, but he did not let her fall.

Darian, for all his many faults, was not prone to violence against women, traitors excluded. He had never touched Fenrir's mother like that. If he had, boy or not, Fenrir would have stuck a knife in his throat. As it was, Fenrir's hand tightly gripped his sword.

"You are drunk. Kapnis, Mel, deal with the count. Sigmund, you…" Darian's eyes shot to Fenrir's. "Bring the girl. It's time we had a family discussion."

Interlogue: Sloth

"I wish we had more time together, sweetling. It will not be long now. There is so little of you left. Just a small bit of humanity resisting all of your basest instincts. Lust. Aggression. Hatred. Violence. Wrath. Soon, those will be all you know. But, as things stand, you will no longer be aware of yourself. Whatever there was of you, sweetling, will be gone. It is a mercy, as your body—bereft of you—may be called to serve me a final time.

"You may be called to battle. I do not relish this, sweetling, but events in the world are forcing my hand.

"There was a time, sweetling, when nothing could spur me to action. I have learned from those times, hence my intervention in the world now.

"When Oletta pierced my body, it damaged more than just my physical form. My mind was also crippled.

"I told you of my pride; how I began to truly believe that I was a goddess, that the Blood Maiden was immortal. That I was superior to my followers and contrarians. That my powers were unrivaled, and I could destroy armies and cities with a wave of my hand. Being so near death, experiencing the very real fear of the end, and the existential terror associated with that, my life, as I knew it, was shattered.

"I grew indolent, listless. I returned to more settled lands, and locked myself away from the world. I no longer gave commands or orders; no longer accepted gifts or visitors. I no longer took lovers, though it seemed as if Wantran had some interest. Perhaps her motivation for saving me? I will never know.

"I was lost, sweetling. It was pure sloth, and it did not suit me.

"My domain stopped its expansion, both on Saiwen and Imsul. The Wasmer were allowed to retreat into the mountains with Oletta, and your Ardia remained mostly unsettled. I cared not. I only emerged periodically to accept a donor. I occasionally experimented with healing magic, injuring one follower and trying to heal him with the power of the next. It was the only thing of use that I accomplished during that time.

"Amorum was hundreds of miles away, but he wrote to me occasionally. His words were those of forgiveness and acceptance, sorrow and love. He was as good a writer as an orator. I never wrote back.

"Intenu continued to lead my school of pasnes alna without input from me. I didn't care, and couldn't gather the energy to care. She continued to search for the man who held her bonds. If she was ever successful, I do not know. We lost contact in what was to come.

"My most trusted captains—Wantran, Yinra, Pinetoe—spent most of their efforts maintaining order in my vast domain, putting down the occasional unrest, and carving out their own little domains.

"During this time, Ultner began to rise in the center of my domain. A man, a god, with powers to rival mine... with the oratory skills of Amorum, as well, and the knowledge to rival Intenu. A charming man who held the hearts and minds of the people.

"I would call it a rebellion, what Ultner started, but it was more than that. It was a movement, a shift in the mindset of the general populace. Ultner evidently taught of freedom, of a release from the bondages that I had created. A breaking of my chains around the necks of the people.

"Was it so bad, sweetling, having most of the world united under a single ruler, a single ideology? Was that not better than a thousand warring factions across the land, with the few peaceful havens—like Aquine—living in fear? That is what freedom begot, sweetling. Violence and anarchy. Chaos.

"Pandemonium.

"Nonetheless, Ultner's own idealogies spread like a great forest fire, and people rose to his standard. They began to assemble, organize, and destroy everything that I had created.

"However, in my lassitude, I hadn't the energy nor the motivation to confront this problem. It was a thousand miles away and seemed like a minor thing. Certainly something that my underlings could handle.

"It was a long while before the extent of the problem became evident, at least to me. My followers feared me, as always, but also lied to me. To their goddess!

"They led me to believe that Ultner was under control, that my various forces from across my domain had the rebellion well in hand. So, I continued to take little interest. I continued to remain slothful, idle, listless.

"During this time, Ultner found his own army of pasnes alna. Some, I later learned, he had recruited as I had. Most, however, came from Intenu's homeland—Menoga, far to the northwest, from across the seas. These were miernes armas, enslaved pasnes alna who were both revered and controlled.

"They wreaked havoc across my domain. Destroying cities, monuments, knowledge. Killing my devout followers and my soldiers, murdering my pasnes alna wherever they could be found. The dispensation of power was so great that the landscape itself began to change. Verdant plains turned to wastelands and deserts. Hills and mountains crumbled. New rivers formed, and lowlands were flooded.

"Still, I did nothing. Still, my followers lied to me. And, sweetling, I knew they lied. I knew it! But, I languished.

"That is, until the day I received word that Amorum had died. That washed away my indolence.

"Tiernum was once a great city near the center of my domain. It was known for its architecture, for the beautiful arches that spanned the city like a spiderweb. Amorum made Tiernum his home as he tried to unite my domain, bringing the people together for the common good. He was largely impotent. My people knew better than to insult him, but without me by his side, he was unable to truly accomplish much.

"Also, he was growing older.

"Because Tiernum had become the seat of the government, it was an immediate target for Ultner's movement. The city was utterly defensible; the walls were great, and the arches were functional, allowing soldiers to deploy to breaches in an instant. Whatever remained of Aquine's great defensive weapons were stationed there. Ah, if only we had focused on science— inventing—perhaps we could have duplicated those weapons and protected Tiernum. Perhaps, then, Amorum would have survived. Perhaps Ultner would never have risen in revolt, would never have forged an alliance with the Menogans and their miernes armas. Perhaps I would not still be on this earth.

"Tiernum held, sweetling, for months. The Book of Amorum says that its namesake won the battle of Tiernum. As always, it was an oversimplification. In reality, the battle was a protracted siege, with attacks testing the vastly outnumbered defenders almost daily. But, the city held! Amorum rallied the people again and again. His voice finally swayed the masses, and he again had the hearts of the people. But, counter to all of his beliefs, the thing that brought the people back to him was war.

"I could only imagine that he recognized this juxtaposition, and that it demoralized him. He was nothing if not a man of principles.

"Eventually, Tiernum seemed invincible—such faith the people had in Amorum, if not me. But it was not to be.

"Amorum was assassinated, killed in the council chamber along with the other leaders of the city. It was said that Ultner, himself, led the infiltration attempt. Not a person in their path survived, and the council chamber was bathed in blood, none recognizable.

"Of course, I did not see this. How could I, wallowing as I was? Everything I learned of the assassination was from second-hand accounts, spoken to me by the broken men of Tiernum. The city did fall, of course, having lost its rallying point.

"Though we had rarely spoken, for years, Amorum's death felt like part of me died. The decent part. The good part. The part that may have deserved some sort of redemption. I was decimated.

"Again, I felt a great urge for vengeance. Stronger, this time, than even when Aquine had been destroyed. And, this time, I had the power to seek such vengeance. I would exact payment for what Ultner had done. I would take it from his flesh. I would rip it from his soul. I would keep him alive and make him suffer.

"I would destroy Ultner, totally and utterly."

Chapter 36

The moonlight twinkled down, bathing the garden in a soft, blue-white light—the type that would lull a person into a sense of calm and security. The winterblooms and frost weeds bobbed gently in the breeze, snow falling in a soft, meandering fashion. Only the crunching of two pairs of boots in the snow interrupted the serenity of this secluded spot.

Emma had taken to spending her evenings in this place. Throughout the days, her head was on fire, throbbing and buzzing while she attempted to organize the shambles of the Army of Brockmore for their return to Ardia, and likely certain death. And, at night, though exhausted, at the moment that her aching head touched the pillow, her mind was lost in a red anger. Anger at Escamilla for ever assuming she would want these worries. Anger at Unael for failing to convince the magnates to support her war. Anger at herself for an endless barrage of failures and bad decisions. And, anger at any god who might have his ear cupped against the door to their world.

But, in this isolated, unmaintained garden, lost in the uninhabited emptiness of the Hold, Emma could sometimes find her calm. It was strange that she could feel so alone when surrounded by others for every minute of every day. Even as she slept, her room was ringed in Apple-ornamented steel. But, here, near an unused portion near the center of the Hold, with no way to reach it without passing dozens of checkpoints and hundreds of armed men, she was given a bit of distance. And, strangely, she felt less alone when actually by herself.

But on this night—her last night in the Hold—she was not alone.

"You are quiet tonight," Lord Unael said, looking up at the moons, both visible at different ends of the sky. In the lunar light, his cragged face mirrored the surface of the celestial bodies.

"Can you blame me, my lord?" Emma asked, pausing during their slow pacing through the garden. She looked at him askance. He'd joined her this night for a reason. Last words of encouragement, perhaps?

"No. No, Emma. Were I in your position, I would be in a constant rage." So, they were more alike than she'd suspected. "But I can respect quiet. Tell me, how is your chaplain recovering?"

Ignatius was, frankly, in poor shape, even these weeks after his Trials. His face had been sewn up, leaving him with two wicked, purple scars on either side of his face. His molars, strained from holding the iron bar in place, had cracked and required removal, lest they splinter and be swallowed. His chest was scarred with the Yetranian Ascension, and the nails that they had driven through his feet still hobbled him. Strangely, with his new lisping whisper, he most often complained of the old pain in his knee rather than a myriad of new aches.

His healing might have been more complete, except that one of the lash wounds had become infected and lingered. He was still abed, though not without a great number of visitors. His faithful were more fervent, and his bravery had even won over some of the unfaithful. Not to mention the native Jecustans who were now clamoring to join Ignatius' fight against Pandemonium, but had yet been turned away.

But that was a problem for a different night.

"He is resting comfortably among the men, in a wagon probably more lavish than anything you have here in the Hold. I'm certain that he is bathing in the attention of his followers, almost making his Trials worth it." She remembered the utter, hopeless fear in his eyes. "Almost."

"I am glad for him. Truly," he added, noticing Emma's disbelieving expression. "The Grand Taneo has long been a thorn in my side, using his divine authority to thwart my mere mortal laws. As terrible as the coming storm will be, I have to say…. It was a fantastic feeling, telling him no." Unael was smiling a wide smile—maybe the first authentic expression of joy that she had seen from him over the past months.

"And I will never be able to thank you enough for that."

"My debts are now cleared. When the dust settles, I still expect to retain my control of the city, though I'll be bereft of nearly every favor and certainly be hated by the most devout Yetranians. Rential, particularly, has been working to usurp me. But, it will be alright. It will be alright." His gaze was distant.

Emma had nothing to say, so she began a slow walk once again. She pulled her coat closer to her body against the chill of the evening, wondering how much worse it would be once her army was again on the march. She should try to take one last bath this night, even if it meant not getting a wink of sleep. How long would it be until she could be alone and surrounded by warmth once more?

"Emma. We never found the traitor, did we?" Unael asked, abruptly changing the subject.

"No, my lord," she said, bitterly. "Somewhere, among my army, is the person who betrayed Lady Escamilla and all of us. The person who allowed fear to penetrate our ranks. We had men try and desert—officers, even. I haven't been as heavy-handed as on the march, but I fear another demonstration will be in order if my army is to survive. At least the Yetranian soldiers are in hand."

"Hmmmm." Unael grunted. "And I hear that Ultner's Fist will not be joining your march?"

The Silver Lady had come to Emma two nights previous. With a formality not usually associated with the blonde-haired warrior, Trina had rescinded on their contract, leaving a great amount of money in Emma's coffers. Emma had even bribed her to stay, willing to use some of Unael's loaned money—which he knew would never be paid back—but Trina had not budged. She'd simply smiled a sad smile and walked away. Ultner's Fist would be leaving them tomorrow when they left Farrow's Hold, heading north to Algania.

"No, they decided to part ways," said Emma.

"Probably a good decision on their part."

"Yes, probably."

The conversation again lapsed into silence, aside from the hacking cough of a soldier somewhere in the distance. The garden wasn't perfectly secluded, as echoes from around the gigantic Hold seemed to congregate here. Last night, Emma had heard an unnamed administrator practicing a speech and a loud couple copulating somewhere distant. The latter had brought her a smile, followed by the sobering realization that she hadn't slept with a man since Fenrir. There was a cute man—another guardsman in the Plateau—who had been flirting with her, but that had been just before she'd lost most of her hand. Afterward, he'd showed no interest in her.

Since then, the thought of love, physical or otherwise, had fallen to the wayside.

The same, as it turned out, could not be said of Unael.

"Emma," Unael said suddenly, grabbing her good hand, not ungently, and turning toward her. His hands were those of an old warrior—powerful, rough, and everlastingly dry. She turned toward him, simultaneously pulling away as if by accident. But he did not release his grip. "This is suicide. Disband your army. Send the men home in twos and threes, or we'll help relocate their families to Farrow's Hold. The gods know we have enough room in this city, though work may be hard to come by at first. You've lost half your mercenaries. Your faithless men desert you. Going

501

back to Ardia will condemn all of you to death." He held her gaze for a long moment, eyes intense with a strange fire. Emma averted her own.

"No. There is no going back. The Yetranian soldiers will return to Ardia regardless, led by Ignatius and the more fervent captains. It is their divine right, they believe, to retake the city. The worse the odds, the greater the glory to Yetra, or so says their damnable book. The men cannot return home, as my agents have said that there are great lists detailing the names and residences of every man who fought in my army. Families have gone missing, and any attempt to contact them would put wives and children in danger." At least, that was the story Emma had ordered circulated among the men, to prevent further desertion. The only path to their families would be over the bodies of the Rostanian Army. "And, this is what Escamilla wanted."

Disorder's warmth flared in her heart, amplifying her headache. Emma had her own reasons to desire a war, though her life would likely be forfeit. And, she knew that Disorder knew she was coming for him. Emma didn't care. Vengeance was a powerful motivator.

"Escamilla. You remind me so much of her, from when we were both young." He grasped her mangled hand with a speed she wouldn't have attributed to the large, older man. "Strong and unflappable, a cold fire burning behind your eyes. Escamilla had that, woe be to me. My life may have been different without her. I was just a young, trumped up lieutenant who managed to get promoted when half the regiment had dysentery. I'd no real military knowledge of any kind—most thick-hided farmers don't."

"How did you meet Escamilla?" Emma managed to extract her half-hand from his grip. She thought about pushing him back, crunching her way back to where Nail and Havert waited in the eaves, but felt a magnetic pressure to learn more about her lady.

"Escamilla came to me—a decade older, a mystery to the idiot boy I was at the time—to sell some rations. Hardtack and beans, surplus from one of her holdings in Draston. At the time, we were at the southern border, near Thaul; this was after they had sacked Kial." Thaul was a sprawling country with a hundred major cities, sharing a border with both Jecusta and Ardia. It had once been a Jecustan conquest, before the empire had collapsed, and Emma knew that they had often threatened to return the favor.

"I had no idea of the range of my authority, and she was surprisingly... understanding. Her visit was for more than to unload a few thousand pounds of shit food. Escamilla came from nothing, like me, and maybe wanted to help. She mentored me, a seventeen-stone plow horse of a soldier... on commanding some, on influencing others. We spent a lot of time together, then. Good time. If it weren't for Escamilla, I would never have achieved what I have achieved. A curse, most times, to be honest. But I wouldn't change it. When Escamilla passed..." Unael's face screwed up with an unrestrained, painful grief, which she realized he must have been holding back for weeks.

He stared at the snowy ground for a long moment, breathing heavily to regain his composure. He still held her hand, though loosely. Emma realized she could pull away now, but instead gave his soldier's hand a small squeeze.

"Emma, don't go. Stay here with me. We can figure this out." He reached a trembling hand toward her face, tucking her red curls back into her hood, brushing her cheek. There was a woman's shriek echoing in the distance. Maybe one of the lovers was getting a bit rough.

"Unael..."

"You and I, we are so alike. Both taught by Escamilla, both desiring freedom from our responsibilities, but resisting because the call of duty is too strong. Gods, Emma. Our obligations bind

503

us together, surely as they tear us apart! Let us find some way around this. Let me help you."

Unael leaned toward Emma, his mouth seeking hers. In that split second, Emma froze—anger battling fear, with resignation moderating the fight. How dare Unael assume that she was some dullard maiden, needing to be rescued? She had led armies, and bartered with some of the most powerful people in two countries. She had risen from being a maid to having thousands of lives in her hands, her decisions influencing whether they would live or die. And, they almost certainly would die. They would die.

As Unael's face approached hers, Emma shivered in a way not attributable to the cold. Maybe she truly did need rescuing.

Unael's lips, cracked and dry, brushed hers. Feeling no resistance, he pushed deeper. His whiskers scraped into the tender skin around Emma's mouth, and the pungent stench and taste of wine filled Emma's senses. Yet, she found that she still did not push away.

She had no attraction to Unael; he was old enough to be her father. But, it would be easy—so easy!—to stay at Farrow's Hold with this man. He was honorable, and he paid his debts. He was respected and wealthy, and would likely do the right thing when push came to shove, just as he'd proved with Pious and the Yetranians. Emma knew that he would eventually fight the growing power of Rostane, and she could help guide him. She could help preserve the lives of her men, assisting them in finding new lives in Jecusta.

While their families were left behind in Rostane, to an unknown fate. While the Rostanians consolidated their power and created more of those Feral—eventually enough to overwhelm any defenses that a divided Jecusta could put together. While Escamilla's murderer still lived.

"Lord Unael…" Emma murmured, pushing away from his grasping mouth with some effort. "Lord Unael, I cannot stay. That is, I must go. Ardia needs hope, and we will have to provide it. Even if the chances of success are slight. Though the hearts of each duchy has fallen, the limbs still resist. Florensians rally in southern Draston, and we have allies yet to be tapped." Emma swallowed a knot in her throat, taking another step back, watching as Unael's soft expression turned to stone. This had been a brief moment of vulnerability and emotion for the man, and judging from his frosty eyes, he regretted it.

Just then, a scream pierced the air, cutting through the moment like a dull axe.

It wasn't a lover's passionate cry. No, Emma has been near enough battles to know that sound—this had been a death cry. And a nearby one, at that.

Unael whipped around, his hand darting to his boot and extracting a knife in a smooth motion that belied his age and girth. A warrior, he was, above all else. Emma drew her own ever-present dagger, though what she would do with it was questionable at best. She looked around the winter garden, trying to discern something in the darkness. With the size of this place, the cry could have come from anywhere. Where were Nail and Havert? Where were the black cloaks?

The night was strangely silent, and Emma could hear little more than the creaking of Unael's boots as he pivoted, scanning the environs for a threat. The numerous towers of the Hold blotted out the starry sky, and the few gas lamps in the garden only seemed to intensify the darkness. There seemed to be something behind every shrub, behind every tree.

Emma felt that familiar warmth flair in her heart—Disorder's curse. Her fear amplified beyond anything she had ever known, her legs shook so much that she fell to her knees. The winter garden, the sole source of comfort for Emma during these past weeks, warped in her vision. The winterblooms became screaming devils; the frost weeds morphed into a thousand serpents. Pandemonium grew before her, tearing its way into her brain and rendering her body useless.

And, through it all, she could see a pair of dark spectacles approaching her. Disorder? Had he finally come to kill her, knowing that she disobeyed him, marching back into Ardia with an army at her back?

"What are you doing in my Hold, demon?" Unael shouted through clenched teeth, his voice quavering as if he fought to master his own terror. Emma managed to raise her head, to see the Lord of Farrow's Hold standing tall and holding his dagger in a warrior's stance. It gave her some small measure of courage, at least enough that Pandemonium subsided somewhat. The devils became terrible primates, and the serpents small if still venomous snakes.

"Your Hold? You have nothing. You are nothing," intoned a voice, it being the gravely sound of a woman who had taken in too much kerena. It was not Disorder, then. This woman was the same thing, though: a Pandemonium-ridden demon.

"Who are you?" Unael sounded strained, and a renewed wave of terror forced Emma down, like a physical force that shattered her will. Her heart, burning inside her, was a child's rattle, thrumming against her wheezing chest.

"Me? I am also nothing. But, if you must put a name to what you see before you, call me Dread." A more accurate name had never be given. Emma's previously burning, palpitating heart seemed to have stopped in a frosty terror.

Just then, a great explosion rattled the Hold as an emerald... power... streaked into the side of one of the visible towers. Emma could barely discern her immediate surroundings, so great was her

506

fear, but she knew that tower. Dignity, it was called simply, being the highest point in all of Farrow's Hold. She had also overheard it called Condescension by some black cloaks, and Immorality by a put-upon serving girl. It was the place where all gathered visiting nobles—including the magnates of all of Jecusta—spent their evenings. And, chunks of that tower were currently raining down all around the Hold. It still stood tall against the blast, though in Emma's twisted mind, it appeared to have been bitten by a demon the size of a mountain.

Unael whipped about, trying to keep his eyes on both Dread and his crumbling domain. The strange silence of earlier was replaced with screams and howls, tumbling masonry, and the clash of weapons as an unknown force assailed the Hold. Strangely, the sounds of battle brought Emma some measure of control, her Lady Emma Breen mask falling into place. Her barrier against fear, which she had been wearing for months now. She fought the force pushing her to the ground and rose slowly, inch by inch, until she was standing on weak legs behind Unael.

Dread looked at her through impermeable glasses, her impossibly pale, delicate features betraying a lineage that Emma had never seen. Not Rostanian, Jecustan, Rafonese, or so on. She smiled, small white teeth reflecting the scant light in the winter garden.

"Tsk, Tsk, Lady Breen. You were warned. That warning still burns inside you, does it not?" Dread pointed a finger at Emma's chest, and heat—a searing, terrible burn beyond anything she could ever have imagined, ran throughout her body. Every vein, every artery, was filled with lava, so much so that Emma only had one reality… pain. Her fingers and toes curled so that she could hear bones snapping. Her muscles in her stomach bunched so that she could feel them tearing. Her eyelids were squeezed shut so tightly that it was a wonder her eyes didn't burst.

Abruptly, she was freed of her agony, finding herself again on the cold ground, knees scraped from having fallen. Looking up, she saw Unael struggling with Dread. Rather, she witnessed Unael slowly being overpowered. Dread, her long, black cloak wafting about in the air, held a red, burning knife that she'd begun inching toward Unael's chest, despite his warrior's arms attempting to hold the weapon back. Not knowing what else to do, her own weapon lost during her convulsions, Emma grabbed a handful of snow with her good hand and launched the hard-packed ball into the side of Dread's face just as she began her final push for Unael's heart.

The throw did just enough to save Unael's life, as the blow intended for his heart instead pierced his shoulder with a hiss and the fierce scent of burning flesh. Unael reeled back, shrieking in agony and falling into the snake-laden ground as Dread turned her attention to Emma, who fought to keep her mask in place, knowing that certain death glared at her from behind opaque lenses.

"Disorder spoke of you, little girl. He said you were brave and canny. Manipulative. Dumber than your predecessor." Dread's words were stilted and choppy, though her diction was perfect.

Dread was not from Jecusta. Not from anywhere in Saiwen, as far as Emma knew.

"Are you… Recherche Oletta?" Emma had squeezed the words through clenched teeth. So close to this strange, terrible woman, the visions of Pandemonium were amplified. Great beasts filled the air in her vision, blotting out the moons and stars while small, sharp-toothed demons danced around Unael's writhing body. Dread seemed almost… mundane amidst all this.

"Ha!" Her barked laugh was like dragging a corpse over gravel. "You think you have an inkling of the powers that are at work here? You know so very little. All of you Ardians and Jecustans know so very little."

"Then educate me!" Emma spat.

"How droll." The flaming dagger seemed to leap back to life in her hand, its blaze renewed. "I could educate you with fire. I could melt your flesh, bit by bit, just enough that the agony would take weeks to end. Months, maybe. I could melt your eyes and burn your ears, leaving you blind and deaf, your only sensation being pain. I could create a symphony from your screams, so that the demons would dance and the beasts would rejoice." Dread took a graceful step toward Emma, and she stumbled backward into the snow—the snow that burned so much like the fire that Dread described.

"But, I don't have weeks or months. Events are rapidly coming to a head back in Ardia."

"Then why are you here?" Emma managed.

"To ensure no interference. You, little girl, were warned. Disorder is far too kind. Far too… given to erratic human tendencies. I am here to ensure that you cease this fight with your little army. That these magnates do not get it in their little heads to interfere." She gestured to Dignity, the tower crumbling and burning as blasts continued to detonate against the once grand structure. "Without leaders, as ineffectual as they are, this country will flounder. We will be back in force, once we gain what we need from Ardia. Besides, domination is less pleasing than chaos. And this…" Dread licked her lips, "is quite pleasant indeed."

Like Disorder, this Dread seemed unhinged, completely unbalanced. Emma recalled that Disorder had been taken by an irrational anger several times while they'd spoken, but he had, as Dread said, seemed to have some humanity. He'd even spoken of disliking killing in their short time together. With his powers, he probably could have fought through a couple dozen guards to kill

509

Escamilla, but had instead opted to subvert the guards through treachery. Perhaps to minimize casualties.

Dread, though, was alien. She was reveling in the destruction around her. Screams still rang out across Farrow's Hold, and battle against an unknown foe still raged. It was hard to distinguish reality from Dread's illusory aura of fear, too, but Emma thought she could make out some words in those shouts.

"My wife! She's burned! Someone help her!"

"Oshwon bastards!"

"My legs! Dear fucking Yetra, my legs!"

Dread abruptly glided forward, clutching Emma's skull with her two hands. Emma made as if to fight, but the strength was drained from her limbs. She could somehow see her reflection in the black spectacles, as well, though they were not reflective. She looked like… she looked like her mother, lying dead following her battle with the flux that had ravaged Little Town.

"Now, I may not have weeks, but I can spare minutes, hmm? What is it that drives you, little girl? What is it that you truly fear?" Dread again smiled. There was no malice in the expression—just a wet-lipped excitement.

***

Emma woke up as if from a nightmare, panting and covered in sweat. Her quarters at Brockmore did have the tendency to grow warm in the summer, and whatever terrible, Pandemonium-ridden dreams she had seemed minor. She ran her hands through her hair,

510

finding it pinned back, held tightly in place in case of a sudden need for her presence. And, a knock at the door showed that she'd had great foresight.

"My lady," called Nail before opening the door. He'd ever been one to worry over privacy, but his brother Hammer yanked him back in case she was indecent. But Emma found herself already dressed in a black and red dress, sleek and silky, emblazed with an apple on the chest. Her monogram.

"Yes?" she asked with bored amusement.

"We've caught the girl. We've caught the traitors. The council is awaiting your judgement."

Without knowing how then, Emma was in the Chamber of War, the stained glass shining brightly over the faces of the gathered traitors. It was... all of them.

Morgyn, murderer of Escamilla, huddled small and meek, looking like a scared girl. She was whimpering. "I had to. I had no choice. I had to protect him."

Feeling nothing at the sight, Emma walked forward, snatching an axe from Braston and gripping it in her hands. Both of her intact hands. Without pausing, she swung the axe overhead, cleaving the girl's skull in twain and leaving the axe buried there. No joy. No satisfaction.

No shame.

"You are a monster! You condemn men to death because of your pride!" shouted the former General Empton before Emma nodded to Hammer, allowing the big man to bash in the general's head with his namesake. The dead man slumped out of his wheeled chair.

Trina Almark glared at her, tears dripping down. "How are you not tired of war? Have you not allowed enough women to die in your name?" Emma yanked back her silver braid and drew a knife across her pearlescent neck.

Ferl simply smirked as Emma drove this same blade, awash in the Silver Lady's blood, into his eye. He was still smirking as he fell to the ground.

"Monster! Florens is gone because of you!" cried Eric Malless.

"Foul liar!" called Opine, looking like less of a hero all clothed in rags.

"Heretic!" shouted Ezram, making the sign of the Ascension.

"Follower of Pandemonium, be vanquished!" Ignatius wheezed around the iron bar driven through his cheeks.

One by one, Emma slew the traitors. Malless, she tossed from a window to emulate the fate of his father, Brockmore somehow occupying a cliff. Opine was hung upside down and bled out in the fate of peasant nobodies. Ezram, she burned alive, ensuring that his soul would never reach Harmony. Ignatius underwent the Yetranian Trials until dead.

Throughout it all, Emma felt nothing. Not anger. Not fear. Not guilt.

Throughout it all, Emma felt empty.

***

Dread's laughter was pure mirth as Emma reeled back.

"This is your greatest fear?"

Emma—having seen what she could become, the Lady Breen who could casually kill without a second thought, glance, or emotion—began to weep. Was that her future, built from constantly donning this mask? A cold -hearted, emotionless killer of men, willing to condemn others to death on a whim? Willing to wield the blade herself?

She could never become that. She never would become that… would she?

Dread continued her gleeful laugh, apparently soaking in Emma's tears as a sort of sustenance for her good humor. "You fear… emptiness? I have seen so much. Fear of death, of the self or loved ones. Fear of dismemberment—which you should have, but don't. Fear of failure. But you fear losing emotions? That is so… perfect."

Disorder flared inside her, and rage replaced her fear. How dare this monster mock her fears? How dare Dread make little of her plight? Emma glared at the pale women from under her red curls, catching a flicker of motion behind her. Again, finding herself without a weapon, she tossed a chunk of snow into the woman's grotesquely laughing face. Her black spectacles were knocked askew, and her burning dagger flickered to nothing.

"Hei wontu!" Dread howled in an unfamiliar language, scrambling to put the things back in place. So frantic was she that she didn't notice Nail limping up until the last moment. His hard-swung blade scraped across her arm, briefly, before she vanished into a black mist, re-forming fifteen feet back. Nail stood in front of Emma protectively, his armor dented and blood running down the back of his head from an unknown wound. Havert and several black cloaks were close to follow.

"You… hurt me! You made me bleed!" Dread was appalled, gripping her arm. If Emma hadn't known better, she'd have said that the woman's mouth curled in terror, and that tears were running down her cheeks.

"We will do more than hurt you, Dread. We will kill you if you do not leave this place." Iolen, haggard and grim, entered the garden unattended. His voice had none of its characteristic sarcasm. Rather, it held an exhausted but potent power. He grabbed two of the black cloaks by their necks and began to gather his magic. The men paled at his touch, but did not struggle.

Dread considered the Savant through her glasses. Considered the bared steel wielded by exhausted soldiers. Considered Unael, motionless in the snow. And, finally, she considered the blood dripping from her arm, her face twisting in a brief grimace.

"Today is your lucky day, but the head has been cut off the snake," Dread rasped, gesturing toward Dignity.

The tower was smoldering and crumbling in a dozen places, looking for all the world like a termite-ridden tree on the verge of collapse. As Emma watched, she could see a figure illuminated by the green flame, dangling from a window ledge in a vain attempt to flee the flames. Inevitably, he fell without a sound.

"You will find, Dread, that a snake can have many heads," Emma said, stepping forward and hoping that her words rang less hollow to others than they did in her own mind.

"A snake that fears biting others is a snake that ultimately consumes itself. And you, little girl, will be consumed." Dread spun about and leapt—in a single, sleek bound—to the wall surrounding the winter garden. She disappeared into a shadowy mist, blending into the night before disappearing entirely from sight.

The nightmare had left, but, looking around, Emma knew that the bad dream was just beginning.

Chapter 37

After they'd battled their way through dozens of warriors, there were none left to obstruct the Offeirs or budredda on their exhausted march to Enorry Falls.

Limner was honeycombed with tunnels connecting the great chambers that made up the below-ground portions of Hackeneth. However, few of these tunnels—those that could easily fit a man, anyway—found their way to the surface.

Hafgan knew why Rian had chosen this particular route for their escape. It would easily limit their pursuit. The exit spat out some couple thousand feet above sea level, emerging from just behind the gushing waters of the falls and wrapping around the mountain. A half a dozen paths split off at a wide clearing cut away from the rock, and those each branched into a dozen more. It would be easy to leave a few false trails and lose themselves in the mountains while evading any real pursuit.

That is, it would have been easy, had not fifty or more warriors blocked their path. Wiscon leaned on his massive axe with a grin, and Rinx, bearing most of his weight on a spear, stood just behind him. Pacing back and forth with a nervous energy, an animal sensing a coming storm, was Hafgan's brother, Yurin. His bastard sword—the weapon that Hafgan had given him after he'd been expelled from the Haearn Doethas—gleamed in the sun and was sheathed in the snow. Standing true and tall.

"Your escape ends here, Iwan," Rinx intoned. He was already engaged in his hedwicchen, probably to dampen the pain of his pierced thigh. It obviously hadn't healed fully since the Cylch. A wound like that might never heal.

"Put your weapons down, and we'll return you to your Pwoll without injury. We will imprison the rest; Leyr would not want the blood of any more Wasmer to sink into this soil. There are few

516

enough of us as it is." Wiscon's face was grim and his voice regretful. He hefted his axe over his shoulder, smart enough to know the inevitable answer.

"Brother, listen. Brother, brother, listen to them," Yurin crooned almost plaintively. He wouldn't look at Hafgan, or any of them.

"You are all pathetic excuses for Carreg Da. All of you!" Rian proclaimed, pushing through their exhausted warriors and waving a bloodied mace at the gathered men. "You subjugate and crush the will of our proud people. You follow a manipulator and a false god, and murder your own kind in both of their foul names."

"You have seen his power, and yet you still doubt the Flawless God?" Wiscon asked, furrowing his brow.

"Such power," said Yurin quietly. "No one can fight such power."

"There are a thousand ways to trick people into believing something. The mountains are not without magic, nor without people who have this skill, rare though it may be," Rian said, all denial.

"If that is what you must believe," Wiscon said, his voice low.

"We all believe what we must," Hafgan answered quietly.

Just as he believed that they were fated to die on this mountain. Better, though, than to die in the Pwoll.

***

517

Though exhausted, the budredda held.

In a tight defensive formation, spears sticking out in every direction, they resisted the onslaught for some time. They were bound to fall, but determined to stand.

Enric's unusually orange-haired face was concentration incarnate, as close to attaining his hedwicchen as he, or any of the budredda, had been. Somehow, he had mastered his anger while in captivity, and now fought with the cold calculation of a trained killer. His precise and effortless jabs wounded and surprised his enemies. Paston, always near his brother-in-arms, shouted instructions and encouragement, though he was prevented from any real fighting because of his arrow wound.

Alwyn, newly anointed as a budredda when they'd filed down his second set of canines, was more tentative. He was frightened, and fought as if his death was inevitable—not with a fierce desperation, but with submission. Hafgan struggled to protect their newest member, but he was too set-upon by these veteran Carreg Da warriors, and his strength was ever waning. Whatever anger had pulled him through the earlier confrontation no longer sustained him.

He could only watch as Alwyn fell, first pierced in the leg, and then decapitated as Wiscon waded into the fray, his enormous axe posing a danger to both friend and foe. At least, it would have, had he not been in his hedwicchen.

"Iwan! It is time!" he shouted, his voice booming and echoing the roar of Enorry Falls in the dwindling light of day. Another casual swipe of his axe cut the hand off a misbegotten budredda, Samuel, who'd been named after the former Duke of Rostane. He fell to the ground, grasping his bleeding stump.

It was indeed time, thought Hafgan. Wiscon roared a command and his men scattered to either side. Hafgan, more delicately, did the same. It was to be one-on-one combat, Haearn Doethas on

Haearn Doethas. One was healthy and whole while the other was weakened, battered, and could not find his center.

But, even exhausted beyond belief, even with his mind clouded from his imprisonment, even without hope for survival, it was not in Hafgan to submit. His fate would not be Alwyn's.

He twirled his silver spear easily in his hands, demonstrating speed beyond what any on this battlefield could muster, aside from Wiscon, Rinx, and maybe Yurin. The weapon still seemed to be a perfect fit for him, and was balanced better than any spear he had ever fought with. It likely wouldn't be enough, but it felt damned good.

Even outside his hedwicchen, Hafgan funneled his attention to his opponent. Wiscon had that look of extreme concentration which gave away the fact that he had attained perfect, empty concentration. Physically, he was intimidating. Several inches taller than Hafgan, the largest Wasmer Hafgan had ever seen, he boasted muscles that stood taut against his tight-fitting war robes. His axe was so large that most warriors couldn't lift the thing above their heads, whereas Wiscon wielded it with ease. He held extra weight around his midsection, betraying his love of the rich imported foods from Ardia, but it did little to slow him.

Having full access to his emotions, Hafgan could not help but be intimidated. Fearful, even. He was the superior warrior, but only in his hedwicchen. Only when his arms weren't already shaking from exertion.

Wiscon sensed his weakness and sought to end the battle quickly with a cross-swipe of his axe. Parrying was not an option, no matter his strength, so Hafgan crouched down and jabbed forward at his leg. Wiscon, of course, anticipated the move and hopped backwards, swiping downward as he did. Hafgan had to roll to avoid being cut, and he stumbled to his feet. The blood soaking his upper arm said that he hadn't managed to completely avoid the blow, after all.

"Iwan, give in now and there will be no more bloodshed this day. I promise this to you in the name of the Flawless God," Wiscon said quietly, his voice betraying that he'd briefly left his hedwicchen.

"A false promise from a false god," shouted Rian from over his shoulder. After only a single pass between the leaders, the fighting had diminished to being half-hearted, as men on both sides needed to see the outcome.

"I do not make false promises," Wiscon answered with a frown.

Hafgan remembered the Wiscon of old. He'd been a prankster, always finding ways to trick the Haern Doethas trainees, and always finding a way to laugh, even when their bodies were being pushed beyond their limits. Once, he had sawed most of the way through Leyr's bedframe so that the thing collapsed partway through the night. Another time, he had tied strings to a few rocks in their quarters, periodically jerking on one string or the other to make a rock jump. He'd been careful to do it only when Yurin was looking, and soon the other young men had thought him even madder than usual.

This somber, wild-bearded Wiscon was a different man. He no longer held any of that joviality. Another symptom of the infection that Leyr had spread.

"There will be blood, my former brother," said Hafgan, echoing Rian. "Either now or later, the people will strain against the shackles of your god. The Offeirs already rebel. How long will it be until the people—the few remaining Wasmer—realize how subjugated they have become? Leyr rules through his silver tongue and the fear of your Flawless God, but the people are not as stupid as he thinks. They remember their faith." However misplaced. "They remember their past." However fabricated. "And they remember those who have fallen."

He assumed a fighting posture. A lazy stance, much like Yurin would take in his random, unpredictable fighting style, with the tip of his spear resting in the light snow. With his training, in his hedwicchen, Wiscon would have a ready defense for any conventional style. Perhaps unconventional would win the day.

Both sides gave up the pretext of battle and lowered their weapons to watch.

"Let us stand here as an example, lending courage to our people below. Even if we fall…." Outnumbered more than two to one, it seemed plausible. "Let our blood flow red down this mountain and our death cries echo through Hackeneth. Through Loch Creed and Sebiant Rhisfel. Through Limner and the falls."

"No one will see your blood. No one will hear your voices," spat Rinx, limping forward from the battle lines.

Hafgan leveled him a glare. "You will have."

With that, Hafgan staggered toward Wiscon, leaning in and then away, moving like a drunken Rostanian down in the warehouse district past full moons. Wiscon again attained his hedwicchen and struck out with a foot. Hafgan darted away, continuing to drag his spear in the light snow. He appeared to be observing the sky, oblivious to the focused warrior in front of him. Until Wiscon struck out with his axe.

Hafgan dropped his spear in the snow and jumped in close— something that was so counterintuitive that Wiscon had not even anticipated the possibility of it. He landed two quick blows, one useless thump against Wiscon's ample gut and one crunching against his nose. Wiscon reeled back as blood spat out. Hafgan dove back to grab his spear, and then stood tall and lazily, doing his best impression of his brother, though Yurin was nowhere to be seen among the warriors.

"Tricks," snorted Wiscon, spitting blood into the snow. "You forget, Hafgan. The hedwicchen learns."

"Then I will need more tricks," said Hafgan, though no more tricks came to mind.

The two warriors circled each other, making several more passes, both wary of the other. Though weak, Hafgan was at home in battle and somehow forgot his weariness. Wiscon, after that first drawing of blood, moved more cautiously. Even detached, he likely remembered that he had never bested Hafgan in sparring.

Wiscon did not tire, and nor did he grow impatient and make mistakes. Hafgan could not land another blow, and the cut on his arm began to ache. His bigger opponent was testing him now, becoming increasingly daring as he realized that Hafgan did not have any more antics. After a particularly brutal pass, where Hafgan stumbled backwards with another small cut on the same arm, he caught a glimmer of surprising movement off to the side.

He had stumbled next to Rinx. The man had always been as vindictive as a cuckold, and with a hole in his thigh, there was little more that Rinx would want to do than stick a spear in Hafgan's belly and jerk it around in his guts. Which was why Hafgan found himself barely deflecting a blow with his spear, taking yet another deep cut on his shoulder as he stumbled to the side. Deflecting a second jab, Hafgan slipped in the mucky snow, falling to one knee.

"Rinx! Cease this!" Wiscon called from Hafgan's left. Rinx's eyes were wild. He was outside of his hedwicchen and lost in a fierce rage, heedless of his weak leg. His was a rage beyond anything that a Haearn Doethas should have been able to experience. He stabbed at Hafgan, brutal and efficient, and the Wasmer could barely fend off the attacks. A few tiny wounds appeared across Hafgan's body—just barely piercing his war robes, but enough to cause bloodloss. He would need to end this, and soon, and then again contend with Wiscon.

He whipped his spear around at Rinx's head, sacrificing a waning defense for a bold offense. But, the blade did not strike because Rinx was no longer there.

"Ya fucker!" shouted a deep voice, its Rostanian accent discordant amidst the mountains.

Rinx was lying in the red mush of the snow, Captain Jalen Yanso's sword having cleaved through his collarbone and nearly severed his arm from his body. The Haearn Doethas howled like a madman. With his good arm, he reached for Hafgan. Yanso drove his sword directly into the man's back with a two-handed thrust, sticking it into Rinx's heart.

Hafgan looked at the human, half stunned and half amazed. He made to say something, but lacked the time before a gang of Carreg Da Wasmer threw themselves at Yanso and bore him to the ground. Paston and two budredda jabbed at the pile, and the battle was rejoined in earnest.

Hafgan barely had time to turn before Wiscon's axe whistled toward him.

"Why…" Another slash that Hafgan sidestepped. "Did…" This one came much closer, but Hafgan stumbled out of the way. "You…" A great overhead blow nearly split Hafgan's skull. "Return!" Hafgan had no choice but to parry the last attack, barely deflecting it, but in a motion that tore his spear from his hands and sent it flying into the churning snow.

Wiscon was breathing heavily now, like a horse past his limit, practically frothing at the mouth. His eyes were as mad as Rinx's had been moments before, as mad as the eyes of all of those affected by the Red Eye that day in the Cylch. The work of the Flawless God.

Hafgan would die, now, at the hands of this madman, ignobly slain without a weapon in his hand, without having put up a real defense. But, again, better than in the bottom of a pit. He spread his arms, accepting of his fate. Rian's screaming in the background tore at his heart, but he would not cower before his fate, nor run.

Wiscon brought his axe back, preparing a cross-body slash that would have the force to cut Hafgan in half. Hafgan closed his eyes and breathed deeply.

"Brother!" croaked a voice, its rough sound cutting through the din of combat.

Hafgan opened his eyes and stumbled back a step. The tip of Yurin's great sword, a gift from his brother, had been struck through Wiscon's back and sat protruding from his ample stomach. Yurin yanked the weapon to the side, gutting the Haearn Doethas and spilling his innards into the snow before he fell.

"Brother…" said Hafgan, barely comprehending what had just happened, so accepting he'd been of his death. Yurin hunched over, his sword dripping red into the crimson muck surrounding them. It was as if the sky was pushing down on him, and he refused to meet the stunned and questioning gaze of his brother.

The Carreg Da warriors fell back, having seen both of their Flawless God-touched leaders struck down, the first by a human and the second by one of their own. Some warleader was roaring commands, trying to regain control, while another was screaming contradictory orders

"Lieutenant, here!" Enric, limping heavily on one leg, handed him his silver spear. It felt odd in his hands, warmer than it should have been after lying in the snow.

"You bleeding fool," said Rian, who followed behind. "You've got a deathwish or something, Hafgan?"

"I think we all have a deathwish, my eternal love," Hafgan said, caring little that her eyebrows had risen alarmingly at his proclamation. He remained focused on his brother, who was inching toward them, shoulders hunched as if he would be beaten. A dog, but one with divided loyalties. Yurin stopped a few feet away, not saying a word. His white robes were anything but, smeared with the blood of Offeirs, budredda, and Haearn Doethas alike.

Hafgan's eyes roamed the battlefield, taking in the gathering Carreg Da warriors, half a dozen paths leading down the mountain, his own depleted and exhausted men, and the plunging Enorry Falls behind him. He felt the pain of his numerous wounds and the weakness in his limbs. With a deep breath, he closed his eyes.

"Paston, listen to me. You are to take the men and guide the remaining Offeirs off this mountain. Form the wedge, cut through them, and follow the southern path, and then head west. I will create a distraction."

Across the field, the dominant warleaders argued as their men stood in disarray. The larger one, a brute of a man with a dozen braids in his beard, pointed furiously—directly at Hafgan.

Paston surged forward, brow furrowed in determination. "No, Lieutenant. We not be leaving you, not again."

"You will not be leaving me," Hafgan corrected him. "Rather, you will be leaving me, but don't expect that I am throwing my life away. I have a plan." A weak and desperate plan, but a plan. "Remember, form the wedge, holding wounded in the center, and slice through them. I will find you after."

With that, he strode forward without glancing at his former to-be bound, his brother, or his faithful following, gripping his silver spear and plucking another one from the body of a fallen warrior. Halfway across the battlefield, the Carreg Da began to notice and shout, with the larger warleader shoving the smaller aside and shouldering his own weapon. Hafgan, without pausing, dropped his silver spear and, taking a short run, hurled his looted weapon at the larger warleader.

The man was too fast, but Hafgan's weapon struck the thigh of a warrior behind him, setting him to howling and rolling in the snow. Without waiting to see the reaction, Hafgan bolted to his right, making a straight path for the mountain walls.

A lifetime ago, Yurin and Hafgan had tried to climb to the top of the falls before enough missteps and near misses had set them back to the bottom, both exhausted and exhilarated. Now, Hafgan placed his hand on the first handhold, finding it easier to grip than he'd remembered. He pulled himself up, but his bloodied and muddied boots slipped almost immediately, his strength finally giving out.

A strong hand pushed him up from behind, and a slender hand grabbed his elbow.

"You're not bleeding leaving me again, dimwit," said Rian, scampering up a few feet and considering Hafgan with her gleaming eyes.

Yurin still wouldn't look at his kin, but his voice held a smile.

"Shall we try for the top one last time, brother?"

Chapter 38

"We need to hurry," Iolen puffed, barely following his own advice. The pasnes alna or Savant or Ardian traitor or Ardian spy—whoever he was—was apparently exhausted. And up to his elbows in blood.

Emma, just behind him, found that she was even more drained, though she had done little more than be threatened and attacked.

And murder everyone she knew in cold, icy blood.

That had only been a vision, of course, but it had felt so real. So very, very real. She could hear the accusations ringing through her ears. She could feel the weight of the axe as it met the paltry resistance of Morgyn's skull. The warmth of the blood as it splattered on her face and exposed arms. And, through it all, she'd felt nothing.

And now she was running through Farrow's Keep, toward the source of the attack on Dignity. Toward whatever had destroyed the tower with great bursts of emerald power.

The black cloaks were continuing to battle the attackers. Emma hadn't gotten a good look at them yet, as her little entourage had managed to circumvent any major engagements, so she still wasn't sure just who was staging this attack. Someone related to Recherche Oletta, certainly, or whoever worked with Dread. Someone who wanted Jecusta so distracted that they wouldn't interfere with the hostile takeover of Ardia.

Ardia was such a small country compared to most of Saiwen, still somewhat on the frontier. It was rich in minerals, had fertile farmland, and boasted a relatively gentle climate. But it was nothing that seemed worth all this trouble. Nothing that would merit an attack from… wherever Dread had come from. From wherever Disorder had come from.

Iolen stumbled upon rounding the next corner in the labyrinthine maze that was Farrow's Hold. Emma managed to grab his arm and keep him from tumbling to the hard stone floor. Though, she hurriedly separated contact with him when she remembered what he was capable of.

"Iolen, you need to rest. It will do us no good if we arrive and you are too spent to do anything but die," Emma said. Nail limped to her side, followed by Havert and a collection of black cloaks who they had gathered along the way. The black cloaks who Iolen had drawn from had remained behind with an unconscious—but still breathing—Lord Unael.

With a cough and a sigh, the Savant relented and leaned against the wall. The clamor of battle seemed lesser here, and there was almost a serenity in the air. Emma had once heard, from a visiting merchant-king, that every great storm had an eye, a spot in the center that was completely safe at least for a short period of time. It was, in fact, the worst place to be. It lulled sailors into a false sense of security, so that they'd lower their guard and assume the storm was over. Too often, men were killed when that eye closed.

"My lady, you should get to safety. You shouldn't be following this… madman," Nail said, his face sad and serious, all good humor killed at the moment when his brother had been disemboweled. "We can go into the tunnels and wait this out."

"The tunnels aren't safe. Nowhere, right now, is safe. Dread may have left, but her minions will fight to the end. And that end will be bloody," said Iolen, closing his eyes in apparent exhaustion.

Nail was right, though. She should leave Iolen to fight this battle. What could she, and a brace of tired soldiers, do to fight these powerful assailants? But, she was compelled to follow, as much by a sick curiosity as a sense of duty.

"Who are her minions? Who is Dread? Who in the fuck are you? What in the name of Ultner's twisted cock is happening in this place?" Emma swore. To Pandemonium with decorum. She'd lived through her literal fears tonight—in comparison, very little seemed to matter.

Iolen smiled a tired smile. "That is a deep question. A very deep question, indeed. The minions part is easy to answer. There are three pieces. The first is the Oshwon, enslaved and mistreated by the Jecustans. They are the primary tool in this endeavor. Most are metsikas—wild mages. You might have noticed their tattoos. Snakes, birds, vines, trees. Leeches and greenies, many of them, with their affinities hidden in plain sight."

"So, that green fire? Dignity? That was the Oshwon?" Havert asked, the usually stoic Sestrian guard seeming shaken to his core. Emma couldn't blame him.

"A suit of armor with half a brain. How refreshing," said Iolen, with a hint of his usual sarcasm.

"Watch yourself, mage. You have no one to suck dry within reach." Nail stepped forward, one hand on the hilt of his sword.

"You'll find that I am never quite defenseless, limper," Iolen said drily. "Now, where was I? The Oshwon, yes. Obviously, they seek to throw off the yoke of their bondage. And, they have the power—if not the numbers—to do some real damage. Dread harnessed this, as well as their common ancestry, to launch a coordinated attack."

"Common ancestry?" Emma echoed. She thought of Dread. Her accent was odd. Her features delicate. Her skin so pale as to have never been touched by the sun.

"Distant. Thousands of years, dating from around the Ascension." He spoke of the religious and heavenly rise matter-of-factly, she noticed, as if it had actually happened. "The Menogans, from the other side of the Great Barrier, fought against

529

the forces of Yetra. Most of the Menogans—most of everyone really—were decimated in the great battle that ended the war. Some Menogans—mages, all—managed to survive, fleeing and hiding to avoid persecution from Yetra's few remaining followers following the war." Iolen rubbed at his temples as if trying to relieve a headache. It was a familiar motion for Emma.

"And they became Oshwon," murmured Emma, staring to connect the story in her mind. So, the ancestors of the Oshwon were Menogan mages. But... "Why did they flee? Certainly they could have turned the tide of the battle. I've seen what magic can do to an army." Iolen nodded at her question.

"The Menoga were the most gifted of peoples, the ability to tap into miernes being widespread among them. But, rather than live in fear of their mages, as you Ardians do, they controlled them. Their mages were both enslaved and revered. Shackled and pampered. When their slavers were killed, the mages fled, cut off from their powers but also finally emancipated. The value of that freedom lives on with their ancestors."

"The path of freedom." Emma recalled Iolen speaking of this very thing, during Escamilla's funeral. About how the Oshwon worshiped the very concept of independence. Had Iolen known that they would rise up like this?

"The path of freedom," he agreed. "It would be easy for Dread to remind them of their past enslavement, these long-ago freed Menogans. It would be easy for her to focus their energies against those who subjugate them. The Oshwon would have little issue getting into position for such a coup; they move practically unseen, little more than spineless, broken servants. With a distraction—support from traitors among the black cloaks, and among your own men—it would be enough for the Oshwon to destroy Dignity."

530

"My… my own men?" Emma gasped. She shouldn't have been surprised, truly. But part of her still held out hope that maybe the mix-up with the guard at Escamilla's door had truly just been a clerical error that no one could trace. And even if there was a traitor, it certainly must be just one twisted soul. But a whole group, enough to disrupt the hundreds of black cloaks on active duty in the Hold at any given time? How could such malignance have spread among her soldiers?

"Don't be so surprised. Certainly a serving girl—as you once were—should know that a bit of mold, when left untreated, tends to spread."

Emma ignored the barb about her past.

"Who was the leader?" Nail demanded. "I'll tear out his throat with my bare hands," he sputtered in a sudden fury. He, like Emma, was probably thinking of that night where Disorder had entered Escamilla's room unopposed and killed their liege lady and Nail's brother, Hammer.

"Why would I know that, limper? You think I am omniscient and omnipotent?" Iolen smirked, pushing himself from the wall and staggering forward.

"Besides, if you just follow me, we'll know soon enough."

***

Lucind's Square, the courtyard outside of Dignity, was a scene from Pandemonium—so much so that Emma feared Dread had returned.

531

She had been to this place several times; it was a great square four hundred paces wide and long in the center of the Hold, carefully landscaped with uniform evergreens lining cobbled paths. Fountains spouted up at periodic intervals, glistening with sparkling water and heated so that they ran even in the bitter chill of winter. Dignity rose far above, a great red tower overlooking the green like a benevolent father. Noble children could always be found here, playing children's games and vexing the black cloaks who were tasked with keeping Dignity safe.

Now, the trees were a slimy gray, though they were hard to make out amidst the ashy mist that choked the air. The ashen trees looked like nothing more than great claws reaching up from the ground, seeking to pull her and her small entourage under. Dignity was only visible as smoldering emerald flashes in the sky as the fires continued to burn. Worse were the shapeless lumps, great heaps of burnt-out black cloaks who had fallen in this one-sided battle.

And the Oshwon were quick to turn their magicks from the tower to their oppressors.

Of the Oshwon, Emma could see no sign. But the mist obscured everything, filling her mouth and nostrils with the stifling taste of death. She wanted to flee back into the Hold, escaping the ash and discordant echoes of a dying battle. Iolen, though, continued forward with confidence, moving toward the waning echoes of battle. He paused only briefly, staring at a haphazard scattering of corpses. These men had fallen to swords and spears rather than green flame. Black cloak had battled black cloak here, traitors battling the loyal. Brothers battling brothers. Emma's stomach heaved at the thought. Iolen pointed to one of the bodies, a man not quite dead.

"Bring him," he commanded imperiously to Havert and Nail. The black cloak groaned, as if understanding his fate. Havert, features twisted in revulsion, looked to Emma.

"Do as he says," Emma said, through dry lips. Iolen would need the injured man's lifeforce for this. She wondered briefly whether this black cloak was a traitor or a loyalist. But, it really didn't matter, given the necessity.

Havert stripped the man of his heavy breastplate amidst groans and weak protestations, and began to drag him along.

The sound of battle grew closer and black cloaks became visible around them, dark shapes swinging weapons at shadows. No green fire lit the air any longer, and Emma couldn't see any of the pale-skinned destroyers. Perhaps the Oshwon were spent, or lacked the resources to continue their battle. She couldn't make heads nor tails of this fight; for all she knew, every man here was on the same side.

But, through the gloom and amidst the earliest rays of daybreak, there was an occasional splash of color. It was almost a trick of the eye, so much did the brain strain to make sense of what was happening. But, focusing, Emma knew it was not her imagination. Here and there, there were men wearing dusty, golden tabards emblazoned with a river otter. A clever, playful river otter, indigenous to the Ingwine River—one of the central platforms for trade in Ardia, and the natural barrier for a major city sitting atop an island. Florens.

That was it, then. Eric Malless, son of the late Henrik Malless, was the traitor. He had betrayed them all.

Emma clutched the claw of her hand so tightly that the muscles might tear. The pain was the only thing that kept her from screaming.

"My lady, down!"

She was suddenly hitting the ashy ground, a heavy, armored body on top of hers. Her face rested in the grainy black dust, but she could see the ground illuminated with emerald, and could feel the blistering heat as a blast of energy tore through the air just above them.

"Amateurs," muttered Iolen, a smirk evident in his voice. Twisting, Emma saw the Savant grasp the wounded man's neck, supported as he was by Havert, and point his finger in the direction of the blast. A single orange ray of light darted from his fingers for a split second, so bright it left Emma blinking away the after-image. A shriek tore through Lucind's Square, rising above the din of battle like a specter. It lasted for the length of time it would have taken for a man to expend the breath in his lungs.

Nail helped Emma to her feet, his face a mask of disapproval. She should leave. She needed to leave. But, even more, she needed to be here. She needed to confront Malless.

Iolen's beam of light had dissipated much of the fog in the immediate area, and Emma got a better look at the square. Maybe a hundred black cloaks—presumably the loyalists—were clustered together near the west end, forming a defensive box that glittered with tired spears. Here and there, individual battles were still being fought, black cloak against black cloak, or Florensian on black cloak. Both sides seemed exhausted as they stumbled around the red rubble of Dignity and swung at each other with wooden arms. Hundreds of bodies were scattered along the square, too, and the traitors seemed to have almost triple the number of men still standing, including the Oshwon.

Fifteen or so pale tribal mages were scattered throughout the courtyard, as well, each guarded by a handful of Florensians. Most had fallen to their knees, exhausted beyond any ability to support their own bodies. Some had fallen completely, unconscious or even dead. Near one of the fallen, Emma could see the bodies of the two pasnes alna who had been tasked with guarding Iolen. Only one or two of the tribal mages still stood, and they did so on shaking, uncertain legs. Emma had expected to see fierce, proud warriors wielding the powers of Pandemonium.

Instead, these men, these subjugated people who worshipped the path of freedom, of anarchy, were exhausted shells. They were almost… pitiable.

Iolen fired another blast of orange light through the heart of one as Emma watched, and the man fell bonelessly to the ground. And then another. And a third. Iolen was surgically removing the biggest threats from the battlefield, and doing so with little apparent effort. One Oshwon, leaning against a tree that still held some green, sent a wan green ball of power at Iolen. The Savant simply laughed as he deflected it with some sort of shield that Emma couldn't see. The wounded soldier was transfixed by Iolen's iron grip, fueling the man's magic and dying in the process.

A group of black cloaks rushed at Iolen from one side while several Florensians came in from the other, with Emma, Nail, and Havert directly in their path. She drew her knife with trembling fingers as her Rotten Apple knights closed in front of her. The first traitor thrust a bloody spear at Nail's chest. Pivoting on his good leg, Nail narrowly avoided the jab while slashing downward at his assailant's arms. The man's wrists were nearly severed as he fell to the ground howling.

Havert rushed at two other traitors, swinging his short sword at the man on the right while simultaneously blocking an attack from the left, knocking away the weapon with his buckler. He continued to bash away at one attacker, his usual precision-level skill trumped by either rage or fear. But, the traitor was skilled, and Havert could not break his guard.

The second assailant circled around the stocky Sestrian, raising his sword above his shoulder and waiting for a clear opening for a decapitating blow. His back was facing Emma; he had discounted her as a threat.

Emma clenched her knife. Another Rotten Apple Knight would not die for her, not this night! She launched herself forward on wobbly, weary legs, stabbing her knife at the Florensian's unprotected neck. It was almost too easy, how the blade penetrated his flesh, cutting skin and severing artery. The man tumbled forward, twisting around, with Emma landing on top of him, bruising her knees against the scorched ground.

She drew back her knife as the man still reflexively struggled, though he was covered in his life's blood. Emma met his eyes for a moment. She knew this man. This boy, rather. Dying beneath her was Jeffers Reband, the same Florensian who had rushed ahead of his fallen party to deliver the news of Rostane's invasion of Florens. The same boy whose father had fallen trying to carry that message, leaving his son to continue the fight alone. The same boy who had marched under her banner for months, fighting alongside Eric Malless and the rest of the Florensians.

"Why, boy? Why would you betray us?" Emma demanded in a fury, drawing close to his bloodied face with tears squeezing unbidden from her eyes. Jeffers merely gargled and reflexively coughed blood onto her cheeks before finally ceasing his twitching struggles.

Her heart grew hot, more so than ever before. Rage overtook her—an unquenchable fury over which she had no control. Emma grasped his bloodied head, gripping his hair and ears. She slammed his head into the frozen ground once. Twice. Three times. Feeling his skull crack beneath her sudden surge of strength. Slowly, only then did she rise and survey the battlefield. Oshwon continued to fall to Iolen's bolts of power. Black cloaks continued to fight one another. Women warriors, armored in silver, had joined the fray, taking on all comers. And Eric Malless stood amidst a group of soldiers shouting commands and pointing in all directions. His young, tired face seemed closer than it should have been. She could almost smell the grease of his hair, and taste the bitterness of liquor on his breath.

Emma tossed aside her slick, crimson dagger and scooped up Jeffers' fallen sword. The thing should have been too heavy for her, but she couldn't even feel its weight. She strode toward the traitorous duke, ignoring everything around her. Ignoring bolts of power that barely missed her, and spent arrows that landed nearby. Soldiers stumbling around her. It was like wading through a dream; everything was moving so slowly, as if underwater, while she strode at a normal speed.

Malless glanced up, noticing a woman dressed in a filthy dress moving inexorably toward him. His face was drawn and tired, his eyes black from lack of sleep or from living in a constant state of hangover for the past months. He seemed scared but determined, a decisiveness behind his eyes and actions that she had not seen in the young man since before they'd fled Florens.

"Lady Breen!" he shouted, his voice ranging out clearly across the carnage. "I won't kill you unless I must."

Emma said nothing, but continued toward him.

"Emma, I warn you. I do this for Florens, and you will not get in my way." Emma gripped Jeffers' sword and bared her teeth. Malless took a reflexive step back. "Very well. Paul, Brian, make it quick!"

Two Florensians, both as dark-haired as their duke but nearly twice the size, moved gracefully toward Emma, both of them with the easy confidence of seasoned swordsmen. To Emma, though, they appeared to be moving in air as thick as tar. Even their expressions—somewhat alarmed, if she were to guess—were nearly frozen. Their faces, young and determined, fanned the flames of her rage.

She closed the distance between herself and the swordsmen, picking the one on the left as her target. Fueled by a fury that she

537

could not explain, let alone control, she lunged forward with a sword that was too heavy and an arm that was too weak. And yet, the blade did not shake in her hand, and it entered into the man's chest straight through his breastplate. She withdrew the blade, and he fell to the ground as gently as a bubble blown by a child.

She whirled around and saw the second man readying a swing, his sword poised to strike her across the shoulders. She crouched easily, glancing up as the sword slowly cut the air above her. Emma scuttled to one side. Jabbing upwards, she took the man unaware beneath his chin, her blade penetrating his skull.

Emma felt herself grinning as his blood rained down on her face.

She twisted to her feet, staring at Erik Malless. He stood, stunned and rooted to the ground, simply staring at the remains of his best warriors. His wet, terror-filled eyes met Emma's and she grinned wider, taking a step in his direction and resting the slick, crimson sword on her shoulder. She barked a wild laugh that sounded sweet to her own ears.

And, abruptly, something heavy slammed into her, carrying her to the ground. Her head jolted against the frozen, ashy lawn and stars burst in her vision. The weight on top of her was greater than just the body of the man who'd carried her to the ground, though. It threated to crush her as her rage left and she realized what she had just done.

The burning in her heart, Disorder's gift and curse, subsided.

Nail looked down at her as Trina Almark, Havert, and three female warriors beat Malless to the ground with clubs and the flats of their swords. The lithe Rotten Apple knight wrapped his arms around her, both restraining her and providing a sort of comfort that she had not felt since Escamilla had passed. She freed her arms and squeezed the footless warrior right back.

538

And then Emma began to sob, her tears cutting canyons through the drying blood on her face.

Chapter 39

Fenrir thought of his mother.

After all these years, her face still shone in his memory. Her gentle, sad smile. Her cool, but mischievous eyes. The way that her jaw would tighten whenever Darian was nearby, and how her brow would furrow when she saw his brothers. Most of all, he remembered her songs… the songs of the Domain. The songs of courage. The songs of endurance.

The day they'd found her, wrists slit by her own hands, sitting in a tub of warm water, they'd refused to let Fenrir see her. Darian, an iron sentinel, had him dragged away by two of his newly-recruited Adders when he'd refused to leave. Fenrir had screamed and cried and cursed and blamed, but Darian had made no move, showed no emotion. No concern. No human emotion.

He was a monster, and monsters needed to be put down.

They stood atop the northern edge of the Plateau, the chill winds of early winter cutting straight through Fenrir's leathers. The moons were just rising, and provided enough reflected light to illuminate the bustle in Little Town below, and even with darkness approaching, lanterned boats and ships navigated the Fullane to the mouth of the Vissas Sea. Far in the distance, Fenrir could see blobs on the horizon that must be war galleons, sitting in readiness for an assault on Hunesa.

Sigmund, unaware that Fenrir was Fenrir, stood just a step away from him, arms folded in a way that concealed his missing finger—men adapted to their injuries. Darian was standing a ways away beneath one of several wooden pergolas, having a hushed, but heated, discussion with Astora. Every so often, a clear word would rise above the wind and sail into earshot, but not often enough to define the content of their conversation.

There was no one else around, not even guardsmen. It was near silent atop the Plateau. It couldn't have been a more perfect opportunity, truth be told. Now was Fenrir's chance to act.

Only one part of what was to come brought Fenrir any pleasure. He yanked off his helmet.

"Hi there, Siggy," he said with a smirk as he decked the man in his oft-broken nose. In the same motion, he disarmed his lifelong antagonist and tossed his sword over the edge of the wall.

"What..." Sigmund struggled to his feet, hand over his face, blood running across his gloved fingers. Fenrir hit him a second time in the gut, and then again in the face as he doubled over. The man dropped to the ground. That should settle him for a while.

It hadn't been a silent exchange, though, and both Darian and Astora turned toward him as he stalked in their direction. It should have been an easy thing to end his father and secret Astora out of the Plateau through the servant passages that honeycombed the walls. With the money Tennyson had given him, they would never have fear of wanting.

And Fenrir didn't look at Astora. He had eyes only for his target.

"Finally getting around to killing me, boy? What did Tennyson offer you?" Darian was all calm.

"They didn't have to offer me anything to want to see you dead. But..." he smirked, "...to answer you, lots of money."

"And why do they want to see me dead? The alliance with the Menogans, I take it?"

"Don't care." It was the alliance, though. Fenrir knew that, and he also knew that Tennyson would not want to see Darian's life spent if he knew the merchant king opposed this alliance. It didn't matter, though. He'd been paid to do a job, not to think. He was a dog, as Tennyson was apt to say. And this dog was keen to assume the mantle of the alpha and protect his pup.

"Right. Coldbreaker the Uncaring. Would you care if thousands of Menogan killers despoiled Ardia? Burning our farms? Raping our daughters?"

Fenrir still didn't look at his daughter, and she still didn't speak.

"Doesn't matter. We won't be here." Fenrir drew his blade.

"You see those ships on the horizon?" Darian turned his back to Fenrir, pointing to the galleons he'd noticed earlier. "They are transports, full of Menogan warriors, held at bay by our own war ships on blockade. With this alliance, the blockade will be lifted, and they will be welcomed into our country. An expansionist people reaching the edge of their own empire, a people we know very little about. People, if it be true, who are known to harness the power of magic in battle in order to subdue... no, to obliterate, their enemies."

"Don't care," said Fenrir. Though, he thought of Merigold, and how she had spattered two men across the wall.

"I will not let this happen. Even now... Oh, there we are." One of the transports glimmered for a second before it became obvious that it was catching fire. "Even now, my Adders serve to fight off this threat. Why do you think I needed to reach into the dregs for protection tonight? Poor protection, I might add." Darian turned back to face him, mirroring Fenrir's smirk.

"Nice story, my lord. It doesn't change things. You die, I live. She lives. Others live." Fenrir's jaw was clenched tighter than a virgin. He should have struck by now. Darian needed to die.

Fenrir was an enforcer. He'd had this conversation plenty of time, albeit with the price being a finger and not a life. He raised his sword just as Darian pulled something from his coat, holding it up in gloved fingers.

"You know what this is, no?" It was a tiny vial of a pinkish, reddish substance. Fenrir paused, feeling his blood run cold—picturing his skin blistering as his muscles melted away.

"Your pallor tells me you understand this is meldus. Imperfect, as a weapon, though we are working on it. But, this shatters easily, and even the fumes are enough to bring down an angry dullard." Darian's lips curled into a sickening smile that held no real glee.

"You would kill your own son?" Fenrir asked, his voice hushed.

"You would kill your own father?" Darian returned, his voice quietly mocking.

The wind picked up around them, father facing son and son facing father. Neither moved; neither spoke. So much had been said, with so much more left unspoken. Fenrir clenched his teeth and noticed his father's jaw tighten, as well. Darian adjusted his grip on his deathly vial while Fenrir did the same with his sword. The light of the white moon seemed almost bloodied.

"Stop this right now, you Ultner-sucking fools!" Astora demanded, stepping between bared steel and lethal chemicals.

"Move, girl," Darian said in his gravelly voice.

"Astora…" Fenrir hissed.

She turned on him in a fury, eyes narrowed. "You! You don't get to say my name. What is wrong with this family? Murderers and monsters! Manipulators and thieves. I would have been better off with my mother, destitute though she is. At least she has some basic kindness…"

"I don't recall that," said Fenrir, unable to help himself. Astora glared at him, but then she cracked a small, sly smile—one so much like his own.

"I said some basic kindness." Her face transformed in an instant then, back to a mask that reminded him of Darian. "But you two would rather kill each other while things are going to pandemonium around us. Look…" She pointed out toward the Vissas, where another transport was catching fire. "What is the outcome of this going to be?"

"Preservation of our country, girl. You know that," said Darian. He still held his vial in front of him, though not as warily.

Fenrir darted forward, shoving Astora to one side while sidling around her. There was no going back, not after drawing steel on his father. Either Darian died now or Fenrir died later, no matter the speech that his daughter gave. He lunged at Darian, his form perfect. Yet, somehow the old man sidestepped and kicked him in the back of his knee, sending him crashing forward.

He pivoted as he fell, staring up at Darian's silhouette against the white moon, raising his vial of meldus. Fenrir knew he was done.

"You think I haven't learned how to defend myself after years around the most elite fighting force in the country? But, boy, I truly didn't think you had the guts."

He lowered the vial, clenched in a fist, and turned his back. Then he walked over to Astora, helping her to her feet. She shot Fenrir another furious glance, the weight of ten years of neglect underlying her gaze.

"But, I would never seek to do the same. Punish you, certainly. But you are my last son, and… I still love you. Contrary to what you think, I am not a true monster," Darian said, shaking his head slowly.

"Are you not? I think I agree with my brother on this one." The harsh voice had cut through the night like a scythe through wheat, and Fenrir twisted to his feet upon hearing this voice that he had not heard for twenty years.

Stepping over a fallen Sigmund and approaching them with a fluid grace was a figure wearing a tight black cloak that flapped in the wind like the crackling of a fire. Fenrir felt his innards turn to water and a sudden urge to fling himself from the wall to avoid what was coming. Then, a flash of hot anger twisted his lips back, so that he beared his teeth at the approaching man much like a grinning wolf. He strode toward this new enemy, death on his mind. As he moved to pass his daughter, Astora stepped back into his chest. He felt a sudden, stomach-wrenching weakness at the need to keep her safe.

Darian didn't move a step.

"Aiden. The rumors were true, then."

"Half of all rumors are lies and the other half twist the truth. I am that twisted truth." He spread his arms wide, and Fenrir could see the portion of his skull that was smashed in, it being only partially concealed by the same strange black spectacles worn by Finn Lo'Argeen. The skull that he had smashed in with a belaying pin on that boat, years before.

Ethan had started the conflict, that day when Fenrir had been forced to accompany his brothers on a 'pleasure cruise' on the Vissas. In reality, it had been a test of Fenrir's ingenuity, in that he had only taken two beatings in three nights. The third night, though, everything had changed. Ethan was the eldest brother, and yet Darian had chosen Aiden to accompany him to Sestria to set up a distribution center and reconnoiter secure locations. It had been a step toward making Aiden the heir apparent of the bulging de Trenton empire, and Ethan hadn't been having any of it.

Fenrir remembered doing his best to stay out of it, hiding behind some lashed-down barrels as the seas became rougher and rougher. Ethan had started shouting, and then shoving Aiden. Aiden, as always, had escalated things until blood began flowing freely. Fenrir remembered that he hadn't been able to keep from smiling, watching his tormentors torment themselves for a change. Fenrir had snuck closer and closer, trying to get a better look at his older brothers' pain. He'd knocked over a lantern, then, distracting Ethan just as Aiden had swung his fist with the full force of a favored middle child.

Ethan's head had snapped to the side and he'd careened into an empty ship hook, the dull metal point nonetheless driving itself into the young man's brain. Aiden had stood over his brother's body, seemingly torn with grief as he'd wailed and howled. He had whipped around after that, and Fenrir had seen madness in his eyes. But it hadn't been defense that had propelled Fenrir to strike with that spare belaying pin. Before Ethan was killed, he had decided—this was his chance. This was his chance to avenge his mother, as these Ultner-fucking bastards had certainly driven her to the edge.

He'd felt Ethan's skull cave in as the bar of iron had connected with his temple. And, as his brother had fallen into the sea, his only concern had been to avoid blame and concoct a story that would be three parts truth and one part lie.

His brothers, he would say, had killed each other.

"You may call me Disorder. Aiden is dead. Brother made sure of that." Disorder nodded to Fenrir, smiling deeply. "You survived my little attempt on your life, and have gone on to do great things. I didn't expect any less from you, killer."

Fenrir's emotions tore at him, escalating from terror to guilt to anger. He fought them, though. He looked at Astora finally, and felt her against his chest, and he fought harder.

"You, Darian, are a thorn in the side of my masters. And, brother is right. You are a monster, though perhaps wearing a different mask than most."

"And you, son? I did not make of you a fratricide; you chose that yourself."

Disorder's voice keened like a wounded mountain cat. "You pitted us against each other! And Ethan's death was a mistake!"

Disorder flashed out of existence in a dark mist, a sudden implosion of humanity. He rematerialized an inch from Darian, who reacted by bringing up his vial, though it would be just as likely to kill both of them as Disorder. He didn't have a chance, though, as a bar of hot redness shot from Disorder's outstretched fingers and blasted completely through Darian's shoulder. Fenrir could smell cooked flesh—a lot like the scent of roasted pig.

Darian fell to the hard, freezing stones, emitting a great scream of agony that carried out over the city. Several screams echoed in response; terrible heart-rending howls that tore through Fenrir's remaining shreds of resistance.

Feral were roaming the Plateau. He could hear human shouts and screams reverberating through the great fortress. Death was filling the chambers below them.

Disorder knelt over a gasping, moaning Darian. He touched a finger to Darian's other shoulder.

"You are a foolish old man. The vote had passed and orders to seize the Plateau were scraped. The Menogans would have come aground peaceably, had your men not attacked their ships. Now, the nobility must burn in effigy of their losses. The council will survive, of course. Most of the councilors, anyhow. It will be easy to blame the man who leads the Adders for a hostile takeover. The man whose general set the Feral against Escamilla Breen's army. The Menogans, then, will be the heroes who slayed the monsters running rampant across the fortress."

Darian struggled weakly, and Disorder casually slapped him down with as little effort as one might subdue a toddler.

Fenrir knew he should do something, but he was unable to act, unable to gather the motivation to even move in a self-preserving fashion. Instead, he wept. For his brother, maybe. For his father, or what should have been. For himself, too, for pity was always his refuge.

His death was overdue. Ultner knew, he'd cheated it enough times. Every time he'd escaped an enraged husband after exploring his wife. Every time he'd taken a man's finger. Every misbegotten adventure he'd had since the botched job, he'd cheated death. And, Ultner knew, he desired it. Fenrir looked again at Astora, and realized what a failure he'd been all his life.

And then Fenrir stopped fighting. He simply gave up.

In a spiral of dizzying colors, his consciousness snapped out of his body and hovered above him, a vulture examining a soon-to-be corpse. Fenrir could see himself, holding his weeping daughter close as his brother knelt over his father. For the first time since killing the duke, Fenrir was truly in his disembodied state, his thoughts stuck within his phantom as his body simply existed below. Phantom-Fenrir.

Disorder still knelt on his father and, without more preamble, he shot another bolt of power into Darian's opposite shoulder, again eliciting a bloodcurdling scream which rivaled those coming from the fortress below.

Phanton-Fenrir saw his body visibly shake itself from his stupor, coming out of the convergence of emotions that had incapacitated him, and which had made him welcome death. With a quick motion, Body-Fenrir brought his booted foot up and across the side of Disorder's face, knocking him off Darian and sending him rolling. Body-Fenrir scooped up his sword on the return motion, pushing aside his weeping daughter and leaping over his maybe-dying father to pursue a violent attack on his disfigured brother.

His overhand strike ricocheted off the stones where his brother had lain a moment before. Disorder rematerialized a foot away in a black mist.

"There is fight in you, little brother," Aiden commented, stepping back quickly as Fenrir swung a riposte in his direction, effortlessly recovering his balance. Fenrir looked like a Ultner-damned Blue Adder, in truth.

"There's always been fight in me, Aiden. You just always had me outnumbered." Body-Fenrir's voice was a monotone, but it was clear.

Disorder grinned a sickening grin, his expression only emphasizing the uneven, shadowed dent in his head. He tossed aside his black cloak—wearing only a sleeveless black vest now, despite the cold. His arms with riddled with ritualized scarring.

"Fine, it's just the two of us. Let's see how you fare, man-to-man, when you can't strike me unawares with a Pandemonium-damned chunk of metal." Disorder drew his own sword, which immediately began to glow a hot red, the air shimmering around it with gentle flames.

Body-Fenrir pursued an attack, unfazed by whatever magic fueled his opponent's weapon. Disorder parried his slash, and sparks flew; Adder blades were made of the best steel, but Phantom-Fenrir hadn't a clue how long they would last against an enchanted sword. But, there was little to be done, as Body-Fenrir had to knock aside a quick riposte with a second shower of sparks that landed on his face. Despite what must have been burning agony, the dancing Blue Adder did not hesitate. He did not even react to the pain.

"You are nothing without Ethan at your back," grated Body-Fenrir in a harsh monotone.

"And you, brother, are nothing." Disorder extended his fingers toward him and Body-Fenrir threw himself down, narrowly avoiding a pinky-thin bar of crimson energy. He sprung back to his feet against Disorder's discordant laugh.

"I could make you dance all night if I wished it. But, alas, I've too much to do, with Darian's little stunt." He gestured toward the galleons burning in the distance.

Phantom-Fenrir examined Disorder, his strange black spectacles seeming to suck up the light of the moons. They were held on with a strap, given that his misshapen skull prevented the things from staying in play by themselves. With a wound like that, how had he survived?

"How did you survive?" Body-Fenrir asked, light on his feet to dodge whatever was thrown at him next. Disorder stood at ease, his burning sword held at the side.

"You mean after you murdered me?" Body-Fenrir nodded. "Truth be told—and why wouldn't I tell the truth, given that you are to die in moments—I remember little. One's head caving in will have that effect. I should have been dead. I was dead, except that someone found me, and not as if by accident. A man with these," he tapped his spectacles, "who could see beyond what was typical. Just as I can now."

Disorder turned his head and looked upward, making whatever passed for eye contact with Phantom-Fenrir. If a spirit, or whatever the Pandemonium he was, could have shivered, his teeth would have been chattering. His body, though, was unmoved.

"Apparently, I had potential. They healed me, to an extent." He tapped his misshappen head with a sword that suddenly wasn't enflamed. "They took me to Menoga; locked me away. Made me into this." He flashed in and out of existence for a split second, as if to demonstrate. When he reappeared, his lips were pulled back in an angry snarl.

550

"And you… brother. You and that pile of old shit laying on the ground are the reason I am this way."

"Powerful," said Body-Fenrir, echoing his mindless thoughts.

"Broken," said Disorder, reigniting his sword and rushing forward, leaping the useless body of his father.

Body-Fenrir stepped forward to meet him.

Phantom-Fenrir watched himself fight. By Yetra's glorious clit, he was good. He was better than good, in fact—he was greater than the best Blue Adder that he had ever seen fight. He anticipated every move that his brother made, moving a split second quicker. Disorder sliced at his feet and Body-Fenrir was already in the air. Disorder threw a punch when their swords crossed and Body-Fenrir batted it away. From his ascended view, Phantom-Fenrir actually thought he was going to win— particularly when he drove his sword into his brother's gut.

Or he should have, anyway, had the dead man not dissipated into a black, shadowed mist and reformed two feet behind where he'd been, immediately resuming his attack. By Ultner's shaved balls, how does one kill a man who can fade in and out of existence like a godsdamned demon?

Another pass. Sparks flew as flames struck steel. Again. A sizzling burn, from Disorder's flat blade, bubbled the flesh on Fenrir's arm, melting right through his leathers. And again. Disorder hissed into nothingness as Body-Fenrir's blade threatened to disrupt his jugular. Neither man seemed to tire, though Phantom-Fenrir knew it was a battle of attrition. He hadn't landed more than a couple of blunt kicks to his brother while he himself had taken several burns. He should run. In fact, he willed his body to run, but it didn't listen. And it seemed that, deep down, he truly didn't want to escape.

The reason, of course, was Astora. His daughter was overwhelmed with smothering fear, and yet moving toward the melee, clutching a table knife as if it held the answer to all of her problems. Disorder's back was to her, his attention focused on his brother as he parried a deadly blow at the last moment. Phantom-Fenrir wanted to scream at her, telling her to run and that she needed to escape this place. That his life wasn't worth saving. But, if his body sent that message, it would just give her away and lead to her death.

Astora raised her knife with shaking hands, up above her head. She had a clear path to Disorder's back, and yet she did not strike. Her arms were paralyzed, tears streaming down her face unchecked. Strike! willed Phanton-Fenrir. Strike now or run away! But it was no use. Her bravery evaporated as quickly as a drop of water in the summer sun.

A wracking sob, with the sound of glass scraping across stone, escaped her mouth, alerting Disorder to the danger. He blinked out of existence and reformed behind her, extracting the knife from her hand with a 'tsk'ing sound as he wrapped another arm around her throat.

"Brother, she looks like you. Poor little bitch." Disorder smiled and tightened his grip on her neck.

"You would harm an innocent girl?" Body-Fenrir asked, his voice flat and his sword unwavering.

Disorder's face spasmed. "There's little I haven't done at this point. And the same could be said of you, Bull. And that heartless old fuck lying on the ground there, as well. He's the worst of us."

"No, you always were, Aiden. Ethan may have been the main bastard, Ethan and Sigmund, but you… you allowed it. You knew better. You were always reluctant, but too much of a coward to stop them. And you could have. You could have saved my knee. You could have saved my mother, if you'd had an ounce of courage." Body-Fenrir's voice was still blank, but it echoed every thought of his consciousness. "You could have used that silver tongue. You could have used your training. But instead you cowered and gave free reign to bad men to torment a boy and his mother."

Disorder's mouth twisted, with a fierce frown and then a sneer. Not at Fenrir, though. At himself. He tightened his grip on Astora and the girl gasped for breath.

"You can stop this now," said Body-Fenrir, tossing his sword to the stones with a clatter. Tact might work, thought Phantom-Fenrir, pushing his body to say the words while somehow maintaining control. Disorder lightened his grip, and his face softened for a moment. And then Darian groaned, causing Disorder to reaffix his mask.

"No, brother. I am too far gone."

He blinked out of sight in a wet cloud, Astora falling backwards upon losing her support, coughing and gasping for breath. Phantom-Fenrir lost track of his body as Disorder reappeared a foot away and lashed out with a foot at his weak knee. The thing buckled, and Body-Fenrir tumbled to the ground. Before he could spin away and reach for his fallen sword, Disorder came down on his stomach with a powerful knee, knocking the wind out of him. Brother knelt upon brother.

"There is nothing to do, Fenrir, but follow my course, the course you sent me on." His voice was vitriolic. "Do you know how you have made me suffer? Look at me! My life has been pandemonium since you destroyed my face. You think I like what I've become? You think this is pleasant? You think I can change because of your soft words?"

He held Body-Fenrir's face down with a strong hand on his neck, his bare, muscular arms rippling with the force of the push.

"It is only right that you suffer as I have."

He ignited his sword then, and considered the flame for a moment before resting the flat of the blade on Fenrir's face, just over his left eye.

His body writhed as the burning metal pressed against his skin, which blistered and bubbled at its touch. The eye itself must have melted immediately beneath the inferno. And yet, Body-Fenrir did not scream, and did not betray what must have been excruciating agony.

From above, Phantom-Fenrir could not feel the pain, but he could see the damaged mass of flesh as Disorder leaned away and drew back the blade. And he began to lose control, too—he felt himself swirling back toward his body in a dizzying, shaking array of colors. For a second, he could feel everything… the brutal, blinding pain of his facial wound, the half a dozen burns all over his body, and the familiar ache in his knee. He shrieked and raged, feeling a madness take him. A rage, a sadness—a piercing cry against Ultner and Yetra and a begging for forgiveness. An emptiness. Fenrir couldn't take it; it was too much. He wrested back control before fully merging back with his body.

Disorder frowned at Fenrir's still-silent and struggling body, and then he glanced up at his Phantom.

"There is something to you, brother. Something I don't understand. But, I will make you howl by the end."

He switched his sword to his other hand, letting up on his grip on Body-Fenrir's neck. The Phantom willed his body to fight. He demanded that his body fight.

Despite his wounds—wounds that would cripple a normal man, both physically and psychologically—Body-Fenrir's arms snapped up, grabbing each of Disoder's wrists. Disorder grunted in surprise.

"Stop this fighting!"

554

"Never," he said, though his voice was a croak.

Slowly, inexorably, Disorder overpowered his brother. He'd always been stronger, always heavier, and he was in a position of power. The red heat of his sword inched toward Fenrir's other eye little by little. Even with him being a Phantom, the flames consumed his vision. Flickering orange, red, and blue, swirling together in a flesh-consuming flurry.

It was a hand's width away.

It was a finger's width away.

And then Disorder recoiled with an inhuman roar, his now-cold, steel sword clanging against the stones.

He stood up, gripping his left bicep with his right hand, neck muscles straining as he glared toward the sky and howled in agony, staggering backwards. Body-Fenrir regained his feet while his Phantom watched. Disorder's arm was blackening now, degree by degree, starting with a spot on his tricep and moving toward his hand and his shoulder. His flesh died, and he felt every piece waste away.

He flickered in and out of existence, his screams cutting off for moments at a time until he didn't reappear.

Disorder was gone.

Darian still lay moaning in his unconscious state while Astora rested on her hands and knees, coughing and hacking. Body-Fenrir stood looking at their savior.

Sigmund Fitra, his face covered with drying blood, stood mere steps from Fenrir, gripping a tiny vial that had once held the essence of meldus.

"You look like… well…. We need to get out of here," he said quietly. He knelt over Darian, checking the man's wounds and then looking up. "The Adders are on their way."

And Phantom-Fenrir finally, inevitably, lost control. His conscientious slammed back into his broken body and he dropped to his knees with the agony of the burns, with the understanding of his lost eye and his hideous visage. Wracking sobs shook him to his core and he curled up on the cold stones of the Plateau. Heavy footsteps approached, but Fenrir didn't care. He was being pulled to his feet then; someone was shouting orders, talking about the Feral. It didn't matter.

As he was guided away, one foot in front of the other, he could only think of his brother. Aiden, twice maimed now and wanting revenge on his family.

And Fenrir, in his pain-laced mind, couldn't fault him for it.

He could only fault him for not succeeding.

Chapter 40

Without the strong arm of his brother or the nimbleness of his to-be-bound, Hafgan would have fallen to his death ten times over.

He sprawled out, exhausted beyond reality, tears squeezing from his eyes by the impossibility of it all. His wounds burned and his head spun so that up and down became the same thing. The ever-present roar of Enorry Falls buzzed in his ears like a thousand maddened bees.

"A little more, brother. We must push… we must push… we must push." Repetitive, just like twenty-five years before. But gentle, and seemingly more and more coherent even as Hafgan lost his own tenuous grasp of reality.

Hafgan battled to his knees, Rian supporting him despite the fact that she stood on shaking limbs herself. They were beyond caring about the cold; though they should have been shivering, the exertion of their bodies pressed them forward. As did Yurin and his gentle mumbling. He was surefooted and focused, almost as if he knew where they were going.

They had lost all signs of pursuit; the Carreg Da, though driven by that huge warleader, seemed to have lost interest before long, particularly after one of the warriors had fallen to what had certainly been his death. From their vantage, it appeared as if they had attracted enough of the forces to allow the budredda and Offeirs to pass, but Hafgan couldn't be certain. He could barely spare enough energy to think of his men—his only path forward was their path upward.

Their little party would have long ago lost their strength, their ability to ascend, except that they traveled a path once tread. Every now and again, in the most impassible areas, there were ropes and spikes affixed to the path, betraying the fact that someone had once forged a road to the top of the falls. Yurin seemed to know each one. Hafgan, in his feverish brain, recalled the story that Taern had shared, that the Dyn Doethas had once sent slaves to the top of the mountain to control the very flow of the falls. Perhaps these pathways were all that remained, the only legacy of those dead multitudes.

Nonetheless, he was thankful. They were so close, though this last stretch seemed like an impossibility.

"Hsssst!" Rian hissed out, crouching down next to Hafgan and gripping his arm, pausing his struggle. Yurin knelt similarly, eyes darting around until they settled on what Rian saw.

The source of Enorry Falls was mercifully only around forty or fifty feet above their ledge, water plunging hundreds of feet to the river below. But, that sight was familiar—what drew the eye instead was a man standing near the falls.

At least, Hafgan thought it was a man. Against the brightness of the snow, all he could make out was a black figure wearing a long coat that flapped in the heavy breeze. The person stood so still that he could have been a statue, apparently gazing out over the valleys below Limner. For so long, the man stood there, watching and waiting for something. He did not move his head, but Hafgan felt that, if any of them moved an inch, the man would notice. And, for whatever reason, gathering the attention of this man seemed like a terrible idea. A fatal idea.

Hafgan shuddered, feeling tears streaking through his facial hair. He struggled mightily to hold back a sob that might give them away. He felt like he was choking, his windpipe clogged with a hundred pebbles. His stomach was a shriveled mess of agony as it twisted about like a serpent. He'd never felt this way before; this was beyond any normal fear. It was beyond terror, even. And the man was not even directing their attention at them.

There was a power in this man. An impossible power. An unfathomable power. The power of a god.

Hafgan's muscles were cramping and clenching, but he dared not stretch them. He dared not move even in inch.

Without warning, the man simply launched himself forward in a great leap into the air that Hafgan couldn't have managed in his prime, let alone now. He plummeted toward the city below, falling as quickly as a man should fall. Hafgan lost sight of him through the omnipresent mist.

"What in the bleeding hell was that?" Rian asked, grimacing as she regained her feet. She was breathing heavily and covered in perspiration. Hafgan realized that he was, as well.

"I think that... I think that was the Flawless God."

***

Enorry Falls originated in a cave—a damp, dark place that nonetheless felt surprisingly welcoming as a refuge. The group walked a few dozen yards into the cavern before collapsing in exhaustion. Rian and Hafgan did, anyhow. Yurin continued to stand, although he tossed his and Hafgan's spears aside with a clatter.

"So, we made it to the top…" Rian said. "I always pictured it being much… grander. Perhaps that there would be some temple up here, or maybe some ancient carvings from a time long past. This, though, is just a cave full of water."

"There is beauty in knowing the truth, though," said Hafgan, closing his eyes.

"Pfft. My life would be better off, had you not shared your truth."

"You would prefer to live a lie?"

"I would prefer to live a lie that I didn't know for a lie, you dimwit." Her insult lacked any real enthusiasm, however. "So, instead, I had to choose between leaving the people behind to flounder, or at least try to teach them something that had value beyond their belief in a false goddess."

"I am beginning to believe that faith is little more than a way to spread values among the people. Traisen spread the value of war and combat with just a hint of honor. Oletta embodied the value of wisdom, knowledge, and logic…"

"Which is why my temple was always so empty. What could compare to the fun of war and battle?" Rian asked wryly.

559

"What indeed? Perhaps, had more people followed you, Rian, we wouldn't be in this cave." Rian was silent at that. Perhaps the statement had sounded too accusatory. Hafgan sighed.

"We should sleep. Tomorrow, we need find a descent on the other side of this mountain."

"No." Yurin's voice was firm. Hafgan's eyes struggled to open, seeing his brother staring, unmoving, deeper into the cave.

"Brother, we must rest. I must rest."

"You will rest soon enough, Hafgan. As will we all." His tone was strange, and Hafgan felt an aura of danger. Had the Flawless God returned?

"That's… ominous," mumbled Rian, apparently feeling the same thing. She gained her feet and helped Hafgan up even as he reached for his weapon. Again, the gifted spear was strangely warm, and he felt a surge of energy flooding through his weary body.

"Rian… where exactly did this spear come from?" He examined the weapon—was it beginning to glow? Traisen's symbol, certainly, seemed to shine softly. Rian's eyes were wide, seeing the same thing.

"I don't know. That fool Ulin had it; he said his people had stashed it away for who knows how long. Said the spear belonged to you, whether you knew it or not. He was half-mad and half-dead, though, so I didn't pay much attention. I had other things on my mind, like killing that bastard Leyr and getting us the bleeding fuck out of Hackeneth."

"Come." Yurin began to walk deeper into the cave.

Hafgan followed, still staring at his weapon.

It was only a few minutes before they came to an impassible wall, when their path diverged from the fast-flowing source of Enorry Falls. There was nowhere to proceed.

"Hold up your spear," commanded Yurin. His voice was clear. It was as coarse as ever, but his words were calm and controlled... so unlike him.

Hafgan did as commanded, feeling almost compelled. He longed to reach into his hedwicchen, but it was unattainable.

The spear began to glow, a soft blue light spreading from under his hands until it consumed the length of the weapon. Similarly, the wall began to glow in the shape of a door, with a circular hole appearing in its center. Without knowing why he did it, Hafgan jammed the spear, the key, into the hole. The wall faded from existence, and the three walked in.

Again, almost as if pushed.

They continued down a path for a time, not speaking. What was there to say? It was all too surreal to be reality. Perhaps Hafgan had fallen asleep, and this was a delusion of his fevered mind. Perhaps Wiscon had killed him, after all, that this was what came after. Perhaps he had never left the Pwoll.

While the walk only lasted a few minutes, it somehow seemed like they had traveled a long, long way. To another world, maybe.

"What is this place?" Rian asked, her voice holding a heavy awe.

They had entered a chamber that was unlike anything Hafgan had ever seen. Pillars, perfectly carved in every style, were visible as far as the eye could see. And the eye could see far, given that it was as bright as day with a light emanating from nowhere. The ceilings, gently arched, were carved beautifully with every major scene from Wasmer history. The fabricated history, anyhow. There was Finlyn, the miner, unearthing the natural phenomenon that was the Cylch. Arwinyadd Anerin, slain from behind by an axe-wielding human. And, as he watched, an image formed, showing Hafgan standing over a fallen Leyr and a bleeding Taern, turning his back on his people.

"You said you wanted a temple at the top of the falls, Rian. I though it a kindness to comply." The voice had radiated from the walls—a quaking sound that seemed to come from every direction.

"What? Who is that?" Rian spun around, her eyes wide. Hafgan, though, just stared at the carving, even as it became more detailed. For some reason, his image was holding the same spear that he held now. And, he could swear that Taern was actually smiling through his rage.

"How do you not know my voice? Are you saying that you have been deaf for all of these years?"

Rian suddenly darted forward, pushing past Hafgan and Yurin, who stood with his arms folded, leaning comfortably against a pillar.

"Rian!" Hafgan shook himself from his revelry, grabbing at her wrist. Rian, though, slipped away. He ran after her as she dodged around the beautiful, ornate pillars. But she didn't go far.

Rian came to a sudden and abrupt pause, Hafgan nearly tackling her down before he could stop himself. She leaned back into him, apparently wanting some comfort that he could not provide. He laid one limp arm across her chest.

"Hafgan… you were wrong. You lied to me," she whispered.

A Wasmer woman stood before them. At least, sort of. She was part woman, part stone, almost as if the mountain had melted around her and formed a second skin. Her face was untouched—it was a rough, weathered face that had seen more than any living being had the right to see. Her arms still seemed to maintain some remnants of the living, shifting slightly at their approach, but always touching a stone podium in front of her. The rest of her was indistinguishable from the granite of the cavern walls.

"Oletta..." whispered Hafgan, falling to his knees as Rian did the same. Oletta, the Goddess of Wisdom, smiled a thin, weary smile, almost as if she understood that the foundation of their beliefs had been rocked, caught in a landslide, and tossed off the side of the mountain.

Yurin barked a laugh which ended with a rough, metallic cough.

Chapter 41

The journey to Agricorinor was without incident.

It only took a few days, riding double and eating scant rations. Merigold was stuck firmly in front of Lisan as they traveled off-road to avoid any Sun Guard or Sestrian patrols, all while desperately hoping to dodge roving Menogan bands. Each of them were showing signs of exhaustion beyond just the physical. Lisan continuously muttered to herself, too quietly to be heard by Merigold riding scant inches away. Ill'Nath never released his hand from his club, and he always had his eyes behind them. Meri practiced questing, knowing that if it came down to it, she would need to draw from her horse to create some sort of defense.

She didn't give the horse a name this time.

But, despite their anxieties, the journey to Agricorinor was without incident. The same could not be said of their arrival.

"Agricorinor will be visible over the next ridge," Lisan announced, her voice taut as a bowstring. "Mane brought me nearby, once, but I got no closer than this."

"It will be nice to finally rest," said Merigold in an effort to assuage the warrior's nerves. "After we find help for Cryden."

"I certainly hope you know something I don't. The pasnes alna do not welcome outsiders, and certainly not those who are on the run from who knows how many soldiers."

"I know a lot that you don't," Merigold joked. Lisan said nothing, but reached for her bow and preemptively began to string the weapon with awkward, gloved fingers. Merigold glanced back at her in alarm.

"We won't need that, Lisan. Please trust me."

"Trust me. Do you hear that?" Lisan asked in a hiss.

Ill'Nath also swiveled in his saddle, holding Cryden in place while setting his eyes on the western hills. There was little in the way of trees around them—just snowy, rolling hills that served to obscure vision in all directions. They kept to the valleys as much as possible so as not to be seen, but this technique also blocked their own ability to scout. Their battered group paused to listen.

The wind swept over the hills with a hiss, and there was a slight creak as Lisan finished stringing her bow. And then there came the whinny of a horse from just over the hill to their west, as well as the jingle of armor in a saddle and someone coughing. Merigold felt her stomach tighten. They were traveling several hundred yards off the road, so any other armored folks making an attempt to be stealthy, out here, meant trouble.

"We need to move, but quietly," Merigold whispered. "Once we pass the ridge, we can make hard for Agricorinor and hope for succor. They will certainly rush to protect one of their own."

"What, Cryden, who is apparently unwelcome in the place? Or you, a wild mage convict?"

"Yetra willing, both."

They started forward again, moving toward the top of the ridge. The horses crunched the untouched snow and cleared their throats. Their packs jingled and knocked together. Ill'Nath shifted Cryden with a loud scraping noise. They must have sounded like a small army, and yet no one approached or raised an alarm. Maybe the ambushers simply focused too strongly on the road and ignored sounds in this direction. Or, maybe they weren't truly ambushers, and instead just a few hunters out for a stroll.

As they were about to crest the ridge, Cryden half-moaned and half-yelled in his feverish way. There was a sudden rush of voices then, shouting out something in Rafonese, and an echo of horses trotting off in all directions.

"Shit," Lisan muttered. "It's time to ride. Let's hope you are right, Merigold."

Lisan drove her feet into the horse's flanks, pushing the beast forward. Ill'Nath, clutching Cryden, had already passed them. Merigold glanced to the west in time to see several dozen Sun Guard cresting the ridge. They must have lain in wait, assuming that the girl with magical powers would strike for the magical stronghold in the northern reaches of Rafon. Merigold only hoped that Captain Tinto was not among them.

If it came down to it, she wouldn't want to kill the man.

Agricorinor rose in the distance, though Meri struggled to take it in during their flight. It didn't seem like much, though, from her vantage. There were fields of roots and shrubs, the type of foodstuffs that even grew in the winter. Groves of trees, evenly spaced, created both walls and shade. And, though it was just at the edge of her vision, she thought she could see a herd of pigs roaming amidst short fences.

"Agricorinor is a farm?" she shouted incredulously.

"Of course, it's a fucking farm. Where do you think you get your powers?" Lisan barked from behind her. "But it's a lush fucking farm for all but the students."

They continued their rush toward the stronghold of the pasnes alna, still at least a mile away. She could start to make out towers, in the distance, that would betray the posh nature of Agricorinor. It only stood to reason that those in power would live lavish lives. There was something happening in the mage's stronghold, too, with hundreds of people milling about in a mass, but she was too intent on her own plight to decipher what was going on.

Doubled up as they were, they could only move so fast, and the armored Sun Guards gained ground steadily. They would certainly catch them well before they reached the hoped-for safety of Agricorinor. Lisan twisted in her saddle and launched an arrow into the center of the rushing horses, but with no visible effect. She wasn't dissuaded, however, and shot a second time; this time, a horse stumbled and flung a Sun Guard to the snow. Lisan grunted in appreciation, but it would not be enough.

Merigold needed to do something, but it was extremely unlikely that tossing some of her discs would do more than take down a couple of horses, especially at this distance. She could fire a beam or two, but not accurately from the back of the horse—and again, the impact would be limited. Plus, if she were to draw from their horse, even just a bit, the creature would almost certainly stumble… if not fall outright.

Merigold gripped her nail-knife impotently. There had to be a way to slow them down. But, what was it? The grip of her nail dug into her skin even through her gloves, and it was a familiar and comfortable biting sensation. And, with that, she knew what she needed to do.

She turned, seeing that the charging Sun Guard were only twenty yards away. She removed her glove, and touched Lisan's neck just as she released an arrow.

"I'm sorry," she murmured. And she drew.

Mane was dragging her from the beach to safety, murmuring pleasantries while insulting her stupidity at being washed up naked on the beach.

She was bent over the thick comforter of a small bed, Mane behind her as he heaved and plunged himself into her.

She was slitting the throat of an innocent woman on Mane's behalf, feeling a terrible shame but doing it nonetheless.

Merigold shook her head and concentrated on shaping Lisan's maenen. Tiny nails, each one the familiar shape of her own knife. She crafted a dozen. Two dozen. A hundred. The orange-burning things floated in front of her like a spike trap. It took far less effort, far less maenen, to craft something that she was so intimately familiar with. And, with a sudden thought, she shot them at their pursuers.

Horses began to fall across the front line, pierced by tiny nails. Men were crushed by their own horses or flung free and trampled by the next line. Merigold flinched at each death, but her lips were a straight, tight line. She had told them, back in Polanice, that pursuit would mean death. And, at the precipice of Agricorinor, she was not going to give in now.

Lisan rested draped across Merigold's back, holding onto her with one arm. She was conscious, but barely, and she said nothing. Merigold held her wrist tightly, lest she lose her grip.

Pursuit had halted. There were still many mounted Sun Guard, but they rode in confusion and had taken to helping their fallen comrades rather than focusing on pursuit. At least, though, Meri had a clear path to Agricorinor. Someone would certainly help them, and then the Sun Guard would turn back rather than approach this vaunted... farm.

Turning back to their destination, Merigold almost yanked on the reins to turn the horse around when she got a better sight of what they faced. "Yetra, you scale-bellied fish-fucker," she swore, and not exactly under her breath. The people milling about in front of the towers, amidst the farms, were Menogan. She could see their brown cloaks hiding their armor—the same cloaks that had covered them during the ambush. They were battling an outnumbered force of bronze-armored warriors, presumably whomever kept Agricorinor safe from more conventional invasions.

The Menogans were staging an attack on the stronghold of the mages. And, from the looks of it, they were winning.

There were flashes of light—of green, gold, and red—dissipating into nothing as they struck near the battling Menogans.

The pasnes alna were attempting to rain destruction down upon the invaders from the safety of their great stone towers, but the Menogans had created a barrier with their own metsikas; an umbrella that protected them from a rain of destruction. Occasionally, a depleted blast of energy would find a gap in the barrier and leave soldiers writhing in pain, but they harmed as many defenders as attackers.

The Menogans were clearly winning, despite the gasconaded power of the pasnes alna. With that barrier in place, there was little they could do. If Merigold were to guess, she had to think the pasnes alna, locked in their towers, would run out of living fuel for their assault before long.

And then it would be over.

No one was safe in Agricorinor, and there would be no one on this continent who could fight off the Menogan metsikas.

With that barrier in place…

The Menogans had not noticed Merigold yet, though, distracted as they were by the battle.

"Ill'Nath. Take Lisan and the horse, and travel east to that grove, out of sight of the Sun Guard. Keep Cryden safe and wait for the battle to be over. Agricorinor must win here. I… I need to help them." She clenched her teeth so tight that they might crack. She was one small girl with barely any control over her powers, but she had spent enough of her recent life being helpless and scared of the dark. She would do what had to be done, live or die. She would stay true to her course.

And even in her thoughts, Merigold realized that she sounded like Lisan.

Ill'Nath, grinning that frightening grin of his, reached into a saddlebag and pulled out… of all things, a small white rabbit. The thing was shivering in fear, completely disconcerted and confused by having been in that pack for who knew how long. Ill'Nath handed it over to Merigold.

"Hush…" she whispered, gently stroking its pure white fur. She looked up at the islander as he led his laden horses toward the eastern grove. "How long have you had this?" she called after him. Ill'Nath shrugged, grinned, and loped off with his horses. Merigold shook her head at his back; such an incredulous man.

Without the vantage of her horse, it was much more difficult to make out the flow of the battle. The snow had fallen more lightly here, and tall grass provided her with some cover as she approached the fight. Her goal was clear. Break the barrier and help the pasnes alna win. A barrier of that size must be maintained by a number of Menogan metsikas. If she could manage to stop even a couple, the barrier should fall. She glanced behind her and saw that the Sun Guard was still in disarray in the distance, while Ill'Nath was all but out of sight in that grove of trees.

She continued, in a crouching run, to cover the remaining distance to the rear of the forces. The sound was becoming deafening, louder than the only other great battle she had witnessed in Florens. But she had never been this close before. Standing tall for an instant, she could see a mass of brown-cloaked soldiers pushing against one another with hardly enough room to swing a weapon. If anyone glanced back here, they would see her, and the lifeforce within this rabbit would not save her. But, thanks be to…. Well, thanks be that no one did.

Finally, she found what she was looking for. Near the edge of one of the man-made tree groves, Merigold could see the telltale signs of a greenie. Three trees had already succumbed, and the ashes were sweeping across the battlefield, making things even more disordered. A half dozen bored-looking soldiers stood around leaning on those strange spears of theirs and watching the battle. Two more Menogans pressed their hands on separate trees, both of them looking upward toward the sky. The trees were slowly being drained of their lifeforce. Leaves curled and blackened, bark peeled back, and branches cracked here and there. These were the metsikas maintaining at least a portion of the barrier.

If they were to fall, the barrier would fall. Merigold hoped.

She quested, feeling the vibrant maenen within the rabbit. Though the animal was much smaller than a horse, its ephemeral reservoir of maenen was still fairly significant. She continued to absentmindedly pet the small, fearful creature as she plotted out her next steps.

There were a hundred yards of open ground between her and the metsikas. She needed to get closer, but the risk was great. Any one of the soldiers turning around could see her, and then she would be stabbed, pierced, or incinerated. But, she also couldn't risk missing. She had one shot at this, so she simply strolled out of the tall grass and began to confidently walk toward them. If anyone turned and saw her, they would at least see someone who appeared to belong. With her silvery blonde hair, they might even mistake her for one of their own.

It was strange, Merigold thought, that she felt so little fear as she strode purposefully toward this battle. Her legs bore her weight without quivering, and her stomach lacked that hollow feeling that she would have expected. She was potentially— likely, even—marching toward her death. And yet, for some reason, she felt at peace with herself.

No one saw her until she was within ten yards of them. A guard dropped his spear, twisting backwards to pick it up. He saw the small, slender girl approaching and just stared rather than calling out. Merigold smiled at him and waved before drawing from the rabbit.

She felt frantic and hungry as she crafted her nails. She launched just a single one, which caught the guard between the eyes. The two dozen more that she launched forward killed or crippled the other guards. The first metsika was just becoming aware of Merigold now, glancing away from his barrier. The burning plate that she summoned cut through his midsection, leaving his guts to spill out into the snowy grass.

The second metsika, though overweight, was faster. He diverted his attention from the great barrier to create a smaller shield. He deflected her burning plate, sending it dozens of feet away, into the legs of the rear ranks of the soldiers. Men went down and confusion continued to rein as Menogans turned to determine the source of the magical attack.

The metsika retaliated, sending a spinning scythe toward her. By instinct alone, Merigold threw up her own barrier, remembering to create more of a cone to deflect the attack rather than absorb it. The scythe ricocheted off and flew off somewhere behind her. Three more followed in quick succession. Two more were blocked, but this metsika knew his work. The spinning motion of the blade somehow propelled the scythe around her barrier, and the blade cut deeply into her upper arm.

With a cry, Merigold fell to her knees and the rabbit tumbled from her hands. It didn't go far, but she lacked the maenen to create another barrier. And, the pain from the burning wound on her arm was so intense that her body shook and her mind splintered. Across her wavering vision, she could see the metsika slowly approaching another tree, his first having been completely drained of life. He moved like a man in his dotage; it must have been exhausting work to contribute to such a barrier. But Meri couldn't focus. She couldn't find her rabbit, her only source of protection. She couldn't think of anything except for the agonizing pain.

The metsika reached the tree and placed his hands on the bark. Soldiers were detaching themselves from the last ranks and approaching the magical conflict warily. Either by spear or magic, Merigold was going to die.

But by fucking Yetra, she would not die on her knees. She would not.

As she pushed herself to her feet, gripping her wounded arm with her opposite hand, a great flash of light and a booming report sent her reeling backwards. Blinking wildly against the stars in her vision, she could just make out a smoking crater where the pasnes alna had been standing. The barrier had broken and the pasnes alna of Agricorinor had pierced the veil.

Above her, she could see that the protectors of Agricorinor were finding gaps all throughout the shield, launching beams of power and creating devastating explosions all throughout the Menogan army. The Menogans fought back, the metsikas continuing to maintain the barrier where they could or sending their own shining powers to deflect and disrupt.

But they could not reestablish the same level of control.

Any joy that an ailing Merigold could have derived from this was lost as she realized that the soldiers still approached her cautiously, and she was going to be in the direct path of the just-retreating army. She stumbled over to the group of guards she had incapacitated with her nails. Two still lived. Two could be fuel for her protection.

Two could be fuel for the destruction of any who approached her.

Ragen had once told her that, if she was ever in a fight, she should hold nothing back. She had seen her father follow his own advice on a day when some travelers had treated her roughly. He'd fought two men, both much larger than him, without any hesitation or consideration for his own well-being. And, he'd prevailed. Merigold would do the same. If she cut a bloody swath through these soldiers, who would dare approach her? She needed to leave an impression before her strength gave out or she became overwhelmed by pain.

She gripped the first Menogan, a young man. Vivid pictures from his life—the memories of leaving his mother and sister behind; of killing his first man, a slave, in a hazing ritual; of boarding a ship and taking a last look at his homeland—became Merigold's. She shoved them to the back of her consciousness and rained death upon the soldiers approaching her.

Nails flew forward, piercing armor, skin, and flesh. Burning plates severed legs and opened bellies. Scythes decapitated and incapacitated. Occasional barriers blocked thrown spears. There was a circle of death around her and none could approach.

She moved to the next guard upon draining the first, collapsing his nerring into nothing. In the brief time between drawing from one and then the next, Meri was nearly crippled with exhaustion, but the maenen from the second guard filled her with exhilaration. Ecstasy, even. She was a goddess among these weak-bodied Menogan warriors.

The sound of hooves behind her spun the would-be goddess around. The Sun Guard had finally organized themselves and gained the courage to approach her, despite being surrounded by enemies. Or, maybe they rode to the aid of Agricorinor. She would never know, as she cut them down like she was a lumberjack and they were simply saplings. Horses fell and bodies were cut, cleaved, and crushed. Blood splattered on every inch of her body, and she found herself laughing in the face of it. As the dead and dying built up around her, she continued to move from one dying person to the next, giving their final moments meaning as their maenen fueled the deaths of others.

The Sun Guard had fallen or fled. The Menogans ran in the same direction, flowing around her as if she were a great, bloody island amidst a river of panic. Another Menogan metsika tried to stop her and she eviscerated the women with no conscious effort. Any who approached her died, further staining her hands, hair, and face with crimson. The goddess—the girl—did not know how long she fought and killed; time had no meaning. Her nerring was distended, stretched, and sickened. Her body was beyond exhaustion, quivering as if she had not eaten in months. And yet, the only thing that mattered was the maenen. The control. The power.

Eventually, with the setting of the sun, perhaps, there were no more enemies. There were no more injured or dying to sap, to fuel her magic. There were only the dead in their multitudes.

And the girl, bathed in blood, standing on weakened legs, desperately searched for more maenen.

She fell, the girl did, into the muck. Laying on her side, she emptied her stomach through gagging and gasping breaths. She prayed and begged that it would stop, her body bucking and shaking with the effort. Her wounded arm swung uselessly at her side, tearing more deeply with every retching and sobbing heave.

The girl heard the crunching sound of footsteps, and she looked up. A man, flanked by a dozen bronze-armored guards, approached. He was older, and balding, but he held an aura of power. His blue robes, rimmed in gold, were fine and untouched by the filth that caked everyone else.

"Who are you?" A deep, booming voice—one that was used to being obeyed. It held a note of disdain, one that would have made the girl bristle, had she been able to answer his question.

The girl thought for a moment. "I am... I don't really..." A thousand memories fluttered through her mind. She was the offspring of a whorish mother. She was a killer of children. She was a scared and gentle person, forced into war. Faces flashed through her mind—a thousand faces from a thousand memories, all of which felt real, though incompatible. Tears ran divots down her blood-caked face.

"Maenen poisoning," the man muttered. "Dumb, foolish woman. So, you don't have any inkling of who you are?"

The girl, with impossible effort, pulled herself to her feet while gripping her wounded arm. She glanced around at the dirty, hard-faced soldiers and the man in the blue robes. She noticed the way that they gripped their spears more tightly when she shifted her weight on wobbly legs. She considered the bodies scattered around her, and the general destruction nearby. Finally, she met the gaze of the insulting man.

"I'm your fucking savior," the girl spat, venom lacing her voice.

The man smirked, though not kindly. "That, indeed, you are." He spread his arms wide to encompass the devastation around them. Ash blew into the girl's face, trying to tickle a sneeze out of her.

"Welcome to Agricorinor, savior."

Interlogue: Ascension

"This will be our last visit, sweetling.

"I know not what else to say. You barely understand a word I speak now. You fear me. You hate me. You would never seek to harm me.

"I might as well finish telling you my story. You have listened, this entire time. And, though you are now beyond comprehension, you deserve to hear the end. And it is good for me to reflect and remember, though it is painful. It may prevent me from making the same mistakes.

"Oh, sweetling. Recalling my past has ripped forth so many emotions, few of them pleasant.

"After Amorum died, I shook off my stupor. I re-immersed myself into my role as leader of those people. I placed the mask of the Blood Maiden back upon my face. I realized that it was a mask, after all those years. That was not who I was. What I actually was was complicated. What was I? In my thirties? And yet, knowing that Amorum had died, I felt like a scared girl again. The same girl who had lost so much in the past, and now had no one to trust.

"But, that girl wanted vengeance. This time, it was a cold, calculating wrath. Not driven by the hot rage of youth, nor the belief that I was invincible.

"How had I truly been so unaware of the state of the world? Ultner's rise had taken place across years. Certainly, I had been fed misinformation by followers too frightened to tell me the truth, but I should have known things were worse. The majority of my domain had been taken, destroyed. Ultner did not seek to control the people, as I did. He sought to free them. And, with that freedom, ever more havoc was wrought on the land.

"With such freedom, the people were filled with lust, greed, wrath, envy, gluttony, and pride. They wanted sex. They wanted wealth. They wanted revenge. They wanted all of that which belonged to their neighbors. They wanted more and more, and they expected to receive it.

"The population of Saiwen was decimated, reduced to a fraction of what it was. In the wake of the wars, pestilence and disease reached out and gripped the continent firmly. Ultner continued to destroy my forces wherever he could find them. Some surrendered, freely giving up my towns and cities. Often, the people rose up in the aftermath of the surrender and murdered my soldiers nonetheless. Sometimes, my soldiers defected and joined with Ultner.

"Soon, my remaining forces were spread thin and vastly outnumbered, war being fought on a thousand fronts. Many of my pasnes alna were killed, and Intenu was missing.

"My chances at regaining my place as the goddess of these people were negligible. But... I felt an obligation to the people. Maybe it was because my near-death experience had changed me. Maybe it was to honor Amorum. But I felt an obligation to help the people, to force them into a peaceful life once again. They had peace under my rule. Granted, it was peace that had been birthed by fear, but maybe, could I once again unite the people, I could change that.

"My one chance was to collect all that remained of my forces—conventional and magical—and cut straight to Ultner. To defeat him and his Menogan allies, destroy their miernes arma. And then, to start over.

"The thought, sweetling, was exhausting. But I knew not what else to do.

"Battles of great armies rarely occur in a single day. There are ruses and feints, skirmishes and pitched battles. Fights for the high ground, and digging in around defensible terrain. My forces and Ultner's were joined together for weeks in battle. A thousand tiny battles, really. Though my veteran army did a great deal of damage, Ultner's army continued to grow. Men joined him on a daily basis, and some deserted me. It seemed as if defeat was inevitable.

"Wantran was again my savior. She rallied my three captains and nine of my most skilled pasnes alna for a covert attack against the miernes arma. Without my knowledge,e she did this, and knowing that I would wish to protect her and my own magic weapons at any cost.

"The twelve, with great skill and daring, made their way past the magical defenses put in place by the miernes arma. And, instead of targeting the weapons, themselves, they attacked the Menogan slavers, the holders of the bonds.

"Nearly all were killed. Having no one to control them, the miernes arma fled. Intenu had taught us that, though the miernes arma were revered and treated with the utmost respect, they were slaves nonetheless, and would always flee if the opportunity arose.

"However, Wantran and the eleven were surrounded by the end. The earth had already crumbled; the green had been exhausted. There were no living beings left to draw from. They were cut to pieces by swords, pierced by spears, transfixed by arrows. Thereafter, they became known as my Martyrs.

"Most of the mythology about me was created after the fact, by the misguided group who wrote The Book of Amorum. But the Martyrs… I named them myself. And I mourned them with all of my heart.

"The warriors on both sides were exhausted from fighting, exhausted from killing. Ultner sent me a message requesting single combat with me. I accepted.

579

"He was not, as depicted, a boil-faced, horn-headed demon with a silver tongue. No, Ultner was a young man in his twenties, relatively handsome with jet black hair and piercing blue eyes. He was softer-spoken than I had expected, and incontestably less certain.

"He asked questions before our battle began. Whether I truly believed I was a goddess. Whether I believed in peace. If I still felt emotions like I had when I was younger. If I was scared. If I could love. It was a far too… human conversation to be having just before we battled. I hated myself for liking the man. I hated him for being likable.

"He asked whether we could allow the armies to retreat to a safe distance first. I acquiesced.

"I had my one hundred donors nearby, and Ultner had his own menagerie to draw from. Animals—cows, horses, goats—and humans.

"As if there were an unspoken bond controlling us, we began our attacks in unison. Clouds swirled in the sky, drawn by our powers as we strained against one another. I sent fire; he summoned a wall of wind to block it. He sent blades of power; I deflected them with my own barriers.

"The lands were torn around us. Men and women, who had crept back to witness the battle, were killed by errant powers. Even those who retreated a safe distance were not immune, so powerful were the forces that stretched between us. The impact of this battle was felt hundreds and thousands of miles away. I later heard that a great sphere of power, shaped by me and deflected by Ultner, ended the lives of two hundred thousand souls in what is now Rafon. The balance of the very world was shredded, and nowhere was safe. The world's population was decimated.

"Ultner and I were utterly, evenly matched. I could gain no advantage, nor could Ultner. Hours passed. Maybe days. I began to tire, and had to use donors to refresh myself. Ultner's attacks became less concentrated, more diffuse. After a time, we were like two exhausted prize fighters, exchanging periodic, ineffective blows. I'm certain that only sheer will kept me on my feet.

"My donors were nearly gone. My own maen was near expended, my nerring nearly emptied. I felt weak, alone. Scared. I quested beyond myself to find power, to find something to allow me to hang on a little longer, and cling to this world for a few more seconds. I needed just a little more. Something. Anything. Sweetling, I have told you before that I fear death.

"Without any warning, Ultner's powers flared like a sudden, violent storm. He knocked aside my paltry defenses; left me bloodied and on my knees. It was the end for me, sweetling. So I thought. I am not ashamed to say that I wept.

"I quested one last time, reaching out beyond myself for any power I could use. Anything… the crumbled earth, the blackened flora, the air itself. And, I was rewarded beyond belief.

"A warm energy filled me, sweetling. It filled my great nerring to capacity and beyond, which stretched to accommodate this strange power. I felt more alive than ever in my life. Stronger. More certain. And, strangely, peaceful.

"I pushed myself to my feet and knocked aside Ultner's attacks. I could sense his surprise across the length of the magical battleground. With this great force pulsing within me, I approached him and bombarded him with a magical storm beyond anything I could have imagined. My power took the form of flames and lightning, beams of power and magical animals. Ultner responded in kind, and our magical storm filled every inch of my vision. It was terrifyingly beautiful to behold.

"But, I had experience beyond that of Ultner. Years of practice and training, and some thoughts on how to use this sudden, limitless power that infused me.

"Barriers, sweetling, are typically used for defense. However, I focused all of my power on creating a barrier around Ultner, a half mile in circumference. Something that I could never have done without this strange power. I enclosed his attacks, trapping his magical onslaughts. I forced the sphere closer and closer to Ultner; he fought, but I managed to restrain him. When I was near his body, I could close the sphere no more.

"The new power, I could feel, was running out. But, so was Ultner's. I could not defeat him, but he could not escape my prison of energy. So, I did the only thing I could think to do. I used my reserves to tear the ground open, revealing a great chasm. I sealed Ultner's barrier so that it would persist, and hurled it into the gap, closing it afterward.

"I had not noticed that the sky had turned as red as blood, that the clouds appeared charred and black. Burnt, it seemed.

"My powers were near exhausted, and I simply sat amidst the ash and crumbling ruin that had once been a verdant, green landscape.

"After a day, the sky was still burned. Survivors began to pick at the battlefield, maybe looking for loot or maybe for survivors, but instead they found me. My army, Ultner's army… they all began to gather around my exhausted shell. They were quiet, at first. Frightened, but still they assembled about me in a great circle. After a time, they began to murmur my name. I heard it repeated again and again. Yetra. Yetra. Yetra.

"With great effort, I stood. A hush cut through the crowd, much like a knife ripping into each of their throats. I looked to the crimson sky, so unnatural, and raised my arms.

"I do not know why I did it. But, I released the remaining power that had filled me the day before. I released it to the world, freeing it from my nerring. It felt like the right thing to do, and it had been so long since I had done the right thing.

"Beams of light rose from my hands; they cut through the sky. The sky was rejuvenated, the clouds cleaned of blackness. The people were in awe. They released their weapons and began to speak to one other.

"The Taneos say that it was my ascension to godhood. And, indeed, from that day, I never aged. In fact, I seemed to lose ten years, and I became as you see me now. The people, those who remained… they worshipped me, and were united in that fact. They stopped warring; they stopped fighting. They began rebuilding.

"The Taneos say that it was Harmony that filled me that day. That Harmony—some primordial power from the times of creation—was the great power that allowed me to win the battle, to cleanse the sky.

"I know not whether that is true. I know not whether those powers exist. I did feel a great peace. A great certainty. Perhaps, sweetling, I was briefly infused with Harmony. And, perhaps Ultner was bathed in Pandemonium. Perhaps, the reality of these warring powers was as Amorum had preached.

"After my so-called Ascension, I made the decision to withdraw from the world. Not based in sloth, as before, but for the good of humanity. So much had been destroyed, and I had been the vehicle of that destruction. The people needed to rebuild… to recover. And, I needed to allow this to happen without my interference.

"Perhaps that power led me to relinquish my grip on the people. Perhaps the events of the previous twenty years…. Well, I am uncertain.

"Over the years, I have simply observed the world. I have walked among the people of the world, unknown to them. For years, things were as they should be. The people worked together as they should. They rebuilt. They rediscovered some of the wisdom lost from my time. They forged alliances and created lasting concords. Certainly, there were petty wars here and there, but nothing on the scale of the thousand warring countries I'd witnessed in my youth. Or my domination of the land and subsequent fall.

"I have quietly taken donors over the years, it is true—typically, those who were condemned, so as not to cause undue suffering and to mask my presence. I needed to replace my maen, sweetling. I told you—my nerring has been slowly draining over the years. And it has gotten worse. Now, I realize my mistake. Feeding on the maenen of criminals and the condemned changed me. Having a good man, such as you, has reminded me of who I am. Or, rather, who I wish I were. It has reminded me of Amorum.

"I regret that my followers—my Erudites and Lanei—lost control and destroyed your town and your life. I regret that I approved it. Telling my people and my generals to bring me strong men to turn Feral, to bring me donors from far away, out-of-the-way villages, was such an easy, impersonal request. I did not realize that I would find you, and that you would have such a profound effect on me.

"I realize now that I need good men. Unfortunately, sweetling—and it hurts me to admit this—it is more important for me to draw pure, good maenen than for you to continue your own life. Though you are good in your own small way, though you have made small positive changes in the menial lives of those around you, the fate of everything rests on my shoulders.

"Over the past hundred years, I have felt something. A stirring, if you will, beneath the surface of the world. A familiar feeling from long ago. A feeling that frightens me.

"I have begun to gather my school of pasnes alna and warriors. My Erudites—warriors and practitioners of magic. Never again will Wantran and the Martyrs' fates be shared by my people; they know how to protect themselves, using both weaponry and magic. They will never be left completely defenseless. My Lanei are the greatest conventional warriors in the world. My Fane. Healers beyond compare.

"I have begun to build my army, and I can only hope that it is enough.

"The feeling I have… It reminds me of Ultner, from that day that the world was nearly destroyed. From the day that I was nearly destroyed. Pandemonium is rising, sweetling.

"Pandemonium is rising, and only if I can unite the world under my banner will the people stand a chance of survival."

Epilogue

The man with one hand reeked. He always did, and he didn't care.

The only problem was that the smell alerted the short guard a moment before the curved sword sliced into his unarmored neck. The short man had half-turned, and the blade didn't have the bite for an instant kill. Instead, the guard was able to gurgle a scream before the second blow ended his life. Yet more blood caked boots that had long been stained brownish-red. The sword slashed down, severing the dead guard's left hand from his wrist.

The man with one hand stepped over the body and met the next guard, who must have been alerted by the scream. This one was good—he was a weasel-faced bastard who wielded two wicked daggers with deft intelligence. It didn't matter, though, because he wasn't good enough. He had too much care in his steps, too much of a focus on self-preservation. The man with one hand had lost that feeling long ago; living and dying was much the same. He cut through the man's left hand so that blood spurted from the limb. Now that they were on even footing—with one weapon each—the weasel-faced man didn't last five seconds. He was blinded by a slash across the eyes, and then disemboweled.

The man with one hand paused, listening. Several long moments passed; only echoes resonated through the comfortable building. It was warm in the space, and pretty cheery with its brightly painted walls and art depicting unnaturally beauteous scenes from nature, all of them likely painted by someone who had never spent a day in the wilds. Even though his senses were dulled, even he could smell cinnamon, pumpkin, and various spices; it was the season for it; Rostanians loved their false scents, especially in the winter.

The apparent solace of the place made the man uncomfortable. He was now a creature of the sewers, a resident of the ruins, more comfortable knee-deep in shit than among real people. He was the king of shit.

When he wasn't out hunting, he spent his time listening from the dark places, from below. Husbands cheating on their wives, wives cheating on their husbands. Children bullying one another. Neglected elders speaking to themselves for some sense of companionship. Criminals plotting their heists and murders, and Taneos committing sins that they'd later condemn. From below, he saw exactly how corrupt Rostane had become.

He listened now, his ears sensitive to any change around him, and determined that his last altercation had gone unnoticed. These people were in disarray, given all that was happening. His hunts had become increasingly dangerous, and he knew this day had been long in the making. He knew that the Feral—as he had heard them called—would be unleashed one day, soon, and today was that day. There was only so much one man could do to dam the flow of a river.

At the very least, attempting to dam this river was enjoyable.

The man with one hand continued to stalk through the building, growing nearer to his destination. He came across a wandering idiot—a man staggering about wearing the face of a twisted, sickly bird. The masked figure staggered back in surprise at the sight of a filthy, blood-covered warrior. He didn't live to respond, though, upon looking down to stare dully at his missing hand, before taking a sword across the throat.

The man with one hand killed two more guards before reaching his destination, which was a much less hospitable wing of the building. He tossed his sword to the stones without much grace. It was easiest to let go of the thing suddenly; otherwise, his hand just seemed to grip it tighter with the need to kill. He fumbled with the keys he'd taken from the belt of the dead guard. He pinned them against the stump of his hand, struggling to find the right key and failing twice before finally hearing the lock click.

He pulled open the heavy door, letting the light filter into the cell. He glanced around, not immediately seeing anyone. Had he been mistaken? Had he heard wrong in his eavesdropping? Stepping into the cell, he was immediately accosted by a small, but fierce figure. His own body was hard, though, and his assailant lacked real strength. Without much effort, he batted down the figure so that she rolled away heavily. Rather than admit defeat, though, she immediately regained her feet and launched herself forward.

The man with one hand appreciated the effort, but he had been dealing with fierce, mindless attacks for months now; he easily subdued her, though this time his goal wasn't to kill. It was counterintuitive, of course, to not kill.

His attacker, the prisoner, pushed herself to her feet again and took two steps back. She was a young girl, her short hair disheveled, eyes staring at him intensely—as if analyzing him for a weakness. Her eyes focused on the stump of his hand. He wanted to ball the thing into a fist and hit her, though the first wasn't possible and the second wasn't an option.

"I'm not going back to Tennyson, you stinking pile of Ultner shit," she spat, her voice cracking from disuse.

"You do not have to," croaked the man with one hand. He had little opportunity for conversation these days, and the sound of his once-refined voice made him cringe.

"Well, what the fuck do you want?"

The girl, Morgyn, was wary, and he didn't blame her. The man with one hand hadn't looked in a mirror for… for months now, but he could imagine that his appearance did not inspire confidence.

"You did me a kindness a lifetime ago. I would repay the favor, with a caveat."

"I do few kindnesses," she said, narrowing her eyes at him.

"Nonetheless, you did. And I remain grateful." Her eyes widened, perhaps suddenly remembering the day that she and Escamilla had freed him from his cell, alone in the smothering darkness beneath the Plateau. Where the man with the red glowing eyes had drained him of his essence, whatever had made him human. Which was why, of course, he was far less than human now, though more human than the rest of them. Enough to know they needed to be wiped out.

"Erlins? I thought… I thought you were torn to shreds. I thought you were dead."

"Erlins is dead. I am the Hunter."

Morgyn appraised him, her greasy face creasing with a ghost of a smile. "Seems a little dramatic," she said.

"It is all I do, girl. I hunt and I kill." He ached to pick up his discarded sword and return to the hunt. He ached to feel blood splattering his face, running down his forearms, to hear that death scream. He ached to kill. But, he resisted, as he had taught himself to do.

"And I sit and I wait. But I don't call myself The Waiter."

The Hunter turned to leave, moving to close the door behind him.

"Wait! Wait!" she cried, throwing arms in the way of the closing door.

"I thought you weren't the waiter," said the Hunter. Morgyn stared at him dully, and then started to giggle. The giggle turned into a laugh, and the laugh turned into a sputtering loss of control, with her wheezing for breath between hiccups. At least the Hunter had some semblance of humor left in him, though he didn't think his comment had been nearly as funny as the girl apparently did.

Her glee soon subsided and the Hunter noticed tears running divots through the old dirt on her face.

"Alright then, the Hunter. Let's get out of here." She started past him, but he held up a finger.

"The condition. I am grateful, but my help is not free."

Morgyn seemed to shrink back.

"Yet another master. What do you want of me?" she asked quietly.

"You are to join me on the hunt. I will teach you to find, isolate, and kill. You have an advantage of being able to fit into small spaces. Together, we can ambush. Together, we can thin their numbers."

"What are you talking about?" She licked her chapped and broken lips.

"We hunt the Feral below the Plateau. We hunt the Feral that live in the spaces below Rostane. And, we hunt their masters." Now, he finally let himself move back toward his discarded sword, reaching for the thing with near desperation sword. His body, tense to the point of breaking, unwound at the touch of the well-worn, well-blooded grip. He felt compelled to leave this place of light and return to the underground.

Morgyn looked small, standing in her cell, body malnourished and weak. But, her face hardened with a sudden resolve; a slight twist to her jaw, a hardening of her deep brown eyes. She gave a single nod.

"Fine, the Hunter. Lead the way."

Merigold's Journal (Appendix)

I've decided to start taking notes about magic. It's confusing, and Cryden, as is typical, just conceals and obscures. He's cocky, though, and lets a little bit slip from time to time. If I'm ever going to get the hang of this power, then I need to make sure I understand it.

Some terms that I need to keep straight:

Miernes. This is the broad, general term for magic. It's basically any type of lifeforce that a person can draw from, whether of plant life or animals.

Maenen. This is the term for the miernes (see, I used it correctly!) contained within living creatures, like animals. I have maen inside of me, which is what it's called when you refer to your own lifeforce. So does Cryden. So does his horse and basically any animal you find. That's my power—but I can draw maenen from animals and people.

Note 1. People who can draw maenen are called, colloquially, leeches. It's a disgusting term, and I don't like it. But... it makes sense.

Note 2. The official term for those schooled in the control of maenen is pasnes maenen.

Nerring. I used to call this my vessel. It is the 'container' that holds the maenen within us all. I like to think of it like a container anyway, but it is very difficult to explain and perceive. I'm fairly sure that the nerring not only holds maenen, but also creates new maenen. So, if I were to draw a little bit of maenen from someone, their nerring should create more. Like the body creates more blood, even after some leaks out.

Note 1. When I quest (oh, I need to define that!), I can see the nerrings, and the maenen, of people nearby. Maybe up to ten or fifteen feet away.

Note 2. Cryden told me that drawing too much from a single person could collapse their nerring, rendering them a broken shell or even killing them.

Note 3. He also said that Feral are birthed from a continuous drawing from the same individual, shrinking the nerring without destroying it.

Questing. The process by which a person is able to see outside of their body and view the maenen of others. It's something that is barely a conscious process; I used to do it all the time without realizing it and without realizing that everyone couldn't.

Note 1. Does this work the same for people who draw from plants? What do they see?

Greenies. This is what Cryden calls people who draw from plant life. I saw some in action in the Battle of Florens, and they sapped life from the very grass surrounding them and hurled deadly power into the Rostanians.

Note 1. I heard Cryden say that the power they draw is called yenas.

Pasnes alna. These are the people who are trained in the use of miernes. Cryden tells me that they are usually in positions of influence around the world, but I've never heard of them before.

Metsikas. These are people who use miernes, but are not trained by any of the schools of the pasnes alna. "Wild mages" is what I think this means. I suppose I was a metsika before Cryden found me. In fact, I probably still am a metsika.

Acknowledgments

First, you are still reading at this point, so first I will beg you to leave a review. Amazon or Goodreads would be awesome. At the very least, you could force me to contemplate my existence by criticizing every one of the above words. Or, you could motivate other folks to read my writing, and therefore encourage me to further neglect my family and continue to write!

Speaking of, I certainly must thank my incredibly supportive wife Katie for continuing to accept me despite my penchant for spending the evenings in writing. She is an awesome sounding board, great editor, and a generally swell person. My beta readers, friends all, also deserve a great, heartfelt thanks. Bill, Adam, Rita, Anthony, Dominque, Kristina, and Morgan, I managed to survive all of your concentrated criticism. Please stop nagging me to write the third book. I'll get there...

I am uber thankful for my editor, Jennifer Collins, for two reasons. First, she does a kickass job editing. Second, she is incredibly supportive and makes me feel like a decent writer. My art team can turn my terrible scribblings into beautifully-realized painting. Rene Aigner, the cover artist, and Dave O'Meara, the map man and designer, I'm lucky to have the two of you.

When I started this journey, I was largely on my own. There was a lot of guesswork and a lot of idiocy. Thankfully, I stumbled into a great community of supportive authors and readers. I have to start by thanking Mark Lawrence and all of the fantastic bloggers from the Self-Published Fantasy Blog Off. If it weren't for all of you, I never would have felt comfortable actually talking about writing, nor connecting with all of the great people in the community.

Speaking of bloggers (yes, I was), I've stumbled across a horde of online influencers who were kind enough to take interest in my writing. First, Petrik from Novel Notions is probably the nicest guy in the world, but also a fantastic, skilled, and honest reviewer. Thanks for the review, interview, and cover reveal for Wisdom Lost! Nikki from TheBookDragon is a killer and dedicated reviewer who also helped repair my bruised and broken ego by comparing me to the gods among fantasy authors. Matt from Darkside Reads is probably my first real fan, and he actually pays attention to me on Twitter! And Alexia from Bookworm Daydreamer was amazing, and was my first blog reviewer. Certainly, there are more, but I'd rather forgot people and get some angry emails.

Finally, I would be remiss if I didn't thank the Grimdark Readers and Authors Facebook group for being so awesome, as well as a great place full of dark, twisted people who like reading this stuff.

Copyright

Wisdom Lost

Copyright © 2019, Michael Sliter

All rights reserved. No part of this book may be reproduced in any form or by any electronic or mechanical means, including information storage and retrieval systems, without permission in writing from the publisher, except by reviewers, who may quote brief passages in a review.

ISBN eBook: 978-0-9998021-2-0

ISBN Print: 978-0-9998021-3-7

All characters and events in this book are fictitious. Any similarity to real persons, living or dead, is coincidental and not intended by the author.

Editing by Jennifer Collins

Cover image by René Aigner

Book design and map designs by David O'Meara

Published by Dragyn Press

DragynPress@gmail.com

Visit http://www.authormikesliter.com/ to sign up for the author newsletter!